Praise for the Edinbur

"Expertly blending elements of Zin[...] ture, Huchu's occult thriller is as e[...] provoking."　　　　　　　　　*—Publishers Weekly* (starred review) on
The Library of the Dead

"Witty, suspenseful, and keenly attuned to real-life socioeconomic hierarchies, this equally entertaining and insightful sophomore outing should keep Huchu's star on the rise."
—Publishers Weekly (starred review) on
Our Lady of Mysterious Ailments

"Everything rides on the shoulders of young Ropa in this post-apocalyptic, near-future Edinburgh where magic, science, and monarchy all hold equal sway. Ropa, at only fourteen, carries an adult's burdens and responsibility with equal parts can-do spirit, stubborn energy, and kicking herself and her friends as necessary. This twisted Edinburgh tries its best to keep her down, but she never stops."

—Library Journal (starred review)

"A fast-paced, future-set Edinburgh thriller. *The Library of the Dead* mixes magical mysteries with a streetwise style of writing. . . . Roll on the sequel."　　　　　　*—The Times*

"I highly recommend *The Library of the Dead*."
—Charlaine Harris, author of the
Sookie Stackhouse series

"Contemporary fantasy, at its best, is both escapist and urgent: this does both admirably."　　　　　　　　　*—The Scotsman*

BY T. L. HUCHU

EDINBURGH NIGHTS
Book Three

The Mystery at Dunvegan Castle

T. L. HUCHU

TOR PUBLISHING GROUP
NEW YORK

THE MYSTERY AT DUNVEGAN CASTLE

Copyright © 2023 by Tendai Huchu

A Tor Book
Published by Tom Doherty Associates / Tor Publishing Group
120 Broadway
New York, NY 10271

www.tor-forge.com

Tor® is a registered trademark of Macmillan Publishing Group, LLC.

The Library of Congress Cataloging-in-Publication Data
is available upon request.

ISBN 978-1-250-88308-7 (trade paperback)
ISBN 978-1-250-88307-0 (ebook)

Our books may be purchased in bulk for promotional, educational, or business use. Please contact your local bookseller or the Macmillan Corporate and Premium Sales Department at 1-800-221-7945, extension 5442, or by email at MacmillanSpecialMarkets@macmillan.com.

First published in Great Britain by Tor, an imprint of Pan Macmillan

First Tor Paperback Edition: 2024

Printed in the United States of America

0 9 8 7 6 5 4 3 2 1

For
Rufaro Huchu

Principal Magical Institutions

Calton Hill Library, incorporating the Library of the Dead: These are Scotland's premier magical libraries, both located under Calton Hill in Edinburgh's city centre. Together, they house an impressive collection of magical texts and books. There is an entrance by the pillars of the National Monument of Scotland, on the summit of the Hill. Alternatively, there's a further entrance via David Hume's mausoleum in the Old Calton Burial Ground. Those who don't practise magic are strongly advised against visiting as punishments for trespass are reportedly disproportionately severe.

Elgin (The): A term mostly used by the alumni of the Edinburgh School (see Calton Hill Library, incorporating the Library of the Dead).

Extraordinary Committee (The): An organ within the Society of Sceptical Enquirers charged with checking the powers of the secretary. It consists of two heads of the four magic schools in Scotland, plus two board members of the Society, and one ordinary member drawn by lottery.

General Discoveries Directorate: An independent division within the Society of Sceptical Enquirers. It supports the Secretary of the Society (currently Sir Ian Callander) in his role as Scotland's Discoverer General.

Our Lady of Mysterious Ailments: An exclusive holistic healing and therapy clinic on Colinton Road. Clients include aristocrats, celebrities and the cream of Edinburgh society.

Royal Society of Sorcery and the Advancement of the Mystic Arts:
England's foremost magical society claims to trace its origins to the
mythical wizard Merlin, though contemporary scholars date its
formal establishment to the late seventeenth century.

Society of Sceptical Enquirers: Scotland's premier magical professional body. It is headquartered in Dundas House on St Andrew
Square in the New Town.

Principal Places

Dundas House: Designed by the architect Sir William Chambers
and completed in 1774, this neoclassical building located at 36 St
Andrew Square in the New Town was once the headquarters of the
Royal Bank of Scotland. It remains the bank's corporate address and
simultaneously serves as the headquarters of the Society of Sceptical
Enquirers.

Dunvegan Castle: The ancestral home of the chiefs of the Clan
MacLeod. It was built in the thirteenth century and is located on
the shores of Loch Dunvegan.

everyThere (The): This realm is a nonplace beyond the ordinary
world. It is where deceased souls go before they can move on. Only
a few of the living can reach and navigate it safely.

Isle of Skye: The largest island in the Inner Hebrides, located to the
north-west of Scotland, and accessible via the Skye Crossing running
between Kyle of Lochalsh on the mainland and Kyleakin on the
island's east coast.

Other Place (The): Little is known about this realm in the astral plane, but wayward spirits can be expelled there. It is believed there is no return for them from it.

Realms Beyond (The): Lying beyond the event horizon of the Astral Realms, these represent a higher dimension currently out of the reach of contemporary magical practice. Though much has been speculated about them, little empirical evidence exists to prove or disprove their existence.

Royal Bank of Scotland: Established in 1727, the RBS is a major retail and commercial bank.

RBS Archives: Located in South Gyle, the archives are responsible for collecting and preserving the records of both the Royal Bank of Scotland and the Society of Sceptical Enquirers. While the premises belong to the RBS, the archivists who work there are employed by the Calton Hill Library.

Principal Characters

Briggs: Coachman and servant to England's Sorcerer Royal.

Callander, Ian (Sir): Scotland's leading magician. Secretary of the Society of Sceptical Enquirers. His role in the Society also makes him the Discoverer General in Scotland.

Cattermole, Fergus (Professor): Vice Principal at Glasgow University and head of the Lord Kelvin Institute.

Cleghorn, Euan: Head Librarian at the Glasgow Library, which holds Scotland's second-largest collection of magical books and texts.

Glasgow is considered by some to be a rival to Calton Hill Library because of its impressive collection of antique handwritten and illustrated grimoires dating to times before scientific magic was established.

Cockburn, Frances: Director of Membership Services at the Society of Sceptical Enquirers.

Cruickshank: Ropa Moyo's magical scarf. A gift from her mentor, Sir Callander.

Diderot, Octavius: Member of the Extraordinary Committee and the board of the Society of Sceptical Enquirers.

Featherstone, Calista: Head teacher at the Aberdeen School of Magic and Esoterica.

Hanley, Mary: Member of the Extraordinary Committee.

Hutchinson, Hamish: Principal at St Andrews College, Scotland's second-oldest school of magic.

Kapoor, Priyanka: Healer at the Our Lady of Mysterious Ailments clinic on Colinton Road. She studied healing and herbology at the Lord Kelvin Institute in Glasgow.

Kebede, the son of Bekele: Assistant to the Grand Debtera of Abyssinia.

MacDonald, Avery: Second son of Dalziel MacDonald and a student of theoretical magicology at the prestigious St Andrews College.

MacDonald, Dalziel: Clan chief of the MacDonalds of Sleat, one of the oldest and most powerful Scottish families.

MacLeod, Adamina: The wife of one of the earlier MacLeod chiefs named Norman.

MacLeod, Edmund: Clan chief of Clan MacLeod and host of the biennial conference of the Society of Sceptical Enquirers.

MacLeod, Fenella: The only child of Edmund MacLeod and a student of esoteric history at the prestigious St Andrews College.

Maige, Jomo: Trainee librarian at Calton Hill Library and Ropa Moyo's best friend.

Maige, Pythagoras (Dr): Head Librarian at the Calton Hill Library and Master of the Books for the Library of the Dead. He holds a doctorate in mathematics from the University of Edinburgh and is Jomo's father.

MacCrimmon, Stephen: Deceased piper of renown in his time. A scion of the MacCrimmons of Borreraig, hereditary pipers to the chiefs of Clan MacLeod.

Mhondoro, Melsie: Ropa Moyo's grandmother.

Moyo, Izwi: Ropa Moyo's precocious younger sister.

Moyo, Ropa: A teenage ghostalker from HMS Hermiston in the south-west of Edinburgh. Ropa dropped out of school to support her little sister and grandmother by delivering messages on behalf of the city's dearly departed. Her activities, including finding and saving missing children, have attracted the attention of the Society of Sceptical Enquirers, an unusual feat for an unqualified independent practitioner.

Qozmos: The Grand Debtera of Abyssinia.

Lebusa, Rethabile (Lady): Member of the Extraordinary Committee and the board of the Society of Sceptical Enquirers.

Samarasinghe, Sashvindu (Lord): England's Sorcerer Royal.

Sneddon (Mr): Librarian at the Calton Hill Library.

Soltani, Esfandiar: Currently the Makar, the national poet laureate of Scotland, and an independent scholar best known for his biography of Robert Burns in verse. He is a non-practising magician married to Sir Ian Callander.

Walsh, Nathair: Deputy head boy and captain of the rugby team at the Edinburgh Ordinary School for Boys.

Wedderburn, Montgomery: Rector of the prestigious Edinburgh Ordinary School for Boys.

Wharncliffe, Lewis: Student of sonicology at the Edinburgh Ordinary School for Boys.

The Somerville Equation

$$y = w(c+a-N)/t$$

y – yield
w – practitioner's potential
c – combustible material
a – agitative threshold
N – natural resistance
t – time

Discovered in 1797 by the polymath Mary Somerville, from Jedburgh, when she was only sixteen. This elegant equation was the first mathematical proof of the Promethean fire spell. Somerville's work is considered by most scholars to have been a key development in the shift towards magic becoming a true scientific discipline. Scotland's four schools of magic also use it to derive their pupils' potential by working out the 'w'.

The Four Magic Schools

These are the only accredited schools of magic in Scotland. They are highly selective and have very competitive admission standards. Qualification at one of these institutions is a requirement for professional registration with the Society of Sceptical Enquirers:

Aberdeen School of Magic and Esoterica, Aberdeen

Edinburgh Ordinary School for Boys, Edinburgh

Lord Kelvin Institute, Glasgow

St Andrews College, St Andrews

I

Boom. Lassie from the slums winds up in a castle. Ain't that a right old fairy tale? If I didn't know any better, I'd have done up my dreadlocks, worn a tiara and called myself princess. Nah, screw that Disney malarkey. I'm just loving the Isle of Skye right now. This must be what being on holiday feels like. Though how would I know? Seeing as I've never done nothing posh like that.

Frances Cockburn wouldn't let me bring my fox, River, along. Her being a boss lady type, with a big ol' stick up her arse, who doesn't want me working in Scottish magic. She said no pets allowed on this particular jaunt, or some such jazz. It's a proper downer, but hey ho . . .

In terms of the day job, it's nose to the grindstone, 'cause I've been seconded to what we call the Hamster Squad. They're the admin gophers where I work. We're helping organize the Society of Sceptical Enquirers' biennial conference at Dunvegan Castle. That's real, important work right there. And it means little ol' me is mixing with the great and good of Scottish magic. But being me, I've also nabbed myself a wee ghostalking side hustle in Skye's village of Dunvegan, just for while we're here. The Society don't pay me nothing for my labouring, so I have to be creative. Inshallah, they'll turn my unpaid internship into a proper apprenticeship any day now. I flunked my last test on a technicality, so all I have to do is to take it again and I'm in, baby. But right now, the island's sea air smells like crisp banknotes to me, and I'm sat in a cottage with a couple in dire need of my skills.

'So, this here lassie be a real magician? We dinnae need none of that,' says the husband, Brodie Budge, all gruff like, tossing peat into the stove.

'I'm a registered ghostalker,' I correct him. Impersonating a registered magician's a big offence.

'Still our shillings you want, right enough.' He sounds proper annoyed, but I can tell he's actually masking shame. Poverty does that to you. Better to lash out than admit you're hard up.

I give his partner, Ellie, a look. She's a wee mouse. Narrow face, long snout, hunched shoulders like she could disappear into that hole in the skirting board. Brodie's kinda the same, but more extreme 'cause he's got actual whiskers poking out round his cheeks. They're that kind of couple who've blended till they resemble each other. It's there in their body language and facial expressions, and a weird tic of flinching at random moments. Too much sorrow's written in their eyes too.

'I've been saving from the cleaning jobs I've been doing,' Ellie says, barely audibly. 'It's got tae be done.'

'If my boat hadnae sunk, I'd be good for it,' Brodie replies, softening.

'Ah ken. You survived. That's all that matters, love.'

'I'm useless. Nae jobs to be had anywhere on this goddamned island.'

'Dinnae be silly.' Ellie reaches out and strokes his arm. 'We'll be alright.'

Folks out here lost everything during the Big Yin. A massive storm that was. The Hebrides were devastated and so was a huge slice of the west coast of Scotland. Fishermen like Brodie Budge lost their livelihoods as Mother Nature devoured their boats. There've even been news reports of debris from broken-up vessels washing up on beaches in Florida. Broke the camel's back, that did. It was always lean times in the fishing trade anyway, with the way fish stocks were decimated round about the time of the Catastrophe when everything went to shit. Since then, people have been leaving the Island of Skye like it was the nineteenth century all over again.

Still, Ellie asked me here to help them, so it is what it is. *Be a pro, Ropa, just like them suit and tie folks.*

Her and him live in this old shepherd's cottage on the outskirts of the village. The whitewashed walls could do with some DIY. Walking in, I was also worried the slate would fall off the roof on top of my head. The room we're in now is pretty glum, with the windows boarded up, and a solar lamp illuminating 'cause the power's gone again. Springs in the sofa poke my behind. Could do with some reupholstering – I'm sure these date from before them two were sprogs. There's wires dangling out of a broken socket in the wall too. It's definitely seen better days, but I still don't see how this pair could afford a pad like this. Reckon one of them must have inherited it.

There's a pink teddy bear underneath the coffee table.

I can smell damp in the air and glance at the black mould painting *Guernica* on the walls. An almighty draught's blowing in from somewhere, cancelling out the fire's warmth.

'Morag said you could help us,' Ellie says with an air of desperation. Good ol' Morag. She's a good egg, my favourite of the staff at the castle, and has had my back since we got there. Her and me have been lounging in downtimes blethering about the myths and legends woven into the fabric of Skye. Half the time I don't know if she's spinning yarns or she believes these tales to be true.

'Sometimes it's best to leave things the way they are,' Brodie complains.

'I cannae sleep nights on account o' that awful racket. Then I have tae get oot each morning and work mysel tae the bone while you're moping and wallowing. I cannae take it anymore, Brodie. It's got tae stop, you hear?'

Ellie breaks away from him and storms off to the far side of the room, keeping her back to us. Brodie clenches his jaw and stays schtum. I'm beginning to regret taking on this gig. Dramarama. *Keep it pro, Ropa*, I tell myself. When emotions flare, I must be the grown-up in the room. Good thing is, I've got tons of practice dealing with my little sister's wild moods.

'How long's this been going on? The haunting?' I ask to bring them back firmly to the matter at hand.

'Couple of months,' Brodie replies.

'A year and some,' Ellie contradicts. 'Started a few weeks after Ava died. Christ, do yous even remember her?' she snaps at Brodie.

4

'What kind of twisted question is that? She was my daughter too. My own flesh and bone.'

'How often does it happen?' I say quickly. I need them to stop bickering and stick to the facts.

'Used tae be odd times. Once or twice a week, maybe. Now it's every single night. I wake up tae hear the sound of my dead bairn wailing. And all I can think about is how I used tae hold her in my arms and rock her tae sleep at night.'

'Both of you hear these sounds?' I ask.

'Aye. I've entered the nursery many times and seen the cot bed rocking back and forth all by itself,' says Brodie. 'But it's nothing tae be afeard of. Ava's soul is just here with us. Cannae you see that?'

'Jesus Christ. Listen tae yersel. It's got tae stop,' says Ellie.

Morag, who lined up this gig for me, didn't tell me the couple weren't in alignment. But I've seen it all. Not everyone who has a resident poltergeist wants it gone. There's people who hold on to the souls of the dearly departed, unwilling to let go. My grandmother told me that kind of situation's none too salubrious. Grief and growth go hand in scythe. Eventually, you have to move on. Try telling that to those who've loved and lost, though. But I also know that the souls of babies don't linger unless they're held by force, by strong emotions. The well of sorrow's a tough place to tread water in. But in the murky waters after loss, there are those spirits who aren't in the light and who may try to move in. That's when shit gets real dark. First, I have to work out which of these is going on here.

A piercing wail comes from upstairs, making Ellie jump.

A cold shiver runs down my spine. It's horrible. A cry that sounds like torture. Nails on a blackboard. A wave of revulsion washes over me. I feel like throwing up but I'm not the sort to waste my tea like that. Ellie yells out and covers her ears, shutting her eyes tight as tears stream down her cheeks. But it's given me my answer.

I grab my backpack and unzip it pronto, pulling out my mbira. The metal keys shine, reflecting the candlelight, 'cause I gave it a good polish earlier. Even oiled the wooden keyboard too, so it looks real swank. I'm headed for the stairs when Brodie blocks my path.

'I cannae let you do this. That's my bairn you're wanting tae kill all over again. I cannae lose her twice, lassie.'

'That's not your daughter, pal,' I respond. The revulsion I feel tells me all I need to know. You don't think these things, your gut tells you in plain Shona and Scots.

'I ken the sound of her voice. Used tae wake me up many nights, changing nappies, feeding her, holding her till she slept in mine arms.' He holds out his hands, imploring. 'She's come back home.' Brodie tears his shirt off and shows bite marks around his nipples. The flesh there is purple-black with bruising. 'I've been breastfeeding ma baby like a father should.'

Fuck me.

I shake my head and administer the pill without sugar coating. His child had moved on long ago.

'The souls of babies don't linger here like those of adults can. Not even in the everyThere, just beyond our plane, whose sharp claws clasp tightly to our own world. In very rare cases indeed they can be held back by another soul known to them. Only usually by a father or a mother. But you're both here, so this isn't the case. Your daughter ascended to the realm of the purest, a place of light and love where babies go. She isn't here anymore.'

'How can you be sure?'

'And how did you know how to find shoals of cod in the barren sea? It's my job to know,' I reply.

The wailing upstairs intensifies. A mix of hunger and anger, known to parents everywhere as the signal their baby is demanding to be fed. Even I feel its awful pull. The way it makes you want to go up to it and serve it. Soothe it. But listen closely and you'll hear something sinister in the notes, a timbre not quite right, the undertone of the damned. Once you hear it, you can't unpick it from the rest of the cries. It's what me and Ellie hear, but not this oaf.

'Listen, Brodie Budge, really listen to it,' I say.

My grandmother taught me the 'Song of Clarity' before I turned ten and I strum it now on the keys of my mbira. Softly and quietly, beneath the loud cries. It's not meant to over-whelm the noise. Instead, I insert the notes like a wedge between the blank spaces within the cries. Prising them apart gently. Stretching the sound out, bit by bit. Brodie freezes in shock, his face going blank. I keep playing those ancient notes passed down across generations. And as I do, with each passing moment, the gaps between the cries grow wider. Then in those spaces emerges something else, the scary sound of the choirs of the damned. Heavy metal. It's deafening. No baby cries like that.

'*Breast milk. Feed me sweet blood. Hungry,*' it demands.

When Brodie's chin hits the floor, I stop playing and push him out of my way, heading up the stairs to the nursery. Ellie timidly follows, a few steps behind.

On the landing up top, I feel as if I've been plunged underwater.

Icy cold.

It's hard to breathe.

But I press on against the pressure front trying to push me back.

The cries grow louder and angrier with each step I take. The sound swells up and surrounds me like a stirred-up swarm of demon babies. It comes from under my feet. Behind me. Presses down from above. I feel it pound my insides like a heavy bassline. It freaks me out, like nothing I've ever encountered.

'It's nae been this bad before,' Ellie says, voice quivering.

I stay calm. Tell myself to focus. Then I hold out my right hand, muttering an incantation invoking the Anemoi, those Greek wind gods, to send an airwave, the shape of my palm, slamming into the door of the nursery, bursting it wide open. From within comes the sound of an angered hornets' nest as I stride inside.

'That's *enough*,' I say with Authority. This is MY realm. Earth belongs not to the spirits but to us beings of flesh.

A dark figure glowers from the white crib in the corner. The music box dangling above it cranks up and begins to play a distorted electronic lullaby. The carousel wheels within it house a menagerie of brightly coloured toy animals. Round and round they go. Faster and faster. The wheel breaks and shoots off, forcing me to duck so it misses and hits the wall, spraying plastic toys everywhere. Holograms of green stars dance around the room. The weight of this dark energy is abominable. I'm overwhelmed by revulsion and loathing.

The spectre in the crib comes to the bars and holds them, its large yellow eyes staring defiantly out. It looks far more simian than human. Feels ancient and terrible.

'*Breast milk. Feed me sweet blood. Hungry . . .*'

'You are not supposed to be here.' I strum my mbira once more.

'And you look delicious. Let me feast on you, my sweet,' it says.

'The only thing you'll be getting is my boot up your back-side.'

I play Musekiwa Chingodza's 'Kutema Musasa' furiously and drive it back against the wall to show my Authority. I must stamp this down quickly, as I do with all spirits who've come over to us from the other side. And I won't allow it to challenge me again. Gran warned me before I set off for Skye that this isle is littered with restless souls from bygone eras, desperately clinging on to the world of the living. There's been much suffering, destruction and death here, and many are angry they didn't have the lives they felt they should have had. This is clearly one of them.

'Don't hurt baby,' it pleads, pinned back by the vibrations of my melody.

Normally, I would bargain, but not today. I have no sympathy for evil spirits that torment grieving parents. Gran taught me that 'cause they've been gone for so long, they no longer feel anything except for the most extreme of emotions. They feed on fear and misery and become ever more malevolent along the way. It's like losing your sense of taste until the only thing you can feel are the hottest chillies 'cause they, at least, set off the pain receptors on your lips. That's better than nothing. Hauntings like this happen to satisfy the spirit's grotesque craving.

'Be on your way, never to return to this plane, nor have dealings with the living for ever more. Do this or I'll cast you out to the Other Place,' I say.

'Bargain with baby, please,' it replies.

'There'll be no bargain, no compromise. You will obey.'

'Obey baby must. Baby curses you,' it says, retreating further into the corner. Its yellow eyes fix on mine with menace.

'Off with you!'

I hammer my mbira's keys and drive the spirit through the wall, out into the darkness where it belongs. It desperately tries to grip on to this reality, but my power is too great. I've cut it off from the tether that held it to this world, so now it falls into the void.

By and by, the pressure recedes. Lightness returns, like a storm's lifted. I survey the nursery this ghost has desecrated. Brodie and Ellie had taken the little they had in this world and tried to make something magical for Ava. But they lost her in that very crib to something banally termed Sudden Infant Death Syndrome. SIDS sounds like a mate's name or something. It doesn't tell you what exactly happened to your baby. You're just supposed to accept it as something scientific, even though it's a diagnosis that belongs more to quackery than anything. I take in the feature wall with cartoonish giraffes bounding west, the toys scattered about the floor, a soft baby blanket. The absence of one who'd been loved beyond all else has sucked the life out of this place. And into that vacuum stepped the spirit I've just vanquished.

It makes me feel mighty low. A real sadness that rips my heart apart.

Ellie sniffles behind me.

'Is it over?' she asks.

'You're free of it now and for ever more,' I reply. 'Gather up these toys and pack them away. Dismantle the crib and set it in storage. Paint these walls something neutral. Grieve. Then move on.' I say the words I think my grandmother would speak at a time like this. Giant boots to fill but I've got fair-sized trotters.

Ellie rushes up to me, grabs my hand and presses money into it. Just another day in the office for me, but I can't not feel this mother's pain. A year of this will have taken its toll on her nerves. Her hands are rough from labouring. Tears fill her eyes, and she trembles.

'You're going to be alright. You are strong,' I tell her. Words have great power. Through them we create reality.

She nods and I break away to pack my mbira, leaving her knelt before the empty crib, weeping silently. I know I should say something more to her, but I won't be here for the next steps. She'll have to find something within herself. Brodie's in the doorway and I signal for him to join his partner. He's ashen and shaking. The spirit had been messing with them both for a while. Now he's lost whatever diabolical hope it dangled.

'I dinnae ken what came over me.' His voice is filled with shame.

'Make sure Ellie's okay,' I say.

'Thank you, Ropa Moyo.'

I walk down the stairs alone, leaving them to face the five steps of grief together; the scab's been opened up again. I make for the door but before I go, I stop at the telephone table and place the money Ellie gave me onto it. They need it more than I do – I know where I'll be getting mine.

II

There's neither dawn nor dusk on the Isle of Skye in autumn. Pale light from behind grey clouds is a mere punctuation mark in the lengthening sequence of nights. You lose your bearings. Not just in the sense of the hours marking the day, but your place in history altogether.

I'm an Edinburgher through and through. Wake me up blindfolded in Granton and I'll tell you the hour from the scent of the air. This is my first time ever outside the city proper. Like, not for a day trip, but actually spending time outside Edinburgh. Scary. I'm used to the rhythms of the city, the bustle and tussling that comes with it. Out here, everything's too quiet for my liking.

Where *is* everyone?

Something uncanny happens to you here.

When you arrive, your mind's racing, doing ninety miles an hour. And then at some point, click: it goes calm. A weight you didn't even know you were carrying's eased off your shoulders. Bless Buddha. Wish my gran and sis were here with me. I think they'd like it. River too, my vulpine compadre. The great outdoors would do her good. It sucks to be away from them but I'm corporate now, innit?

My boots squelch as I approach the castle, having got into the grounds via one of the lesser-used entrances. Wet toes. Rains all the time out here, and when it's not, the ground bleeds water all day long. There's the smell of rotting things, mulch and compost, with fallen leaves and twigs carpeting the ground. The Isle of Skye's an old man badly in need of a dash of talc.

'Ropa, where have you been?' Cockburn asks, all brusque.

'I've been going to and fro in the earth, and walking up and down in it,' I reply.

'I already told you, this is not a holiday. You are here to work. Try not to forget that. This shoddy behaviour will reflect on your internship evaluation.'

Frances Cockburn's a prick and she don't like me none. Great thing is, the feeling's mutual. But, unfortunately for me, I've been seconded to her chain gang to prep up for the conference being hosted on the island. Normally, I'm working direct under Sir Ian Callander, Scotland's answer to Mandrake the Magician, or otherwise known as the Secretary of the Society and Scotland's Discoverer General. Alas, I was shunted here as an extra pair of hands since the investigatory work I normally do for the General Discoveries Directorate ain't much needed here of all places. I thought it'd be a chilled gig but, man, was I wrong. Spent days lugging furniture about till my back was sore. Whatever happened to job descriptions and all that malarkey? Oh, that's right, trade unions were banned after the Catastrophe. No more bargaining, collective or otherwise; now you gotta do what the boss man tells you to do and haud yer wheesht.

'Oh, there you are, Ropa. I need your help in the big tent,' Carrie says, one of the Hamster Squad, toddling over with an almighty stack of boxes so high she can barely see where she's going. 'Give us a hand already.'

'Go on,' Cockburn says. 'You need to keep a close eye on this one, Carrie. No slacking. The guests will be here soon, and everything should be ready.'

'I'm on it.'

I grab a box and am amazed Carrie was lugging these solo down from the castle. So heavy. We make our way slowly down towards the jetty 'cause the road's all slippery. There's an old sign about boat cruises for seal-watching on one side of the road. Dunvegan Castle looms above us, perched upon a rock, masked by smirr that's been going all morning. The light drizzle's fine until it catches your eyelashes, half blinding you. Waves crash into the rock, spraying more water into the air. I'm losing my grip, half slipping and sliding, by the time we make it to the big tent opposite the Laundry Cottage on the grounds where some guests will be staying.

'I see Cockburn's busting your nuts again,' Carrie says.

'We were just teabagging.'

'Language, please! The Society of Scrotum Enquirers expects its young ladies to be prim and proper,' she says with a laugh. 'No, seriously, we all get hell off Cockburn. Comes with the job. Tip from me to you, newbie, study your dossier and you might just survive this with your hymen intact.'

I groan. The dossier is this thick file with the photos and details of all the top magic practitioners attending the conference. Sure, lanyards are a thing, and all the attendees will be displaying their names, but Cockburn insists the Hamster Squad, plus me, study everyone in the file. This is just so that in the morning you don't offer Earl Grey to Doctor Norwell, who prefers lapsang souchong, which we happen to have 'procured specially' for him. We, the said Hamster Squad plus me, are here to cater to their every need. We have to anticipate, etc. So, I've had to learn tons of stuff, like where all the bathrooms are, and touristy information about nearby attractions in case anyone wants to go on an excursion. To sound knowledgeable about places I've not even been to see. We'll make reservations at the top restaurants on the island if any of the VIPs want to go. In addition, we also have to know the programming by heart. It's a lot to take in for a first-timer like me. Carrie and the others have done this a couple of times already – they're the young magicians who do the Society's admin at HQ in Edinburgh.

'Don't look so glum, Ropa. This is a great opportunity. Where else do you get to see so many leading magicians in one place?'

'—'

'A couple of years ago, we had a lad called Felix Erskine working with us. He caught the attention of *the* Craig Shoemaster, and now he's landed a gig making a mint in Glasgow. Can you imagine working for Shoemaster and Sons? That's why every fledgling magician wants to start at the Society. It plugs you in with all the big players in Scottish magic. You couldn't pay for those sorts of contacts . . . Put that box over there. No, behind the table. Abdul still hasn't set up the sound system. The first guests arrive tonight and we're behind schedule.'

We've put in a week of work setting this place up. Doesn't feel like that was enough time, even with the help of the castle's own staff. It's a mad rush to the finish line now. Carrie told me it used to be easier when the castle had more of its own staff, but cutbacks . . .

She snaps her fingers in my face.

'Wake up, Ropa. Unstack those chairs and arrange them in rows,' Carrie orders. 'Where's your head at today?'

I'm a bit zombified after my late-night excursion banishing evil spirits.

'Dead yesterdays and unborn tomorrows. Why fret about it, if today be sweet, my darlings?' quotes a man at the entrance to the tent. 'I think she needs a nice hot cuppa to set her straight. It's too early, even for me,' he continues.

He's short, portly and balding. To compensate for this follicular challenge, he wears a luxuriant moustache, greyed to match the goatee on his chin. He has piercing eyes, filled with mirth and mischief, and the bushiest eyebrows I've ever seen. The suit he has on is a big middle finger to the grey, gloomy weather, and our staid Society, looking like someone's poured a few packets of Skittles on it with its multicoloured polka dots. A matching tie and black shirt only serve to high-light the vivid colours. Muddy white loafers on his feet complete the look. I'd thought everyone here would be crusty and conservative, but not this guy.

'Hi, Esfandiar. You being here must mean the big boss is back?' Carrie says.

'Does it?' he replies with a laugh. 'I made my own way. He left me for his young intern! The scandal.'

Carrie laughs and cups her mouth, while giving me a wee side glance. I'm not in on this joke – I've never seen this bloke in my life.

'Are you going to help us or just stand there?'

'I'm not cut out for menial tasks, little dove. My hands are far too soft and my constitution too delicate. But today, and only today, I must steel myself, summon up the courage of the ancients, and see that Ropa Moyo here is dressed in the finest Callander tartan.'

'What's this about and who are you?' I ask.

'If you'd bothered to read the bloody dossier then you'd have known Esfandiar Soltani here is Sir Ian Callander's husband,' says Carrie with mock outrage.

'And since you're his apprentice, you are to wear his colours,' he says, smiling widely. 'Never mind the damned dossier, I am but a footnote in the great man's entry.'

'You'll get your own full-page spread one day,' Carrie says.

'Unlikely, since I'm a third-rate practitioner, if I can be considered one at all. My parents forced me into magic, but I prefer other, more wholesome, pursuits. Still, I must make an appearance at these things, if only for form's sake. Oh, Ropa, you'll soon learn it gets dreadfully boring at events like this. I sincerely hope these dour magicians haven't rubbed off on you yet. Carrie, find someone else to do your hewing and drawing, I am borrowing Ropa for a bit.'

Fancy that – my gaffer's got a spouse, dour as he is. Chalk and cheese. I almost smile but wear my poker face instead.

Carrie tuts and pretends to make a fuss but I'm grateful for the escape. My fingers are freezing, and I was dreading the labouring today. Let's see what get-up this guy has in mind for me and then maybe I can sneak off for a nap after.

'Come straight back here when you're done,' Carrie says, seemingly reading my thoughts. Busted.

I follow Esfandiar Soltani out the tent and back onto the road, veering over the bridge above the burn, past the lavatories, onto a path through the woods. Some of the trees were broken during the Big Yin and trunks lie on the ground, roots sticking up. A voice whispers in the woods, tenderly talking to the plants, and I realize it's only Murdo the gardener in his overalls. Strange fellow, that one. He shrinks away from touch, won't shake no one's hand, but he's nice enough so long as you don't push him.

My poor toes get wet again. I'm not sure Esfandiar fares any better in those loafers he has on, not that he seems to care. He carries an air of leisure about him, one arm behind his back. The gentleman flaneur. You could easily picture him strolling down a promenade in Paris or browsing the Grand Bazaar in Istanbul. He has a dreamish air. Head stuck somewhere in the clouds, feet barely touching the ground.

'So, what are you doing at the conference if you're not into these events?' I try to strike up conversation. Cosying up to the boss's better half can't hurt.

Esfandiar is startled. He frowns like I've offended him.

'*My friend, let's not think of tomorrow, but let's enjoy this fleeting moment of life,*' he replies, somewhat cryptically. 'Omar Khayyam,' he adds for clarification. 'The universe was composed in verse and remained so until man discovered maths and now all colour is gone, only ones and zeroes remain. How's your grandmother?'

'Fine, last I checked. You know her?' I'm proper surprised now.

'She's dear to me. But we've long since lost touch. Last I heard she was in seclusion, away from the problems of society. I'd love to share a glass of sherry and watch the sunset with her again one day . . . But enough of old people's woes. You must be bored.' There's sadness aplenty in his voice.

'No, I—'

'Go on, in you get. We don't have all day, darling. Well, we do, but you have work to do, and I'd much rather be idle, thank you very much.'

We enter through a wooden gate leading to the Keeper's Cottage, which is just a short walk from the castle. It's fenced off, separate, though still on part of the castle grounds which extend across the tarred road and beyond. Used to be that this place was the home of the grounds-keeper who looked after the castle, or something like that. It's in good nick and Callander's staying here for the dur-ation of the conference. Haven't seen much of him since we arrived, though. He picked me up in his Bentley and packed me off on the electric minibus, along with Cockburn and the Hamster Squad. I spent most of the journey here sat by the window, watching the Highlands go by. Didn't see too many cows or sheep or crop for all that. It was a wasteland filled with forlorn folk wandering the fringes of the motorways, like the Highland Clearances were taking place all over again. The black blight's bitten into the wood-lands too, affecting pines and firs. Kills everything it touches, like the countryside's rotting away, and there's naught no one can do. It was a lot grimmer than I expected. Give me the city any day.

'Enjoy the calm before this place gets mad, Ropa,' Esfandiar says ruefully. 'Too many young hopefuls, sharks really, elbowing through, hoping to score a connection that'll kick-start their magical career or take it to the next level. It's overwhelming. The schmoozing and canoodling, arse-licking and backstabbing. Welcome to the world of conference. Be on your toes, lassie, or someone's sure to step on them . . . Apart from that, it's all rather boring, as I said.'

'Thanks for the tip.'

'My husband is very fond of you, you know?'

'Not like he's ever shown it.'

'Oh, Ian's a fuddy. But that's hardly his fault. You'll see tomorrow. This place brings out the troglodyte in all of us. Magic does that.'

'You say that, but you're still a magician,' I point out.

'I've got the qualifications, I'm ashamed to admit. But I haven't cast a spell in over two decades. I can barely tell you the difference between a Promethean lustre and Zeusean levin nowadays. I pass my time as a man of leisure in this life filled with the most incredible cares. Poetry is more my speed. Give me wine and verse, and my worries disappear. Before you ask, there's no money to be made in poetry. That's why I made sure to marry well.'

'So you married Sir Callander for his money?'

'It's Sir Ian, dear girl, and no, I married him because he has an ear for poetry and helps to fine-tune my own doggerel. He knows everything from his Homer to his Hafez, Rabbie Burns all the way to Rumi, Ferdowsi and Jackie Kay. And you must promise not to tell anyone else this: he is especially partial to crude limericks once you've got a dram of Craigellachie down his throat.'

I find it impossible to imagine my mentor having fun, let alone reciting vulgar poetry.

'I've never heard of anyone getting shacked up for love of verse.'

'Sylvia Plath and Ted Hughes . . . Though that's not a very good model, is it? Ours is a more enduring partnership. Right, let's get you spruced up and looking the part,' Esfandiar says. 'I love the orange dreadlocks by the way. They're so autumnal. Reminds me of a beautiful poem, "Your Orange Hair in the Void of the World" by Paul Éluard. But you're going for anime, aren't you? Isn't that what we young people are into these days?' He laughs at his own joke.

Esfandiar is only in his fifties, which must be young for a wizard, I guess.

The Keeper's Cottage is slightly secluded, surrounded by hedge and mature pines. A few remain standing after the Big Yin. I can see why Callander gets this pad when he stays. It affords him some privacy away from the conference activities at the castle. However, the interior is disappointingly modern. Bright laminate flooring and flat-pack furniture, not the antiques you'd want in such a place. The walls are painted a light grey and it's clean but definitely lacks oomph.

Still, it's better than the digs me and the Hamster Squad are staying in.

Esfandiar leaves the room and returns in a jiffy with a leather travel case.

'Let me see what we have here. I hope I got your size right. Ian was useless when I asked him. It's bloody hard to pick something out when all you've got to go on is hand gestures to say she's about this tall and a waist this wide. He was right about one thing, though, you're skin and bone, not an ounce of fat on you.' He pats his pot belly to make the point. 'You can have some of my lard if you wish.'

Then he hands me a kilted skirt, blouse and tonnag.

'I ain't wearing that,' I say.

'I wouldn't like to either, but we're all stuck with it this week, I'm afraid, darling. You and me both, if that's any consolation. Huff and puff if you will, but there's simply no getting around this. We're with the secretary, therefore we're required to wear his clan tartan.'

'I'll freeze my tits off in that. And where am I supposed to store my catapult and ammo if I ain't got no pockets?'

'Hand me the tonnag. I'll give you this three-quarter-length coat instead. It's got all the pockets a girl could ever want or need. I know this because it belonged to your grandmother and she was very partial to it, but she forgot it after a soiree on our estate long before you were born. Oh, and you're supposed to wear this pin too.'

I can't find an excuse, so I take the gear he's handed me and head to the bathroom to change. Yahweh, that massive tub! I wish I could soak in it for a bit. Beats queuing up early in the morning for the one bathroom I share with the Squad. It's alright though. We're holed up inside the castle proper, which is something, has to be said. And since I don't get paid for my work, I mean to pull off a heist. That'll be my remuneration. Fair's fair and all that. I simply have to find something no one will miss. A girl's got to get paid, after all.

III

So, it's finally start day and I've been posted to gate duty. I'm already wishing I'd brought leggings 'cause of the nip up my kilt. Pity Esfandiar didn't hook me up with a new pair of boots either. I look weird with this old pair on. But the coat's proper cool, he was right. It's a few sizes too big and the sleeves cover my hands, so I have to roll them up – I can live with that when it's this gorgeous kente cloth, whose oranges and greens match my tartan. I'd take a selfie and send it to Gran, but she don't see too good, so instead I send a voice note with a description. Must be her and Callander were tight back then, although she doesn't tell me much about them days. Neither does he. I'm gonna have to grill her when I get back. I'm sure I'll have better odds doing that than trying the gaffer.

I'm stuck in a sentry box by the castle's wrought-iron entrance gates, which have funky Celtic symbols drawn on the black metal. There's a car park across the road, and some kind of shop or shelter that's been stripped bare. The wet tar shines as a sliver of sunlight slices the heavy clouds. I'm really hoping the weather improves. Cockburn shunted me out here instead of having me do duties inside the castle. But I'll have the last ha-ha since I get to meet and check out all the attendees as they come in.

I was up all of last night too, studying my dossier. I keep it next to me today, just in case. Cockburn insists we greet the important guests by name, identifying them before they say who they are. Personal touch, blah, blah. At least I'm good with faces. Aurora, who I'm working with on gate duty, doesn't seem bothered with any of it. She's pissed 'cause she wanted to be working inside, thinking out here the guests just breeze by, but inside, you have time to make a connection. And who knows what it might do for your career down the line? I still think it's better to be here – the first faces everyone sees. Maybe we'll find out whose strategy wins the day. *For shame, Ropa, you're thinking like them already.*

So far, I've met Hamish Hutchinson, the principal of St Andrews College, one of the four schools of magic. He drove through the gates in a sporty electric car. The bigwigs get to drive in, while plebs have to park across the road. It means the honchos avoid the beggars and orphans from the area who mill about the entrance seeking alms. I gave him a lanyard but he blanked me, then thanked Aurora instead. Sigh. I'm also dishing out tote bags filled with the programme, a special conference edition of the *Monthly Sceptic*, mugs, pens and fudge. Well, not every bag is complete. I've pinched fudge from a few and given it to the orphans, and will see if I can get them leftovers after dinner too.

How could I not? These dirty kids, snot on their faces, dressed in virtual rags. I thought my boots were pretty bad, but the stuff they wear on their feet doesn't deserve to be called shoes. People walk past them, like they don't even see them.

'Ropantasmatron!' Jomo Maige shouts excitedly, emerging from behind a bush somewhere. Dude's all resplendent in the flowing white uniform which acolytes of the Library wear. It's good to see my bestiest amongst all the elite of Scottish magic.

'Hey, man,' I say.

'A bit more enthusiasm would be nice, Ropa. Aurora, you look like the morning star.'

'Mr Maige, you're so suave,' she mocks, handing him a blue staff lanyard – all the librarians count as that too. Ordinary guests get green ones, castle staff wear purple.

'Euan Cleghorn, the head of the Glasgow Library, is giving a talk on "Lost Texts and Where to Find Them" this afternoon. I can't wait. Sneddon was telling me about a lass called Genevieve Something who goes around the world seeking lost grimoires for our collections. Isn't that amazing?'

'A kind of librarian Lara Croft?'

'Maybe I can train to do that one day,' he says.

I'm not sure Jomo's built for action, but I give him an encouraging nod. Were it up to me, I'd keep him locked away, safe in the Library, where the world can't get to him. Sweet kid. The fuzz on his lip and under his chin is really coming along as well. It curls like his huge 'fro. I've been told I have to attend a couple of talks too, as part of my internship, but the choice is narrower for me 'cause I'm only allowed to attend the ones that ain't oversubscribed.

'Looks like the gang's started the party without me,' Priya

yells, crossing the road from the car park. The mad grin on her face spells trouble, and I would know, she's my kickass bestie. The only one of us who's an actual magician by profession. That lass and me have been through some mad adventures, but this time we're all about the hobnobbing. She's got bags dangling off the push handles of her wheelchair and there's stacks of posters on her lap. She's desperately trying not to drop anything as she moves towards us. The bottom hem of her trousers rides halfway up her shins, showing she's wearing different-coloured slouch socks. Fluorescent green and rose red garishly jarring. I love it.

A queue's forming now, with folks staying in the accommodations dotted outside the castle trickling in for the first day's activities. Most of them are staying in the stretch between Dunvegan and Orbost. Although more than a few come through from Portree as well. Aurora shakes off her mood and helps me to process them all as they arrive. Gotta cross everyone off the register before they get their pass.

'Which talks are you attending?' Jomo asks Priya.

'There's one just before lunch on the advances in teleportation spellcraft. I read a paper in the *Monthly Sceptic* that suggested using wave function collapse to fool subatomic particles that they are in a different region of space could be potentially groundbreaking. It could be used in the excision of tumours and cancerous growths without the need for invasive surgery or chemo. It's early days, but the theory sounds fascinating.'

'Those theories are wildly speculative and unlikely to have any practicable application,' a mansplainer in the queue opines, having overheard. 'Richard Schabas, who's giving that talk, isn't exactly known for his rigour. I would suggest you go to Strang's talk on Cochrane's Fluxions, which I'm certain will revolutionize our understanding of—'

'Your last name wouldn't happen to be Strang, perchance?' Priya cuts him off.

The mansplainer tuts and shuts it, wearing the aggrieved look of a man unfairly treated. There's laughter from the back of the queue, but Aurora spares him too much embarrassment by keeping the line moving. I quickly check the list and see only two people have signed up to the talk on fluxions, but the teleportation event, which it clashes with, is fully subscribed.

'I *was* going to his event, but I won't be anymore,' says the woman next in line. She gives me the sense of thunder rumbling off in the distance.

'Have a longer lunch instead,' Priya suggests. She's a bubbling burn you wouldn't wanna whitewater raft in. All magicians give off a vibe you can tune into, like them old wireless sets with shiny knobs.

She and Jomo leave not long after, going through and abandoning us to the drudgery of getting all the remaining guests in. A few have shown up on the wrong date and their passes won't be valid till later in the week, so I have to deny them entry, unless they upgrade to a full pass. But in the main it goes well, until three ruddy-coloured, broad-shouldered men with ginger hair appear, jumping the queue like this was London, where I've heard they do that sort of thing. But they don't look like no Londoners as they are proudly attired in full

Highland dress, complete with the flying plaid and a purled fringe dangling down to the calves.

It's odd how no one in the line complains. No Scot worth their sodium chloride lets queue-jumping go unchallenged.

These men give the impression of musky horses and flashing steel. An older, cruder style of magic perhaps, which is a mix of earthiness and metallurgy. You feel something of a magician's power up close to them, pushing against your sixth sense and forming something in your mind's eye. The same way photons reaching your eye are turned into images by the brain.

'Names?' I ask.

'Dalziel of the MacDonald Clan. These are my sons, Avery and Boyd.'

'I can't find your names on the register,' Aurora says.

'Is that how it is then?' Dalziel says in a booming voice. He has a powerful frame and a large noggin. 'It's the MacLeods mucking with us again. Is this conference still about Scottish magic, or has it degenerated into a partisan affair?'

'You tell them, Dad,' Avery says.

'We have every right to be here,' Dalziel shouts.

I'm taken aback 'cause I don't know nothing about this beef. It's not like I've been to this conference before. Nope. Not my problem. My job is to keep things moving. And I must say, it's kinda satisfying being the gatekeeper for a change.

'You three stand aside. We'll let the others in while we sort out your story,' I say.

'No one else is going in if we aren't.' Dalziel's proper radge.

He bangs his fist on our poor desk and sends our paperwork flying.

Bloody hell. We've only just started and we have a situation already.

'Please, gentlemen—' a fellow in the queue starts to say, but one look from Dalziel MacDonald silences him. I text a quick SOS to Cockburn. Other folks in the queue will start to get annoyed and that's how shit gets out of hand. But the MacDonalds don't look like they're budging any time before the second coming. If this was my own show, I'd tell them where to go stuff it. But I'm with the Society, so I have to act professional.

A few minutes later Cockburn comes through briskly, sharp as always in her grey suit. She holds three lanyards with 'GUEST' written on them, instead of names.

'Frances, must we do this every single conference?' Dalziel asks.

'You haven't been to one in over ten years, if I remember correctly,' she replies.

'And that makes me less of a member? You'd do well to recall all that the MacDonalds have done for Scottish magic.'

'It means that you may not be aware we are now fully computerized, and we no longer accept registration via carrier pigeon.'

'Well, we're here now.'

'Come along then. I have a lot of work to do prepping for the guest of honour, who's due this evening. These passes will let you into any events that aren't already fully booked. And you have access to the usual spaces.'

'Then I'm certain you'll have us quartered accordingly and include us in the dinner tonight. I very much look forward to seeing this Ethiopian fellow everyone's been going on about,' Dalziel says, pushing past Cockburn with his sons in tow. I wonder what's brought them to this conference after so long? I can see they're going to be trouble.

IV

The hulking mass of Dunvegan Castle stands solid and grey in the fading light. The sessions are done for the day and many attendees have left, while those that remain linger at the bar on the ground floor talking magic. I've been summoned to the courtyard to stand beside Sir Ian Callander, where we're waiting for the guest of honour. But they're running late.

'I see Esfandiar's worked his sorcery on you,' Callander remarks, looking me over in my livery. He's also in tartan, so we're matched rather nicely, as planned. His husband, similarly attired, is yakking with other VIPs.

My feet are killing me, but at least I got the chance to change into a dry pair of socks. Overtime pay, anyone?

The lawn in the courtyard is, mercifully, wet but not soggy. There's slabs laid upon it in a square pattern. Must make it awkward for the gardener when he comes to mow.

The bulk of the building runs behind us, large windows looking down towards the sea. The MacLeods have had this place for eight hundred years, so I'm sure the mortgage must be paid off by now. It's a hybrid building, the amalgamation of five distinct structures erected by different chiefs through the ages and glued together to become what it is now. At least that's what Morag told me. If Victor Frankenstein was an architect, this would be his style of building.

We're stood by the crenellations of the castle wall looking down onto Loch Dunvegan. Rusty old cannons point to where the Sea of the Hebrides cuts inland to create this saltwater loch. The high tide laps gently against the scraggy rock below and from here we can see all the way across to the shore on the other side. Lights burn in the houses and cottages stretching out to Uiginish.

Callander's impatience grows. He's not the sort of man used to being kept waiting. Welcome to my world, sir.

Our host, Edmund MacLeod, the current chief of the Clan MacLeod resident at Dunvegan Castle, is on our left. He's a rotund man, sat on a chair I brought out for him after he complained he didn't like standing. He has pale skin, dark eyebrows and a distrustful air, as though he expects the enemy to pounce any moment.

'How much longer? This is getting ridiculous,' MacLeod whines.

Callander turns his head, as if listening to something far off in the sea none of us can hear, and replies, 'Soon.'

I bloody hope so.

Montgomery Wedderburn, rector of the Edinburgh Ordinary School for Boys, is deep in conversation with his fellow educator, Hamish Hutchinson of St Andrews College. They're standing near the South Wing, with several other men hovering near them, listening keenly to their discourse. I imagine they're held in high regard since every practitioner here would have passed through one of those four schools . . . except for me, but then

I'm not a real magician. Not yet, anyway. Wedderburn removes his golden monocle, fishes out a hankie from his breast pocket and cleans it while pontificating on something.

I next spot Professor Fergus Cattermole sipping bubbly near the door with Priya and several others. He's a vice principal at Glasgow University and head of the Lord Kelvin Institute, which is part of the uni. It's the only school affiliated to an institute of higher learning, so it grants degree certificates to its graduates. Cattermole is in full academic dress – a gown of black watered silk, with a square collar and lace on it. He's also wearing a trencher cap with a silver tassel, looking like he's going to a graduation ceremony. A man approaches him, and I recognize him from the dossier as the Royal Bank of Scotland's Chief Risk Officer Les MacLaughlin. Carrie told me that it used to be the RBS Chief Executive who came to these things, but because of strained relations the bank stopped coming. This is their first year back after a long absence, and only because of services I rendered to them. Work I did for the RBS archives a few months ago. Relations might be thawing, but they're still not prepared to send their main man over in case it pisses off the king. Scottish magic is still in the doghouse.

The person I really want to see is Calista Featherstone, the head teacher at the Aberdeen School of Magic and Esoterica. My sister, Izwi, got a scholarship there, and I'm hoping to hear word on her progress. Unfortunately, Mrs Featherstone hasn't turned up yet, and instead all I get is the MacDonalds sulking in the corner. They look tense, ready to kick off at the slightest offence, and are chatting in hushed, conspiratorial tones. What's their beef with the Society and the MacLeods?

Avery, the younger son, is particularly distracted, checking out Fenella, Edmund MacLeod's only daughter. She's a ghost walking among us, with the same anaemic look as her father. White hair and a grace that makes it seem as though she's floating through the gathering.

As I look around, I recognize more folks from the Society. Members of the Hamster Squad scurry about the lawn carrying trays with champagne and canapes. Keeping the attendees lubricated is all part of the job. Cockburn hovers around too, seemingly engaged with the other guests when in reality she's keeping an eye on the staff. Luckily I'm off her leash for the time being, sticking with Callander for the evening. He won't let me drink the champagne – I'm only fifteen, after all, too underage by his book. Even though, this being Scotland, when I turn sixteen next year I can legally marry, it'll be another two years after that before I can have a pint . . . legally. Go figure. I make do swiping the other treats coming through. And I also get properly introduced to important folks as his intern, which is super-dope.

Suddenly there's an audible gasp, followed by the shattering of a wine glass somewhere near the stairs leading down to the sea gate. We turn collectively, and I'm horrified to see what looks like a massive tsunami wave headed straight for us.

As the wave barrels along at a steady clip, washing over the small islets in the middle of Dunvegan Loch, I'm proper bricking it. But Callander seems to have this sangfroid thing going on, as do some of the other magical honchos watching it. Getting ready to bail, I wonder why I'm one of the few people here with any sense of self-preservation. The roar of the tsunami rises to a crescendo.

'About bloody time,' mutters Edmund MacLeod, ponderously rising from his chair.

I see it: a tiny craft is being carried aloft by the tsunami. It looks like a surfer from here. The noise of the water is still deafening but I notice the wave stays within the limits of the loch. Save for the uninhabited islets swallowed in its wake, it doesn't touch land on either side. The grey water rumbles on, drawing nearer, towering over the castle as it narrows to fit the course.

Then it stops in front of the wall.

'That's a new one,' someone behind us says.

'Swell,' comes a droll reply.

From this close up, I can see ripples in the water as it cycles down from the crest. The wave maintains its position but recedes gradually in height, backwash flowing up the channel. It lowers until the small papyrus boat riding the crest lands atop the castle wall. The craft looks so flimsy, I'm shocked to imagine it making an ocean journey.

A man, apparently in his early twenties, wearing a white traditional Ethiopian suit with yellow, gold and red trim, leaps from the boat and lands on the lawn.

'Sorry we're late,' he says. 'And please forgive the theatrics. We had to make haste. Navigating in these overcast skies is very difficult. You see neither sun nor stars, and we got lost at the Isle of Man. I mistook Peel Castle for this place.'

I can only imagine what the poor islanders of Man must have thought about it all.

Behind him a wizened old man, back bent, dressed in the robes of the Ethiopian Orthodox Church, shuffles to the front of the boat. The young man holds out his hand, but the old man hesitates. He seems worried about the distance between the boat and the lawn. His assistant intuitively grasps this and so kneels, offering his thigh as a step. And using this, the older man finally descends.

Once on the ground, the old man seems even tinier, overwhelmed by his voluminous vestments and delicate as a thing made of porcelain. His sharp eyes home in on Callander.

The old man gives off the vibe of the rising of a sandstorm whose grains are sharp razor blades. It's a dense storm, humming like angry locusts, blotting out the sky. A power that overwhelms everything in its path. It can devour every leaf and blade of grass if it so chooses.

Callander steps forward, with me in tow, and stops before the Ethiopian magicians. They barely reach his navel. I stand just behind him, solemn, trying to look the part.

'Scottish magic has the honour of welcoming the Grand Debtera of Abyssinia, Qozmos, to our seat. Our peoples have a long history of friendship and mutual aid, and long may this continue through the ages,' Callander says formally.

'Dunvegan Castle opens its doors to you,' Edmund MacLeod proclaims. Nice rhetoric, but not every door is open. The apartments on the second and third floors are off limits, save for a select few personal guests of the MacLeods. It's still a private residence, after all.

The assistant whispers into the old man's ear. The Grand

Debtera nods and the assistant replies, 'Your welcome pleases us, indeed.'

There's polite applause from the magicians behind us, and the secretary moves in to shake the Grand Debtera's hand. The old man's eyes meet mine briefly and his eyebrows raise a fraction, almost in recognition, then he quickly turns back to Callander. I've always seen Callander as a great battleship parting the waves, and physically the Ethiopian magician seems frail and weak before him. But at that moment I recall a story I heard the other day, on my favourite military history podcast.

It told of how, in the early twentieth century, Ethiopia was divided, with many rival warlords vying for power. Amidst this chaos emerged the young noble Ras Tafari Makonnen, who rose to supremacy, unifying the various feuding factions. Unlike the Ethiopian leaders of the past, he was mild-mannered and soft-spoken. But by the mid-1920s, there were still those powerful enough to resist him, among them the great general Balcha, governor of Sidamo, who saw no reason why he should bend to this young upstart. And so Tafari, who would later become Emperor Haile Selassie I, finally ordered Balcha to come to the capital, Addis Ababa. Sensing danger, Balcha arrived with a host of several thousand soldiers and camped outside the city. He had the strength and resources to start a civil war. But he did not enter the city, forcing Tafari to send emissaries to ask him to attend a banquet in his honour. This he did, but only after getting Tafari to agree to him bringing six hundred armed bodyguards along too. Balcha knew that past Ethiopian leaders had used banquets to entrap their rivals, and he was wary of being murdered or arrested. Tafari simply replied that he was honoured to host a great warrior of renown. But Balcha, who was still suspicious, directed his men not to get drunk and to remain on high alert for the ruse that was sure to come. He declared to Tafari that, should he not return to his army that same day, orders had been given that they should sack the city. This was his insurance.

At the banquet, Tafari was deferential towards Balcha. He had songs sung in praise of the general and seated him in a place of honour. All this slowly convinced Balcha that the young leader was afraid of him. So he began to plot how he would return to unseat Tafari and take power for himself. It would all be so easy. After the banquet, Balcha returned safely to his camp with his bodyguards, ready to push forward with his plans. But when he arrived, he found not the bustling camp he'd left behind, but only smoke from doused fires. All his men, every single one, were gone. Surely there must have been a fight? Why hadn't he heard anything? Where were the bodies? Balcha soon learnt that, while he was feasting, Tafari had sent a trusted ally, Ras Kassa Haile Darge, with an army to Balcha's camp, using a secret route. He'd arrived not with force of arms but with gold, money and trinkets, and proceeded to buy Balcha's men off. The general's men gave up their weapons quickly and scattered into the desert, loaded with cash. Balcha wanted to follow and rally them, but Darge's forces blocked the way. He then thought of taking his six hundred back to the capital, but Tafari's troops would be there, waiting for him. And so Balcha, realizing he was out of options, humiliated himself before Tafari. He was stripped of his governorship and exiled to a monastery. Before Balcha entered his exile, he warned his contemporaries, 'Do not underestimate the power of Tafari. He creeps like a mouse but has jaws like a lion.'

I sense this same cunning masked in meekness in the Grand Debtera, Qozmos. I sense the might of the vast desert coming off him and feel awe.

The assistant retrieves an ornate wooden box from the papyrus boat, and the wave fully recedes. The loch finally settles back into high tide, with the boat moored at the rocks below.

Callander next introduces me as his apprentice, with Qozmos's assistant interpreting. It makes me feel rather important and my head swells up to the size of a pumpkin.

'I'd introduce you to my husband too, but he has a way of getting lost in the crowds,' he says, looking for Esfandiar Soltani, who's now regaling a group of students.

'The girl reminds me of someone I once knew, sir. You have chosen your successor well,' Qozmos responds through his assistant. But I think something is lost in translation there. 'The heavens are pleased too that I should introduce your left arm to mine. Kebede the son of Bekele is my assistant. I pray our hands clap to the song of the ages.'

The assistant reaches out to shake my hand and smiles, revealing pearly-white gnashers. His curly hair bounces in the light evening breeze.

'You must be famished after such a long journey,' MacLeod

says, cutting in, maybe a wee bit gruff at not being at the centre of things, even though this is his castle. 'Let's go inside and eat.'

'Yes, it was simpler when planes more commonly circled the earth. Now we make do as we must,' Qozmos replies.

'Father, will you not introduce me as well?' the white-haired lass says to MacLeod.

'Not now, Fenella,' he snaps.

She retreats back into the crowd, stung. There's a whole bunch of other important people jostling for position to meet the guest, but just then, from the tower, the ghostly sound of bagpipes begins to drone. The piper's nowhere in sight, only his haunting notes filter down to us. I've heard rumours a spectral piper resides in the tower and can be heard playing some nights. Morag swears by it, but I ain't seen nothing since I got here.

The Grand Debtera pauses and closes his eyes to listen to the music. His serene stillness holds us rooted fast.

One might have expected national anthems or some such jazz on an occasion like this. Instead it's the 'Piper's Welcome' playing. A clever compromise. Had 'March Forward, Dear Mother Ethiopia' been played, then 'Flower of Scotland' would have had to follow. Its omission would have been obvious. But those lyrics – 'That stood against him/ Proud Edward's Army/ And sent him homeward tae think again' – used to rally the separatists, and while it's not banned or anything like that, no one plays it anymore. Nothing's forbidden here. We are free.

The flagpole above the tower at the northern end of the castle stands empty. Choosing either the Union Jack or the

Scottish Saltire would compromise the Society and the MacLeods with it. The king doesn't make fine distinctions in such matters; he prefers the bone saw to the scalpel.

Best let sleeping dogs lie, methinks.

Nah. Stop fretting. This gig's supposed to be a doddle. Endure this posh wank, kiss arse galore, rinse, repeat, go home. That's how it'll go down.

The piper entrances us right up till the final note blows away on the breeze to distant shores. We then begin to make our way into the castle. It's slow progress, with various practitioners pressing to have a quick word with Callander, or trying to attract the guest of honour's attention. His assistant has a hell of a job translating, while Qozmos smiles gently. At last, they are rescued by Cockburn, who clears a path, shooing away the eager young magicians desperate to make connections. A couple have their phones up, taking photos. But the small, select number of dinner guests, like Rector Wedderburn, show no such compulsion, 'cause they know they'll soon be in a more suitable environment to make their presence known. Status means access.

'There'll be a presentation and drinks after dinner in the drawing room. You'll all get your chance then. Now, please, make way,' Cockburn says.

With her taking charge, we make faster progress across the courtyard. We're nearly at the door when an almighty crash of thunder booms in the sky. Instantly afeard, I look up over my shoulder. The thunder starts to sound like galloping hooves pounding up in the clouds. Then an ivory glow shines through, as if the sun's risen a second time.

I hear the sharp crack of a whip.

'Hiya! Hiya!'

The light above us moves at an incredible speed. Horses neigh. The sound of their galloping comes smashing against us in waves. Cockburn, clearly alarmed by this interruption to her smooth planning, scans the Hamster Squad, seeking explanation. But we're all equally baffled. Callander bites his lower lip. Dalziel MacDonald smirks, still back in the corner of the courtyard, as if he knows something the rest of us don't.

Finally, breaking through the clouds, a small dark object plunges towards us at a steep angle. Ivory light trails it like a comet's tail. Behind that is a plume of dreadful black smoke blighting the sky.

'All part of tonight's activities,' says MacLeod, trying to regain control of the situation. But it's clear from his tone that he's been wrongfooted like the rest of us.

The dark object in the sky soon resolves into four horses pulling a stagecoach.

'Looks like Christmas's come early this year,' someone tries to quip.

Waves of warm air roll over us.

The wheels of the stagecoach glow red hot. Now it's close enough to see the driver whip his charges.

The warm air turns to industrial blasts of heat as the stagecoach descends. It arcs to the east, driving past the castle, then veers back on approach. The coachman's face is covered by a mask, and he wears a bowler hat. Soon he cries, 'Hoo, hooooo,' pulling back on the reins to slow his horses.

Sparks fly from beneath their hooves.

The heat blasting us becomes unbearable as the horses touch down on the lawn and the stagecoach plunges after them. There are cries of alarm, people leaping out of the way, as the coach's wheels burn tracks into the grass. The driver battles to halt the stallions until the coach eventually stops in the middle of the grounds.

A chemical smell then washes over us. Metal, plastics, coal, hydrocarbons, toxic substances all in one. It's overpowering. Several people in the gathering cough. All but the most stoic fan their faces or cover their mouths. My eyes sting and start to water.

The driver applies the brakes on the carriage and, whip in hand, jumps to the ground. He's wearing a greatcoat that is so bulky and square, you can barely see his frame beneath it. His long arms make him seem like a great ape. Moving with an arrogant air, he ignores the people he nearly trampled under his carriage. Instead, he goes straight to the door – on which I spot a royal insignia, no less – and opens it.

Folks whisper amongst themselves.

None dare approach.

All the while I'm racking my mind, wondering who I might have missed in the dossier.

It's hard to make out the occupant of the coach from this angle. All I can see is a hand holding a china cup of tea and another the saucer. The passenger inside slurps their beverage loudly and smacks their lips with satisfaction. When they are done, they toss the cup and saucer onto the lawn, then a cane with a silver tiger's head appears in their hand.

The carriage sways as they get up.

He steps down, bending to fit through the door, and one hand grips the carriage, cane landing on the first step. Out he comes, until he's standing upon the singed grass in his fine leather brogues. He wears a top hat with a red stripe and has a cape draped around his shoulders. I receive the impression of unbridled menace, rivers of blood, marching boots signalling a seismic event, horns, cries of despair, gunpowder smoke hanging in the air. Victory at all costs. Conquest after conquest. A relentless force that bends the world to its will.

The man gives us a twisted smile.

His eyes are dark and fierce.

Shadows dance upon his face.

He regards us slowly, turning his head left, then right, before returning to the centre and finally fixing his eyes upon Sir Callander. He moves as though he's got all the time in the world. Like he's the laird of the manor just arrived home.

'GOD. SAAAAAVE.' The man pauses and strolls casually, until he's standing toe to toe with Scotland's top magician. He throws the left side of his cape back, revealing his blazer, the royal insignia emblazoned upon his breast pocket. 'The . . . king.' The word 'king' he says quietly, with reverence.

Callander stands for a second and then replies at last, 'Long may he reign.'

'Long may he reign,' says MacLeod with gusto.

'Long may he reign,' says Wedderburn.

'Long may he reign,' says Cockburn.

'Long may he reign,' I say, and swallow.

The words flow into the crowd, gathering momentum, that

twisted smile never leaving the interloper's face, until they morph into a chant: 'Long may he reign, long may he reign . . .'

V

After the chant dies down, we're all kinda anxious. Well, except for the Grand Debtera, who wears a bemused look as Kebede tries to explain to him what is happening. The distress on Cockburn's face is proper freaking me out. So I can be sure the new arrival wasn't anywhere in the plans. She's been drilling us all week, there's no way she'd have missed someone this important-seeming.

'I'm touched to see Scotland display so much affection for her monarch. That she remembers how he single-handedly dragged her out of the abyss, when the lawless looted and murdered openly on the streets of Edinburgh, Glasgow, Aberdeen, Inverness and Dundee. When women in the villages and towns were dragged out of their beds at night, it was he who stood as their protector. When children were starving in the Highlands, he was the father who fed them. He brought order out of chaos. And so, it pleases us to see you gathered, sipping champagne and enjoying the fruits of the king's peace,' says the new arrival. His voice is firm and commanding.

With his cape thrown back, I can see the shoulder of his jacket is adorned with raven's wings.

Niccolò Machiavelli once said, 'It is better to be feared than loved.' That's the playbook this man and our king use to rig the games they create for us. It's impossible not to be awed by this raw display of might. He's undoubtedly impressive, with a thick monobrow over dark eyes. The way he moves is energetic, and he has a certain vivacity and ambiguous allure. Everyone loves a bad boy, and he has that Freddie Mercury magnetism. His magic seems to come with bells and whistles, seductively different from the Presbyterianism of the Scottish sort.

'Scottish magic has the immense honour of welcoming the occupier of the Merlin Seal, Lord Sashvindu Samarasinghe, England's Sorcerer Royal, to our biennial gathering,' Sir Callander announces, gesturing towards the man himself, trying to defuse the situation.

'And the chief—' MacLeod starts.

'Does it? Really?' Lord Samarasinghe cuts him off. 'Then where was the invite to the fellows of the *Royal* Society of Sorcery and the Advancement of the Mystic Arts? It seems such a strange welcome to us when practitioners from abroad are feted, but your cousins down south find themselves ignored.'

'My Lord—'

'We are not finished!' His voice rises and falls as he speaks. It's like seeing a deadly cobra swaying in front of you. 'But we forgive the administrative oversight, as we have done many a slight in the past. Mercy and compassion is the way . . .'

Someone grabs my arm and I turn. Carrie.

'Inside, *now*,' she says.

I sneak back into the castle, away from the drama. Seems like the Hamster Squad's been drafted in to fix something. Before we reach Cockburn, who's also come inside, Les MacLaughlin from the Royal Bank of Scotland corners her. He dabs his sweaty brow with the sleeve of his suit.

'I must excuse myself. My wife's just texted and there's an emergency at home. I apologize. I must go,' he says, abruptly withdrawing, headed for the exit.

Cockburn straightens up and brushes invisible flecks off her suit. She's trying to compose herself. Hard to do while still being able to hear Lord Samarasinghe's voice outside rattling off a list of grievances. In his account, you get the sense *they*, our neighbours down south, are the victims in all this jazz.

'This is a catastrophe,' Cockburn moans.

'What do we do?'

'Follow me to the dining room.'

We make our way up the narrow stairs and then through the corridor lined with portraits. There's a couple of young magicians lingering, strategically positioned to intercept their marks as they pass through. Cockburn shoos them away, telling them to wait until after dinner and for the reception at the bar. Nearest the door leading to the dining room is a familiar-looking middle-aged man. I rack my brain and then realize it's one of my favourite authors, Rossworth Rupini. He wrote *Rich Sorcerer, Poor Sorcerer*, which is a brilliant practical guide for busigicians seeking to make a buck in this cut-throat economy.

He's a huge personality, but his scuffed shoes and the

mending on his suit don't seem to reflect the wealth and success he claims to possess in his books.

He flashes a charming smile at Cockburn.

'Frances, you look radiant,' he says, stepping up to kiss her, but she pushes him back.

'I'm rather busy at the moment.'

'Yes, that's why I'm here.' He nods his head. A priming technique taught to travelling salespeople.

Classic Rupini, from his chapter on converting No into Yes. There's a technique to building rapport which he emphasizes in his work. Mirror your mark's body language. 'Jam your foot in the door before they shut it.' I love the shamelessness he has. If he can flip Cockburn right now, it'll be all the proof I need that his teachings really do work.

'You see, I'm trying to penetrate the English market, and was astounded to learn you'd not reserved a seat for me at the dinner table tonight. Obviously this was an error. I'm certain important people will wonder where I am if I don't attend.'

'I've already announced there'll be an open reception afterwards,' Cockburn replies, annoyed, probably because this American doesn't know the difference between England and Britain. 'You may make your connections there.'

'I'm giving a sold-out talk at this—'

'Mr Rupini, I really am pushed at the moment. Perhaps we can discuss this at a more suitable juncture.'

That's the door shutting for anyone here, but the author, being the ultimate salesman, doesn't buckle at the polite dismissal.

'There'll be other dinners this week. I'm sure you'll get me a seat at one of those,' he insists. Then he gives me a wink. 'Get yourself a ticket for my talk tomorrow. You'll learn the latest trade secrets, young lady.'

So much for his talks being sold out. I nod along, but I'm not really feeling it. I was dying to go before, but seeing him now in person, unfiltered, he's a lot less impressive than how I'd pictured him. He doesn't appear to be doing all that great, going by the standards he sets out in his work. Me, Carrie and Cockburn escape him quickly and shut ourselves in the dining room.

'The chef's already complained we're running late. He's got nine courses to run through,' Carrie says.

'He can bloody wait,' Cockburn snaps.

She's finnicky at the best of times, but the stress is really getting to her right now. Before this gig with the Society, I was working for myself. You know, self-employed, living the dream, a modern entrepreneur. Now I can admit, being at the bottom of the food chain's got its perks – I can kick back while it's all hitting the fan, 'cause the buck ain't even in my postcode. Ha-ha. It's a beautiful feeling and I'm digging seeing Cockburn roasting under the pressure.

The table in the dining room seats twelve, but if the guests don't mind rubbing elbows, we can add two extra chairs. It's got lush seats, padded for extra comfort. And it's all under a candelabra with six LED lights, although we have candles for tonight. Reminds me of the Library of the Dead, but more modern. Kinda ironic since the Island of Skye's the sticks.

'We're going to have to revise the seating arrangements

again. I've already had to bump Theodore Wilke to make way for Dalziel MacDonald.' She stares at the table intensely, as if her life depended on it. 'The good news is, with Les MacLaughlin gone, I won't need to get rid of anyone else in order to accommodate Lord Samarasinghe. All we need to do is to shuffle people around.'

The last time Cockburn'd had us in here, prepping for tonight, she'd explained to us the traditional seating arrangement. Edmund MacLeod sits at the head of the table, since this is his castle. Sir Callander goes opposite him, at the other end of it. Then the heads of the four schools of magic take honoured places on the table's shoulders next to MacLeod and Callander. These are rotated at every conference, in order not to show preference to any of the schools. It's all a delicate balancing act. In the past there've been serious disagreements in this area, 'cause of the perceived primacy of the rector of the Edinburgh School, which rankles the two newer schools especially. The problem is that any slight to a particular school ripples out to its alumni too, in this snobbish world where status is everything. It even caused a mass brawl at the conference of 1932, when the principal of St Andrews was snubbed by Sir Richard Simson, who at the time served simultaneously as Secretary of the Society of Sceptical Enquirers and head of the Edinburgh School. The result was that, to this day, no head from any of the four schools can hold the post of secretary at the same time. This was meant to diminish the Edinburgh School's stranglehold on the institution, but to date only St Andrews has had an alumnus in the post. That said, their secretaries tend not to last very long in the role.

Cockburn had seated the Grand Debtera in the middle of the table, on the side facing the windows. That way this key guest could converse easily with the two halves of the table, and conversation would flow around him. And seeing as he spoke no English, Kebede was placed next to him to translate. Otherwise, it was unlikely the assistant would have been included.

The real headache for Cockburn now is where to seat the English Sorcerer Royal. He is, after all, a representative of the sovereign. It's essential that attention is paid to this status. So much pressure, with mere minutes to go before dinner. Cockburn must decide quickly. She mutters us through her thought process: Edmund MacLeod can't be bumped from the head of the table. The lairds of the Highlands and Islands are especially prickly about how they are treated by folks from the lowlands.

Reseating Sir Callander is equally problematic. He is the head of Scottish magic. The Society fiercely maintains its independence within the Union and considers Scottish magic equal to English magic. I've heard rumblings that the English magicians, who are wealthier and far more numerous than their Scottish counterparts, are of a different opinion on the subject. It's telling they are a 'royal society', whereas the Sceptical Enquirers are granted no such status. Another quirk of this arrangement, as I've learnt, is that English magicians wishing to practise in Scotland are subjected to a rigorous conversion course before they're admitted into the Society. English magic, on the other hand, has no qualms integrating practitioners from the former Commonwealth, so long as they hold accreditation and qualification from their relevant juris-dictions.

Removing Callander from his place would, de facto, be an admission that English magic was superior, rendering Callander's position untenable.

This is the circle Cockburn has to square: to create a new seating arrangement in which no one's fragile ego is bruised. No wonder she's flustered. She runs through various permu-tations, looking to us for support we can't give. Then she finally settles on a solution.

'I'm going to move the heads of the four schools to the middle of the table.'

'And the other guests?' Carrie asks.

'I'll sit the Sorcerer Royal on MacLeod's right-hand side as an honoured guest.' She sweeps her hand diagonally across the table. 'Then I'll have the Grand Debtera at Sir Callander's right. That way the two external heads have equal status at the table. And you will all bend over backwards to ensure they have a pleasant stay. Is that clear?'

Carrie sucks in air through her teeth.

She's thinking what I'm thinking.

'Out with it,' Cockburn snaps.

With this new arrangement, Cockburn may have managed to diffuse tensions, keeping Callander and Samarasinghe far apart. And hopefully the host, MacLeod, can keep the Sorcerer Royal occupied with wine and stimulating conversation. But according to the English, Samarasinghe has equal status with the Ethiopian Qozmos and is the equivalent of setting an altogether different landmine under the dinner table. The state's 'One Nation' policy is very real. But this arrangement also sets the English guest above the MacDonalds. If this were, say, a conference at a dodgy hotel in Stirling, then MacLeod would certainly have been bumped down, keeping the clansmen equal. Now you get two centres of gravity. I hope we don't get spaghettified by the pull between them.

'I don't see any other way,' Carrie replies at last.

'Of course you don't. Now, handle the seating. I still have to ensure Lord Samarasinghe and the MacDonalds have somewhere to sleep tonight. That won't be much fun since every room here is already taken.'

There it is. We can only stand back now and hope this thing doesn't blow up in our faces.

VI

Finally, we're sat around the table and no one seems to be kicking up a stink. Yet. The rest of the Hamster Squad – Carrie, Abdul, Sinéad and Aurora – are lined up by the wall behind the table, like old-school butlers or something. Sin gives me a wink, since I'm sat at the table too, like a top magician. Hardly my fault. Cockburn would have had me serving, but Callander insisted that it's tradition for the secretary's apprentice to attend dinner. My status seems to hover between intern and apprentice depending on the situation. When it comes to work given to me, I'm an apprentice. Remuneration for that work, I'm an intern. It's a scam. Anyways, since the gopher is usually of the Edinburgh School, unlike me, Cockburn's counterweighted my presence by also slotting in a prefect from the school this time.

The kid from the Edinburgh School looks like he belongs here, also unlike me. He engages in conversation with the guests next to him while I'm still in a panic trying to figure out the cutlery in front of me . . . Earlier, when we set the table, Abdul had explained you go from outside in. But what if I mess it up and end up looking all ignorant?

Keep cool.

It's a right sausage fest here too. Of the fourteen at the table, me and Mrs Featherstone are the only women present. This Society thing's an old boys' club, no question. Then again, so is this whole magicking bollocks anyway. Somebody play some James Brown in here.

I'm surprised when there's suddenly a call for grace before dinner.

Must be tradition, or it could be they're doing it for Qozmos, who's a man of faith.

'Some hae meat and canna eat, and some wad eat that want it, but we hae meat and we can eat, sae let the Lord be thankit.' Esfandiar Soltani recites the Selkirk Grace. Only apt since he's a poet. He goes on to read an original poem he wrote about the friendship between magicians all over the world. It's beautiful, a wee bit sentimental, delivered with lots of heart. Only a philistine wouldn't be moved by it. Turns out he's the Makar, Scotland's national poet or something. Didn't know we had one, so it goes to show . . .

After he's finished and sits down, the Hamster Squad moves in to fill our glasses with water and wine. Quality silver service right there.

All my life, I've been looking after my sister and grand-mother. I've been rushing about, running errands, chasing shillings. Feels nice to be waited on for a change . . . Also feels a bit awkward . . . I could get used to it, all the same. Soft life goals.

The dining room's a splendid space. It's not the grand hall of the fairy-tale castle. No. It's just the right size for a large family, throwing in a few friends if need be. The MacLeods are a large clan, so presumably at some point in history one could expect randoms dropping by. It has a Prussian-blue rug laid upon the floor, contrasting jarringly with the lush velvet the walls are adorned with. And portraits of long-dead MacLeods in powdered wigs and Victorian dress hang around the room too. The one woman depicted on the wall, Adamina MacLeod, with jet-black hair, looks to be in her twenties and is gazing at the painter with much sorrow written upon her face, as though she'd been forced to sit for her portrait. I eye an ornate cabinet with intricate carving, which then starts me wondering how much I could get for the ivory-handled cutlery. Or maybe I should go for the clock atop the fireplace mantle? Nah. Too obvious. I want something no one'll notice, and it's got to be something I can move quickly on the market. My connections in the Edinburgh underworld can help with this, for a commission.

Broad windows look out past the courtyard to the sullen sea.

The candlelight reflects off the glass panes. It's nice.

'I am rather curious about the nature of Ethiopian magic, which surprises me in the way it clings to its theological foundations, in spite of the great advances in science. Perhaps you'd care to explain this, if you can forgive my boldness.' Wedderburn strikes up conversation as the Hamsters bring in the first course. I recall the ontological explanation of magic. Some stuff about a divine deity or deities creating the universe through powers akin to magic. 'Let there be light', that sort of thing. And as a result we can also do magic by virtue of being creations of said deity or deities. It's the sort of hocus-pocus not practised in Scotland for over two hundred years.

Kebede translates the question for the Grand Debtera, who waits until the waiters have finished serving.

Sin announces: 'The chef wishes for you to know that tonight we'll be serving a menu with fresh, locally sourced ingredients. We'll start with crispy chicken and seaweed crackers.'

Then she swiftly withdraws to stand against the wall with the rest of the team. I swear I see Abdul swallow, 'cause this stuff is well appetizing. I wanna take a pic of it but resist the temptation to whip out my phone.

'Magic is akin to our appendix, a vestigial organ from when God created the universe. All forms of magic begin from this standpoint – from God's use and endorsement of magic. While I am very much aware certain traditions reject this altogether, is it not strange that only those creatures made in the image of God can practise magic? Has anyone seen a beast of any sort work a spark into existence?' His words carry an absolute conviction that can only come through faith.

I recall the many arguments against this theory of magic. You'd be barred from the Society if you professed similar beliefs here.

'I agree that most magical systems are founded upon belief in a pre-scientific precursor. But surely, since our spells work without any sign of a god's involvement, this should be proof enough that magic doesn't have divine origins,' Wedderburn replies.

The Grand Debtera smiles, nodding slowly, as Kebede interprets the assertion.

'In which case I find it most curious that Scottish magical incantations invariably cling to Greek gods in their wording. All magic is an act of worship, aimed at something greater than ourselves. Whether we admit it or not is the sole difference.'

The table bursts into laughter. A brilliant retort, even though, in actuality, the spells Qozmos refers to only use the names of deities to fix a concept in the mind. This helps to harness the practitioner's will. It's very different to invoking a supernatural being to do the magic for you.

'Are your Ethiopian magicians, therefore, members of the clergy?' MacLeod enquires.

'The debtera are not ordained. We aren't priests. We are lay members who assist in the services of the Ethiopian Orthodox Tewahedo Church and perform music. Isn't music the ultimate magic? Traditionally we were astrologers, fortune-tellers, exorcists and healers within the community. So we are very much tied to our Orthodox faith. We see no reason why magic and faith should ever be separated. It has served us well for two thousand years and will do so until the end of time,' Kebede states for Qozmos.

This is a not so subtle reminder that their civilization is far older than ours.

'Indeed, when we built our own occult Library, we sought masons from Ethiopia to carve it out in the style of the great stone churches of Lalibela. We hope you will visit one day. There's some interesting Christian art and symbols left behind by those masons, especially in the upper section,' says Dr Maige, head librarian at the Calton Hill Library.

'The Kingdom of Prester John is always happy to help its Christian allies,' Qozmos replies, leaving half the table in stitches again.

I wonder why, then realize what he's referring to. In the Dark Ages, a myth arose in Europe about a legendary Christian kingdom lost amidst the lands of the Muslims and pagans in the Orient. It was supposed to be a place of pure faith and incredible wealth, with a strong army. Ethiopia, being an ancient Christian nation, became the focus of this belief, and European kingdoms sought to make alliances with it on that basis. This was something the Ethiopians subsequently played to their advantage against rival kingdoms.

As the conversation flows on, the Hamsters work, clearing the table, filling cups, bringing the next course.

I pinch myself to make sure I'm not dreaming. Here's me sharing a table with three bigwigs of the magicking world. I desperately want a selfie. It's killing me.

'I must contest a point you made earlier, sir,' says Esfandiar to the Grand Debtera. 'Music has its merits, undoubtedly. But real magic is to be found in the word, in poetry. That's why ancient incantations belong to the spoken word. It must be uttered into existence.'

'Our Muslim brethren would agree with you. That's why in the old days, when the persecution against the new religion increased in Makkah, the Prophet Mohammed, peace be upon him, sent them to Ethiopia to seek protection.'

Qozmos explains that the Negus, the king who ruled then, had a reputation for justice and wisdom. Some of his ministers called upon him to expel the refugees, and so the umma

– the Muslim community – sent one of their number to speak to the Negus. This was Ja'far ibn Abi Talib, the cousin of the Prophet, who told the Negus that his people had been steeped in ignorance. That they had been worshipping idols, committing abominations and living their lives in darkness. That was until Allah appointed a messenger from within their community, a man of integrity whose word could be trusted to guide them into the light. The Negus asked Ja'far if he could share any revelations that his cousin the Prophet had received from God, so he recited the 'Surah of Mary'.

'And make mention of Mary in the Book, when she withdrew from her people unto a place towards the east and secluded herself from them; and We sent unto her Our Spirit, and it appeared unto her in the likeness of a perfect man,' Esfandiar recites in his melodious voice. The Quran is revealed in verse, the perfect medium for a poet like him.

'And because of that particular verse, the Negus vowed he would not return the Muslim refugees back to Makkah,' Qozmos concludes.

'Utterly fascinating,' Lord Samarasinghe says, raising a glass. His demeanour's now pleasant, charming even. Gone is the frightening bluster he arrived with.

The history buff in me's savouring the convo. Loving being a fly upon this wall. I never thought highly of other magics. For a while Gran tried to teach me Shona magic, but it didn't work out. I play the mbira to talk to ghosts and stuff, which isn't considered real magic by the Society, but that's about it. Maybe one day I'll pick it up again, though.

The Grand Debtera speaks about the circle of sacred magic

that flows through all creation, like a current whose ultimate origins have no beginning and end. In this way, all receive the spark of the divine. About how the Caliphate emerged after the Prophet Mohammed's ministry. It was the Muslims who drove innovation in magic, mathematics and science. Then the Hindus added a zero to mathematical theory, a fiendishly tricky concept that has since become commonplace. These innovations were next taken up by the Europeans who designed their own magic systems. Now, that magic swirls around the globe, touched and modified, refined by all who come into contact with it. The Debtera speaks of his fondness for the empiricism fundamental to Scottish magic and expresses his scepticism towards its *scepticism*. He says he prefers an openness to those things which lie beyond the tools offered by the scientific method.

'Can you measure the weight of a grain of salt in the astral realms?' he asks rhetorically.

The courses of amazing nibbles keep on coming. Fancy-sounding food such as Drumfearn mussels with asparagus, Waternish prawns with organic carrots. Glazed Torvaig beef brisket with peas and pickled mushrooms. Sin announces each dish and my only gripe is I'm still hungry. Each plate's only got a bite or two on it. Callander chips in with an anecdote about the eighteenth-century James Bruce, who explored the Blue Nile Basin and lived in Gondar for a time. Not to be outdone, Lord Samarasinghe points out that Ethiopia was the first African country to establish an embassy in London. He's keen to remind us too of the role of the British in assisting Ethiopia to resist the Italian fascist invasion during the Second

World War. Samarasinghe grows animated as he talks about this, and becomes kind of endearing. I didn't expect to feel this way towards English magic's biggest cheese. It's disorienting, as though a different person has stepped into his body and taken the driving seat. At points he breaks off, complimenting the hosts for throwing such a wonderful dinner.

Then the spotlight shifts.

'I wish to enquire about Ms Moyo's opinions on the development of Scottish magic. I'm certain our honoured guests would find such discourse edifying,' Nathair Walsh, the Edinburgh School boy, suddenly declares in an RP accent.

I nearly choke on my almond sponge. That little twat. I've been happy enough chowing my grub and listening to the experts talk. What the heck do I know about anything?

'I don't want to bore anyone. The evolution of magical science is well known to everyone at this table,' I deflect, hoping that's the end of it.

'Your ignorance on these matters reveals itself through your unfortunate phrasing, Ms Moyo. Allow me to correct you, if I may,' Nathair replies pompously. 'No serious practitioner uses the term "magical science" anymore. It suggests a kind of pseudoscience one associates with magical thinking. The hierarchical ordering, where you place magic before science in your taxonomy, is self-evidently flawed. We are not alchemists. Science does not proceed from magic. Science can't be a product of magic. Rather, I prefer the more accurate term "scientific magic", which demonstrates that magic is the *result* of scientific thought – not superior to it. It is a branch of science, a hard science, equal to physics or chemistry or biology. It is founded upon systematic observations, experiments, and uses mathematical principles, drawing across multiple disciplines. In fact, scholars like Lamont and Watt have suggested that magic is the ultimate practical application of science. And so, in future I'd advise you not to embarrass yourself by employing dubious terminology.'

Earth swallow me whole. Like, who cares? But the cat's got my tongue good and proper and it's hard to know how to respond, since I know the douchebag knows more about these things than I do. I probably look like a muppet. Wishing I'd not been invited to this bloody dinner now, I'm a right whopper.

'Young man, you may think you sound original, regurgitating worn clichés, but I assure you *that* debate was already stale back when I was in school. Long before you were born,' Mrs Featherstone says with a laugh. I give her a grateful look. 'Montgomery, I'm surprised you still teach this sort of thing at the Edinburgh School.'

'Along with ancient Greek and Latin too,' Professor Fergus Cattermole joins in. 'Magic appeared long before science, and it's perfectly legitimate for a practitioner to give primacy to the original discipline. Science happened *to* magic, not the other way round. We can dance on this pin's head all night long.'

'I shudder to think what they teach their students in Glasgow and Aberdeen,' Hamish Hutchinson weighs in, throwing his hands up. 'Anything goes, it seems. A sort of postmodern relativism, eschewing rigour.'

'Critical thinking is an essential component in the magical scholar's arsenal. That's what we've been teaching for three centuries now. Pity you lot weren't around for the first two. My student Mr Walsh has presented a well-reasoned argument. I believe it's up to Ms Moyo to formulate her own response,' Wedderburn adds.

The fault line between the four schools cuts through the woodgrain of the table. The Doric School and Lord Kelvin on one side, Edinburgh and St Andrews on the other. Meanwhile Kebede speaks rapidly, translating the debate for Qozmos. Poor lad's barely eaten, since he's been at it all night.

I'm out of my depth.

I should chill.

'Ms Moyo comes into magic via a rather unconventional route, so I've heard. She can't be expected to know these things,' Hutchinson says. A burn coated in placatory language if ever I've heard one.

It's for this reason I'd turned to Niccolò Machiavelli before I came to this conference. He said: 'I'm not interested in preserving the status quo; I want to overthrow it.' So screw these old farts. I'm radge now and aware I should really stay silent . . . but I can't. Not this time.

'I know what I need to know, and I've done things your precious little pupils couldn't even begin to imagine. So you can go fuck yourself,' I say.

There's a murmur around the table. Gasps of shock and indignation. Abdul's eyes pop out of their sockets, and Mrs Featherstone gives me the subtlest of nods. The Sorcerer Royal bursts out laughing, tears running down his cheeks.

'Well, well, it seems this little kitty has sharp claws,' he says.

'This is most inappropriate,' Wedderburn protests.

'You did point out the girl had a right to respond in her own manner, and now she's done so,' Mrs Featherstone replies.

'And in so doing has chosen, unprovoked, to insult a principal of one of the four schools. This is intolerable. Sir Ian, what do you intend to do about it?' Hutchinson is absolutely fuming.

Callander shrugs, then turns to me, saying, 'Ms Moyo, I'm sure you misspoke. Kindly withdraw your comments and apologize to Mr Hutchinson.' It's all polite, but not really a request. That's why I prefer folks from my slum. At least they're up front and direct.

I grip my napkin on my lap and shake my head. He might be my gaffer, but I don't owe these other bellends nothing.

'Very well. Leave the table, young lady. I'll have a word with you later,' Callander says.

I get up, throw my napkin on the floor and get out of the bloody room.

VII

My piss is still boiling like Vesuvius about to let loose on Pompeii all over again. I'm wandering the castle in a blind fury when I bump into Priya. She's peering round corners from her chair, looking proper shifty. Jumps out of her skin when she spots me.

'Awkward. I've got two exes at this conference and it's been a mission avoiding them all day. Easy enough for you bipeds, but I have to navigate the stairs. Like, hello, are we in the sixteenth century? Hang on . . . why you looking so glum, hot lips?'

'I'm good,' I reply.

'Aren't you supposed to be hobnobbing with the great and mighty?'

'I got kicked out.'

'For what?' Priya's mouth is wide open, halfway between surprise and disbelief.

'Nudging the head of St Andrews College towards autofellatio.'

She giggles.

'I can totally see why they'd take exception to that. Screw 'em, hen. We're here to have a good time. That means we can't miss the reception, it's going to be fun. Please tell me you at least waited till after dessert before you got yourself kicked out. I'm Hank Marvin starvin' out here.'

I recall I'm meant to pinch leftovers to feed the orphans who're hanging around the castle entrance later. Will see if Carrie and Sin can sort that out for me, and I file it in my to-do. My radge-o-meter's dialled down a notch since I bumped into my pal. Priya's a real diamond. I'd rather be out here with her anyway. Truth be told, I should go to bed, but she insists we do the reception 'cause Jomo's told her there'll be some presentation he's super-excited about.

'We've got to support him,' she says. 'Emotional blackmail notwithstanding, *mi amore*, I've missed you.'

Priya rattles on about a talk she went to earlier by the Rwandese practitioner Isaro Uwimana on the loss of indigenous languages and its impact on magic. She gives the example of the word 'tree' in English, which conjures up a different image in Kinyarwanda. Magical incantations are rooted in language – there is no outside language. Empirically, the power yields of spells have been measured and found to be subtly different, depending on the language the practitioner uses. Studies of bilingual magicians have also shown this. The speaker commented on the need to preserve indigenous languages or risk losing more magical formulations. Which includes right here, where Scots and Gaelic have given way to English and the effects on Scottish magic are discernible.

I find all this fascinating, but it's not the same as being at the dinner, listening to the top practitioners chatting. Well, that boat's sailed for me now. I don't regret what I said, though.

'I'm hoping to corner Isaro at the reception. The work she's doing is something we've been discussing in the healing field too. Our current thinking is that linguistic rapport with one's patients may have positive outcomes.'

Sounds rather obvious, until Priya goes on about the need for clinical trials to give definitive proofs.

Sneddon appears with Jomo in tow. The older librarian is a gentle bear – big and broad with a soft voice. He's always out of breath 'cause of the extra pounds he's carrying. But in the Library, you hit him with any topic you wanna research and he'll find the perfect book for you. Hits you back with barbs sometimes too. But unlike, say, Dr Maige, Sneddon's comments are always good-natured. Jomo's my best mate, right enough, but Sneddon's my favourite librarian.

The two of them are lugging something bulky, covered in a red silk cloth.

'If you enjoyed that particular talk, then you may want to attend tomorrow's session on Sharia-compliant magic in Kyrgyzstan and the Central Asian states,' Sneddon says, having overheard Priya. See, he's always recommending cool stuff.

'I'd check that out, but it's clashing with a talk Lethington's giving. I can't afford not to be at the boss's thing. I still have to go back to work next week, you know?' Priya replies.

'And what about you, Ropa?' Jomo asks.

'I'll be doing Society business.' I can at least make running around for Cockburn sound important.

'Suit yourselves. Now you really ought to be moving along if you're coming to the reception. It's going to be a tight squeeze. The room's too small; happens every single conference.'

The two librarians walk off and we follow soon after. The drawing room's a warm salmon colour, giving off a calming vibe which is upset by the young magicians who've come in early to stake a place. They chat loudly, bragging about their 'discoveries', clearly desperate for attention. We took out the furniture earlier to make space, and the only chairs remaining are by the wall with the massive painting of Sarah MacLeod and her kid. They must have burned through half the family fortune on portraiture alone, these MacLeods. I considered nicking a piece, but that'd be too obvious. It's not like their pics are in high demand either.

Back when I was a-burglaring with the Clan down in the Auld Reekie, I didn't waste as much time thinking about a caper. Just went out and did it. Indecisiveness is a horrible thing. And this place is a buffet-type situation alright, with so much loot on display. I must be really losing my touch.

We'll find something.

Me and Priya stick ourselves in the corner. I wanna be as unobtrusive as I can, since I'm sure Callander owes me the mother of all rollickings. Let the baby shark magicians prowl for a patron, 'cause there are numerous conference veterans about. Folks who've been coming here since they were at school. They form familiar circles and moan about how it was all so much better in the old days.

All this bitching I hear makes me wish I was drunk or something.

This is the world I've been fighting to become part of.

It's sublime and silly simultaneously.

But if I still want to keep my family above the waterline,

then I have to make it. And I begin to regret my outburst at dinner. Didn't exactly win friends and influence anyone back there. Maybe I should re-evaluate how I'm reading Machiavelli. Normally, I'm cruising by on Eastern martial texts which emphasize subtlety. But my pal Nicco's more of the bull in a china shop kind of guy when it comes to political theory. Let me stick with it though, 'cause I heard he delivers a mean pizza when it comes to landing an argument.

Folks begin to stream in. This thing's about to start.

Nathair Walsh passes by in the company of some other Edinburgh boys, fresh from the dinner. It must have finished and I feel a pang. He spins round when he spots me. Tosser. I'm surprised when Lewis Wharncliffe pops in after them. I didn't expect to see him here as he's not the scholarly type. He helped me on my last gig, saving some kid called Max Wu from their school. Glad to see the zit situation on Lewis's face is much improved, although he's been left with some angry red battle scars courtesy of Madame Le Puberty. Cool lad. I've got all the time in the world for him. He heads to our corner and gives me a fist bump.

'Dude, at dinner, I heard you—'

'It's all true, Lewis.'

'Wow . . . and *I* thought I was radical. Gotta up my game. Nice to see you, Ropa. I just came to this for the rugby. There's a competition the day after tomorrow and I can't wait to cream the Kelvinites. No offence, Priya.'

She rolls her eyes.

'Anyhows, gotta dash. We'll catch up soon, yeah?'

Lewis leaves just as Cockburn shushes the buzzing room.

She's been at it since dawn but her Duracell's still going. Say what you will about her, the lady puts a shift in. I have to admire that . . . It takes a minute for folks to settle. Everyone from the dinner's now present save for Lord Samarasinghe. Must be because he only likes the sound of his own speech.

'Thank you all for coming to this wonderful reception which brings together the finest practitioners from Ethiopia and Scotland. And England,' she adds quickly, glancing around. 'We acknowledge our friends from abroad who could also join us. And we have a long week filled with activities and talks, but tonight is really about the intercourse between two particular and peculiar schools of magic for humanity's benefit. So I'd like to welcome Dr Maige, head librarian at the Calton Hill Library, to get the ball rolling.'

Polite applause.

Dr Maige is in his crimson gown with kanga cuffs. The white gloves on his hands add a touch of class. Tonight he's also wearing a three-peaked biretta, heightening the quasi-ecclesiastical nature of his bibliothetic vocation. The robes play well against those of the Grand Debtera and his assistant. It's as though this is the meeting of two primates of the ancient church.

The head librarian speaks warmly of the friendship between all scholars of magic. How the study of science is the bulwark against superstition and enthusiasm. That cooperation between magicians all over the world is for the benefit of all. In this he highlights the role of Scottish magic in shaping the world today – the discoveries made in various fields that have advanced humankind. And tonight, Dr Maige is pleased to present a gift: the loan of one of Scotland's most precious books, for a period of ten years, to benefit Ethiopian peers in magical practice.

'In addition to this loan, we undertake to teach our colleagues the advanced methods we have pioneered for preserving knowledge. We do this so they too can fill their libraries with the finest minds available in their sphere.'

The last bit is too literal for my liking. I know exactly how the Library creates books – using those deceased minds. Sneddon nudges Jomo forward, carrying the silk-draped slab of meat that constitutes a book from our Scottish Library of the Dead. You can feel the hum and pulse of it. The lure of arcane knowledge. After my experience trying to read one, I'm pretty wary of these 'books'. I much prefer dealing with 'texts', which are the printed materials held by the Library. It's strange seeing a book out in the real world. I'd been told they were for reference only. That they could only be studied by top magicians within the controlled environ-ment of the Library.

There's barely suppressed fury on Euan Cleghorn's face. The head of Glasgow's library appears to be taking deep breaths to compose himself. Must be tough seeing a rare object shipped off halfway across the world.

Jomo presents the book to his boss, his father Dr Maige, and then removes the silk covering it. He bows and walks three steps back before spinning round to return to his place off stage. Dr Maige holds the book aloft, turning it from side to side for everyone in the room to see.

'Behold, the *Alexander Buchan*. Through this book the

mysteries of the weather and oceans were refined and modernized. We hope that during the period of our exchange, our Ethiopian counterpart's knowledge in these matters will be refined too. When you read these books, you not only learn from them, they also read you. So their ideas are constantly updated by means of their readers. Our overseas friends will receive this book and learn from it. And when it returns to us in ten years' time, we too will learn the things it has learnt from them. That is a precious thing.'

I totally get why these practitioners from the desert are interested in climate science. It can be a matter of life and death where water is scarce and the weather unpredictable. Whereas Scotland isn't short of a little rain. They'll have a hundred and fifty years of Scottish learning on these matters now.

Dr Maige hands the book to the Grand Debtera, who passes it to his assistant.

'This is a most worthy loan, and it pleases us that you favour us so. But the currents of the ocean do not only move in one way. The wind does not only blow in one direction. Knowledge must forever flow. For if it doesn't, and only remains in one place, it becomes a stagnant swamp. Then it grows putrid and becomes distorted. That's why this moment is important. In sharing what we know, we are renew—' Kebede stops to translate and rethinks the term before proceeding '—revitalized. The waters of the world's oceans are one, even though we give them different names. The knowledge of all humankind, too, is one. And so we give with the same pleasure with which we receive your most precious offering. From us you will receive an ancient grimoire, whose teachings are known only to a few. It was written in the crepuscular zone between life and death. For the wise, it restores those who are lost. We loan to you, in good faith, the profound teaching from *The Book of the Shaded Mysteries of Solomon as Recounted by the Queen of Sheba.*'

There're loud gasps around the room. I've not seen this text mentioned in any of my learnings. 'Damn,' Priya whispers. 'That's some heavy artillery and a coup for Dr Maige.' The excited voices rising in the room confirm this.

'King Solomon was the wisest man who ever lived. Upon his death he journeyed to realms beyond the twilight zone, which some here call the everyThere. It is known that once a soul has crossed this threshold, it can never return to us. But the wisest man did. He returned to his favourite queen to give her knowledge of higher places. Realms even the most astute astral projectionists cannot access. This book holds the key to understanding the Realms Beyond.'

A feverish applause breaks out, excitement all round. The Realms Beyond lie over the event horizon of the infinite astral realms. It is said that therein lies the ultimate reality from which our worlds are projected. That is the source. Even Gran, who knows much about the astral plane, has mentioned that the only Realm Beyond we can access is the Other Place. That's the place of perfect dark, where we banish errant spirits to. Nothing comes back from there.

Qozmos holds out his hands, palms upwards. A minor entropic shift occurs, and in his hands appears the small box Kebede carried out of their boat earlier. The Grand Debtera then raises his hands and suspends the box in the air. It sits there steady, as though upon a shelf.

'What's happening? I can't see anything,' Priya says, blocked as she is by the folks standing in front of us.

'The wooden box is opening,' I whisper.

It's like a chrysalis cracking open to reveal life inside, as it unclasps itself in the air. It opens from all directions in the most confounding manner, as though there are more dimensions than the three we experience. Every side is simultaneously the lid, yet somehow it still holds together. Not quite breaking apart, though it should. A miraculous light shines forth and the scroll is then finally revealed.

I feel pure ecstasy as the light touches me.

Elevated.

As though my soul's been pulled out of my body into those Realms Beyond.

This lasts half a minute before the box knits itself whole once more, swallowing the scroll. I feel as though I've been floating and now suddenly find myself under gravity's sway again.

'What is it?' Priya asks, urgently tugging my elbow.

'It . . . it, it was beautiful.'

'Bummed I missed it now,' she complains.

'Talk to Sneddon. He's got to bump us to the front of the queue to read it in the Library.'

'That's just what everyone else in this room wants,' Priya says. 'Fat chance we get in before the head honchorati.'

Qozmos steps back from the scroll box and gestures for Dr Maige to retrieve it from where it's hovering in the air.

Normally the head librarian is reserved, straight as a ruler, but right now he's positively beaming. Jomo and Sneddon then approach in a coordinated step and receive the box from Maige.

'We'll secure this in the castle library. It will be guarded all night before we can then take it to Edinburgh in the morning.'

Jomo's face is all tight and there's a solemnity about him. I know it's his eagerness to please his demanding dad. I guess that's the bonus of not having any parents, like me. I don't have to impress anyone. I can be myself.

Cockburn retakes the stage as the librarians leave. The room applauds again and she gives it a moment to settle, then signals to Sir Callander waiting in the wings.

'Thank you very much. Next up—'

Suddenly the room goes black. Power cut.

'Stay calm, everyone. It's just an outage. This is an old building but the backup generator should kick in moment-arily,' says Edmund MacLeod. 'It won't take long at all . . . Anytime now really . . . It normally should have . . . Someone check the—'

There's an awful scream followed by a thud from the corridor.

Jomo!

I make a dash for the door, bumping into people along the way. Can't see nothing.

'What's going on?'

'Why isn't my spell lighting up?'

'Mine too.'

Voices surround me in the dark as I fumble my way towards

the door. *Knapf.* Hit my knee against something. I push my way out into the dark corridor, grab my phone and turn on the torch. Dim figures appear further along. I rush towards them, trying not to stumble.

'Quick. We need a healer here,' shouts Avery MacDonald. Him and his father are knelt over a fallen body. Oh no. Two bodies on the floor.

'Priya,' I yell above the commotion.

'What's going on?'

'Why can't I cast a spark?'

'Use your phones like that lassie is doing.'

More people finally fish out their phones, turn on their torches and spill out into the narrow corridor. The light improves but the moving shadows make this thing a right horror show. No, no. This is worse than I thought. Sneddon and Jomo are on the floor. A dirk pierces Sneddon's chest. And a massive puddle of blood blossoms underneath them. I fight the urge to scream. Please, whatever deities are out there, not Jomo. Where is Priya? She should be here quick. But rubberneckers are blocking her wheelchair.

'Make way for her, she's a medic,' I shout. 'Out of the way, people.'

Oh, my days.

I finally look for the scroll . . . It's gone.

VIII

Lethington arrives moments before Priya, who finally gets through the bottleneck at the door. So much blood. I'm pacing back and forth with my hands on my head. What do I do? *Think, Ropa.* Priya takes the medkit from beneath her chair and tosses it to Lethington. Then she gets to work on Jomo, while the more experienced consultant healer deals with Sneddon. The two of them are completely zoned in on what they're doing. This is life or death.

The translator, Kebede, bursts through next. Fury flashes in his eyes as he takes in the scene and realizes that the Queen of Sheba's scroll is lost. Gone is the serene layman; he looks like a hurricane. Just the kind of artillery I need right now.

It snaps me out of my funk.

'Come with me,' I yell to him.

He responds immediately and we make a mad dash through the corridor, me talking as we go.

'Whoever's done this is getting away as we speak. Go downstairs, out the entrance, and up the road to the main gate. I'll head upstairs.'

We've lost precious time. I shouldn't have frozen like that.

This place is massive. If we don't move quickly whoever's

done this will be long gone. I'd rather take action now and deliberate later. I run to the end of the corridor, through one room and then up the stairs. Adrenaline's coursing through my veins. We're not supposed to enter the MacLeods' private residence upstairs, and I spot CCTV cameras as I go. They may help later.

Slow down. Turn off my torch. Don't want to be an easy target.

Dagger at the ready.

I draw my catapult from my jacket pocket and load up a nice smooth rock. Picked them up from the pebbled beach for the katty. It's a good size to crack someone's skull with, and I'm really praying I'm the one to catch this bastard.

Awfully quiet up here.

The only noise coming through is from the commotion below.

Breathe quietly. Step lightly. Spidey senses on high alert.

I bump into something and it falls to the ground, breaking. My leg feels wet. Must be a vase. There's a radical entropic shift and I drop to the floor instinctively. A pneumatic *pfft* speeds over my head, blowing my dreads back. The soliton wave crashes into the wall behind and I fire my katty blind in retaliation. The stone ricochets against the wall. I immediately roll to the other side to change my position, hugging the wall tight. I squeeze behind a cabinet which is solid enough to block any projectiles coming my way.

A second concussive blast clears out the space on the floor where I'd just lain.

Clever.

They daren't cast a thermosphere 'cause the colour of the flame would help identify them – different magicians produce different colours with their spellcraft. But the soliton doesn't leave any such trace.

I, on the other hand, have no qualms about being identified, so I incant a quick Promethean spell, sending white sparks shooting down the corridor. They catch the assailant ducking into a room on the left.

'They're over here,' I call out, hoping someone from downstairs will join in. Then I follow.

I'm already feeling foolish I came up here on my own. Every magician in this place is better trained than I am. But I'm an investigator with the General Discoveries Directorate, making this my job. So I follow, ducking as I go and firing a concussive blast to clear the room. But they've already headed up the stairs to the third floor. Gotta be careful I don't get something lobbed at me as I go up. Looks like a storage area up here, with old furniture and boxes. Kinda dilapidated. They're up a ladder to the roof now. I can't let them close that hatch, so I fire off a thermosphere and hope MacLeod's got buildings and contents insurance in case I go all *Carrie* on this place. My spell's weaker than normal. Strange. Works all the same, though, as they flee, leaving the hatch open.

Katty back in pocket. Grab my dagger instead and I'm up that ladder in a jiffy.

I come out on the lead roof. This fucker's parkouring on it like James Bond in Mexico City. They vault over the array of solar panels, footsteps clanking against the lead. I fire off another Promethean spell for illumination and they spin round, sweeping their arm before running in one swift motion. My sparks die out a second before I'm hit by a fine mist of water.

Some of it gets into my eyes. Stings like a bitch. But I still manage to see they're very slightly built. Dark suit and ski mask like a ninja.

I'm blinking, pushing on half blind now. *Don't be a static target.* I hide behind the raised solar panels, trying to buy time and hoping for backup.

'There's nowhere to run,' I yell. 'This place is packed with magicians. Leave the scroll and I'll let you go. That's a promise.'

'I wish I could, lassie, but the Black Lord needs it for his return.' What's that voice? Man or woman? Such an unusual tone. They must have disguised it.

'No one can touch you if you give up,' I shout. 'I'll square it with Sir Callander.' I'm bullshitting to buy time. 'We can still make this right.'

'He's coming to save you all and build us a better world.'

'What do you mean?'

'Hold fast.'

They then step off the ledge and leap down to the viewing gallery below. I peer over. They're not getting anywhere unless they're Peter Parker or something.

'Stay there. You're going to hurt yourself,' I say, desperately hoping someone will hear me.

But as they leap they're incanting, floating like a flying squirrel, until they hit the ground and roll to break the fall. It's not quite flying, more of a controlled descent. That's a new spell on me. I then watch them run up the tarmac on the road leading south, which'll take them to a gate.

Can't let them get away.

Kebede appears on the bridge below. The one that joins the castle to the drive up to the main gate. He moves with a cold efficiency.

'There,' I yell, pointing at the receding figure.

He takes off quickly, making a crazy twenty-foot leap down onto the tarmac in hot pursuit. His robes flow in the wind, but don't impede him none. Looks like a white wraith tearing across the castle grounds. I run along the roof in the same direction, but gotta be careful. There's holes in it. Panels that don't look too steady. It's in some state of disrepair. I wanna play the spotter, but in the dark, with all these trees, I can only see so far. I vault over the partitions marking different sections of the castle.

Then I'm out of runway.

It'll be too late if I go back down the hatch, through the castle to the ground floor.

Improv time. This one's for Jomo.

The southern face of the castle's layered like a cake, with a pipe running down to drain the gutters. I climb up to it and then shimmy down the drainpipe. Whoops. Phew. All the way down to the roof of a wee annex. Walking along that takes me to the second floor, where I go to the other end and begin to climb off the ledge. Gripping like a gecko, I hold on. Okay, here goes. It's a fair drop down to the base rock supporting the castle. But if I can make it there, I can then slide along it to the ground on the other side. I'm proper scared now, 'cause if I don't make it, I'll fall into the sea.

I should have taken the stairs.

No way back in now.

This was a dumb idea. The rock below's concave and slippery. I need the *Prince of Persia*'s rewind button. My arms are getting tired, I'd better pull myself back up. *No!* I lose my grip and fall to the rock below – can't find my footing and next I'm tumbling towards the sea. I quickly incant an anemoic cushioning spell Priya used in a chase ages ago. In response, a grey airbag suddenly forms below me like a mist atop the water. I slam into it and it bursts, then I hit the ice-cold sea.

It's bloody freezing as I go under. I resist the urge to take a breath.

I start kicking my way back to the surface. Gasp as I make it there. Then I'm swimming, headed for the shore. My boots and clothes are a drag but still I push on, against the current of the burn which brings fresh water into the sea. The water gets shallower and I finally make land, half-stumbling my way out. Teeth chattering. I'm well drookit as I drag myself onto the tarmac.

Seawater drips down my hair and clothing. I cough a fair bit, and wipe the mucus from my nose with the back of my sleeve. Strange, there's no breeze blowing around. An eerie kind of stillness in the air.

Then I take off after Kebede, hoping he's got the bastard. My wet clothes are heavy and my feet slip inside my boots, but I ain't got time to worry about any of that. Noisy footsteps sound just past the Walled Garden – that one's a spooky space which I've heard boosts your magical powers, so I gotta be careful. Is that the thief? Maybe they didn't head for the gate. I veer right, trampling through the flower beds. A root sticking out catches my foot and I nearly fall. I still follow the sound though, past the polythene tunnel nurseries on my right. I'm running along the path when an almighty blue thunderbolt hurtles my way.

I spring to the side and let off a thermosphere spell.

Then I scramble up and hide behind a sycamore. Hard to control my breathing. I'm shivering bad.

Footsteps crunch against the fallen autumn leaves.

I pop my head out and fire a concussive blast speculatively. It catches someone and they groan. *Yes.* Before I can celebrate, their thermosphere hits the tree. The heat from the blaze is intense. If only I knew how to cast that Zeus spell, I'd send a thunderbolt their way, see how they like that.

'Is that you, Ropa?' A distinctive Ethiopian accent. 'I could have killed you.'

'Kebede?'

'Over here,' he says. A bright blue light fills the air. 'I didn't mean to. It's dark and you attacked first.'

'I bloody well didn't,' I reply strongly.

I take a peek to make sure it's safe before stepping out. Death by friendly fire was never on the cards for me. The grim look on Kebede's face tells the story. Total disaster. And his nose is bleeding.

'Where did they go?'

'That way, I think.' He points to the side gate with barbed

wire bristling atop it. Hovering over the palm of his other hand is an orb of blue light.

'Okay, we have to go after them!'

'I can't. They did something to trap us inside these grounds. It's a magic I've never seen before.'

His light gets brighter, the orb doubling in size. At first I don't quite see it, my eyes are still adjusting. Then it's there. A pale reflection coming from the air above. It goes all the way up and around, tracing the boundaries of the property. It looks like that weird force field the aliens in *Independence Day* had around their ships.

Kebede points to his bleeding nose, picks up a rock and throws it, and it bounces off the thin reflection of light. Maybe we can break through with more force? I take out my katty and aim.

'Careful. The ricochet will take your eye out – I've already run into this thing with my face. Fire at an angle if you must,' Kebede warns. His eyebrows twitch. He's agitated. 'I'm sorry. I didn't actually attack you. I was trying to breach that force field with lightning but my spell bounced off and came straight back at me. You were right behind me. I only realized when you shot back. I've tried everything but I can't break this thing down.'

I know mistakes happen on the battlefield. We don't have time to kiss and make up, though.

We've wasted more time. The barrier preventing us from chasing any further gives them a proper lead – they could be in the village by now. And there're plenty of other places they could go. A hideout in the woods. Or they might have doubled back and headed the opposite direction towards Coral Beach. The longer we delay, the likelier it is they'll get away. Best make a move rather than remain static.

'We'll have to go around this. You go that way and I'll try the other side. Send up a flare if you find a break in the barrier. Once we make it out, we'll hunt them down.'

IX

We meet again in the woods at the northern end of the property. There's no way out. Like, what the hell? It's got to be one very powerful practitioner to pull this off. Putting us inside a glass jar like we're ants. I've already seen one magician make a tsunami and another fly a stagecoach through the sky today. There's levels to this game.

What the—?

Palpitations.

I begin to feel claustrophobic. Hemmed in. *Breathe. Breathe. Breathe.* Flashbacks from the last time I was trapped like this in a big old house called Arthur Lodge. Couldn't get out that time either. I could only go as far as the length of my intestines. Gross. I don't need that flashback right now. Please.

'Are you okay?' Kebede's all concerned.

'Yeah, sure. I'm fine. Just, er, trying to figure this thing out. Aye. Thinking.' *Get a grip, Ropa.* 'I'm good. Let's get back to the others.'

My mind's screaming. I push those memories back inside a hole and plug it up. It's still game time. My heart slowly settles as we walk down the footpath to the driveway. Now we have to go back and report our failure. My failure. Kebede was simply helping out, but this is a Society issue now.

'When we received your invitation to this conference, there were those among the debteras and clergy who did not wish for us to come,' Kebede says.

'Why's that then?'

'They thought it unwise. You people have already taken so much from us. There was a time when you went around raping, looting, pillaging, plundering peoples who'd done you no harm. Everywhere you went you stole priceless magical relics.'

'That sounds like us, alright.'

'You called yourselves Christians, yet you looted our churches. Places where the faith had been practised while you were still living in caves. In 1868, when your army defeated Emperor Tewodros II at the Battle of Maqdala, you committed sacrilege. Tewodros was so humiliated that he committed suicide, damning his eternal soul. Your soldiers ransacked his treasury, but gold and silver alone were not enough. Precious jewels couldn't satisfy your appetites either. You wanted to feast on our nation's soul. So you seized our processional crosses and illustrated manuscripts. An attack on our faith. And you auctioned these off. They say you even had an expert from the British Museum there to bid for the choicest cuts.'

Kebede curls his lips, scunnered like. But this was hundreds of years ago. Who cares? Seeing him now, though, it seems that memory is still fresh. I recall some proverb, shit about the axe and the tree. Only one of them forgets. The way he keeps saying '*you*' makes me feel guilty. I wasn't even there.

'Then you took our sacred *tabots* too. Do you know what those are? No? Eleven wood and stone tablets passed down since biblical times. These represented the Ark of the Covenant itself. No one but the priests of the Orthodox Church were allowed to see them, let alone touch them. But your soldiers did, with their bloodstained hands. We have not forgotten how you carted them off, placed them on your ships and brought them here. These things mean *nothing* to you and *everything* to us. For more than a century we have asked you to give them back. For more than a century you have answered *no*. And yet you make fine speeches, host elaborate dinners, and call us *your friends*.'

The light shining through the castle windows casts dark shadows across his visage. This is no longer the amenable assistant of less than an hour ago. Still, I have to ask:

'Knowing all this, why then did you come and present us with this precious scroll?'

'Hope.' He pauses at the entrance. 'Our civilization has endured for two thousand years. We are a patient people. Our enemies have been ground to dust while we withstood. And so, despite great opposition, the Grand Debtera, Qozmos said, "This is a new age. The world has been broken again, as it was before. And it's being remade anew, as it has before." He planned to come here and offer true friendship. There were those who said he should bring a lesser token, but he wanted to bring *The Book of the Shaded Mysteries of Solomon as Recounted by the Queen of Sheba*. It contains secret knowledge for calling back spirits who've crossed the threshold beyond the every-There into more inaccessible realms.' Kebede quivers with rage and I step back, away from him. He clenches his left fist and breathes out to calm himself. 'The Grand Debtera believed that only by showing you that we are truly willing to share our knowledge, and our culture, might we neuter the avarice embedded in your hearts and show you a better way. He thought that with this grand gesture we could at last begin the necessary steps to restore those wrongs. You could keep the gold and jewels you stole in past times. Those are mere trinkets. But you have to give back our sacred *tabots*. They belong to *us*. I guess he was wrong about you people, *yet again.*'

I picture every community who met Europeans with a warm welcome and received bullets and germs in reply. Yep, that's how we roll.

'I'm sorry.'

'No, it is I who am sorry for you.'

He clenches his jaw and walks through the door.

What an almighty clusterfuck. Kebede doesn't need to say it. The ramifications of what's happened tonight are dire. Obviously the Grand Debtera can't return home and face his people now. Not when his mission to reclaim the *tabots* has resulted in the loss of yet another precious artefact. His position would be untenable. This goes beyond magic into politics, and relations between Ethiopia and Scotland would be poisoned for a hundred years or more.

And I've landed right in the middle of this mess.

The garden is now filled with folks in fancy suits and

cocktail dresses. A few are still sipping from champagne flutes, as they look around assessing the situation. All these magicians, yet me and Kebede were the only ones to give chase. An older man in a Turkish suit, fez and all, approaches.

'What the bloody hell's happening?' he asks. 'Is the reception still on? Young lady, you're with the help, answer me. I have a very important—'

I walk past him, but there's so many of them about. Fucking toffs. The thief's getting away and no one's lifting a finger. They're so used to other people doing the dirty work for them. I'm filled with contempt, Ganga forgive me.

I follow through into the hall where Cockburn waits for me at the top of the stairs. They've got candles and lamps burning. Still no electricity.

'Well?' she says.

I shake my head. I'm shivering badly, teeth chattering. The cold's bitten deep into my bones 'cause of these wet clothes.

'The secretary wants to see you immediately,' she continues. 'You are with the General Discoveries Directorate, after all. This whole thing falls within your remit.' And there goes my pseudo-holiday. Almost wish I was in the Hamster Squad proper.

'I have to see Jomo first.'

She frowns. 'Hurry then. Time is of the essence.'

My muscles cramp up further 'cause of the cold and it's a mission simply climbing the stairs. I leave wet footprints on the polished floor. When I reach the top, Cockburn touches my sleeve. She mumbles an incantation and I feel warmth return, as well as an unusual burst of gratitude towards her. Steam hisses, rising off my clothes and boots. In less than a minute I'm dry. Well, except for my hair. Magic doesn't work well on the human body. It's much easier to perform on inanimate objects. I brush off the sea salt crusted onto my clothes, a good amount falling onto the floor. They still feel crusty and scratchy against my skin. But I'll take that over being soaking wet any day.

They've put Jomo in a room on the second floor. His dad's staying up here as a personal guest of the MacLeods too. All that matters to me is Jomo's alive. As I rush in, I see him sitting upright, plump pillows behind him, in an old-school four-poster bed. Rich people and their eccentricities. Who still uses these? Never mind. Rector Wedderburn's standing by the bed and watches me give Jomo a bear hug.

'You had me worried, man . . .' I run out of words.

'Right. I'll leave you two to it then. I hope you feel better soon,' Wedderburn says, exiting the room.

'What did he want?' I ask as the rector disappears.

'He came to check up on me. He's actually a really nice guy. Sometimes we play chess when he visits the Library. If he's got time.'

That's cool of Wedderburn. I guess since his job's looking after a bunch of teenage boys, an extra one isn't a big thing. Jomo's still shook by everything, though. I take a glass of water from the carafe on the bedside table and make him drink some.

'How badly were you hurt?'

'Priya says it's a concussion. Someone rattled my brain and

I got knocked out. Nothing major. Is Mr Sneddon okay? No one's telling me anything.'

'I don't know yet.' I feel a glimmer of hope, though, despite all the blood there was. Jomo wasn't the one who got shanked. Lethington's a great healer. If anyone could save Sneddon it'd be him. 'I don't know what I'd do if anything happened to you, Jomo, you're my chummiest.'

'Phew. I thought for a minute there you'd say you've been secretly in love with me all these years.'

I punch him in the arm. Hard.

'Ouch. I nearly died, man. You should be waiting on me hand and foot.'

We laugh our heads off, tears streaming out of my eyes. This dork.

The door swings open. Dr Maige, Jomo's dad, steps into the room looking like thunder incarnate. There's no softness about him. Not an iota of compassion as he towers over his son.

'I'm so glad you're laughing as if this is one big practical joke. Is that it, Mr Maige? Is life one big game for you?' he says.

'No, sir,' Jomo whimpers.

'I ask so little of you. You had one simple task. Take the scroll to the castle library and guard it till morning. It seems even that was beyond you.'

'Come on. It's not his fault,' I protest.

'I'm talking to my worthless son, if you don't mind, Ms Moyo . . . Do you know why my vestments are red? *Answer me*, Mr Maige.'

'No, sir.'

'To be a librarian is the supreme vocation, a privilege above anything you can imagine. When they make the head librarian's vestments, they mix a vial of his blood in with the dye. It is my own blood that colours my vestments. I am prepared to die for the Library and protect its treasures. That is what we *do*. What generations of librarians through the ages have also done. Maybe this is my fault. I've always been too soft on you, and you're not half the man I was at your age.' He exhales long and loud. If he could breathe fire, I'd be toast. His voice then softens, almost cracks. 'I wish it was not Mr Sneddon who died tonight. At least he was worth something.' I can't believe what I'm hearing. But Dr Maige hasn't finished. 'He was a great librarian whose name shall be forever etched in our rolls. You are a disappointment to the Library – and to me as its head.'

Dr Maige gives Jomo a long, contemptuous stare, then leaves as abruptly as he came in. He bangs the door on his way out.

The room is completely hollowed. All the oxygen sucked out. Bloody hell. *They killed Mr Sneddon.* I met him the very first day I joined the Library. He did my paperwork and everything. The librarians can be a weird bunch, but he was a good egg. Always keen to help if you couldn't find a title. He could be droll if you caught him on a good day. Now he's *gone.* Just like that. I can't believe it.

As Jomo trembles with emotion, I hold him. Then he lets go fully and weeps. For the second time tonight I'm drenched in salt water. *Let it all out. There you go.* Nothing else for it. I might not have a dad, but I'm pretty sure if I had one and something this major happened, he'd be more concerned about whether or not I was okay. Dr Maige's a right psychopath. Numbers and books, that's all he cares about.

'He hates me, Ropa,' Jomo says between sobs.

'No, he doesn't. He's just a dick, that's all.'

'He's right, though. I am useless.'

'Don't be silly.'

'It's true, Ropa. I can't do half the things you do. If I was more like you . . . then maybe he'd . . . love me.' His voice hitches.

'You don't have to be anyone else except for yourself. Trust me.'

He bawls for a while, poor lad. Still sniffling, he finally pulls away from me and throws the covers off. Then he swings his feet off the other side of the bed.

'I have to find that scroll, even if it kills me,' he says. 'I'd rather die trying.'

'Steady on, Jomo. You're in shock and you need to rest. I'm on this. We'll square it together. Okay?'

I have a good idea where his strengths lie. Adventuring ain't one of them. Back when we were in school, before I bailed from the system, I'd fought his battles. He's smart, gentle, kind and loyal. Dr Maige may not appreciate this about Jomo, but I do.

'We can start by you telling me everything you saw tonight,' I say.

'It was dark.'

'You received the scroll. You headed into the corridor. Did you see anything before the power went?'

'No. It was normal. I'm sorry, Ropa. I wasn't . . . I was just so happy that I was doing something so important. I never imagined anything would go wrong.'

'The lights go out. Then what happens?'

'I reached for my phone so I could turn on the torch. It's really hard to get to your pocket when you're wearing that librarian gown. But I got to it. Once I'd unlocked it, there was a bit of light from the screen. I was still trying to find the torch function when something whistled past me. So I turned to Mr Sneddon . . . Oh my God, he's actually dead. And I couldn't help him.' He bursts into tears again. I stroke his shoulder.

Really don't want to be pushing him on this right now, but I need to gather all the intel I can before the trail gets cold. I give him a moment.

'Sorry. I still can't believe it . . . It was so dark. That dagger sticking through him . . . It was horrible.'

Jomo's wrong on one factual detail. It wasn't a dagger, it was a dirk – a long Scottish straight blade. A dagger's shorter – that's what I carry. King's law here is that women can carry a blade up to six inches in length, but a dirk's twice that. Details like this matter.

One of the first places I checked out when I arrived at the castle was the armoury. I'm into military history and love weapons and stuff like that. Morag'd told me they had a fine collection so I had to see it. They have a number of swords, including some from India and the Far East, which they keep alongside an impressive array of traditional Scottish weapons. I really liked the broadswords, but I couldn't carry one. You need to eat your oats for sure to wield one of those. I went giddy over the Great Sword of Dunvegan, which belonged to William Long Sword. He was the seventh chief who got killed back when. It's one of only two surviving claymores from that era. A massive two-handed sword that can kill you at about four and a half feet. William Wallace used one back when he was Mel Gibsoning. I also noticed a few dirks in the collection.

'I need to know what happened next, Jomo.'

'There was nothing I could do, Ropa.'

'We can't turn back the clock. What you do right here, right now, that's what matters. You're brave. We'll sort this together, yeah?'

'I screamed,' he says, embarrassed. 'I thought they were going to kill me too. And I froze. Couldn't move a muscle. The next thing I remember is waking up in here with this lump on my head.'

'Listen to me. Next time something like this happens, you run, Jomo. Run like the wind. I don't care what anybody says. None of that macho bollocks. You run, you hear?'

He sniffles and nods. Poor lad. I'm just glad he's alive. But I've picked up what I can from him right now. Not sure what I can use of it, though. At this stage, I'll hoover up anything, throw it in the blender and see what sort of smoothie comes out. I have this and a foggy picture of what the murderer looks like. And their mention of the 'Black Lord' needing the scroll for his return. What was that? This is about more than the scroll itself. For the first time in my life, I wish the fuzz were here. It's just us, though. This wanker killed Sneddon and I'm going to make them pay, even if I have to hunt them down from here to John o' Groats to Land's End. But first we need to get this damn barrier down, and I'm sure Callander will know how to do it.

X

Cockburn was waiting impatiently outside the room, and now rushes me downstairs to see Callander in the castle library. It's tiny. Then again, it's a private collection. This is my first time here, 'cause they keep it locked. Too many precious texts and artefacts for prying magicians. It is still the best magical library on Skye.

It looks more like an office to my eyes, with a cosy fireplace and garish chartreuse wallpaper. The bookshelves have locked glass doors; you can see but you can't touch. A portrait of John MacLeod looking dapper in a powdered wig hangs over the fireplace. He was the man who drew his family into the proper magicking world. Before that, Skye had been an isle of myth, legend and rampant superstition. John MacLeod was admitted into the circle of Humeans in Edinburgh, the one that would later become the Society in the eighteenth century. He then returned determined the practitioners of the Highlands and Islands should join the modern age. It was his immense influence that made the Society look outside the central belt. And it's why his family remains central to magic here.

A pendant light with six bulbs dangles impotently. Instead the room is well lit by a solar lamp in the corner. Callander's sat on the desk near the window. He looks calm and in control, despite the dire situation we find ourselves in. Edmund MacLeod's behind the desk, leaning back in his office chair. Qozmos is inscrutable in an armchair to the right of it.

There's also a chesterfield sofa on the opposite side of the room where the four heads of the schools of magic are sat. Wedderburn occupies the arm of the sofa. Feels like I've been summoned to the headteacher's office, which happened many times when I was in school. That's why I had to bail. No miseducation by the man for me.

I stand on the rug in the middle of the room, directly in front of Callander.

Kebede comes in soon after me and heads straight to the Grand Debtera. He kneels and bows his head, speaking in Amharic. Don't need to know the language to understand he's reporting on our failure. Qozmos listens, still as a statue, then places his left hand on Kebede's shoulder and makes a sign of the cross with his right. Once he's finished, he gestures for the assistant to rise.

'Before we begin, I really think the young lady ought to apologize about her conduct over dinner,' Hamish Hutchinson says.

'We have matters of greater import,' Callander replies irritably.

'Yes, I suppose. But, be that as it may, I see no reason propriety shouldn't be observed.'

I'm seething. But I bite my tongue. It's been a long night.

Dr Maige enters the room and takes the free wing chair next to Qozmos. That's when Cockburn shuts the door.

It's understandably tense in here.

'Why don't we have any light still?' I ask. This whole thing was timed to start with a power cut, but surely they could have fixed it by now?

'The line from the mains has been cut and the fuses wrecked. We have two backup options, a biomass generator and solar panels. Whoever did this poured cement in the generator and also tampered with our lithium battery array,' MacLeod replies.

'So they wanted darkness to cover their heist and made damn sure about it. But I'm curious as to why, in a room filled with powerful practitioners, none of you could conjure a simple fire spell. It seems rather convenient,' I challenge.

'My, the girl is clever. It sounds to me like we're all suspects now,' Professor Cattermole says, all amused.

'It's a legitimate question,' Callander replies. He's not in the mood for humour. 'And we would all do well to remember that the Fairy Flag is housed in the drawing room too. You wouldn't know this, Ms Moyo, but it's a relic of the Clan MacLeod which opens up portals to other worlds, and possesses properties that have a powerful effect on any prac-titioners in its vicinity. It's something the clan has often used to their advantage during battle.'

'But only in the direst of circumstances. The founders of my clan defeated the Fae who held sway over these islands long ago. In Iceland, to this day, they have to appease the fair folk. They don't have full control over their domain there. They can't build where they want or construct roads and dams in certain parts. Skye was the same when our ancestors first got here. The Celts lived in fear of their vicious and capricious fairy overlords. At that time they called them the Sidhe. Some here still remember them as such. I'm sure you've felt how otherworldly this place is. Skye lies very close to the hidden places, something the Fae took advantage of to gain a foothold in our realm. But my brave ancestors vanquished them, confiscating the magical flag that allowed them to overlap their world upon ours. Our victory extended to the nearby islands, including the big one where you live, young lady,' MacLeod explains, and not without pride. 'The Fairy Flag protects this castle too. When our enemies, that heinous clan you all know, tried to set fire to this place in 1938, the flag stayed true. No MacDonalds breached its walls or the damage would have been so much worse. Over the years, there've been other attempts, but with the flag here, this place will never be put to the flame.'

Interesting . . . But I frown, trying to get a handle on how all that is relevant to no one conjuring a spell when the lights went out.

'Recall your Somerville Equation, Ropa.' Wedderburn launches into lecture mode. 'You are familiar with the term "natural resistance"? It varies in different locations, but the greater the NR, the more difficult it is to perform a basic Promethean fire spell. The flag's properties increase this effect across the castle, although it's most intense in the drawing room, then diminishes with distance. That's why no one could conjure a flame.'

But Qozmos had still been able to levitate the scroll. Makes him extremely powerful if he can still do magic in an area with heightened resistance to it.

MacLeod speaks again. 'This is your first conference here, so you wouldn't know this, but one of the highlights is the full moon ceremony in a few days' time. The flag is currently shielded, as is the case outside wartime. Though you can see it, it's as impenetrable as though it were in a bank vault. But once a year, under the first full moon of autumn, the lock on its casing opens briefly, and we can unfurl it to celebrate our victory over the wicked Fae.'

'That means whoever did this probably knew exactly what would happen, because of where we were all gathered, in the same room as the flag. They were a few steps ahead. That takes careful forethought and planning,' I say.

Callander grunts in agreement.

I'm trying to read him. His arms are crossed and the tone of his voice earlier sounded cautious to me. I report directly to him, when I've not been farmed off to Cockburn, and when I started my internship, he made sure to remind me about loose lips, as though we were at war. I should play my cards closer to my chest.

'The main problem we have to deal with first is that we are trapped here. Some sorcery is preventing us from going past the perimeter. Whoever took the scroll will have gotten far by now,' Kebede says.

'What do you mean? You *can't get out?*' Mrs Featherstone asks.

'It's some kind of force field,' I reply.

'Around the entire property? How's that even possi—'

'I did that,' Sir Callander says. 'As soon as the power went off, I had a sense something was amiss, so I erected a Newton

Barrier along the perimeter of this estate, or as well as I could recall the dimensions. Even now, as we speak, I'm holding it together.'

It was Callander all along! But how? Ah, so it seems even in a room with high natural resistance, you can still pull off a spell so long as the effects of it are to appear elsewhere, removed from that room. Interesting.

'But this means no one can get in or out.'

'You haven't thought this through. Where will we sleep? We can't get to our hotels.'

'I have a meeting in Portree tomorrow morning.'

'Why weren't we consulted?'

'The legal implications. This constitutes false imprisonment.'

'I had to act decisively,' Callander replies to them all.

'You should have made me aware, at the very least. Now I have extra mouths to feed for God knows how long. Where will I put them all?' MacLeod protests.

That's his problem. As for me, I'm glad Callander's bought us more time. It means the person I chased didn't get away. They are still somewhere on the property. Now I'm kicking myself because there were all those people in the gardens who I didn't check properly, since I assumed the thief was gone already. They might still be hiding out in a hole somewhere on the property. Maybe they're skulking around trying to find a way out too. The alternative would be to double back and blend in. If it were me, that's what I'd do. And I wouldn't want the scroll on me, I'd stash it in some thicket or foxhole and wait this thing out. I'm itching to leave the room so I can track them down ASAP.

'We need to blanket search the property immediately,' I say. 'This includes going through everyone's stuff. And I mean, everything.'

'That'd be illegal, and it would cause offence among the many upstanding practitioners gathered here. I'll get my staff to scour the grounds – they'll go through every nook and cranny until they find this thief.'

'Murderer,' Dr Maige corrects MacLeod.

'Yes, quite right. We'll have them by the morning, and I'll string them up the old way.'

I dig his enthusiasm, but I get the feeling it ain't going to be a walk in the park. Schemers make contingencies. Callander's element of surprise will only serve us for so long. The murderer will be planning their next move now they can't leave, and it's crucial we get to them before they make a play.

'Rest assured we *will* find your scroll,' MacLeod addresses Qozmos. 'In the meantime, I suggest we let everyone know to be on the lookout.'

The Grand Debtera's been real still so far, listening to Kebede's translation. He's no longer the witty, jovial grandpa he was playing at dinner. It's almost scary to see him like this. There's a sandstorm coming for sure if this thing doesn't get resolved. He begins to speak in a soft monotone, with his assistant translating.

'Know this. If the scroll is not returned to us soon, I will tear this castle apart stone by stone and fling it into the sea. And when I'm done, I'll level MacLeod's Table and salt the earth, leaving this island a barren rock.'

With that bombshell his only contribution, he gets up and leaves the room.

Heavy stuff. MacLeod's Table is a flat-topped hill across the water. And I don't think this biblical threat was metaphorical at all.

'Surely you wouldn't allow him to do that,' MacLeod whines. 'He can't. Can he? This place has stood for eight hundred years!'

'The scroll's much older than that,' Featherstone replies dryly.

'The schools will assist in any way they can,' Wedderburn says. They might each be independent, but his Edinburgh School behaves like it's the head of the pack.

'I'm more concerned about the fact, and I very much hope I am mistaken here, that the secretary wishes to leave this matter in the hands of this girl,' Hutchinson says, pointing at me.

'What the secretary chooses to do is at his own discretion. He is the Discoverer General of our Society,' Cockburn replies.

'*Some* of us are on the Extraordinary Committee, Frances. It's our duty to speak up whenever there's an issue.'

'The girl is more than capable. It was only this summer she saved some boys at my school who'd got themselves into a bit of a magical pickle,' Wedderburn says. 'And I don't know of anyone else here who is in law enforcement.'

'Your view of the girl doesn't sway me at all. I'm sure we've got someone who is more qualified. And she really ought to apologize about her conduct earlier.'

'That more qualified person is me, sir. I will run this

investigation personally, with the aid of my *capable* assistant. I hope that is to your satisfaction. Now give us the room,' Callander says sharply.

Cockburn immediately opens the door. The heads might grumble, but they leave anyway, Dr Maige following after them. Edmund MacLeod shows no sign of wanting to move, and I notice Cockburn waiting impatiently, still holding the door open.

'You too, sir,' Callander says.

There's a coldness about him now. But in a crisis, especially in a crisis, everyone should know where the power lies. That's what Callander's flexed by kicking them out.

The laird of the castle gets up rather reluctantly. Booted out of his own library. Throughout the meeting he'd been trying to assert his own control too. This whole thing's going to get messy with egos floating about. I was happier stacking chairs and handing out tote bags. The gaffer waits until Cockburn has exited and shut the door behind her. Just us now. The two members of the General Discoveries Directorate here on Skye. It's an independent body within the Society, and as the Discoverer General, Callander is tasked with tackling all magical malfeasance. He sort of roped me in to work for him a while back and I've been here ever since. Gets a bit hairy at times and it pays zilch, which is the going rate in this economy . . . but it's a job, I guess. Callander uncrosses his arms, rises and moves to sit on the sofa. Then he instructs me to sit opposite.

I'm grateful 'cause my trotters are complaining now.

Callander holds out his left hand and a square dram glass appears. Then he holds out his right, conjuring a bottle of

The Macallan, a thirty-year-old single malt. The bottle alone's worth more than the caravan I live in. Sigh. He pours himself a shot, swirls it in his glass and downs it in one. Then he immediately pours a second, more generous round, and the bottle disappears back into the ether.

'I promised Esfandiar I wasn't going to drink until conference was over. Don't tell him about this.'

I zip my mouth and throw away the key.

The air in the room's oppressive and heavy. I'm so exhausted.

'Do you know how often I've sat around these people and wished I could tell them to play with their nether regions as you did earlier? All the time, Ropa. But I can't because I'm more than me. It's not about my feelings or what I want. I am my office, and that demands decorum. My emotions can't get in the way, or else . . . Let me put this another way. You are exceedingly good at what you do. You've more than earnt your place at the table. But you need to understand that when you speak, it is my voice that comes out through your lips.'

'Then maybe I should be the one to say the things you can't say out loud.'

Callander pinches the bridge of his nose.

'That is not how you win with this lot. You've got to *play the game*. What happened at dinner was out of character for you. I've long admired your forbearance.'

'That's for the forefathers . . . What's suspicious to me is how you anticipated all this. You must have done, putting that barrier spell up so quickly.' Even Callander is a suspect as far as I'm concerned. Don't matter he's the gaffer.

He looks at me wearily. I immediately regret saying what I just did. Maybe I'm taking it too far.

'Sorry,' I say.

'Don't be. A good discoverer is cynical, distrustful, inquisitive, sceptical. It was only in the early twentieth century they changed the name of my office from Witchfinder General to Discoverer General. Before that, office holders used to round up unregistered practitioners and burn them at the stake. The world's changed somewhat since those halcyon days. For all its grandiosity, the Society is nothing but a collection of schoolteachers, administrators, academics, businesspeople of every hue, magiformaticians, zoomagicians, and healers, of course. Hell, even Marxists. After the events of the Catastrophe and our defeat to England, Scottish magic was neutered. That was the price we paid for peace. Our militants exiled or executed. In reality we are just a professional body now, no different to the Royal Institution of Chartered Surveyors or the Chartered Institute of Editing and Proofreading, or, disgustingly, the Association of Chartered Certified Accountants. I observed what you and that Ethiopian boy did tonight. No one else rushed off with you. We've lost our teeth and maybe you are the last person here worthy of the witchfinders of old.'

Great, now I'm a *witchfinder*? Thanks a lot, universe. Kinda feel sorry for all those poor women (and some men) who were tortured and killed back in the day. Ironic how, like everything else, this office has been sanitized. That's how it goes. Murderers become honourable soldiers, or worse, lords and kings. Charlatans morph into clergymen. Usurers are now respectable bankers. Rent-seekers become landlords. Dig deep enough into the history of anything and you'll hit festering pus. That's what makes us human. I'm still going to do my job right, though. No point getting all hung up about the sins of the past. That's what's got us here.

'I suppose we could go round torturing everyone until we get a confession,' I jest.

'Don't tempt me.' Callander gulps his whisky and winces. 'Tell me everything you discovered tonight.'

I give him the full play-by-play. Everything me and Kebede did. Problem is, I've got no real leads, apart from the vague awareness that I need to start with people who weren't at the reception. That's gonna take some serious nosing about. I also need to figure out who has something to gain from this. Take it apart, thread by thread. I at least have a shadowy sense of what the thief looked like, and the name they mentioned too.

'When I was on the roof, the person I was chasing said something about a Black Lord. Does that mean anything to you?'

'In this country there are more lords kicking about than commoners. I know a Lord Black, but he's a genial farmer who seldom takes his seat in the upper chamber. He's given more to managing his estate than bothering with the extra-natural.'

I tell Callander I'm super-worried about this element. In my time chasing arseholes, I've heard of the Tall Man who was to come. Got rid of him. Then there was some cat calling himself the One Above All.

'What if they are some kind of profane trinity targeting the magical world,' I speculate. With nothing to base it on yet, I need to go down all avenues.

'Hmm . . . That's a bit of a stretch. You need to focus on the more immediate issue at hand. Mr Sneddon's murder and the robbery. I'm going to lean heavily on you for this one, Ropa. We don't have much time. The castle has very limited supplies. Or one of the attendees will declare they have some medical condition and need their drugs from outside. MacLeod will grow impatient with catering for extra guests at his own expense. And I don't even want to think about Qozmos. For as long as the Newton Barrier is up, I can't sleep either. I constantly have to renew the spell with my will or else it'll collapse. Time is of the essence, Ropa. But you get a few hours' rest now – you look tired – and let MacLeod's people start the initial searches. First thing in the morning, you'll find this person and we'll deal with them.'

This feels very real all of a sudden. Instead of planning my own heist, I have to look for stolen property. You couldn't make this up. Yep, we are so screwed right now.

XI

Some castles have that medieval fortress aesthetic. Not this one. Maybe it offered protection once. But if it weren't for Callander's barrier, rampaging Vikings could ransack it in no time. Dunvegan Castle feels to me like the inbred cousin to a big block of council flats with a few additional fancy architectural features. It's the McMansion of castles.

It's really late and I'm on my way to bed in my little room on the ground floor, near where the old kitchen used to be. That's where the dungeon is too, though it's accessible from above. You can picture all the servants scurrying about down here like rats, back in the day when the MacLeods could afford them. Yep, the rich keep you under their feet, literally. Something's felt off since I got here. A malevolent presence. I breathe a sigh of resignation. I can't really escape them, it seems, and old buildings like this are wont to have a spectre or two in attendance.

The older ghosts become, the more mental they get too. That's why it's important to help them move on. I think of our world as a teaching zone. You don't wanna be that old geezer who still hangs out by the old high school trying to relive old glories. That'd be super-creepy. There's infinite realms out there waiting to be explored. The ghosts that linger have issues. Naturally, I'm wondering if I can use the ones around here. See if they saw something.

Yawn.

Bloody knackered now. Callander told me to rest while MacLeod and his people search the grounds. I hope they find something, but in the meantime, I'll use my gift. Scottish magic looks down on ghostalkers like me, they don't even consider it real magic, but the dead are with us still. They can help us or harm us. Try as we might, we can never wish them away. It's too soon to speak with Sneddon's ghost – newbies are always confused, especially when they are victims of foul play. I doubt he would have seen anything useful in the dark anyway, especially since Jomo didn't. No, I need someone else, and so I grab my mbira and head outside the castle, down the stone steps leading to the sea gate.

It's dark outside. Still no power yet. In the distance, I hear voices and catch glimpses of folks with lamps tramping through the gardens. Their lights blink in and out of my field of vision, distorted by the trees and shrubbery. But I'm not interested in them. Instead I turn my attention to the sullen sea and focus on the woman in white wading through the ocean. This isn't the first time I've seen her. Every night, sometimes several times even, she makes her way from Dunvegan Castle, down the stairs and through the sea gate, and drowns herself. Then she reappears in her pristine nightgown and does it all over again. This time she can't get as far out. She's stuck by Callander's barrier, and is studying it.

I cough and she turns to me from the shallows where the

Ethiopians' tiny boat floats lazily. Dark, sorrowful eyes pierce me. I immediately recognize her as Adamina MacLeod, from the portrait I saw at dinner. This is the first time she's seen me see her, and she seems surprised by it. I reach my hand between the iron bars of the gate and beckon her to me. In less time than it takes to blink, she appears in front of me, and stares, clearly unsure if I really do see her. Ghosts can be pesky and needy, and so over the years I've developed ways of avoiding their attention. I pretend not to notice they're there. It's become second nature to me, 'cause if they know you see them, then they're all over you, badgering your arse for this and that.

'Must be exhausting walking into that sea all the time. It's not exactly the Maldives,' I say, all gentle like. I am a wee bit wary, since I find folks who've topped themselves taxing to deal with. So much pain.

She continues to look at me with those large, sad eyes, carrying agonies that've been borne for centuries. A gruesome cross. Her long hair's blowing in a non-existent wind, and the Jane Austen nightdress she's wearing flutters about too. She cocks her head to one side but remains silent. I start twanging my mbira so I can hear her speak. A tune called 'Hurukuro', which my nan told me was great for opening dialogues.

'I need your help,' I say.

She turns away from me and makes to go back into the sea.

'Please, I can help you cross over to the other side. Bargain with me. What's keeping you here? I can fix that.

All I need to know is if you saw anything unusual happen in the castle tonight. There's been a murder and I need to find out who did it.'

'There's been many a murder in this accursed castle. Many a dark thing has happened here, many a love lost and a life too. Nasty business these MacLeods, but the curse the Fairy King laid is upon them. They'll pay for what they did to the original inhabitants of this place, and soon they will lose what they treasure the most. And with that all their power and prestige too. Now leave me be, I've harmed no one,' she replies with venom.

'What do you mean by that? What's going on? What will they lose? Please.'

The ghost glances over her shoulder and looks up to the highest part of the castle, the one with the flagpole. Then she looks back at me, shakes her head and floats down into the sea to drown herself again.

I'm so frustrated, but I head back inside the castle anyways. I wish I could compel her to tell me more, but Gran warned me to respect the wishes of the dead and the damned. You can't force them to bargain if they aren't causing anyone any harm and no one has brought a grievance against them. That's an important rule. As far as I can tell, the only person Adamina hurts is herself. I'll have to find another way.

I'm wishing I was back in my caravan, bunking in with Gran. I miss her scent. Whenever you're stressed out, she always knows the right things to say. She's got a boyfriend now. Well, she doesn't call him that. He's her 'companion'. *Ropa, are you jealous?* A wee bit. I've had her to myself since

Gramps croaked. This new fellow makes her laugh. That used to be my job. The worst thing is, they've started watching *Wallander* without me!

'Excuse me.'

Jesus. I nearly jump out of my skin.

'I didn't mean to startle you,' Mrs Featherstone says. She's sat in a chair in one of the alcoves off the corridor. The window beside her stares out into the black night.

She dresses in red all the time, though she's neither little nor from the hood. Red hair, red lipstick, red-soled shoes. Bloody hell.

'You surprised me, that's all,' I say.

'It's good to see you again. Our first encounter was all too brief. I've gone on to hear many fine things about you. Your sister, Izwi, shares some of your talents. She's progressing much faster than we thought possible. I'm certain she'll catch up with her age-mates in only a year or two.'

'Thanks for giving her a scholarship.' Callander arranged all that and I'm happy sis is getting the magical education I'll never get. It's taken a lot of financial pressure off me. And because the Doric School has her in boarding, I've only got to worry about feeding me and Gran during term time. They even provide uniforms and stationery for her. Makes my life way easier. Doesn't stop me missing her, though.

'I brought Izwi here as part of a choir that's meant to do a presentation.'

'She's into singing?' I can't believe she's here! Why hasn't she messaged me about it?

'It's not that type of choir. For more complex spells, you

need to have magicians working together in concert. One person can't possibly hold all the information needed to make it work. So each magician takes part of the spell. Why do you think witches' covens were a thing? We teach our pupils the value of working together in Aberdeen. The Edinburgh School is all about the pursuit of individual goals at all costs. We foster a more communal ethos. The point I was trying to make is, I'd hoped to surprise you by bringing her here. The performance may not happen anymore because of this barrier. All the same, I wanted you to know she's staying in a hotel nearby, with the other students.'

'So near yet so far! Thanks for bringing her, though. I hope we can get this all sorted quickly so I can see her.'

'You're welcome. Goodnight, Ropa Moyo. The rest of us are still waiting for Frances to sort out our accommodation.'

I leave her staring out the window. My ticker's filled with yearning for Izwi. She had to go off to school. It's for the best. But our cara's emptier without her moods and humour. It's not the same hearing the sound of her voice on the phone. I've got a phantom itch, a part of me is gone. I miss her so much.

When I open the door to my room I'm surprised to see a figure lightly snoring in my single bed.

Am I in the right room?

Of course. That's my backpack on the floor. But there's also a wheelchair.

'Oh, hey.' Drowsy voice. 'I was wondering when you'd come down.'

'Priya, what are you doing in here?'

She moans and tries to raise her head from the pillow. Too heavy, she slumps back down. I take off my clothes. Never had no jammies so . . . I lift the covers.

'Move over, squatter.' I budge her towards the wall and get into bed.

At least it's been warmed up. They don't bother heating our rooms, so the last few nights have been well Baltic. All the Hamsters complain about this. But this is nice and cosy. I throw an arm over her and shut my eyes. Zonked but my mind won't stop racing. There I am with Sneddon, back in the Library of the Dead last month. Then I hear him haranguing me for picking an author he doesn't rate. There we are in the cavernous reception and he's bugging me about a title I want to renew 'cause some plonker's got it on reserve. Moments where he shushed me and Jomo. The way his double chin wobbled when he laughed. The little things. We weren't tight or anything like that. I try not to shed any tears for him. A small hole in your hull can sink your boat.

'Sorry I commandeered your spot,' Priya says in the morning.

'Pay me rent and we're square.'

An odd raspberry light filters through the window. This place has weird skies. One moment orange. Lilac the next. It's like a painter's changing his mind about the canvas every five minutes. Priya's got her face in front of mine. We lie on our sides, knees touching. I can almost taste her morning breath. Not too bad actually. It's nice sharing the bed with her. Guess I'm so used to the cramped-up space in our caravan, I feel lonely on my own. Even in a tiny room like this.

'Cockburn made alternative sleeping arrangements for everyone, after Callander raised up the barrier, and I asked to bunk in with you. Did you know your legs move about at night like you're running away from something? Restless Leg Syndrome. Warm baths with essential oils might help.'

'It doesn't bother *me*.'

'I'll have to put up with being kicked about then. I'd have thought you'd have run it out of your system last night. Last I heard, you'd been spirited away to have a meeting with the big boys.'

'Thank you for saving Jomo.'

'You don't have to thank me for that. I wish I'd been part of the chase instead.' She gets all sombre. 'You heard about Sneddon by now? Lethington's virtually the Greek god of medicine, Asclepius reborn, but there's little anyone can do to fix a blade through the heart.'

I grimace. Death, bodies. Not my thing. Give me ghouls any given Sunday.

'So, what's the plan, Jessica Fletcher?'

'We're in a right shitshow, lass. At least you're not on my list of suspects 'cause you were right beside me. Time to get up. We've got to find the Black Lord's minion.'

XII

Me and Priya set out to retrace my steps around the castle grounds last night. I notice a version of the Union flag now flies full mast on the pole. The old Union Jack of 1801 was the amalgamation of the flags of three kingdoms: England, Scotland and Ireland. Never mind Wales, they didn't get a strip, since they were already part of the Kingdom of England. Fitting a dragon over the whole thing would've been awkward anyhow. Since Northern Ireland went its way, we've removed a cross, and resorted to using the King James version of 1606, which was originally designed for the navy.

The MacLeods must be perturbed to have it flying this morning. A clear signal to London that the lairds, on this isle anyhow, don't want no bother. It'll piss off a number of Scottish magicians, though, for sure. Anyone harbouring separatist tendencies is likely to catch a fit. Well, they can take it up with the Sorcerer Royal and see how that turns out. Most folks have been sucking it up, as evidenced by everyone going round saying 'God save the king' to each other this morning.

Yep. Long may he reign and all that.

We bypass my watery leap in our rehash of last night's chase. The tide's gone out, but the invisible barrier is still holding some water near the castle. Seaweed floats atop it. Maybe my imagination, but I swear the air's also a wee bit stale. No morning breeze comes through.

I once heard on a podcast about this Biosphere 2 experiment from back in the day. Kind of like the Eden Project they built out in Cornwall before the Catastrophe. It was supposed to be an isolated sphere with everything necessary for life within it. Biosphere 1 was Earth itself. But number 2 failed. Seems Sir Callander has inadvertently restarted that experiment in the castle gardens, this time with us as guinea pigs. I hope these trees are pumping out oxygen fast this morning.

I'm seething by the time we get to the nurseries. The search party MacLeod sent out trampled over everything. There's footprints all over the soggy earth and it's impossible to read anything meaningful.

I shouldn't have gone to bed before I'd checked, I should've pushed on.

My Italian pal Nicco said: 'It's better to act and repent than not to act and regret.'

I'm in the latter category just now. The key's to keep most stuff in the former one.

'What's next, Mrs Fletcher?'

'Are you going to keep calling me that?'

'I thought you said you and Gran were well into *Murder, She Wrote*.'

I roll my eyes, imitating Angela Lansbury.

'Let's go over to the front gate. I need to see if the orphan children hanging round there can help me with something, since they're still on the outside,' I say.

'It's proper echoey under this bubble. Makes me feel like shouting just so I hear my voice bounce around,' says Priya. She cups her mouth but doesn't go through with it.

She's right, though. It's weird walking around with this dome above us. Must do something to the light too, 'cause there's a sepia tinge in the air, which varies as you move. Maybe it's because of refraction relative to the sun's angle in the sky. It's not like Callander explained any of this to me. And even if he did, I doubt I'd fully understand the spellcraft on display.

There's a subtle distortion to the trees outside the barrier as you move. Didn't notice that last night, it was too dark. There's a slight reflection too, of things on this side. It's like a ghostly mirror. The waterfall, a neat feature in the garden, has dried up and the road up top is probably flooded since the water has to go somewhere. But that's a good thing. If the water from the burn kept flowing towards the sea, we'd drown in this enclosure.

'What's over there?' Priya says, pointing at a pine near the fence.

We head over, sinking into the soggy ground as we go. I swear this place could do with better drainage. My wet toes feel kind of itchy and I wiggle them inside my boots.

Right by the base of the barrier is a hole in the earth, nearly a foot and a half in diameter. Perfectly circular. It's starting to fill up with water. I stick my hand in all the way to the bottom and feel the eerie texture of the barrier. When you hit it, it's like your hand's pushing back against you. Same warmth, softness, everything. It's repulsive.

'Our suspect attempted a Huttonian earth-moving spell. They were trying to get out of here. That or they had a sophisticated drill rig, which I very much doubt,' says Priya. A healer will always try to give differential diagnosis.

Gran tried to teach me magic to control the earth. It's very difficult and I never mastered it. Her style of magic isn't the scientific sort, so it's hard to make sense of it . . . This hole is a good indicator that at some point last night, or early this morning, someone tried to get away. But the footprints every-where show the search parties already came through here. We'll have to check what they turned up. Narrowing it down to a specific practitioner will be tricky, seeing as me and the odd castle staff member are the only ones who aren't trained in this.

We're finished inspecting the hole when a robust fella approaches carrying a bunch of roses. He's dressed in chinos and a purple windbreaker.

'I know you've been avoiding me, Priya,' he says. 'Please, I just want to talk to you.'

'Jordan, it's over. What more is there to say?' Priya's frostier than Bobby Drake.

'Give me a second chance. I love you, baby.'

Whoa.

'Don't embarrass yourself.'

'Is this because of her? She your new girlfriend or some-thing?' he asks.

'As a matter of fact, she is. Now kindly bugger off. Cheating twally.'

'Yeah, piss off. And stick those roses where the sun don't shine, you tube,' I say, jumping into the fray.

Jordan looks like a wounded puppy. He's got that posh-boy thing they do when they can't get what they want, and soon enough he frowns like a petulant teenager. There it is. I take the handles of Priya's wheelchair and lead us away. I don't ask questions, she doesn't need to tell me nothing. I'll always take her side over some toff twat.

'I guess we're officially an item now, pal,' I say. 'You're buying the ring.'

'But I can't kneel.' She guffaws until I catch it too. Our laughter bounces off the walls of the barrier.

We reach the main gate and it's not just feral orphans milling about outside. Someone's opened the gate, but no one's getting through. Scores of practitioners who were due to attend today's events have to dodge street kids throwing rocks at the barrier for fun. Can't hear them, though. The rocks don't make a sound on our side either. When the kids see me, they stop and point to their mouths, rubbing their bellies. They're hungry. I've been nicking what I can to give them something to eat since I got here, but not much good now. I mouth the word 'sorry'. Nothing I can do from this side.

If sound wasn't an issue, I'd have them scouring the area and seeing if there's a getaway car or bike stashed nearby. I reckon last night's assailant would have had some means of transportation ready. If they can find it, we could then trace it back to its owner.

Check my phone. One bar of reception. Oops, even that's gone now.

The network inside the castle's dodgy, but it's usually okay outside. That's how I'd been making my calls.

I check a couple of texts I sent out to Gran and Izwi last night. They still haven't gone through and I haven't received anything today either. Hail Mary full of grace. I send Izwi another one explaining the situation, and asking that she get the orphans food if there's leftovers where she is. If this one does get through, I can use her as a channel to get useful info off them. I promise to pay in fudge for any relevant details.

Right now, it looks like the siege of Dunvegan Castle has begun in earnest.

One of the practitioners outside is gesticulating madly, but I can't make out what he's saying. He's Peter Hernandez, one of our speakers for today. I bet if he doesn't show he won't be getting that fat honorarium the Society dishes out. There's going to be more angry folks like him before the day's done. This nightclub's full.

The tap-tap of a cane approaches behind us.

'Isn't this an exquisite thing of staggering beauty?' Lord Samarasinghe says.

He walks past me, brushing me aside, even though there's plenty of room. Total douche. Then he stops in front of the barrier, taps it with his index finger and runs his hand playfully along it, grinning. There's a curious kid somewhere inside him. I recall he wasn't present at the reception last night, which puts him damn near the top of the list for me. He's intimidating. Not in appearance – he's actually the best-looking person at this conference. Strong jaw. Not too many people can pull off a monobrow the way he does. But it's that air of menace he carries. Fortunately for me, Priya's nearby, and that gives me more guts than a Highland cow.

'I have the most profound admiration for the parasitic genius of the Scotch. The Kerr-Newton Shield. An imaginatively applied magicization of Newton's third law. "For every action there's an equal and opposite reaction." See, there's nothing material to form the actual barrier. It doesn't exist in the strictest sense, since when no force is applied to the region there's nothing there.' He speaks with his back to us. 'Rather, it's a region of potentiality, inverting forces applied to it, thereby giving the appearance something *is* there. It's so elegant. But tell me something, poodles, is Sir Callander really sustaining this super-unstructure all by himself? It must be draining.'

He turns and gives us his twisted smile. I'll show him a fucking poodle.

'Lord Samarasinghe, I'd like to ask you a few questions,' I reply instead. 'Where were you last night?' Direct attacks unsettle folks. You can catch them out that way.

His amusement turns to mild bemusement. Eyes dart between me and Priya, almost as if deciding which toy to play with. He lets go of his cane, but it doesn't drop, just remains balanced upright, its tiger's-head handle staring at me, jaws wide open.

'Indeed, you are Callander's little project. We've heard all about you. How, in his immense charity, he took in an unqualified urchin and made her apprentice to Scotland's foremost witchfinder – not *the* foremost witchfinder, I'll have you know. Last night I was thinking you are much skinnier than I'd imagined. Emaciated. So much less impressive in person.'

The Sorcerer Royal moves closer, towering over me. Personal space is a concept he's clearly not heard of. This morning he's not in his cape, but he still wears a blazer with raven feathers on the shoulders. He's also got a white armband round his left bicep. The purple stripe running down the side of his trousers adds to the militaristic bearing.

'You didn't answer my question,' I persist.

'And you, Ms Kapoor. The little healer who's taken it upon herself to be an aide to said urchin. Must get you into all sorts of adventures,' he says, ignoring me. He's clearly used to being in control of whatever encounter he's in. This is his way of showing me his power. How petty.

But he's playing with us. There's that evidently English arrogance about him. I step in closer until we're touching, looking right up his clatty nostrils. Lord Samarasinghe's taken aback. He steps away from me, crinkling his nose like I'm howlin'. And then he speaks, looking right over my head.

'You know, I chose to fly because I can't stand the travelling in Scotland. Not by road. The squalor, the deprivation, those dreadful accents. The *smells*. It distresses my delicate disposition. But even from a great height, soaring above everyone, I couldn't help but notice that the bleak blight's spread has swallowed up further swathes of farmland. Itinerant labourers drifting across broken motorways searching for sustenance. Hardly any sheep or cattle in your fields. I'm no agronomist, but you lot should be starving by winter. It'll be the Seven Ill Years all over again.'

He's right, I saw that plague too. The abandoned farms. Overgrown fields. Furry black and grey fungi colouring what should be fields of grain. But I can't be distracted by that right now.

'That's not what I asked.'

'You'll do what you've always done in the past. Turn to England, bowl in hand. I despise beggars. It's demeaning. Look at them.' He points to the poor people milling about beyond the barrier. 'But to answer your question, poodle. You wanted to know where I was last night? It's hardly my fault if you people can't look after your own stuff. Do I have a sign that says "Lost and Found" hanging round my neck?'

'Strange, isn't it? How you show up to the conference uninvited and all of a sudden things go missing. If it quacks like a duck.'

'It's your first time too, if I've been correctly informed. You ought to start investigating yourself by that logic . . . given your criminal record. Granted, you don't have any actual convictions. You're still too young for the penal system. But you are known to associate with some rather unpalatable characters.'

I try to respond but stutter. He's caught me off guard. Clearly he knows things about me he shouldn't. Stuff even Sir Callander didn't bother checking out before I started interning with him. If they'd come out, I doubt I'd have been given this opportunity. But I know this play. It's not strong enough kompromat to shake me off. Let's spar a bit more and see what happens.

'You are well informed,' I acknowledge. Honesty is the only way to diffuse something like this.

'The wise raven sees all and knows all. Nevermore,' he replies with a raised eyebrow.

'What do you want the scroll for? If this is a ploy to

embarrass Scottish magic then you've miscalculated. The Ethiopians don't seem to draw much of a distinction between us. To them we are just one *United* Kingdom, and they're still bristling over their stuff you've got in the British Museum down in London. This will backfire. I advise you to give the scroll back.'

Lord Samarasinghe's shoulders heave and he starts laughing. Loud and hearty. Then he stops abruptly and bares his teeth. I have to fight the urge to look away as he stares me down. Soon, though, this gives way to something resembling pity, as if he truly feels sorry for me. His emotions vacillate so rapidly, it's disorienting. Then he picks up his cane once more.

'This is comedy gold. I've enjoyed our little chat, poodle. But clearly you're nowhere near as smart as I'd been led to believe. Pity. After last night's performance, I even thought you had potential. But if you'd been in the loop, you'd know they caught your suspect in the early hours. They are holding him in the dungeon.'

XIII

Okay, Samarasinghe's pulled the rug out from under my feet. I'm paddling in the air like those old-school cartoon characters before they drop. Made me look like a right mug. The upside is the guy's been caught. Yay. Let's verify that and get back to normal life.

Someone should have told me, though. Means they don't think I'm important enough to bother with. Wankers.

Morag waylays us at the entrance. She's well past retirement age and shorter than I am. Whiskers on her chin, wart on her nose. Keen eyes and sharp ears, though. Knows everything about the place, having worked for the MacLeods since she was a teenage girl. She's been great to me since I got here, the best one of the castle staff to deal with as we've had to coordinate with them on various things. This is their turf after all; we're just passing through.

'Oh Ropa, lassie, this isnae fair at all. Our Murdo wouldnae hurt a fly, he wouldnae.' She's distraught, tearing at the tufts of hair springing from her balding head. 'You work for Sir Ian Callander. You tell him.'

Murdo? He's the suspect they've caught?

'I'll do what I can, okay?' I reach out and hold her hands.

'Bless you. I'm gaun out of my heid.'

'It'll be alright, Morag.'

Nothing hits you more than a mother's pain. Poor Morag's still in her maid's uniform, still working even though they've got her son locked up in the dungeon. Anyone else would walk out or kick up a stink. But poverty does that to people. You learn to take it. Skye isn't exactly a place filled with opportunities.

It seems wrong she'd be asking me of all people to help. She's worked for the MacLeods her whole life and Edmund is the third chief she's served. You'd think there'd be something there. Some loyalty to their own. But if I know one true thing about the rich and mighty, it's that as soon as you're no good they'll discard you like used Kleenex. They are nice enough when they want something from you. Praise and compliments. Put a foot wrong, though, and see how quickly that all changes.

Her son's always wandering about in his overalls. He might be slow, but he sure as hell has green fingers. At least that's what I've heard. He's the reason the castle gardens are in such great shape, even after the devastation wrought by the Big Yin. Seems happier with them hydrangeas than when he's dealing with people. Never looks you in the eye. It makes him seem shifty if you don't know him, but that's just how he's wired. We've all got our quirks.

'Dinnae let them stitch up my boy,' Morag begs. 'I should have packed in my work here a long time ago, but there's nae other jobs to be had out here. Our wages are late coming in half the time. I'm sick of it.'

'I'm on it. In the meantime, I need you to check if there's a missing dirk in the armoury – could you do that? I'll come find you later, okay?'

She raises my hand to her lips and kisses it before hobbling off. I wish I could give her a cast-iron guarantee, but you can't do things like that. Folks take it literally. Then when you don't deliver, everything's your fault. It's cruel. Best to give her something to do. Make her feel like she's helping out. Which she is.

'I hate to say it, but we can't be sure yet that the gardener didn't do it,' Priya says, once Morag's out of earshot.

'You think he knows Huttonian spellcraft? I wonder which magic school he went to,' I reply sarcastically.

Priya raises her eyebrows, considering my words. I'm already on the march, the scent of fish right up my nose as something sure doesn't smell right. Murdo's no gymnast, wrong build and everything. Couldn't have been him prancing up on the roof last night. I've seen him lumbering through the gardens, steady as an ox.

Access to the dungeon where Murdo's been stashed is just next to the drawing room. I have to go through a narrow and confined passage of rough stone and dirt. This material is the original stuff they used to build the castle. It's . . . No. My heart's starting to beat fast. Can't move. A visceral terror feels as though it will overwhelm me. Not now, not now. My thoughts are racing so fast I can't catch them. Too dark in here. I can't breathe.

'Hey, you okay?' Priya asks.

I need air. What's that tingling? I'm going to die. Here.

No. I look stupid. God, I'm shaking. I can't control it. So dizzy. I slump against the wall. Too tight. Make it stop. God, make it stop. The walls are closing in, I'm going to be crushed in here.

I don't want to die.

Heavy.

Those rocks. It's all closing in on me. Can't get air.

'It's okay, Ropa. I'm right here. Take it easy.'

And just as quickly as it starts, it stops. I can breathe again.

I've made an arse of myself, haven't I?

'Hey, hey, it's okay. You're alright.'

'I'm good,' I say, smiling. 'It was a wee wobble, that's all.'

'You sure? Let's go back out for some air.'

'I said I was fine, okay? Geez, can you let it go already,' I snap at her.

'Wow. Alrighty then. I was trying to look out for you. No pressure.'

I regret sniping at Priya almost as soon as the words come out of my mouth. She looks hurt by it. Rightly so. I'm not quite myself the now. Felt like the whole world was crushing down on me. That's nothing new, though, and I'm fine now.

'Sorry,' I say.

'Don't be. I want you to know I'm your pal and you can talk to me about anything. Anything.'

'Cheers.'

I straighten up and detach myself from the wall I was leaning on. Feels strange. Like I've just regained control of my body again. The tingling sensation in my fingers is gone. What the hell? But I'm not going to think about what it might've been right now. Storm's over, let's get back to work.

Priya hangs back as I head on into the dungeon. The passage is too narrow for her wheelchair.

It's dark and dank in here, so I light up my torch again. I'm inside a small cavern, and in the middle of it there's a deep hole covered by a metal grill with a padlock on it. I shine my light down the hole and see Murdo curled up at the bottom of a pit. It's a long way down. The dimensions are tiny, though. I've seen roomier graves. The way he's lying makes him seem like a child – he's clearly suffering down there. It's said the dungeon was placed next to the old kitchen so that when they locked you up, you could smell the aroma of food cooking as you slowly starved to death. Certain kinds of cruelty require a perverse genius.

The prisoner looks up, covering his eyes with his forearm.

There's blood on his temple.

His clothes are also torn, with some bruising and swelling on his lips. They've roughed him up a bit. Reminds me of bad encounters with Edinburgh's bobbies. They let you know who's boss for sure. Fear's written all over Murdo's face. Confusion too. I bet all the times he's helped out in this place he's never once thought he might end up in its dungeon. The village of Dunvegan's got a small police station. But with no cops about until the barrier's lifted, this is as good as it gets.

'Murdo, I want to talk to you. Can you tell me who did this to you?' I ask, speaking gently.

He shakes his head.

'Did you steal the scroll and murder someone?'

He nods nervously.

'He's already confessed,' Edmund MacLeod says, coming in. 'I'll have to ask you to leave. This place is off limits now.'

'I work in the General Discoveries Directorate. That means I get to ask him questions.'

'Go on then. Tell her you did it, Murdo,' he says.

'It was me, boss,' the gardener replies without hesitation. 'There. Satisfied?'

'Where's the scroll then?'

'He burned it, didn't he? Knew he was about to get caught and set about destroying the evidence. It's a sacrilege.' MacLeod sounds annoyed he has to answer to me.

'Where did he learn to do magic then?'

'Murdo was caught standing by the hole. He tried to bolt when the lads apprehended him. If it wasn't him, he'd have no reason to run. Look, don't you think there's anyone more disappointed by all this than I am? I've looked after him and his mother, who's worked here since I was a little boy. They're practically like family to me. It broke my heart to learn he was behind this.'

His 'disappointment' sounds hollow to me. 'What else has he stolen?'

'The scroll. I've just told you that.'

'I meant before this. He's been employed here for years, surely he's stolen something else from the castle – if he's a thief. Maybe you forgave him for it? Now he's a recidivist.'

'I don't see the relevance of this. We caught him trying to sneak out. And he confessed. That's all the proof anyone needs. We'll hand him over to the Ethiopians to do what they please and that'll be the end of it.'

I'm a thief. Well, I was. It's complicated. Takes one to know one. I clasp my hands together in a steeple under my chin. So, the gardener steals a precious scroll, murdering Sneddon in the process. But he's never tried to take anything else from the veritable buffet of loot in this castle. Sniff, sniff. I smell bullshit. You can get anyone to confess to anything if you give them a good laldy and MacLeod's lads clearly gave it to him proper. Simple man like Murdo wouldn't know how to handle himself under that kind of heat. It's downright cruel what they've done. Where I'm from, I've seen plenty of people stitched up and sent to jail for shit they ain't guilty of.

See, a gardener spotting some alien burrow near his fence would surely have gone over to check it out. Whoever'd done it, he would know it's his job to fill it in again. And I imagine he'd have been a wee bit pissed off by it. There's tons of work to be done in autumn, all those fallen leaves, preparing the gardens for winter. Someone randomly digging up a hole in the perimeter was one extra thing for him to deal with. The same way he had to pick up after littering guests.

'Why don't we check the CCTV footage from round the castle. Even if there was no power, we might have something from last night. Maybe spot someone in the wrong place.'

'Impossible. They broke into our security and destroyed the hard drive too.'

Great. Without video evidence, we have to concentrate on what's in front of us now. But it tells me this was someone with intimate knowledge of the castle and its security.

'Even if I accept the premise of what you're suggesting, which I don't, that'd still mean I have to believe some highly implausible things. If Murdo *had* burned the scroll, why did he still try to run?'

'He's not the sharpest tool in the shed now, is he?'

'Okay. Show me the ashes. The scroll was contained inside a wooden box. Let's see the ash, including the metal clasps and nails holding it together.' The strange way it opened suggests it must have multiple hinges.

'Uh, erm . . . we're still working on that.'

'A gardener would have used a shovel if he wanted to dig his way out. This man doesn't know magic, and wouldn't know where to sell a magical artefact either. He hasn't even bothered with the antiques you've got in here, if he hasn't stolen anything before. You clean him up and let him go. This isn't going to be the quick fix you're hoping for. Murdo is not your scapegoat.'

'You don't tell *me* what to do, young lady.'

'I'm more inclined to believe that the owner of this castle, who's heavily in debt, might have a stronger motive. Look at this place. Your lead roof's about to cave in. I've heard those cost loads to repair. When was the last time you had proper renovations done? It's not exactly hanging by a thread, but I see the wear and tear. Like the wallpaper that needs replacing in your own apartments. Threadbare carpets lining the corridors. I heard you used to run this place on grants and now they've dried up. As for tourists, forget it. Who comes to Skye now anyways? That used to be a huge part of your revenue stream, I bet. Staff here get their wages late some months, I've heard, 'cause there's no money to pay them. They tend to talk about things like that and I'm real good at listening.

Maybe a valuable artefact to sell on the black market would offset some of your outgoings. Save you from selling off the family silver. Once we lower the Newton Barrier, you might think whoever's holding the scroll gets off scot-free. But not on my watch. Now get Murdo out of here and patch him up.'

MacLeod huffs, but he's not blowing down straw houses anytime soon. His pale face turns beet red. His hands are shaking. The emperor's naked after all. Strutting about like everything's kosher, when you're just another petty aristocrat rolling in debt you can't pay. I'd rather be a commoner. But still, he gathers his nuts in a sack and tries once more.

'This is my castle. You don't tell me what to do,' he growls.

'In case you missed the memo, I work in the General Discoveries Directorate. That makes me a witchfinder. It means I get to point fingers. If you want them pointed at you, it would be my pleasure.'

He swallows hard. I brush him aside and leave the dungeon. Sod this for a game of marbles. This thing ain't over till the scroll's back with its rightful owners and Sneddon's murderer's in the nick.

XIV

There's two-hundred-odd grumpy folks about the castle this morning. Tons more fuming outside the Newton Barrier. Them ones in here have had to sleep on the floor with dusty quilts, and queue up to use the bathroom. There are others who simply want a toothbrush or change of underwear. Most are angry toffs for whom this is a ghastly ordeal. A few days in my slum might change their minds – give them the gift of perspective.

Cockburn's the most stressed-out person here, in this, our *Titanic*. Think of it as a luxury cruise gone wrong, and Cockburn's the one telling the band to keep playing, as she desperately scrambles to schedule an alternative programme. I appreciate her efforts, though. Anything to keep the natives occupied. Stops them rioting. I'm in the entrance hall, listening to folks grumbling about this very fact. Bothers me that any one of these people might be the figure I chased last night. I tune in, surveying them keenly, hoping something will give the game away. Their build, or manner of walking.

'I heard he might be challenged to a duel over this,' one says.

'It'd be madness to go up against the secretary. Not at a time like this when we need to present a united front.'

'Easy enough for you to say. Have you tasted the dishwater they're giving out and calling coffee? It's dreadful.'

'The horror.'

Moan, moan, moan. Nothing out of the ordinary then. I check my phone and see the messages I sent to Gran and Izwi still haven't gone through.

The light filtering through the windows is a strange tinge of grey. Cockburn's stood at the top of the stairs, trying to calm folks and give them the order of the day. Easier said than done. Most want to know when they can leave. Everyone's got a reason why an exception should be made for them. She's having one hell of a time convincing them it's beyond her control.

'If everyone cooperates, we'll get through this soon,' she says.

'I slept on a carpet. My back hurts. My chiropractor—'

There we go again. I actually feel sorry for Cockburn. She's doing her best but she's now being swarmed by angry market stallholders, who attended the conference to sell their goods.

'Are we getting refunds or not?' asks Hector Beaton of the Barra Association of Magical Suppliers. BAMS is the premier group for retailers of the esoteric across Scotland.

'The market *is* still open, and you're encouraged to sell your products.'

'To whom? This pathetic crowd? We've sunk in significant costs. Merch, transport and logistics. If we don't move stock, we're screwed. I'm not being unreasonable when I say this year you've got to waive your stall fees and give us full refunds.'

'Add some compensation too while you're at it. Lost earnings, it's called,' someone shouts.

'Please, everyone, this is an unprecedented situation. We're doing the best we can. Right now, I've noted your concerns and will be discussing them with the organizing committee to chart the best way forward.'

Poor Cockburn. It's not like contingency planning could have factored in the scenario that you might just wind up in a giant fishbowl. At least she's the lightning rod for their discontent. I watch for a bit, then I have an idea what I need to do next.

It all boils down to money. Crass as it may seem, that's the lubricant that keeps the wheels of Scottish magic turning. The same could be said for every other brand of magic, to be fair. Doesn't matter what high-falutin' malarkey they wanna dress it up in, it's all about the cheddar. I guess the same goes for every other profession too. Accumulation's the name of the game. I know these inescapable facts 'cause I've been riding this hamster wheel since I was nine. All that bollocks about the betterment of humanity, making new discoveries, contributing to knowledge, everything is really a by-product in the quest for more money. Call me a cynic, but we're all of us trapped inside this thing with no emergency exits. I used to have all these silly dreams way back when, about how I was going to do something that helps people. Thought I might make life better for everyone who lives in my slum. But you can't do any of that without chasing the cheddar. Kinda reminds me of this thing I heard the other day about a village in Gloucester. Once a year they bring everyone out to Cooper's Hill, which is steep as hell. Then they roll a seven-pound wheel of cheese down it, and everyone goes after it. You should see the videos online. They stumble, fall, run and roll. The whole thing's dangerous and undignified, but still they chase that roll of cheese down that hill. Most who turn up get nothing. But for the lucky few . . . well, seven pounds of cheese is a lot of calcium. We're all on that hill, flailing, hoping it's us who hits the jackpot. And if I can find out who stands to gain the most from the illicit sale of that scroll, I'll be one step closer to finding Sneddon's murderer.

Chase the cheese.

There are a lot of tradespeople here dealing with sales in all things magical, and those are the kind of folks who will know who might be interested in buying magical artefacts on the black market. Priya and me head outside and bump into Rector Wedderburn strolling through the gardens, with a gaggle of kids in tow. It's a diverse group of young people, including Fenella MacLeod and the MacDonald boys. Current pupils and alumni from all four magical schools follow him. They descend the gentle slope of the road while we are going up it.

Wedderburn walks leisurely, one hand behind his back, discoursing as he goes. 'The future of Scottish magic belongs to you, the young. Can you return it to its former glory, or are we doomed to continue this decline? There are those who claim the best we can do is to manage the decline. Others, on the opposite side of the aisle, argue that only by discarding post-modern impulses and returning to our Enlightenment roots might we yet again become that shining beacon of progress.'

His pupils are keenly engaged, following every word, as though siphoning the wisdom of Socrates from the source. Wedderburn draws a spider's web, ensnaring the youth in his philosophizing, and they dangle off it. No doubt they leave inspired with all these high notions. Thinking they're original when in fact they are indoctrinated. That's what school does. I didn't get to go to no fancy magic school. The Edinburgh Ordinary School for Boys is yet to take on a female student in its three-hundred-plus years. Still, I can't help but feel envious of them. I have to scrape by and figure out every single thing myself. Would be much easier if I had a dominie like Wedderburn holding my hand. Callander's okay as a mentor, but he's too busy doing his own thing to pay attention to me.

'Hello there, our intrepid discoverer. How goes it?' Wedderburn says, breaking off from his talk and stopping.

It was never a good thing when I spoke with the head teacher at my old school. Now they're all over me like the proverbial rash.

'And as always you have Paula Ka-something alongside you.'

'It's Priya,' says Priya. 'Priyanka Kapoor.'

'Ah, yes, how silly of me. Lord Kelvin's finest rugby player in a generation. Pity you don't play anymore after your accident. It's a fierce rivalry when Glasgow and Edinburgh clash. I'm not sure if the other schools have enough players to field their teams given everything that's going on. We'll see how that goes.'

'I'm sure we'll still beat you,' she retorts sharply.

The Edinburgh boys laugh, but Wedderburn hushes them instantly. Lewis makes eye contact. He clearly wants to say hi, but maybe not with the others about. I get it, teenage peer pressure is a brutal thing. Nathair Walsh smirks at me for no reason. Them lot have this superior air, like they know the future's been laid out on a red carpet and they simply have to stroll onto it.

'Comportment, gentlemen. When you wear that uniform, you are to behave. It's a privilege being in this position. Take Ropa Moyo here, for example. She's a promising young lady with aspirations of being fully admitted into our ranks within the Society. But she is home-schooled and has to take the long way round.' Great. Now I sound like a charity case. 'I'd forgotten to check, Ropa. You've been due to take a test to admit you onto the register. Refresh my memory, has it been sorted now?'

'Not yet.'

Proper bummer. I've been trying to get this lined up for weeks. 'Cause I ain't got no certificates, Callander, Cockburn and Wedderburn made me take some test. Theory and practical. I did alright with the theory but flunked the practical on a technicality. I was asked to produce a single spark but made a flame with the Promethean spell. They haven't given me a chance to retake it and I get fobbed off whenever I ask about it. Everyone's always too busy.

'You ought to see to it, so your paperwork is in order. I think we may find time for that now the perpetrator's been apprehended. Will you be advising Sir Ian Callander to drop this barrier? Our fine boys were instrumental in helping catch the gardener. They discovered him as they were out on their morning run.'

Funny how MacLeod had made it seem like it was his own staff that had caught him. But this means it was these toffs that beat the crap out of Murdo. I'm seething.

'You caught and assaulted the wrong man. The gardener has nothing to do with any of this.'

'Maybe it was a move by the Fifth School,' Lewis says.

'Which school is that?'

'It's this super-secret—'

'Mr Wharncliffe, after the mess that got your friend Max Wu expelled, I'm surprised you're still spouting conspiracy theories. Scotland has only four schools of magic, and they are all represented at this conference. You'd do well to remember that. I guess all will be revealed under the silver light of the full moon. Have a good day, Ms Moyo. You too, Patricia. Come on, gentlemen,' he says, proceeding with his gaggle.

As they pass, Lewis casts a timid, friendly glance back towards us.

Priya's bristling, but she don't say nothing. No point going over it. We have a giant tuna in our fryer and that's got to be our priority.

'You know anything about a Fifth School, Priya?'

'Never heard of it,' she replies. 'Let's try to get some real leads.'

The Barras have been set up in the Round Garden, which borders the New Garden and the Water Garden. Shaped like a wheel, it has a central point with radiating footpaths and green lawns that make it perfect for an open-air market. There's stalls and tents arranged in a circle round the central feature. The bright installations the busigicians have set up give off a carnivalesque vibe.

There's a tall monkey puzzle tree at the fringe of the garden which also has tables set up under it.

'This don't look like any place I've ever been shopping,' I say.

'I thought you were all about farmers' markets and that middle-class shit, Ropa.' Priya chuckles.

'Nicking from them, maybe. I can't say I've seen one like this before.'

'The magical market started in Glasgow, and that's why they call it the Barras, even when it's out here. Before all this red tape around who may or may not practise magic, busigicians used to trade next to regular market stalls. You could buy your eggs at one stall, fruit at the next, then get some miracle elixir at the next. I like coming here on conference days 'cause you can get a great selection of herbs from Herbert the Herbologist. He comes every year, and if there's anyone who can get us information, it'll be him,' Priya says.

Herbert's tent is the one made of creepers growing up some netting. Some of them are flowering, with a particular purple bud I've never seen before. There's a sweet scent wafting from within. Other stallholders try to get our attention, waving bottles of potions, powders, bones and no small amount of unsavoury-looking objects. They're selling laboratory equipment and consumables – pipettes, volumetric flasks, test tubes, beakers, burettes, magnifying glasses, thermometers – and other stuff you'd find in a standard school laboratory. This is scientific magic, after all. Gives me a right hard-on. But my pocket's too empty to even bother asking the prices.

'The latest in beauty potions, ladies. I've got a cream that'll make everyone think you're the most desirable woman in the room, harnessing the miraculous might of pheromones,' one seller shouts.

'How about making a cream that gives you half a brain, Ashraf,' Priya replies. She turns to me. 'The market's great, but you've got to be careful. Lots of stuff's legit, but they'll try it on if they think you're gullible.'

'Genuine unicorn horn from the Glencore Valley,' cries another seller.

'Chen, you've been trying to pass off that narwhal tusk since the last conference.'

'Someone will buy it. You'll see,' Chen replies cheekily.

'May I interest you in Dirac's *Lectures on Quantum Spellcraft Theory* from 1966? It's still the authoritative text on the subject,' says the bookseller in the tent next to Herbert's.

'Name one person who actually understands anything he said in there, Kwame?' Priya says. Then she turns to me: 'The only people who buy that one are pretentious senior-year students who put it on display alongside Hawking's *A Brief History of Time* to show they're smart. I know 'cause I've also got a copy in my flat. Dirac's unreadable.'

I might not want that one then, but the prospect of owning my own grimoires is enticing. Not that I can afford to. Knapf. Even if I could, where would I put them in the caravan I live in with Gran and Izwi? We've hardly got room as it is.

We hit Herbert's stall and he beams on seeing Priya.

He's a tall man with a bushy beard that reaches all the way down to his belly button. He's wearing a safari suit, like Roger Moore who's let himself go. The tent is filled with strange aromas. There doesn't seem to be any order to it all, as though he didn't bother organizing his merch. Nothing's labelled either. There's herbs in packets and others sat in plastic containers. Bottles with dried powders and others filled with strange liquids.

'Careful, you don't want to touch that with your bare hands,' he says when I reach for some sweet-smelling petals. 'Paralyses your nervous system in fifteen seconds, and you forget how to breathe, unless you've got the antidote, which you must inhale while you can still breathe. If you don't know what you're looking at, I'd advise you step away from the poisons section.'

I withdraw my hands and put them in my jacket pockets.

'Long time no see, Herbmeister,' Priya says, huge smile on her face.

'Who gets you the best stuff from the great jungles of the Amazon and the Congo, places where the locals will—'

'Shut it, Herb. You grow half this stuff in your greenhouse in Selkirkshire.'

'And what's my greenhouse called?'

'The Amazon and the Congo.' Priya shakes her head.

'There you go. So I'm not lying to you, am I? Lethington came by earlier and scooped up my middlemist red. I'd love to know what he plans on using it for. It'll be years before I come across another plant. I do have an equally rare corpse flower, though, if you're in the market for something special?'

'Today I'm looking for something else, I'm afraid. You'll have heard about the scroll that was stolen last night?'

'Nasty business that. Everything I trade in's legit, above board and all. I keep my nose clean and arse wiped with a sponge scourer. Moving rare texts is more Kwame's thing.'

The bookseller, who was listening in from his stall next door, comes over. He wears a pinny with the name of his business proudly displayed: 'Kwame Boateng's Rare Books and New Texts'. It's printed on the background of an open scroll. The T-shirt he's wearing has a quill embroidered upon the chest. I notice he's wearing what look like fake glasses. I wouldn't trust a bookseller who doesn't wear spectacles either.

Kwame wipes his hands on his pinny and enters the tent, looking round conspiratorially.

'Those of us in the legal market have long complained about unscrupulous practitioners swooping in. Only last week I attended the auction for the Marquess of Linlithgow's library. Since the old man croaked, leaving his heirs a fine inheritance of gambling debt, they've been selling off chunks of his estate. It was an incredible collection too. Five hundred years' worth of material. I couldn't even get my hands on a single volume. Not fair, is it? The books were divided into lots, and no one could afford them. Even the Glasgow Library wanted some, but they couldn't compete either. And that's with their deep pockets.'

'Aye, I heard about that one. There were some handwritten recipes I wanted too. I didn't bother, though. Beyond my budget,' Herbert chimes in.

'There were some shady types at it. A rough-looking fellow

with a Doncaster accent working on behalf of some anonymous bidder over the telephone. Scooped up every single volume, offering double what any reasonable dealer might have. Didn't leave us honest folk any crumbs. If I know anything about this, those irreplaceable books will have been carted off abroad as soon as the money changed hands. It's a shame that.'

'Any idea who's behind it then?' I ask.

Kwame lowers his voice. 'Rumours here and there. Nothing you could bet your house on, mind you. But there's long been chatter among the bookish community about nefarious goings-on to undermine Scottish magic. How do you destroy a people's magic? You cut them off from their knowledge, of course. That's what the Spanish did with the Mesoamerican codices. Destroyed their libraries, burned their books. When was the last time you heard of anyone using Aztec or Mayan magic? That was all wiped out. The Egyptians never really recovered after Julius Caesar burned down the Library of Alexandria. The Caliph Omar merely dealt the coup de grâce. They went from being top of the world to Third World, innit? Hitler bombed the National Library of Serbia – and how are the Serbs doing lately? Same goes for the Krasinski Library in Poland. Oh, but them Poles really are unlucky. In 1794 Czarina Catherine also seized their books in the Zaluski Library and carted them off to St Petersburg. And we all know what happened when the communists got hold of them later on. Then there's the Islamists who burned down the Ahmed Baba Institute in Istanbul. This sort of thing's happened throughout history—'

'Okay, I get it,' I say. 'But who's going after Scottish magic this hard?'

Kwame leans in till his face is nearly touching mine.

'Fella going by the spectacular moniker of the Black Lord, that's who. Don't ask me who he really is or where you can find him. I don't know nothing, and I've said too much already.'

He abruptly turns and retreats within his stall.

Black Lord. I feel a tingle of excitement.

We've heard that name before, haven't we?

XV

Everywhere I look I see shady motives. Everyone's got an angle. And applying my pal Nicco's political treatise to this gig's making me even more paranoid. You start seeing ill intent round every bush. I've got to be sharper on this than any other gig I've pulled; Callander is relying on me. *The Prince* says: 'There are three kinds of intelligence: one kind understands things for itself, the other appreciates what others can understand, the third understands neither for itself nor through others.' I guess by the end of all this we'll see where I stand on Nicco's scale.

'Where to next, *Jessica*?' Priya asks.

'You're so annoying right now.'

'Well, you kinda look like her . . . if she had orange dreadlocks and black lipstick. Lighten up, Ropa. We'll crack this.'

'This pond's too small for all the sharks swimming in it. Makes it hard to figure who the murderer is when everyone's got sharp teeth.'

'That's why you need a little help from your friends, Ropacetic,' says Jomo, joining us. We'll be karaokeing the Fab Four next at this rate. Behind him is Lewis Wharncliffe, hair all ruffled like a rock star, which is fitting since he's studying sonicology at the Edinburgh Ordinary School for Boys.

I notice Jomo's removed his vestments and is dressed casual, without a coat. I know how proud he is to wear the uniform of the Library, it means everything to him. He wants to be like his dad. Fat chance at this rate, though. He flashes a smile, but his eyes aren't in it. I've known this dork all my life. There's a darkness settled on his soul since this all kicked off.

'Why you not in your uniform, man?'

'My fa— The head librarian has suspended me for dereliction of my duties as a junior employee of the Library.' Sounds like he's quoting something his dad said to him. 'It's the first step before he sacks me. He's just following protocol, otherwise he'd have done it already.'

'Get out of here,' Priya says. 'You serious?'

Jomo shrugs, resigned to it.

'He can't be seen to be giving me preferential treatment.'

'Nearly being killed and getting knocked out in the process constitutes dereliction of duty in the librarian's manual?' Lewis says. 'Goes to show, you can't please some folks, hey?'

'It's okay. Seriously. Maybe if we can find the scroll and who . . . you know, did for Sneddon, then they might reconsider. I'm having nightmares about it, but I can't sit around this castle doing nothing.'

'And that's why we're all here to help out. I've been itching to go again ever since I helped you guys with that Max Wu thing in the summer,' Lewis says.

'We don't need you this time round. Not after you

Edinburgh boys tried to pin it on the gardener,' Priya replies sharply.

'Walshy and the lads got a bit carried away. For what it's worth, I wasn't cool with it at all. It was clear to me he wasn't smart enough to pull off a caper like that. But the others wouldn't listen,' says Lewis, holding his palms out.

'Did Nathair Walsh put you up to this? To muscle in on our investigation?' I ask, staring at him.

'No, of course not. The lads all low-key loathe you and they don't think you should be here at all. I'm risking everything to be seen with you right now.'

'Wow, Lewis, you really know how to reassure a lass,' Priya deadpans.

'I just want to help like last time. I can be deep undercover,' he says.

'Very heroic of you,' Priya replies. 'So what's with this Fifth School you mentioned earlier?'

'Rumours, whispers, that kind of thing. As well as the four official Scottish schools, I've heard there's another one out there somewhere. A super-secret school that's a rival to the mainstream ones. It operates from the shadows. The practitioners it trains know each other by a look or handshake, or something like that. I figured they might have sent a spy to . . . I don't know, to mess with us, I guess.'

Some things never change. The first time I met Lewis he rambled stuff about some secret society called the Monks of the Misty Order, and now he's come up with another one. He's been helpful to me in the past, but this one's too far-fetched. A whole school operating in the shadows in modern Scotland? Like, how do you educate a bunch of kids without anyone noticing they're missing from regular school?

'This is ridiculous. Some secret school no one's heard of? Tell me, Lewis, do you have anything to back up this conjecture?' Priya's snark is a ten on the scale.

'I'm just trying to help.'

Give me strength.

'I know you mean well, Lewis, but we need facts. I can't go to Callander and start spouting about some secret school right now. Is it maybe tied to the Black Lord?' I ask.

'The Black who? Never heard of him.'

'Let's stick to what we know for now, alright?'

I need help, but *everyone's a suspect.* Jomo was the closest person to the scene of the crime. But he's also my friend. That's why PIs in noir flicks have to be loners. Alkies too. But I wouldn't know anything about human nature if I concluded Jomo was in on this. He's the closest thing to a Hare Krishna monk I know. Wouldn't hurt a fly. And what would be his motive anyway? Money? Not his thing. A wonderful new book for his collection? He practically lives in the greatest library in the world. The scroll was coming his way anyway. Nah, ain't him. I hate the fact I'm even considering it, but I have to cover every conceivable angle. Still, he's too close to this gig. I'll give him wee tasks to fob him off so me and Priya can do the heavy lifting. Lewis can keep an eye on him. I'd feel safer knowing he had a magician by his side. If they turn anything up, that would be a bonus.

'We *could* do with your help on something else, lads. I need the two of you to ask the castle staff if anyone saw anything out of the ordinary last night. After that, you can try the students. If anyone mentions some geezer called the Black Lord, tell me immediately. And Lewis, I want you to find out who has access to the armoury and check with Morag whether there's definitely a dirk missing from there.'

'And what are we doing?' Priya asks.

'Going for a walk in the woods. There's an angry librarian who we need to have a word with.'

There's a commotion outside the main gate. We don't hear it, but we see the aftermath. Someone's electric car has crashed into the Newton Barrier. The front's dented, but could have been worse if they were driving faster. The driver's protesting, seeking sympathy from the orphans milling about. She gesticulates angrily at us too. Nothing we can do for her in here.

I ignore her and check my phone. Still no reception. I'm getting serious withdrawal symptoms now. It's just a matter of time before I curl into the foetal position or start screaming. I wish Callander could have conjured his field without messing up the network. Gauging by the number of folks I've seen checking their phones, I'm not the only one suffering.

A fir tree's split in half where the barrier came up. One half's fallen inside, slanted against the other trees, the other lies across the road.

This woodland section of the gardens is my favourite spot. Yellow and orange leaves carpet the floor, decaying into browns and blacks. Some of the trees appear golden in this strange light. We squelch through the mud. My feet are still super-itchy right now. It's proper torture.

'I should've brought my all-terrain, off-road chair instead of this one,' Priya says, stuck in the mud. 'It's not like I planned for any excursions this time round. It's hard enough getting about inside the castle. It could do with a few ramps and a lift.'

I help push her out of the rut. I have to rock the wheelchair back and forth a bit before I build enough momentum to get her moving again.

'Cheers, pal.'

'Don't mention it.'

'Morag won't like it when I leave muddy tracks on her floor.'

'I'm sure she'll be dealing with boot prints too.'

It's gorgeous out here, though. Rhododendrons. Bressingham Beauty. Chicago Royal Robe. This mix of flora from all four corners of the globe. This far in, if you look out to the castle, it's obscured by tree trunks and branches, leaves ready to be shed. The sun's muffled behind thick clouds. Regardless of its location in the sky, all we get is one long twilight. Moss grows on tree bark. It makes the woods feel ancient; everything on Skye seems to have been dragged from another era.

The further up the path we go, the quieter it becomes. We eventually arrive at a wee clearing with a bench carved out of a fallen tree trunk. Euan Cleghorn's sat there reading a book, concentrating intensely. The hem of the emerald robe of his vocation is muddy. He carries on reading even when we approach, and I try to be polite and wait, but he doesn't seem interested in engaging with us.

'Mr Cleghorn,' I say at last.

'Euan is fine with me. Hasn't anyone told you never to interrupt a man reading Walter Scott? I've devoted myself to finishing all his novels. This is my last one.'

'Sorry to disturb.'

'You don't really mean that. It's just something people say to be polite. So, for propriety's sake, I will say it's quite alright.' He uses a bookmark and closes his copy of *Castle Dangerous*. I notice the head of the gold ring he wears on his left pinkie is in the shape of a book. Pretty extra.

There's dignity in his bearing. A certain studiousness. Round spectacles and a bald head help give that effect. Then he smiles, something one seldom sees with Edinburgh librarians. Even Jomo smiles a lot less than he did before he joined them.

A beech leaf falls onto the ground between us.

Euan bends over, picks it up and inspects it.

'I couldn't help but notice you didn't exactly seem pleased at the reception last night,' I say. 'You were bristling when the book from the Library of the Dead was given to the Grand Debtera.'

'The books are supposed to be reference material only. Never to be taken out of the secure confines of the Library,' he replies. 'At least that used to be the idea. I don't know anymore.'

He frowns. This is a true bibliophile alright.

'It was a fair exchange, a temporary loan. I don't see why you should feel that strongly about it,' Priya says.

'You don't know the half of it. I envy such blissful ignorance. If you knew, you'd be "bristling" alongside me.' He pats the spot on the bench next to himself for me to sit on.

I politely decline. The wood's wet, and right now I'm standing over him. I have the high ground. As soon as I sit next to him, I become a little girl to be lectured. Basic psychology.

'Suit yourself, but this may take a while,' Euan says. 'You've been to the Library of the Dead in Edinburgh, undoubtedly. And you've seen Dr Maige preening about, acting as though he's, in your youthful parlance, "the bee's knees". The one thing he doesn't tell his patrons is that while the Calton Hill Library is as Edinburgh as the S-bend flushing toilet, the Library of the Dead they hold rightfully belongs to Glasgow.'

Priya and me exchange looks. I'm not 'Weegiephobic' like some people I know in the Auld Reekie. Priya studied there so she's halal too. But we're not buying any of this.

'You lot have your library and we have ours. What's the beef?'

'*Ours?* You've already picked a side without first listening to the facts,' Euan says, opening his book once more and starting to read.

I realize my blunder straight away. Can't be helped, it's a tribal thing. Callander was right. I have to remember the cloak of my office. My language matters. Weegies easily get galled by snooty Edinburghers, though I don't put myself in that category.

'I didn't mean it like that.'

'You'll have to wait until I finish reading my chapter, then we'll see if I still feel like talking to you.'

Dick move, Euan. Priya gives me the look that says 'chill'. Ah well. I sit on the bench next to him. His lips draw back in a suppressed smile. I start reading over his shoulder to get my own back, and he gives me the side-eye, but ploughs on regardless. It's grim reading on page one hundred and thirty, I'll tell you that much. Something about a guy threatened with torture. They (whoever the baddies are) want him to reveal the purpose of his journey. But the guy is hardcore, and says something gangster: '. . . they shall tear the flesh from my bones ere they force me to break the oath which I've taken.' It appears this is in a letter and the hero's called Bertram.

By the time we make it to page one hundred and fifty-six, I'm getting into the story. Seems this Scott guy wrote a banger.

Then Euan places the bookmark back and closes the book before I gain any closure for my efforts.

'I will tell you how it is. During the Great War, Edinburgh suffered Scotland's first blitz. German Zeppelins reached the Firth of Forth on the evening of Sunday the second of April in 1916. They dropped twenty-four bombs in thirty-five minutes, killing thirteen people and injuring many others. There were no air defences back then. The attack alarmed the librarians at Calton Hill, who requested the Society reinforce their location. In Glasgow, unfortunately, our library isn't secured in a bunker under a hill; it's in a sandstone building in the Merchant City. There's a basement, but that wasn't enough to protect our stock from air raids.'

He seems genuinely distressed. That's what happens when people walk around carrying the weight of history. Must be a relief whenever you can pass it on. Then maybe, collectively, we all wind up shouldering the burden for things that had nothing to do with us in the first place.

He tells the story of how, after the Clydebank Blitz by the Luftwaffe in March 1941, the Glasgow Library was sufficiently distressed to seek aid from Edinburgh. It was agreed then that their 'texts', that is paper books and documents, should be moved to various country estates belonging to friends of magic for safekeeping. The 'books', or rather the flesh-and-bone creations, would instead be evacuated and secured in the bombproof fortress that is Calton Hill Library.

'It was all done on a handshake,' says Euan.

That's the same thing the Russians did on NATO enlargement after the collapse of the Soviet Union. Never ends well.

'As you'll have figured out by now, our books have still not been returned. The Edinburgh librarians used our collection to bolster their status, positioning themselves as the pre-eminent library in Scotland. We have started making new books in Glasgow, but our heritage, our historic material, is tied up at the Calton Hill Library. Each year we ask for their return and they refuse, claiming that we agreed to a permanent loan. The books are still considered ours, but they "hold them in trust". It's disgraceful the way they carry on. There's a difference between our two institutions. Theirs is filled with mathematicians and ours prefers philosophers.'

Yikes. I can totally see now why Euan was pissed at the reception. It's one thing to take the books but a different order of douchebaggery to start divvying out stuff that's not yours. Possession being nine-tenths and all that. It seems to me, though, that Euan has inadvertently confessed to having a very good motive for causing problems for Dr Maige and the Library. But he was in the reception room with the others.

Maybe he found a disgruntled operator he could rope in for the job? Glaswegians ain't averse to a bit of sectarianism now and again.

'So, this is a hostage situation? The scroll for your books?' I prod.

Euan contorts his face with revulsion.

'I'd never wish for harm to befall any of my brothers in the letters. You won't find what you're looking for here, Ropa Moyo.'

He picks up his book and the curtain falls.

Priya cocks her head, signalling for us to get a move on. I'm with her. There's nothing else of value I think I can squeeze out of Euan Cleghorn right now . . . We are living in a troubled age. The sea of time takes our filth, swirls it round the world on currents. We relax, thinking the shit we dumped is gone. But there's the swell and churn. Incredible gyres. The uncontrollable forces of chaos at work. When we least expect it, when the trade winds and currents align just so, it's all vomited back onto our laps. That's what history does to us. Old hurts, buried for decades, centuries even, spilling out with a vengeance. And someone out there's exploiting our fractures. Pulling strings from the shadows.

I walk away over the soggy earth, pushing Priya's chair. The land around us grows old and weary. Amidst the hubris and debris, I push on, cogs turning in my head. Euan Cleghorn has a motive. I'm gonna have to find the means.

XVI

Priya heads off, scouring for grub. We've been on the go all day and missed our lunchtime rations. Yeah, they're actually calling them 'rations', like this is a war situation. Top that off with a body odour problem inside the castle and it's no fun. There's bored folks lounging with little to do. Dodgy mobile reception means people actually have to interact with one another. It's terrifying.

A few have formed spontaneous study groups, of all things. Others debate the latest techniques with foreign attendees. A few tour the gardens but the still atmosphere quickly wears them out. I'm used to crowds and general deprivation, so I don't much mind the press. But these magicians are the elite. A lot of them ain't taking it too well. Cockburn's running a skeleton programme now everything's tits up. Even I can admire her tenacity. I still don't like her, but I can respect her hustle.

'Any progress, Ropa?' she says, cornering me on the first-floor corridor. 'That Ethiopian lad is going round asking people questions too and it's confusing everyone.'

'Free country,' I reply. 'But he won't get very far, knowing this lot. I'm working my end the best I can.'

'How much longer?' The exasperation in her voice excites no small amount of Schadenfreude in me.

'We'll sort it. You hold off your hordes and I'll work the angles.'

Cockburn shuts her eyes like a martyr, inhales deeply and exhales. Her nerves are shot.

'Frances, there you are. You must come and see to this,' a woman calls from the end of the corridor.

Cockburn gives me an imploring look before she leaves.

But somehow she steels herself, and a few steps in, she has that same officious, uber-confident gait. Heels knocking loudly on the floor. Did we just make a connection? Nah. Don't fool yourself, Ropa. As soon as she gets what she wants she'll flush you down the bog. Been in the rodeo long enough to know that it's in the bull's nature to throw you off and trample you.

Still, we're on the same team for now. And I have my work to do. If not for the likes of Cockburn, then for Callander, 'cause he's my guy.

First, I need to verify everything Cleghorn told us and I know just the man to talk to. I find Dr Maige in the library. He's stood at the window staring out at the sea. His crimson robes are impeccable, and light reflects from the thick wedding band on his finger. Reckon I could get a few bob for that. Stop, that's not what you're here for, Ropa. Stick to the mission. I go up to Dr Maige and stand beside him, taking in the view.

A seagull flies into the Newton Barrier and soundlessly snaps its neck. It plops down into Loch Dunvegan, where the corpses of several other seabirds float on the water.

'That's been happening all day,' Dr Maige says. 'Poor creatures. It's not their fault.'

'You're into birds?' I ask.

'I've been birding since I was a young boy. In Tanzania I could tell you the name of every bird by hearing its call alone. Here it's taken me much longer to learn their names. It's far easier to grasp and retain such details when you're young. No matter your age, the awe you feel seeing our avian friends soaring never goes away. Nature's exquisite engineering.'

There's a disconcerting softness in his tone. Grief does that to you. He's taking Sneddon's death hard, it seems. Be that as it seems, there's one other person he ought to be thinking about.

'You're too hard on Jomo,' I say.

'And he's too soft. The world is a hard place. The weak get flung into the gutter. People see me in these robes and make the wrong assumptions: that I am gentle, meek, agreeable. That's what they want librarians to be, but we are made of sterner stuff.'

That reminds me of something Machiavelli also observed. The wise Italian said: 'Everyone sees what you appear to be, few experience what you really are.' I think that's accurate in this wankerish clique. Dr Maige wears armour like an armadillo. The thing about armour is it's heavy and weighs the wearer down. Yes, it protects you – for a while. But there's a cost. It blinds you in certain ways too. You can't see the full picture from behind your visor. All you catch is snapshots of a hostile world, and from that you draw your own assumptions. Carrying all that weight eventually exhausts you, and the determined enemy will find a chink if they prod long enough. I know, 'cause I'm wearing my own armour too.

'I used to walk ten kilometres to school, back and forth, every day. Barefoot. It didn't matter whether it was raining, or the sun was blazing. Every morning before I went to classes, I had to do my share of work in the family fields. There's never been a day, since I turned six, that I haven't woken up at four in the morning. I did two hours' hoeing and weeding, then I ran those ten kilometres on an empty stomach. If I got there late, I was caned. No excuses. That's how it was back then. A teacher called Mr Sanga took an interest in me, and I owe him a debt of gratitude for the rest of my life. He noticed my aptitude for mathematics and gave me extra problems. Because of him, I developed my love for books. I soon exceeded his knowledge in the subject, and he arranged a bursary for me in Dar es Salaam.' Dr Maige stares out at the sea, not meeting my eye. Poverty embarrasses you like that. 'So I became a poor boy at a fine school. I helped my parents by doing odd jobs for wealthier pupils whose pocket money was far more than what my own father earnt. I was their cobbler. If they wanted contraband from outside, I took money and risked myself, climbing over barbed wire to get them what they wanted. Soon the teachers, too, noticed I was useful and found tasks for me. Weeding their gardens. Cleaning their houses. Tutoring their children in maths. Though I was a child myself, I sent my parents money to put my siblings through school. I couldn't afford to put a foot wrong, I didn't have the luxury of making mistakes. I walked a tightrope with a heavy load strapped to my back, juggling at the same time. You think I'm hard on Jomo?'

'He's not a mini version of you. He doesn't have to go through what you did.'

'No, but with the opportunities laid out for him he should be better than I was.'

'He already is, and maybe that's what scares you.'

Dr Maige looks at me briefly, then returns to gazing out at the view.

Everything about him is straight lines and right angles. It must be oppressive, even for him. I guess that's what happens when you've lived your life like a robot. You can't straighten out the world with the mathematical theorems he's devoted to. It's too muddled for that. I fudge through, though, fumbling for more questions.

'Did Sneddon have any enemies you know about?'

'He spent most of his time in the Library working. It's unlikely.'

'You lot do have extreme methods. Anyone he shushed the wrong way, perhaps? Or maybe a boyfriend or girlfriend with whom he was having issues?'

'I don't take an interest in my employees' personal lives, unless it impinges on their obligations towards the Library.'

He really didn't know him then. I wonder if he wishes he did. Dr Maige avoids intimacy. But I'm not like him and I do wish I'd got to know Sneddon better. I look back now at all those times I passed through the reception at the Library and said 'Hiya', without stopping for a chat. Come to think of it, we only ever spoke if I wanted something, or when the Library had issues with me.

What were we to each other really?

But I know what this is. I've seen it many times whenever I've been ghostalking. This is what happens after someone's gone. The regret. Ruminations over missed connections. The yearning for an impossible intimacy. All too late. I wonder if Sneddon will choose to return and haunt the halls of Dunvegan Castle. Or maybe he'll move on to the biblioparadise that awaits. A realm within the astral plane where every book written and unwritten sits on shelves high enough to touch the sky.

Trying to get to Sneddon's ghost won't help me just now, though. The ones that die of a traumatic event are often confused in the beginning.

Either way, I hope I get a chance to say goodbye to him.

'I spoke with Euan Cleghorn earlier,' I venture.

'You don't need to tell me what he said. The Glasgow Library is wrong. This is not a tale of two cities. It's about doing what's best for Scottish magic. Having the books in the secure, specialized facility of the Library in Edinburgh is what the head librarians who came before me put foremost in their consideration. If Sir Magnus Carmichael were still alive, the one who ran the Glasgow Library when that loan was made, he'd inform his successors of the truth of the arrangement that was made back then. I cannot undo precedent. But if Mr Cleghorn and his peers *are* behind the violent theft of the scroll, it would be a betrayal of their vocation. I don't need to tell you what the ramifications of all this would be. So please find that scroll. I will render any assistance necessary to this end.'

Two sides to every story. Only one of them can be true.

XVII

My mind's overheated. Oil's leaking. The gears are grinding up against one another. Springs pinging out into nowhere. I need to let stuff settle a wee bit. It's kinda like when you're studying hard for an exam, and you keep going over and over the same stuff. After a while nothing gets in. It's the cast-iron law of diminishing returns. I sneak away from the madding crowd and retreat into the little room me and Priya are sharing.

Staying in a castle sounds swell and all, but the servants' rooms are a notch removed from the dungeon. The paint's peeled 'cause of the damp. Piping they didn't bother to cover up runs along the walls. The only decoration's a small mirror whose frame is chipped. Doesn't help either that Priya's scattered her gear about. I try to open the window, but it's jammed shut.

Plonk myself on the single bed and veg. When you have a problem, it helps to stop banging your head against the wall for a bit.

It's getting to me that my little sister's so close but I can't see her. I guess that's even more of an incentive for me to get this thing done. The sooner Callander drops this barrier, the better. Then I can see Izwi. Yay. The hard part is pulling all these pieces together. I wish I was one of them types who can look at a suspect and start rattling off all kinds of random shit 'cause they've seen a cornflake on their shoe. Wouldn't that make life so much easier, Mr Holmes?

Knapf. Welcome to the real world.

But I have my own way of reading people. Understanding the things they say and, even more importantly, the stuff they do. You need that to survive down in Edinburgh. Learnt my trade with friendly thieves and cut-throats. They don't give you no certificates when you graduate, but it's an education all the same.

I need to leave it for a wee while, though. Recharge my batteries. There's been one thing I've been meaning to do. It'll take my mind off things. I thought while I was here I'd get a chance to practise my spellcraft. I flunked my last test to become properly registered in the Society, and Cockburn's trying to get me kicked out, so I have to be at the top of my game next time. If I hadn't been so busy chasing my own tail, I'd have been badgering some of these practitioners for tips. Still, I'll pinch a bit of time and go over Barrington Clifford's awesome guide, *The Advancing Practitioner's Handbook of Self-Defence*. It's the one that comes after *The Able Practitioner* . . . I don't know why they do this, though. I mean, both volumes are pretty slim. They could just publish one long thing, then you don't need to have two books. That's the trick they use to siphon cash off us. I'm wise to that, which is why I use the Library.

I want to learn to wield lightning like Kebede did. I'm really gonna need it, I can tell.

Let's see what Clifford has to say about it.

'. . . the discovery which propelled mankind out of the caves into civilization. The second such advance came with the harnessing of electric power. It is electricity which powers the technological age . . .'

Hmm, interesting, but I'm sure Clifford's skipped taming the horse, the steam engine, the printing press, the ship of the line and a gazillion other things that moved us forward. I get the point he's making, though.

The leap from fire to electricity is the leap from Prometheus, a lesser deity, to harnessing the power of the king of the gods, Zeus. As such, we require Zeusean spellcraft to hurl thunderbolts at our enemies. Kinda ironic since he's the same dude who punished Prometheus for giving us fire in the first place. Clifford says that in order to understand electricity, we have to think of the American polymath Benjamin Franklin. I know he had links to the Scottish Enlightenment. He even visited Edinburgh a couple of times. If my phone was working alright, I could just look this up. Give me something, old hippocampus.

I guess Plato wasn't playing when he said mobile phones would diminish our ability to form memories.

Franklin did say he met 'men of genius' in Scotland, didn't he?

The picture of Ben flying a kite during a storm is described by Clifford as demonstrating that fine line between genius and idiocy. The author isn't averse to dishing out burns now and again.

Ah, yes, I remember now. Franklin was pals with David

Hume. They spent time together. And Hume is the foundation upon which modern Scottish magic was set up. His scepticism and empiricism is what scientific magic is all about. The two men were penfriends back in the day. I wonder if they talked about electricity.

So, Clifford says electricity was already known during Franklin's time. The success of any spell is contingent upon the practitioner's comprehension of the precise scientific phenomenon necessary to create the intended effect. That's why it's more powerful than superstition-based magic, which is hit and miss. If you don't understand the science, you can say the words of a spell all you like and nothing will happen. So, I have to learn about the underlying principles from Gilbert, Coulomb, Ampere, Ohm, Faraday, Maxwell, Edison and anyone else who was messing with this stuff. The great thing is I've encountered some of the concepts before, through my independent learning. The simple way in which Clifford breaks it down helps an awful lot too.

On the battlefield, using the Zeusean craft is to summon something devastating from nature's arsenal. We revert from harnessing electricity to light our homes and power our industries, to utilizing it for terror. He goes on to describe how pernicious this is to the morale of opposing forces. The light, heat and resultant thunder strike terror into the hearts of all but the most hardened of troops.

Clifford also warns on the drawbacks of using it on the battlefield. It's notoriously difficult to direct lightning, since the laws of physics dictate it finds the nearest conductor. The presence of metal, such as soldiers' helmets, rifles, buttons, etc., can help it find its target. But equally, tall trees, tanks, artillery and even positive charges on the ground can misdirect a strike. Friendly fire by novice practitioners is not uncommon, and nor are self-inflicted injuries.

'Wear thick rubber-soled shoes before attempting this spell,' Clifford writes. 'DO NOT ATTEMPT DURING STORMS OR FOG OR PERIODS OF HIGH HUMIDITY WHEN ELECTROMAGNETIC ACTIVITY IN THE ATMOSPHERE IS HEIGHTENED, CREATING AN IONIZED ENVIRONMENT.'

Alrighty then.

Let's try something small first. My boots are wet, might not be a good idea to try this out while wearing them. I take them off, together with my socks. The skin on my feet is peeling now. Eww. I find Priya's flip-flops under the bed and put them on. Then I pick my spell from a list of options Clifford offers.

As directed, I point my index fingers at one another, holding them an inch apart.

'Static small, I invoke the Lord of the Heavens, Zeus, may your thunderbolt spark between my fingers.'

There's a crackle.

A brief flash erupts between my fingers.

Then I'm hit with a mild tingle as it passes through my body.

I try again, this time holding my hands further apart, and get a similar result. It used to be that I had to try a spell over and over before it worked. But when you learn the general principles, it gets easier to master the next one, so long as it's not a complex spell. I don't mess with those yet. Right now, I'm just pleased with this result.

The next step Clifford suggests is to learn how to direct the 'electromagnetic discharge' to a specific target. I try that a few times and end up zapping myself. The hairs on my arms stand up, static building on my clothes. I can definitely see why there's a high likelihood of injuring yourself with this spell. If I had the cash, I'd buy a taser instead.

The air in the room feels charged.

The more I practise, spontaneous discharges start occurring between objects in the room. I have to be careful now, especially given the metal frame of my bed. Static electricity on the bedding isn't a smart move either. That's why people get zapped by dryers. The last thing I want is to mess up and for something in here to catch fire.

I watch a few sparks dance in the air before I decide to stop.

It's a lot of fun. And it's helped me destress. The next step will be for me to learn how to use high-voltage discharges out in the field. I memorize the spell. There'll be time for that when all this is over.

XVIII

There's dark circles ringing Callander's eyes as we settle for dinner back in the grand dining room. His eyelids close a little too long when he blinks. He's asked Sin to bring him an espresso. Esfandiar is trying his best to put on a brave face, but his fidgeting gives the game away as he pats Callander's hand. It's been more than twenty-four hours since the secretary's slept. The Newton Barrier requires constant maintenance.

Hyenas circle this table and I intend to watch every one of them. Callander needs to be at the top of his game. The situation's got people worked up, both in here and outside. They were crowded at the door demanding answers when he came in.

The Ethiopians declined to join us for dinner tonight. They are staying with Callander and Esfandiar at the Keeper's Cottage, where I imagine things must be mondo-awkward. Part of me worries the Grand Debtera will tear this place apart with us inside, just as he threatened. Their places at the table have been given to Mr and Mrs Gupta, friends of the Colquhouns, who've not attended this year but are great patrons of the Society.

Lord Samarasinghe, also present, has a mischievous look. It's as though he's taken stock of our finest practitioners and decided he doesn't rate them. And it doesn't take long before he lobs a turd onto the dinner table.

'Forgive my ignorance, but I've been informed, and I pray I've received wrong information, that you Scotch still maintain the primitive practice of duelling. Was I misinformed?' he says.

'I'm not sure who told you that, but the last duel in Scotland was fought with flintlock pistols in 1826 somewhere in Fife,' Wedderburn replies.

Esfandiar Soltani turns very pale. He leaps into the conversation.

'I hear tonight we're supping a more traditional fare.'

The Sorcerer Royal gives him a wicked smile.

'My mistake. You see, I was under the impression, and I still can't quite get my head round this, that your Society allows members to duel for the position of secretary.' He opens his palms innocently.

'I don't see why—' Esfandiar begins but is cut off.

'I was addressing your better half, sir,' Lord Samarasinghe says. 'Is it possible that I could challenge you for the honour of your post?'

'No, you may not,' Callander replies sharpish. 'Only a member of the Society of Sceptical Enquirers may, and you are not one of us.'

'Ah, so I wasn't wrong after all.'

A hush descends upon the table. Any side conversations have ceased.

Dr Maige steps in. 'My Lord Sorcerer, there hasn't been an actual duel for the position in five decades. Yes, the rule remains in our statutes, but it's only ever used now in a ceremonial sense. A magician who feels they would like to take on the role issues a challenge in front of us, the librarians. We then go back and forth polling the membership as to who they prefer to be secretary. It's all very democratic. The two magicians then accept the outcome. No one ever presses for actual combat in this age.' The librarians are the keepers of the rules, so he knows what he's talking about.

But Samarasinghe isn't about to let the matter rest. He's a dog with a bone and grows even more excited. Monobrow raised, twinkle in his eye as he swirls the Châteauneuf-du-Pape in his glass. Mr and Mrs Gupta stiffen as though wishing they'd not been invited to the table tonight. I imagine these have been tame affairs filled with mutual back-scratching in previous years.

'See, I heard a story about how you ascended to the role, Sir Ian . . .'

'Oh, please, that's all water under the bridge. Everyone involved has moved on,' Wedderburn replies contemptuously, shielding his friend.

'On my way here, I passed through Renfrewshire to meet my old friend Sir Robert Latimer. The poor fellow is a recluse now. I'd heard he never ventures further than the boundaries of his estate, he's a broken man. He was your mentor, was he not, Sir Ian?'

Callander scowls but does not reply.

'He told me about how you challenged him to a duel and

muscled him out of the role you occupy. He'd won the vote, but you insisted on combat. The old man was practically weeping as he told me this. It was most distressing . . . Oh, here comes our supper. I'm famished. Being imprisoned in this bubble does wonders for one's appetite.'

What do you do when a lord's farted at the dinner table?

You pretend it didn't happen.

Everyone's all tense when the Hamster Squad brings our starters. Spiced lentil and butternut squash soup. It's delicious and I feel better right away. I can't help but notice that Callander's irritation has infected his side of the table, though. Lord Samarasinghe chats heartily with MacLeod and folks down their food at his end. I admire his ability to act as though nothing's wrong.

What a vile man.

But that's power. It doesn't notice when it stomps all over you. It doesn't care. In England, the Sorcerer Royal is a personal appointment by His Maj. I can totally see why someone like Samarasinghe was his first choice. He embodies the bellicose ethos of the Sandhurst Club, those fine gentlemen officers with iron fists in velvet gloves.

Soon enough our bowls are cleared, and we start on the main course. Good old-fashioned beef stroganoff. Thinking on past successions, I recall the story of how Dr Maige's mentor choked to death on this stuff, which was how he got the role. We walk over the corpses of our friends and enemies to get the things we want. It's nature. So, with all these meta-phorical beefs going on around me, I tuck into my meal. This scran's scrumptious. Hail, Mother Russia.

I'm not used to fine dining. It makes me think again of the starving orphans out in the cold. I know what it's like to go to bed on an empty stomach. Gran tried the best she could for us, but it was never enough. To this day, I can't stand seeing food go to waste. But the folks here have no such qualms and some only pick at their plates. Food is sacred. I make sure my plate's polished every single time.

Mrs Gupta strikes up small talk with me. I can already tell she's one of them philanthropic types, always making a show of helping the lower classes. Our chat consists of her telling me about all the wonderful things she's doing for 'deprived communities in our inner cities'. It goes on like this until we have our cranachan, which is amaaaazing. Mrs Gupta insists it's entirely the wrong dessert for the meal we've just had, though. The choice of wine didn't meet her approval either.

I'm hoping with our bellies full and blood sugar levels restored we can all be zen again when Lord Samarasinghe pipes up once more. What's his game?

'Chief Edmund MacLeod, I am heartened by your warm hospitality. Allow me a moment or two to address your table. Breaking bread together is a fine way to remind us of the things that really matter. The issue with the Ethiopian scroll is a problem for us all. Thank you, Ropa Moyo, for making me see this earlier today.' What the actual? I wish people wouldn't try to use me to score points. 'England can and should help in these types of situations. Sir Ian Callander's incredible barrier has been a triumph, but it is now becoming a threat to us all. I'm sure you feel the temperature rising. At this rate, we'll be slow-cooked to death in here, just like those proverbial frogs in a pan.

'Around the globe, few people bother to make a distinction between the Scots and the English. We all look the same to them. We are the product of a union that has endured for three hundred years and will surely endure for three hundred more. But we must evolve too, as we've always done. Union means United. A United Kingdom. That means no more petty divisions. No more borders. No North versus South. One nation, one people, one king, one flag, one destiny. This is our common future. Together. The problem with the old Union was it didn't go far enough. We kept our separate judiciaries, with different laws for the people of North Berwick and those of Berwick-upon-Tweed. A different education system, manipulated to sow division and hatred in the hearts of our children. The list of insidious maladies is too long. Some subtle, others more difficult to ignore. Like different political parties, especially those that stood for a separate Scotland. Those whose MPs sat in Westminster and enjoyed the salary and benefits but cared nothing for the welfare of their kin south of the border. It was always going to end in catastrophe, dear cousins.

'But right here, right now, we have a chance to set things right. No more divisions. We should at last unite English magic and Scottish magic. Bring back that beautiful British magic that built the modern world. Together we achieved so much and united we can do even more. To this end, I shall remain here in Scotland until we are properly unified. Forever.'

A stunned silence falls upon the table. Folks shuffle in their seats awkwardly, unsure of what to do. MacLeod, especially, is stupefied since this is happening in his home. But is he really, or was this pre-planned? I try to read the room. Factions vying to push out Callander, maybe? It's hard to imagine this bombshell dropping without someone else at this table knowing what was going to happen. The Sorcerer Royal surely wouldn't blunder in without a base already receptive to his sentiments. The English were always adept at 'divide and conquer'.

Lord Samarasinghe holds his hands together, interlocking his fingers to show his vision of unity. He has that air of conviction fundamentalists are wont to have. Nothing in this world's more dangerous than a person whose idea is so complete that they believe nothing can stand in its way.

It dawns on me he's calling for the abolition of the Society of Sceptical Enquirers. It's brilliant rhetoric, stirring stuff, but you've always got to read the small print. There would never be an amalgamation with the English Royal Society of Sorcery and the Advancement of the Mystic Arts in which our side would hold any real power. The numbers don't add up on our side of the equation. There's more than a few concerned faces at the table, but no doubt others see an advantage within a new order if they can position themselves shrewdly. We would become an appendage of English magic. A small slice in a much larger pie. Calling it British wouldn't change that reality. The Society of Sceptical Enquirers has been trying not to get swallowed up by this particular black hole for years.

I'm seething. We're not bloody Wales. This is Scotland.

Again, I think there's simply no way Lord Samarasinghe would have fired this salvo if he didn't already have support. Who's in bed with him? No one here's coming out to say anything. And could this have anything to do with the disappearance of the scroll?

Some time ago I met an English magician in Edinburgh. He was hunting the Paterson fortune, which had been appropriated by the Society. I believed then that the king was making a move and told Sir Callander this. He told me to stay schtum about it. So we did nothing. Although I'm not sure what we could have done anyway.

Up till now, Callander's been playing a delicate game, desperate not to attract London's attention. Now it seems that was all in vain. London is here. If it has an inside man, it'll be the magician who challenges Callander for the secretaryship. A new leader could change our course for sure. The future of Scottish magic is at stake here. Callander must let go of the Newton Barrier and save his strength for the battle to come. But if he does that and then the scroll is truly lost, he's damned us with the Ethiopians and will be disgraced that way too. It will bolster the case for his ouster by making him seem incompetent. People have already questioned his judgement in erecting this barrier in the first place. So it *has* to work. We're wedged between the devil and the deep blue sea now.

Sir Callander clears his throat.

'Thank you, Lord Samarasinghe. You've given us a lot to think about. But now I believe it's time for tonight's entertainment. Ladies and gentlemen, the rugby will be played in the courtyard.'

XIX

Me and Priya find a nook near the old well in the courtyard. I should toss a mini-penny in and make a wish. Nah. Too wasteful. I make my own luck like a leprechaun. Haven't yet had the chance to give Priya the juicy gossip of what went down at dinner. Too many ears about. Also, she's moaning about her tea. No cranachan for her. And tuna and cucumber sandwiches ain't exactly gourmet. The chef's not pandering to the plebs. No lie, it feels great to be on the other side of the fence with the chosen ones.

Gotta be careful, though. This is how they suck you in. It's easy to forget which side you're really on when they throw you a few crumbs.

Lord Samarasinghe's carriage had dug tracks into the lawn. With everything going on, no one's fixed it, especially since Murdo the gardener was beaten up. At least he's finally out of that pit, which he should never have been in in the first place.

In the absence of TV and the internet, a crowd's gathering to watch the rugby.

Not just in the courtyard either. More folks stand at the windows of the castle on two floors. A curtain's open upstairs in the MacLeods' private quarters, and I imagine that's Fenella. The castle staff, too, are watching from the wings. I'm not sure how they'll fit two teams on this tiny patch of grass. There's neither markings nor posts here either. It's no Murrayfield. You only have those square blocks lying on the lawn.

The Newton Barrier ominously reflects our artificial lighting, filling the air with an eerie bronze glow. Further off, I can't help but see the ghostly woman in white wading into the sea. Adamina's off to top herself for the zillionth time. She looks over her shoulder before plunging into the water. I swear she's doing my head in.

Esfandiar joins us, pale as a sheet. I ask if he's okay. He shakes his head and doesn't seem able to speak. Instead, he watches the square blocks on the lawn of the courtyard levitate, forming a pyramid. Four blocks on each side, the lowest level raised a foot and a half from the ground. And each block is separated by a couple of feet. Three on either side of the intermediate level, one at the top, plus a couple of others in the middle. You'd need strong legs to jump from one to the other. I remember seeing something like this a while back when Priya and me got in trouble with some topiary hedges.

Dr Maige goes into the empty centre of the pyramid and places three leather balls of varying sizes onto the lawn, just below the apex. He has a whistle on a string round his neck. I know the librarians have a role as adjudicators in the affairs of magicians, but it's a bit bonkers this role extends to sport. But what the fuck do I know?

Priya's getting all excited. She points to two men wearing

blazers and vintage school caps sat behind desks set up next to the South Wing.

'That's the scorers getting ready. Lord Kelvin vs the Edinburgh Boys is always a thriller.'

I'm thinking, if this is rugby, then American football is *football*.

Right on cue, an Edinburgh student approaches us. He's looking all smug. Oh, that's just Lewis Wharncliffe. I remember he mentioned he was only here for the rugby game.

'I wish you were still playing, Kapoor. It'd even up the odds a little,' he says.

'We've still got a strong squad.'

'From what I've heard about you, you were good enough to make our team. I'm not so sure about the rest of them.' Then he turns to me. 'You know what they say about the Lord Kelvin Institute? Nothing good can come out of a school named after a guy who once said, "There is nothing new to be discovered in physics now. All that remains is more and more precise measurement."' Lewis sniggers. 'Get it? He thought they knew everything about the universe. Funny, isn't it. Einstein hadn't even been born yet . . . Hilarious, right? Never mind, you don't get it.'

The comedian waves his arm dismissively. Priya snorts. Nothing like a bit of school rivalry.

'Listen, yeah,' Lewis says, lowering his voice, 'I'm rooting for you with everything going on. There's gonna be a full moon soon and when that happens—'

'Wharncliffe, are you warming up or not?' Walsh shouts at him.

'Aye, captain.'

Lewis turns abruptly and jogs off to his teammates, who are doing stretches on the grass. All this talk of lunar stuff's getting grating. It's not the Apollo missions I'm on, and I don't believe there are werewolves roving about this castle.

'Darling, can I chew your ear for a sec?' Esfandiar says at last.

'Nibble away,' I reply.

'I don't know *what's* going to happen anymore. My mother warned me not to marry a magician. She said they're more trouble than they're worth. And she'd been married to my dad for forty years, so she knew a thing or two about that. Ian says he's fine but holding this bloody barrier together's not doing him much good. He's no spring chicken, I can tell you that. None of these dreadful people appreciate the sacrifice he's making. All I hear is gripe after gripe.'

'We're sorting it.'

He gnaws at his upper lip. I get what's at stake. It can't be easy going through this when someone you love's on the line. There's something else Esfandiar wants to say but he's not coming out with it. That's his business. The cogs in my noggin are turning and I'm watching everyone here for the least hint that might give the game away.

The Edinburgh boys start moving forward. They are captained by Nathair Walsh, with Lewis and one other lad on the team. They're wearing cotton shorts, vests and knee pads, but are barefoot. No rugby boots in sight. No posts either. Dr Maige signals for them to take to the field.

'Lord Samarasinghe mentioned you by name, Ropa. That

did seem just a little off to me. Have you been consorting with him? It makes me wonder whose side you're on.'

'Do you even need to ask me that? I've been *consorting* with everyone. It's in my job description.' Had anyone but him asked me this, I'd have been miffed.

'Okay, okay, I had to make sure.'

'She's solid, and you need to back off,' Priya says.

'I'm sorry . . . It's just that, well, this whole thing is utterly dispiriting, and deeply concerning.'

'For us all. But I won't let Sir Callander down. My position is tied to him, remember? I'll let you guys know as soon as I find something. For now, we need to keep our cool.' And I need to decide on my next move.

'Ian is very fond of you, you know? He speaks highly of you often, which is rare. You know he can be a tight-arse.'

I feel all mushy hearing that. Not like Sir Callander ever says stuff like that to *me*. He's always gruff, grunting orders and being all dour-like. I'd still pick working for him over working for Dr Maige any day, though. So, I'm happy to hear this from his husband. Means a lot to me, that.

The Kelvinites take to the field too, their players ascending the floating pyramid. They are playing on the east with their backs to the castle, while Edinburgh is on the west with the sea behind them. One of the Kelvinites occupies the corner block and the other two step onto the middle block on the tier above. All three of the Edinburgh boys remain on the lower tier: Lewis near us, and Nathair Walsh and the other boy occupying the further blocks.

'That should be interesting. The classic Tudhope opening

against a Sproat,' Priya says. Her hands tightly grip the armrests on her wheelchair. She wants to be on that field, I can tell.

'Meaning?'

'The Edinburgh boys are playing cautious. You've got Magnolia up top for Lord Kelvin, and she can cast like a demon. So instead of matching her mano a mano, they've left Nathair down, so they can concentrate on clearing the base. That leaves the apex free. Risky, but if they can win an early dismissal, they can turn this three vs two to their advantage. If not, they'll get picked up.'

Not sure I get any of that. Sounds to me like she's saying the Edinburgh players have ceded the high ground for some strategic reason. I have the same sense of bewilderment I've had before trying to watch cricket. Footie's more my kind of thing, 'cause my granda, rest his soul, was well into it.

Dr Maige takes a position outside the field as the three balls levitate. The largest and the medium-sized one hover in the gap, equidistant to the competitors. One's the size of a pumpkin and the other's more like a small melon. The third, roughly the size of a tennis ball, rises to a space above the apex block. Dr Maige points to the two captains, Walsh and Magnolia.

'You all know the rules. I want a good, clean game. This isn't sumo wrestling. Obey my commands at all times. The balls are yours but casting directly at an opponent, whether inadvertently or on purpose, will result in the automatic disqualification of your team. Let's play rugby.' He blows his whistle.

Walsh wastes no time nimbly leaping to occupy the free square in front of him. He's just in time to dodge the mid-sized ball swooshing past, which brakes and remains stationary over the square he's vacated.

Priya groans.

'That was so predictable. They fell for the bait and now Edinburgh holds the duster.' I'm totally blank here. 'The biggest one's called the puggler. The cantaloupe one's the duster, and your smallest one's the mollyrag. You can hold the duster and puggler for three passes, but you can't do that with the molly. Understand?'

'Nope.'

'You'll soon get the hang of it.'

The players scurry about, shifting positions on the floating squares. There's a coordination to their movement which I think is tactical but find very confusing. Magnolia's hopped across her tier, using the blocks to gain momentum before vaulting up to the highest block. The player beside her has shifted down to the base to help out his teammate.

Magnolia desperately shouts instructions down to her team when she notices no one from the Edinburgh boys has switched tiers.

She grabs the mollyrag in her left hand, takes aim and throws it at Lewis, who ducks but still catches it on his back.

'Yooowl,' the crowd howls.

'Point – Lord Kelvin. Every strike's a point,' Priya explains. 'Not much use if you've given up two balls, you sausages.'

Once activated, the mollyrag zips about the pitch in a random fashion, going for any player. I see why they have to stay on the move. Walsh and Lewis have been weaving and dodging the zooming mollyrag as they inch towards their opponents at the base. There's a striking confidence in the way they move. The sort of simian skill that'd make prancing about a dilapidated lead roof easy. I make a mental note of this. The spectators roar with delight, cheers echoing back from the Newton Barrier. The vibrations fill the air.

'Mid-tier advance!' Magnolia shouts down to her team.

'That's not going to work now. If I were her, I'd descend and attack from the rear,' Priya says, proper frustrated. 'We're ahead on points but will lose players.'

Lewis and Walsh hop onto a square holding one of the Lord Kelvin players. They sandwich him, impeding movement left and right. 'Sacrifice the square for two,' Priya yells. There's a loud whoosh as their remaining player launches the puggler. The trapped Kelvinite sees it coming and tries to escape by leaping forward, since he's blocked on either side. But he's caught mid-flight by the puggler, which lands with a thud, and he falls to the ground.

'Timber!' the crowd roars, and applauds. One half of it anyway. The other jeers.

The knocked-out player crawls off the field and stands near the spectators, brushing dirt off his uniform. Priya covers her eyes.

'I can't watch,' she says.

She's like a chess player who's several moves ahead. All I see's an open game, with balls zipping about. Players scrambling. The other Kelvinite player evades the Edinburgh boys, hopping square to square. He goes up a tier then back down again, hunted by the pack. Each time he evades them, it buoys his supporters, who cheer wildly.

This is less rugby and more a weird form of dodgeball with magic. I still don't get the rules. But it's exciting. My heart thumps every time the hunted player makes a move. Looks precarious up there, you'd have to be really athletic jumping around like that. I can see why it'd be Priya's thing.

Magnolia spots an opening, suddenly leaping from the top tier, arcing all the way towards a base square. The one in the corner where Walsh is standing. She hits it without touching him, but the square rocks with force and he's thrown off balance. Anyone else would have fallen off, but Walsh leaps to the right, taking the next square. The arrogant smirk never leaves his face.

I now realize Magnolia was baited as she tried to even the odds. They weren't really trying to catch the other Lord Kelvin player, this was a ruse to bring her down. And on that wobbling square, she's hit in the face with the duster, knocking her to the ground.

There's wild cheering from the Edinburgh supporters.

'It's much harder to cast the balls vertically than across. She was hoping they'd try to launch them upstairs, but the Edinburgh boys kept the game at the base. Then Magnolia ceded her advantage, joining her base too late. Now it's three on one. They might as well throw in the towel; the round is lost. "The rabbit", that's the last player in this situation, can only try getting more points to achieve a dignified score for his team. But there's no way he can outrun three "foxes",' Priya explains.

There's a more relaxed, methodical approach by the Edinburgh boys, who are in full control. The Kelvinite moves frantically, delaying the inevitable defeat.

But I can't let myself get too into the game, I have to remember why I'm here. I start scanning the crowd again, looking for anything familiar, and that's when I notice the woman in white, out of the sea again and now staring longingly at the tallest tower by the keep. There's something in there that she wants, and I see a shadow in the window. I recall the ominous piping played on the first night of the conference. Reckon with everyone's attention taken up by the game right now, I can do a bit of snooping in that other part of the castle that's out of bounds. And I want to speak with the MacLeods' resident piper and see if he has anything I can use.

'Where you going?' Priya asks, grabbing my arm.

'I need to spend a penny,' I say.

'The game's still on. That was just the first set.'

'When nature calls, what can you do?'

She lets go and I make my way through the spectators.

'Fight till the end,' someone yells in the crowd.

Everyone likes to root for the underdog. From the sound of it, the remaining Lord Kelvin player is still at it as I go back inside Dunvegan Castle.

XX

ENTRY IS STRICTLY FORBIDDEN

Since when has that ever stopped me? I open the door and go inside. Just my luck, a shitload of stairs await. Fortunately I've spent so much of my life tramping up and down hilly Edinburgh, my thighs are built like an Olympic cyclist's. There's blackened walls in here. Smoke damage? This section's even more run-down than anywhere else I've been in the castle. Cobwebs in corners. Dust so thick I practically leave footprints behind. There's tins of paint stacked to one side, with some ladders and sheets. Maybe someone tried to do a bit of DIY a while back.

I shine a lamp borrowed from downstairs onto the big old sign.

DO NOT PROCEED

UNDER ANY CIRCUMSTANCES

Something creaks and I damn near shit myself. Left hand on the lamp, right on my dagger. Ought to have brought

Priya with me. But I didn't want to disturb her rugby. She was well into it. Without the distraction of the game going on, I might not get another chance to check out this tower, though.

I've visited other realms before, so I know when I encounter a warped space. The atmosphere in this tower's off. The light from my lamp's travelling weirdly, almost like it's hitting invisible patches in the air, making the beam uneven. Uncanny. Creepy as hell.

The stairs narrow at points and then open up again. The top is only supposed to be a few storeys up, and I should already be there, but the stairs keep stretching out further than what's possible. A gut feeling tells me that stopping before I get to the top isn't a good idea. You can't half dip into liminal spaces.

A gust of cold wind hits me. Glad I didn't pick a candle as it would surely have been snuffed out by now. You don't want to be making this ascent in the dark. *Keep going, Ropa.* Let's find whatever secrets the MacLeods are hiding up here. Each landing leads to the next and then the one after that. They all look the same. Blackened walls, grime, a disturbing atmosphere. It's like this part of the castle's a vortex, sucking in the ancient darkness of this isle.

At last, I make it to the top.

A broken door dangles off its hinges.

Here goes.

There's nothing sadder than the sight of a lonely ghost in an empty room. He stares out the window, watching the rugby below. A yearning for life, perhaps. I know from my ghostalking how acute that feeling can be for the dearly departed. The everyThere, where ghosts are parked until they choose to move on, is a desolate realm of inertia. A place where nothing's ever supposed to happen, forever. Still, some, like this ghost, cling on to our world for a taste of life they can't have anymore. It's bad for them. Not good for us either. No one likes being haunted. The relations between the living and the dead have, throughout history, been regulated and mediated by mystics to protect the living from any undue influence. It's not unknown for the dead, whether through malice or mere meddling, to cause harm. Even in cases where they seek to protect loved ones, the law of unintended consequences still applies. Our world is chaotic enough without them interfering.

I catch my breath at the door, watching the deado. It seems unaware of my presence.

It's grey, and dressed in tattered grey tartan.

Drones from its spectral bagpipe are thrown over its shoulder, and the blowstick's attached to its mouth. I see through it and notice it has no arms, just hands placed upon the chanter. It has no legs either. Ghosts may choose whatever form they take. They're often sentimental about this, presenting themselves as they once thought they looked. But older ones lose perspective on what it is to be human and form hideous shapes. That can be freaky as hell.

Very slowly, the piper's ghost swivels to face me. It has such sad eyes.

I take off one strap of my backpack, slide it to my front and retrieve my mbira. I hold it up for the ghost to see. We are fellow artists. I can't hear them speak language without this instrument, which syncs the harmonics. Otherwise all you get is booga-woogaring.

'You played beautifully last night,' I say. 'But what's a piper without a band? Care to jam with me?'

The thing about linking up with ghosts is you have to find the right tune. Much easier to do with the newbies. Oldies like this have different tastes. I usually have a knack for it, but this time the tune escapes me. I sweep my light around the room. Yahweh. In the corner's a shackled skeleton. The skull's got hair, and rests precariously against the ribcage. Both femurs are broken. There's a mess of smaller bones on the ground too, a useless ball and chain round the shinbone.

Skeletons don't hold together unless you wire them. By the time the flesh's rotten and the ligaments and connective tissue are gone, they fall apart.

'Is this you?'

The ghost just stares.

Strong, silent type – that's how I like them. A cheer rises from outside as the final whistle goes for the game. Already? How long have I been in here?

Then the song comes to me and I play, trying to capture the tone and prosody of the human voice. 'The Dark Island' is a timeless, gut-wrenching melody. I approximate it as best I can with my mbira. The ghost sways, forty-five degrees to one side, then the other. Like a pendulum swinging. My song carries strangely, distorted in this warped space. Then I hear that haunting drone of the pipes. It bores through every fibre of my being. The force of it ripples out from my centre, through flesh, to the tips of my hair. As though the piper were playing out from within me into the world. No piece of music's ever hit me like this before.

My hands are shaking as I keep time with a superior instrumentalist.

Those bagpipes and my mbira channel currents from a time gone by. Spectral fingers dance on the chanter. The sound is the tired wheeze of an old man's final exhalation. Overwhelmed, I weep as I play because it dawns on me that what I thought might be a malevolent presence is in fact a trapped soul.

Who are they and why are they here?

The ceiling opens up to a cloudless night. Stars sweep across it. Constellations galloping. The whirl of beautiful forgotten things and broken vows. And when the ghostly piper finishes his tune, I truly know what it is to be elevated by music.

I pause to recentre.

The music lingers in the silence as if it has changed the shape of the air.

'Tell me your name,' I command.

'I am the lone piper. The man who once dared to dream.' The sound comes out of the holes of his chanter, dripping like honeyed milk. His lips never leave the blowstick.

'Tell me about your dream.'

'A slipper. Silk. Her ankle. Kisses I never had. The children we never bore. The life we could have had.'

The melancholy in his voice has a resigned tinge to it. This ghost has been here for centuries. But I don't feel anger from him. Instead he radiates dejection and misery. There's something dark tethering him. He's not tied to the everyThere like other ghosts, but bound to this castle.

He splays his fingers but can't let go of the bagpipes.

'Set me free. I want to rest.'

'Tell me your name and your story.'

I need more info and I'm trying to figure out what Gran would do. This is not the usual situation. I'm not sure if my Authority alone is enough to free him. Helping souls like this is what I do. At least until I get in with the Society proper and move on to better things. If this ghoul is trapped here then it would be Edmund MacLeod's business. Should I try to override this by my Authority, what would be the consequences?

When in doubt, I normally go with my instincts. It's about doing what feels right. My pal Nicco M. is all about doing what works for you, morality be damned. But other people's pain isn't collateral damage. I can't treat it like abstract theory.

The ghost tells me his name is Stephen MacCrimmon. His family were the hereditary pipers to the MacLeods. They were based in Borreraig in Duirnish on the northwest of the island. Stephen claims they were the greatest pipers ever. I'm pretty certain there's at least a dozen families across the Highlands and Islands who make the same boast. Ain't my place to judge, though. He tells me they founded a school where pipers from across Scotland came to learn their trade.

'I was born with the sound of bagpipes playing. They are as natural to me as hearing the wind.'

That explains why he took up his calling.

The room tilts at an angle and I put one foot forward to stop myself falling over. I have a sick sensation deep in my bowels.

Stephen MacCrimmon was a hit with the ladies, as good musicians can be. The usual story then. He fell in love with his chief's wife and, even worse, she fell in love with him. It was chaste, he swears. Soulmates meeting in the wrong circumstances. But Skye is a small island, word gets round. Needless to say, the chief got radge and went all medieval when he heard about it. He ordered Stephen imprisoned and tortured. His punishment was to forever play music, serenading a lover he could never be with. Like Tantalus of the myths. Doomed to be so close to the object of his desire, but never to attain her. From the window he would look down and see the chief's wife standing in the courtyard. Alone in this tower, it was the only thing keeping him sane. He had his bagpipes and played the sweetest melodies ever heard, hoping the notes would caress his lover. And touch her the music did, for when she'd had enough of her lover's torment one foggy winter's morn, the chief's wife walked out the sea gate and waded into Dunvegan Loch, never to be seen again. In his anguish, Stephen kept playing to lament his lost love and soothe his rival's anguish, for he knew the chief loved her too. But the chief was only further enraged. He had Stephen ritually murdered and his soul bound to the castle, proclaiming that he would play for the MacLeods for as long as Dunvegan Castle stood.

Poor Adamina. So this is her lost love, whom she looks up to the tower for every night.

'Release me,' he begs. 'I grow tired of existence.'

'I will do what I can, but first you need to tell me what you saw last night. Who killed Mr Sneddon and stole *The Book of the Shaded Mysteries of Solomon*? You see all the comings and goings-on in this castle. Tell me something. Anything.'

Stephen draws back from me in the tilted room. Eyebrows raised; fear written all over his face. He shakes his head. I hate that I'm taking advantage of his desperation to get the information I need. Gran wouldn't like it. She's all about helping the unfortunate dead without conditions. It's a great ethos, but in the real world, commerce rules. Sod my conscience, I'm growing soft. That won't do. We all live in Machiavelli's wet dream these days.

'Once you tell me, you'll be free of all this. Perhaps you'll find your love again in the great beyond.' I dangle a carrot.

'Foul things this place has seen. Better to be blind and let it go.'

'My job is to uncover those very same things. Tell me or I walk.'

'Promises were made in secret places pitting daughter against father, the young against the old. Men would be as gods. The dead would rise again. Eternity theirs as desired. Knives thrown in shadows. To the heart. Olympus will stand tall as all you know falls.'

'Talk sense, man. I want a who, not gibberish.' Not for the first time, I wish these ghosts wouldn't talk in riddles.

'Sorcery knots my tongue. A woman and three men running inside of a corridor. Young they were.' His face contorts with effort. 'Two islanders and two lowlanders. Another from the south waited within. All I can say I've said, now release me as you swore.' He rushes towards me, the tattered rags he wears flailing about. He's desperate.

Then the room rearranges itself, with the ceiling and floor seeming to have swapped places. Up has become down. The stones defy the mortar holding them fast and move like pieces of a jigsaw puzzle. We are stretched out like rubber bands. A perverse camera obscura. I suspect this is opticology, illusory magic mentioned in the texts I've read. It's not something I have first-hand experience of, though. They used it for kicks back in the day, to create mazes for aristocrats to play in at their country estates.

Outside the window's pure blackness. It's as though we're in space without the stars.

I turn and see through the doorway two red scampering lights bounding up the bleakness of the staircase.

'Who's there?'

'Flee, fly, scarper,' Stephen cries, vanishing in an instant.

This is not good. What on earth can spook a ghost like that? *Ropa, you eejit. You should have brought Priya with.* The room rearranges itself once more. Bricks peel off into the nothingness, leaving a debris-strewn field drifting in the void. Even the everyThere gives me less heebies than this. I pull my scarf Cruickshank out of my pocket and fix him around my neck.

What are those red lights bounding towards me?

What's wrong with this place?

I step over the void onto the remaining islets of flooring. Down below, a tiny speck of white light shines like a beacon, and the stairway has truncated into drifting sections. I need to get out of here. I hop, skip and jump my way across the disintegrating fabric of unreality. Making it onto the landing, I take another step and leap.

I land hard, a jarring force rattling my bones. Ouch. My legs are shaking. But I can't be dealing with that right now.

Those ruby embers are the eyes of a tiny person. An ancient being with pointy ears. Sharp nose. He moves on all fours, squintways like a crab, and hops across the void, scurrying upon the remaining bits of walls. Vertical or horizontal, it makes no difference to him. He opens his mouth wide, parting it all the way to his ears. Rows of sharp teeth appear and a forked tongue flashes out.

'You're not supposed to be here, witch,' he says in a spine-chilling voice.

'Keep away from me. I work for Sir Ian Callander, the Secretary of the Society of Sceptical Enquirers. We are guests of the MacLeods, and I have the right to be here.'

'In that case, you must be nicely marinated. I'll enjoy eating your liver. You bear the mark of our kin killer.'

'Kin what? You've got the wrong—'

He hurls himself from the floating wall, pincer-like claws reaching for me. I grab Cruickshank and flick him at the wee fella, and my scarf forms a fist, punching him before he gets too close. The blow knocks him back, but he's nimble and lands atop a floating windowsill. He glares at me and moves more cautiously now, hopping from block to block. The deconstructed debris of the tower is all around us. The wee fella snarls, tasting the void with his forked tongue.

He called me 'kin killer'.

The Isle of Skye used to be inhabited by the Sidhe who we know as the Fae. That's why it feels like a different dimension, even though it's in this world. The MacLeods may have defeated the fairies, but who's to say they didn't take a few prisoners? That must be why this tower feels so strange. A warping of the agitative threshold defined by the Somerville Equation. The presence of this creature must be causing it, since the Fae aren't of this world. The last time I met one, a brounie, I was trapped inside a spooky mansion in Edinburgh. And the brounie met with a bad end. That's maybe why this little fella is riled with me. It's a bitch when your past actions come back to bite you in the arse, long after the fourteen-day return policy is up.

This guy sure doesn't resemble the pics of Fae in children's books. Their form's warped by being held captive for too long in this realm. Poor Stephen, stuck here for centuries with this guy.

The white light below dims a fraction. Almost like a door being slowly shut. Is that my only exit? I need to get there before it closes completely.

'Let me eat you like my kin was eaten by the voykor you sicced on him,' he says petulantly, stomping about. 'Immortals don't live again once they die. I shall feast on your body first, then on your soul.'

'I ain't the edible variety, pal,' I reply, running down the stairs and leaping onto a floating stone lintel. Cruickshank straightens out over my shoulders, helping me balance like a pole, so I don't have to use my hands as I walk across the narrow block of stone. Looks like I'm made for rugby too. I use my free hands to grab my katty and load up, then I kindle a Promethean spark in the rock and fire. It explodes as it's about to hit the wee fella, peppering him with shrapnel.

He shrieks in pain and rage. I'm already bolting, leaping onto another floating bit of masonry. A second pair of red eyes emerges in the distant void. Then another. Then another. The darkness lights up with these tiny creatures all baying for my flesh. It's an infestation. They're absofuckinglutely everywhere.

I must get to the white light. So I jam on it, running through the floating debris that is the tower. It's like hopscotch with demons on your six. I slip, trying to land on a block, and I'm about to plunge into the darkness, but Cruickshank grabs hold of it and swings me over onto the next block.

Cries of 'kin killer' explode around me.

It's terrifying.

I shut my eyes briefly and yell 'Prometheus', setting off a shower of incandescent white sparks. The creatures yell with rage. But if it blinds them for a bit, since they're accustomed to the dark, then I've bought precious seconds. A few, stunned by the light, lose their perch and fall into the blackness.

But this only pisses off their kin even more, who curse at me.

I'm about to make my next move when I feel teeth sink into my left hand. I cry out, grabbing my dagger with my right hand, and stab the bastard in the eye. Blue blood sprays onto my clothes as I shake free, and barge into an incoming one which has fallen off a block from higher up. My left hand's on fire. Teeth marks through the flesh into bone. What a dick.

I keep on running. The white light's narrowing, while one of the bastards is flying out towards me. I hold a forearm out to block it, knife ready to stab. He slams into me and bites my arm. I wince, expecting pain, but there's a metallic sound and cracking bone, then his teeth fly out of his mouth. What the . . . He howls in agony, and I kick him off into the darkness. I can't believe this shit. Gran's coat is undisturbed, kinda like real armour. How does . . . The one that got me went for the bare flesh. Fucking A. If this coat can withstand those sharp canines, I just need to worry about my head, neck, hands and legs. Doodle that. I'm still running, trying to maintain balance. And the floating masonry's speeding up.

As I run, I yell out all the spells I know. I'm shooting off fire, lightning and concussive blasts of air. It's a lot easier casting in here because of the heightened agitative threshold. But no matter what I throw out, there's too many of these bampots coming at me. I spring a couple of feet to grab the floating flagpole. Slide down it like a firefighter and drop down onto the last bit of flooring.

Nearly there now.

'Kin killer, kin killer, kin killer, kin killer, kin killer . . .'
Their rage echoes through the void.

The gap's almost closed.

A few more feet, that's all I need. Nearly there when I'm
tackled by one of the little critters. Next the whole swarm's
bearing down on me. Sparkling red eyes. Chattering teeth. I
try to shake the bastard off me, but he's gripping into my
flesh with his claws. It hurts. Cruickshank slides down my
neck, onto my waist, and prises him off before throwing him
into the air.

I use every ounce of strength left in me to leap through
the sliver of light . . . And I land on the hard floor just as the
door slams shut behind me.

I scramble to get as far from it as I can, and I hear the
Fae clawing and banging from the other side. Looks like they
can't get through. Phew.

Panting.

What was that all about?

My hand's throbbing and my calf's bleeding. Those arseholes did a number on me. I'm relieved to have made it
out. Okay, now I get why they forbid anyone from going
in there. A warning sign showing sharp teeth and claws
might have been a nice gesture. Health and safety. I can't
believe anyone would knowingly live with this horror in the
house.

I feel . . .

Woozy.

Hey.

What the . . .

I shake my head. It's getting harder . . . to . . . keep. My. Eyes. Open.

A pair of legs in heels is standing over me. Let me sit up. Can't. What the actual?

'You shouldn't have gone in there.' It's Fenella. Why's there ten of her?

I try to—

XXI

Jackhammer's pounding my noggin. The light's too bright. Agony all over. That means I'm still alive. Hip, hip, ouch. My throat's dry. I move my lips and feel a straw placed on them. I start sucking and taste something bitter. It's disgusting but I'm so thirsty I don't care – I'd drink my own urine at this stage.

'I'm only stepping out to the toilet, she tells me,' Priya says. 'Nope, you were off doing your thing without me as usual. If it weren't for Fenella giving us the MacLeods' antivenom, you'd be dead, you fanny. Thank god for kelpie poop. That's what you're drinking right now.'

I try to reply but can only croak.

Jomo's stood at the foot of the bed.

'I see you decided to go one up on me, man,' he says.

'That was a right nippler and all,' Priya says. 'Drink some more of this.'

'It was highly irresponsible. She's very lucky she made it out, few people do. Not if they don't know what they're doing in there in the first place. The last thing any of us needs is more collateral damage.' Fenella speaks, sitting by the window. 'And it'll be a full moon tomorrow night, when the Fairy Flag is unfurled. It gets the prisoners very agitated, so this is a dangerous time to be there. It reminds them of their defeat and how they're cut off from their home world.'

'Thanks, guys,' I manage at last.

Priya tuts. She's proper fuming but I'm in too much pain to care. I raise my left hand to check. It's neatly bandaged. So's my calf, going by the feel of it. Perks of having a healer for a pal. But the clock's still ticking, I don't have time to lie about. There's work to be done. I should get paid for this. There can't be that many people out there risking life and limb gratis like I do.

Still, it's rewarding being back in the normal 3D world where the rules of physics apply.

'What's all that happening in your tower?' I ask.

'That's not what we call that part of the castle . . . Never mind. After my ancestors defeated the Fae, not all of them made it back to their realm. They were cut off when the path was closed. For a while we held them as normal prisoners. We even thought we might find a way to live with them eventually. But it wasn't to be. A madness infected the remaining ones after a while. They can't go home, but we can't let them loose in the world. So we keep them locked up.'

'That's cruel.'

'What's your plan then? A final solution? Our clan was sworn never to do anything like that again. Not since Eigg.'

Umm, that. I'd read about it before coming here. In the sixteenth century the MacLeods had had one more incident in their series of running beefs with the MacDonalds. Them days these things didn't play out on social media, it happened up close and personal. Some stuff about a bunch of MacLeods who wound up on a small island called Eigg after a storm. They nicked some cattle, as was the way in those days, and molested the MacDonald women. Real classy. Taking exception to this behaviour, the MacDs broke every limb of the MacLeod chief's son and cast him out to sea in a boat with no oars. A sure way to kill a bloke slowly. Somehow that boat made its way back to Dunvegan carrying the dead lad, and it pissed his pa off mightily. The old man promptly sent his warriors to Eigg to exact revenge. The islanders caught word of this and fled to the Cave of Francis, which has only a slither of an entrance, making it hard to find. They chilled in there for three whole days while the MacLeod warriors got to the island and ripped everything apart. But they couldn't find no one. So they grabbed what bounty they could and razed every home on Eigg, before setting sail for home. They'd only just taken to the sea when a MacDonald lookout, checking to see if the coast was clear, gave the game away. Monster of a bummer. The warriors came back ashore and sealed up the entrance to the cave with heather and stuff. Then they set fire to it. Thick smoke filled the cave, killing every man, woman and child inside. Four hundred members of the MacDonald Clan. It was barbaric what the MacLeods did then.

'I'm sure your lot still did messed-up stuff even after Eigg,' I say.

'You think the MacDonalds are any different?' she replies.

'I've seen how you and Avery look at one another. Your dad's going to be miffed.'

Fenella blushes, cheeks cherry red, stark against her pale complexion. That's all the proof I need. The MacDonalds – Avery and his dad, Dalziel – were the first to get to Sneddon and Jomo after the scroll was stolen. I still haven't had a chance to speak to father and son about it. If their reception here's anything to go by, there's no love lost between the MacDonald and MacLeod Clans. Their ancient feud seems to be very much alive and well. But Fenella wouldn't throw her beau under the bus, I imagine, if he was guilty of theft. It's not like the dead librarian, or the Ethiopian scroll, are a direct loss to her clan. But wouldn't she have factored in this meaning that the MacDonalds were sabotaging their rivals? As far as the Highlands and Islands go, the MacLeods are the centre of magic. I can imagine that position would rankle with some. Still, I saw the way Fenella's father dismissed her when the guests arrived. There's something going on between them too. Could this be why the piper ghost said something about enmity between fathers and daughters or the like?

I force myself to sit up despite the pain.

My poor hand. Biting's a craven way to fight, Fae or no. Especially when you've got numbers on your side. Those brounie bastards deserve heather and flame.

'I'm glad you're okay,' Jomo says.

'We'll compare battle scars when we're old. Right now, there's work to be done.'

'I have confirmation the missing dirk was one from the castle collection of antique blades.'

Fenella stiffens up. You can get weapons from anywhere and a kitchen knife would have done the job. To specifically use a weapon owned by the MacLeods makes this personal. It's an attempt to frame them, surely?

'I need you to be straight with me, Fenella. Do you think the MacDonalds have something to do with this?'

She hesitates, then folds her hands and places them on her tummy. Makes her look like a kid. That's what she is, though. Everyone in this room too. Some of us have lived a little and that's the difference. You can't compare me to Rapunzel here.

'You need to tell us everything you know. A man's died and my friend's nearly had her tooshie torn off by your goblins while searching for answers. This is serious,' Priya says, proper annoyed.

'I don't know,' Fenella replies, appearing afeard. 'Avery and me go to St Andrews together, that's all. He wouldn't do anything like that.'

'What about his dad?'

'Avery's scared of him. He's angry all the time and mean. Maybe him, but not Avery. He's a sweet lad.'

Stealing the scroll and framing the MacLeods for it might settle old scores for the MacDonalds. Motive. Malice. Fragile egos. That would be one way to sully their rivals' reputation and ensure the MacLeods lose their status in Scottish magic. I'll have to check up on them. It's real late, though, and there's one more thing I need to iron out with Fenella.

'I don't much care for brounies, that's your business. Your family can play prison guards all they like. But you've got to let Stephen MacCrimmon out from this hell your family's made for him. I can't let it continue.' I don't ever want to go anywhere near that tower again. Imagine what it's like being jailed there for centuries.

'I agree, but you'll have to speak to my father about that,' Fenella replies. She looks at each of us in turn. 'It's one of the reasons I hate this place. Secrets and lies. When you live in a house where people were tortured and starved, and the blood's soaked into the fabric of the place, it's hard to sleep at night. I'd rather be anywhere but here. Don't you dream of a better world? If you could, wouldn't you turn the clock back to a better time?'

Someone bangs on the door. Deffo not their knuckles rapping. We stop talking, and they only start banging again more forcefully.

'What?' Priya shouts.

The door's swung open. Lord Samarasinghe's coachman stoops, enters and proceeds to block the doorway. He's so broad there's no way through.

'Hey, I didn't say you could come in,' Priya protests.

'I were asked to bring you to milord's accommodations for a chat, Ms Ropa Moyo.' He has that thick Yorkshire accent.

'No, you need to rest, Ropa.'

'I can handle this, Doc,' I reply.

After the Sorcerer Royal's performance at dinner, I'm keen to hear what he has to say. I might feel like a train wreck, but the grind don't stop for no one.

XXII

The surly Yorkshireman moves with purpose, as I limp along behind him, my hand throbbing. He slows, allowing me to catch up. There's a brusqueness to him. When you're built like a Soviet T-35 rolling through the castle grounds, you can afford to be like that, I guess. Wish I was that buff. I've tried to engage him in convo, but it seems gruntish is his second language. The lord's got him well trained. Pity, 'cause the help often knows things about their masters even the masters don't know about themselves. I've experienced that with Morag and the castle staff. Once you get them gossiping, everything comes out.

'You at least going to tell me your name?'

'Briggs.'

'First name or last name?'

He grunts.

'They're not big talkers where you're from, I can see that much. It's Doncaster, right? What about Barnsley? No? Okay then. How about Scunthorpe? That's more Lincolnshire, isn't it? Give me something here.'

'Nearly there,' he says.

'Great. Umm, wait. Do you mean where we're going or you talking about your home? I'm confused.'

He shrugs. Prick to the nth power. I'm still bugged by what the piper ghost said to me earlier. I had my arse kicked but now I think about it, I know there were at least four people involved in the crime. A woman and three men. Two lowlanders and two islanders – sounds like a fancy cocktail. Finding this quartet might unlock things. But why four people? One or two to take out the power. Another two to take out Jomo and Sneddon? But Jomo was knocked out and Sneddon outright murdered. One uses a knife and the other their fists? I don't know. But who walked out of that room? And who was the other from the south, waiting within? This is super-bugging me. I wish my ghostly informant could say more, but there's little chance I'm getting back into that part of the castle again. Once bitten and all that jazz. Ouch.

It's a short stroll downhill, veering by the conference tent to the Laundry Cottage where Samarasinghe's quartered. It's plum pickings given the accommodation situation. Can't remember who was bumped to make way for him. The cottage has a great view of the sea and western face of the castle, but unfortunately that's obscured by the tent at the moment. Hang on . . . *Another from the south waited within.* Who's more southern in this place than the English Sorcerer Royal? And he's been making moves against the Society of Sceptical Enquirers since he arrived uninvited, so who's not to say he has native allies in place? I've got to tread real careful here.

The cottage chimney's spewing smoke. They've got a fire going, which is odd. It's not even cold. Not since the barrier came up. And the smoke can't rise any further than the

Newton Barrier, so it spreads like a rolling cloud, tracing the force field's outlines.

'We'll all choke to death if you guys keep on polluting like this,' I point out.

The coachman's not bothered.

I smell sabotage. Reckon if they keep this up and it messes with the asthmatics and such, Callander might be forced to let down the shield. That or it'll be Eigg and a load of smothered clansmen all over again. I'm going to straighten this out with the Sorcerer Royal. If not, then I hope the plants here enjoy smoking. It's a large garden . . . I'm finding excuses 'cause I'm a wee bit intimidated by Lord Samarasinghe – I'll have to steel myself. Power can smell fear and it most definitely doesn't respect weakness.

The door opens just as we get there. Rector Wedderburn of the Edinburgh School steps out with Hamish Hutchinson, head of St Andrews College. 'Evening,' Wedderburn says as they leave. I wonder why they were here and think of the challenge made to Callander at the dinner. It seems the Sorcerer Royal is holding court tonight. Seeing them two here makes me mighty suspicious. Lord Samarasinghe wouldn't have made the move he did during dinner if he didn't already have backers, traitors embedded within the ranks of Scottish magic's elite practitioners . . . Nah, I might not know Hutchinson well, but I've observed Wedderburn for a while and know he's loyal to Callander and committed to the independence of Scottish magic. Both are products of the Edinburgh School and he dismissed the Sorcerer Royal when he said the last duel was fought in the nineteenth century.

Seems more likely to me that he's come down here seeking to use his influence to limit Samarasinghe's manoeuvres.

The coachman steps aside to let me in first. It's then I see the game the Sorcerer Royal's playing. I'm the outsider here. Much more likely to be suspected of duplicity, and now I've been spotted visiting England's top magician under the cover of darkness. That'll set tongues wagging and Esfandiar will probably have a go at me again.

Blundered into the trap like a right sap. Nothing for it now save for having my wits about me. I go into the open-plan living room, joined to which is the kitchen. Lord Samarasinghe's sat in an armchair by the fireplace, feet in slippers raised upon a pouffe. His eyes are closed, brow furrowed in concentration. He moves his head to the rhythm of classical music playing off a gramophone. I've only ever seen pictures of vinyl records. I don't like the sound, it's low quality. Too crackly. I can't believe anyone would listen to something that awful.

Briggs shuts the door and stands in front of it menacingly.

The other sofa in the room's a two-seater near the kitchen, which is the back of the room. Samarasinghe's turned his armchair the other way, so if I sat there I'd be behind him. He's not even bothered acknowledging my presence yet, and the music rises to a crescendo, with violent crashing noises. Then it just keeps going, refusing to end. My leg's sore as I limp to get closer and attract his attention.

His chest rises and falls with the music, and he breathes loudly through his nostrils. I think he's lost in it. Each to their own, but classical music ain't my thing. I'd rather listen to bairns beating pans together.

After the brass pomposity finally draws to a close, the needle makes noise tracking the end of the record. Samarasinghe sighs melodramatically, waves his hand, and the needle rises up and returns home. The record stops.

'Thomas Arne. Isn't it exquisite? Music from an era that stirs the soul. A time when men were men,' he says.

'You asked to see me?'

'I hear you're an artist. The byra, is it called? Peculiar. Do you have it on you? Can I see it?' I shake my head and don't bother to correct him by saying it's the mbira I play. 'Pity. Not that it matters in the grand scheme of things. It's not the sort of percussion instrument they'd play in an orchestra. That takes refinement. But you are a musical person, so you understand these things. You really ought to listen to Edward Elgar or Henry Purcell. Come to think of it, I might take my gramophone to the castle and play Handel's 'The Arrival of the Queen of Sheba' for those Ethiopians. Do you think they'd like it?'

'I'm not into any of that.'

'I see . . . Orchestral music is the reflection of the soul of the volksgeist. Everyone comes together and plays their part in front of the conductor. It's about harmony, togetherness, and it's precise, controlled. Each instrumentalist knows where they stand in relation to the rest. I don't much like jazz. Do you?'

I'm confused right now. He brought me out here in the middle of the night to talk about old-people music? I'd better take control of this conversation. I get straight into it.

'What do you know about a magician in England who's

hoovering up magical texts from Scotland?' I ask. 'Only a man with deep pockets could have sent a Yorkshireman to snap up every book in the Marquess of Linlithgow's library.'

'Jazz thrives on bedlam. It's the antithesis of the natural order of things. The product of a decadent culture. I've tried listening to it and had a headache for days afterwards. The pieces I heard were sonically tugging in all different directions. The players were making it up as they went along, like toddlers. Even if you label it improv, all it represents is the inability to imagine civilization. The state, like the orchestra, demands an unwavering, unnegotiable, purposeful unity. Everyone knowing their place, doing what needs to be done. All under the benevolent guidance of the conductor, who is truly king amongst musicians. Don't you agree this is the superior way of doing things?'

'Whoever bought the Marquess of Linlithgow's library might be responsible for the theft of the scroll. Perhaps they didn't find what they were looking for in his collection and thought the scroll might have it instead.'

He smiles, patronizingly. I feel a chill travel through me as he bides his time, studying me from head to toe. I've got his full attention now. It feels like being devoured by the leviathan's pet tiger. Those intelligent, knowing eyes. The monobrow. It takes everything I have to stop my knees knocking.

'Why did you ask me here?' I say instead.

'Take a chair and sit over there.' He points to a spot at the other side of the fireplace.

My leg's hurting, and I really need to sit down. But

everything with the Sorcerer Royal is a power game. If I retrieve one of the bar stools by the breakfast bar and sit where he's asked me to, I've ceded something for nothing. But if I remain standing here, I'll just look like a plonker. Heads he wins, tails I lose. If this is a coin toss, then I shouldn't let it land. Keep it spinning. So I go over to the kitchen, grab the bar stool and take it right next to his armchair. This way I'm sat above him and he has to look up to me.

He grins in recognition. There's that annoying, superior air again.

I realize right away I've made a blunder. I'm directly in front of the fireplace and now I'm roasting. It's after midnight and I've had a long day. My wits ain't half what they're supposed to be. Pride keeps me hanging on, though.

'The fire's creating smoke, which is going to make it difficult for the people in the bubble to breathe.'

'Is that so?' he purrs.

'Kindly put it out.'

'The indefatigable Ropafadzo Moyo.' Lord Samarasinghe chuckles. 'Do you know why I wear epaulettes made of raven feathers?' He opens his hand and closes it into a fist. The fire dies.

I don't know how to score this game, so I give him nothing back.

'The Sorcerer Royal occupies the Merlin Seat. The raven was his mark, and he wore a feather-like cloak. It's myth, of course, but what's true is that the raven finds himself, in religion and folklore, wise and knowing. He penetrates through secrets. Sees all. Knowledge being the ultimate power. And magic is merely a higher form of knowledge. In Norse mythology Odin has a pair of ravens, Huginn and Muninn. They flew all over the world, bringing him back information. My ravens brought me word of you a while ago. Precocious, resourceful, a leader and a fighter. I like that an awful lot. Were this a meritocracy, it's young people like you, the cream, who'd rise to the top of our discipline. Sadly, this isn't always the case. These old farts won't make way for new wine and so we stagnate, then decline. If you ask me, the way Scottish magic treats you is abominable. An unpaid internship for a novice with your obvious talents? A caster of the áspro flame, no less. They should be biting your arm off to have you in their ranks.'

It stings like a bitch when they use the truth to get inside your head. I bite the inside of my cheek then lean back a bit. It's very confusing when a bully like Samarasinghe tries to flatter you. *Precocious. Resourceful. A leader and a fighter.* There's not many people out in the castle that have nice things to say about me, no matter what I do. Not Cockburn, or Hutchinson. Even Callander's got limits on what he does for me. Nothing's been handed to me by the Society. I've had to battle for every crumb I've got . . . But all these savoury nothings Samarasinghe's telling me, I know he's using them to work me. Bollocks to that.

'Flattery don't work on me.'

'I was being candid. It seems my observations cause you distress. Interesting.'

I preferred him better when he was being a knob. At least

that way it was clear where he stood. But it's nice to have someone *see* you. Nah. I ain't in school no more. My life doesn't revolve around adults patting me on the head, telling me I've done well. I'm long past expecting gold stars. Gran once told me that being grown-up means you have to put your head down and get on with it. Even when no one's watching.

Except, the raven's been watching, it seems.

'I don't like being spied on,' I tell him.

'Word gets round when there's real talent.'

Stop acting nice and tell me what you want already. I'm even more suspicious now, 'cause as far as I'm concerned, everyone, and that includes the Sorcerer Royal, is on my list. And he's damn near the top of it so far.

There's a sincere look about him right now which unnerves me, though. It's that fundamentalist claptrap. Like he actually believes the hogwash coming out of his mouth like a broken sewer pipe.

'That's all well and good, but right now, the only thing I care about is finding the coward who killed Mr Sneddon and getting that scroll back.'

'They also told me you have locking jaws. That when you bite, you don't let go. A real British bulldog. Remarkable. You know, my father worked in insurance all his life, and was successful in a staid, middle-class sort of way. My mom was a self-employed quantity surveyor. Neither was into magic. I'm the first practitioner in my family. Contrary to what most people believe, I didn't take the smooth bourgeois path up the hill. I'm a Brummie. You can't tell by my accent. That's the price I paid at the toll gate on my way to the top. It costs you a little something of yourself. If there's anything you should take from our conversation, make it this one fact. My parents lost everything they'd worked to build after the Catastrophe. All gone in an instant, like sandcastles in the tide. We survived on food banks and charity. Can you imagine what that's like for a family in Edgbaston? My father had to go with us, as my mom said she'd rather starve than show her face at one of those places. That was her nature, fierce and proud. On a good day we had two meals, on bad days, well . . . You know what it's like. The humiliation was too much. My father chose to swing rather than face up to the fact he couldn't provide for his family. I used to think he was a coward, but that was unfair of me. He was a proud working man. My mom followed soon after. She died of a broken heart. So there I was, barely sixteen with four younger siblings to take care of.'

'I know what that's like,' I volunteer without thinking.

'Not easy, is it?'

'We do what we must.'

'Stiff upper lip. That's us – you and me, Ropa. We don't mope and moan – we get on with it. I was the oldest in my year when I read magic at Featherstonehaugh. It wasn't easy doing that, with everything else I had going on at home. Got in on merit alone and worked my socks off. I had an aptitude for it and discovered two new spells even before my final year. The king took notice and raised me to his side. Not bad for a lad from Birmingham, don't you think?'

I find myself agreeing. This powerful magician, is he kinda

like me? If this is all true, then it seems Lord Samarasinghe knows what the streets are like. He made his own way into the profession, rising to the pinnacle. I can see why he gets me. Despite myself, I find myself warming to him. I uncross my legs and shift on the stool. What if he's not the bully I thought he was? Like, he could just be the guy who comes across wrong 'cause he's from the West Midlands.

He looks down at his slippers, almost as if he's embarrassed by what he's just told me. I'm really beginning to think he might be alright. Careful. Now I'm tussling with myself.

'I know I'm better than every other magician in this place because in England our practitioners are stress-tested. We take the very best, based on ability. There's much the fellows of the Royal Society of Sorcery and the Advancement of the Mystic Arts would love to do for you, Ropa. We don't ask for anything in return. This is our way. For centuries, we've sought to be the home of the most talented of magicians. It doesn't matter who you are or where you're from. If you show promise and are willing to work hard, you'll find a home in English magic. I know you're self-taught. Look how they sneer at you out there. We can give you the pick of any school of magic within England. You'd advance so much faster with access to the finest instructors, leading experts in their fields. Tuition, no problem. How about a bursary? You need help looking after your grandmother and sister – fine, how about a house and a small stipend to help you along?'

My head's spinning. This is everything I've ever dreamt of. I could become a real, actual magician, not just a ghos-talker.

'We'd also ensure your grandmother has access to the finest medical care in the world. The king's personal physician happens to be a good friend of mine. It's not that hard.'

I'm speechless.

Am I dreaming?

This isn't at all what I was expecting when I came down here. I want this more than anything, but how can I leave Sir Callander in the lurch? He's not perfect, but the man did save me from being hung by the neck until I expired, once upon a time. And there's this whole scroll–murder case thing I'm yet to crack. Could I leave all that behind? Leave the slum and make my way down south? I need to get healthcare for Gran, too. She doesn't moan much, but she's falling apart. It's been stressing me out for yonks and Samarasinghe can sort it . . . Tempting. My thigh's jiggling.

'I'm sorry. I can't,' I blurt out eventually.

'Why are you so loyal to them when they clearly don't give a damn about you and yours?' He looks genuinely baffled.

Thing is, Lord Samarasinghe claims this offer's purely charitable, but I know from the streets that there's always strings attached. They might be ones you can see, or worse, those you can't. My pal Nicco cautioned: 'Men will not look at things as they really are, but as they wish them to be, and are ruined.' I'm staring the gift horse right in the gob. I suspect this is how it starts. Before you know it, the raven's asking you to help out with a bit of information. You're dependent on him, so you've got no choice. One little favour soon turns into a velvet collar round your neck. No, I've got to nuke this thing, else I'll be tempted. I get up off my bar stool abruptly.

'I met an English magician once in Edinburgh. Went by the moniker Tom Mounsey. It didn't end well for him. Goodnight, Lord Samarasinghe.'

He chuckles and turns his attention away from me. Then he snaps his fingers and the fire starts up again. That's me dismissed. I walk across the carpet with a heavy heart. I've gone and blown the opportunity of a lifetime and feel sick to the pit of my stomach. The coachman opens the door, steps out of my way, and I leave.

Once again, I find myself on the outside looking in. And I'm still none the wiser about that slippery Englishman's involvement in this case, or what he might have planned for Callander.

XXIII

Right, next stop the MacDonalds then. I hope they're serving burgers and fries. Sigh. It's late and I'm in turmoil. If I don't find something else to do before bed, I'll be rushing back on my hands and knees to Samarasinghe to tell him I've changed my mind. This must be what martyrdom feels like. I dare say, it feels good to say no to one's betters . . . even if it means cutting off my own nose.

There's a strange peacefulness about the bubble tonight. Through the smoke, the sky has a greenish, limeish hue. Awesome colours filtering through the invisible barrier. That's the aurora borealis out there.

Takes my breath away, how it reflects on the black water.

This weird island has a trick or two up its sleeve. An ancient, savage beauty that surprises you. This aurora's the icing on the cake. I hope Izwi's seeing it too, wherever she is. I check my phone, but still no messages.

Ah well, let me take this picture. I'll foreground the castle and see how that comes out.

Approaching footsteps disturb me.

'Amazing, isn't it?' Jomo says. 'The Merry Dancers, some call it. It's supposed to be fallen angels or sky warriors doing battle up in heaven. Sneddon told me it's that. He was hoping we'd get to see it during the conference. The funny thing is that if he'd not been – you know – we'd have left the next morning and missed this. Now I get to see it without him.'

'Maybe it's merely charged particles from the sun striking the Earth's atmosphere and releasing photons,' Lewis replies.

'Which do you prefer?' I ask.

'They're both true. It's just a question of perspective. Photons if you want to be scientific. Fallen angels if you believe in magic. There's a bit of both in all of us,' says Lewis, and I decide he may just be a romantic.

'Could be the mint milkshake from Jasper's,' Jomo says with a laugh. He stops when a figure emerges from the dark, clerical robes flowing behind. It's Kebede.

Tonight he's also got an elaborate gold cross dangling from his neck. It has a solid cross set within, bound by a second made of latticed wire, then a third cross outside it like a halo. Obviously it represents the holy trinity. Kebede's all grim as he approaches.

'I've never seen anything like it,' he says, looking up. 'When you come from an arid village as I do, green is a sacred colour. Surely this is a good omen for things to come.'

'I can't read the sky like that.' No augury for me, it's not going to get us where we need to be. But tomorrow will be a different night with the full moon out, like Fenella said.

'How's the Grand Debtera?' Jomo asks.

'You're the boy who lost the scroll,' Kebede points out with contempt.

'I'm sorry—'

'Hey, you don't have anything to apologize for, Jomo.' I eyeball Kebede. 'We're all on the same side here.'

He holds my gaze. I'm like, okay then, I can go for ages . . . It's getting a bit silly by the time he eventually turns away, kissing his teeth.

'Lewis and Jomo, what have you got for us?' I ask.

'So, as I said before, the dirk was taken from the MacLeods' armoury definitely,' says Jomo. 'It belonged to the twenty-second clan chief, Norman MacLeod, also known as "The Wicked Man". A real nasty character, he kidnapped a hundred of his own people and tried to sell them off in the Americas as indentured servants in the eighteenth century, because he was heavily in debt at the time. Human trafficking and, get this, all he had to do was trump up charges that they were criminals to get away with it. Ironically, they called the vessel he put them on "The Ship of the People", as though he was doing them a favour or something. Norman MacLeod was their chief, oathbound to protect them, and all he was interested in was lining his own pockets.'

I can't help but think of the current chief of this clan who also finds himself in a financial pickle. 'The Wicked Man' – could this point towards 'the Black Lord'?

'But the lock was broken, which means it could have been anyone,' Lewis adds.

I immediately think of the MacDonalds again. They more than anyone else here have an incentive to mess with Clan MacLeod. Using the dirk to tie in the MacLeods is a very clumsy move, though. I really need to have a word with them now, see what they have to say for themselves.

'Was the lock broken using physical force or magic?' I ask.

'Magic. The break is too neat to have been forced manually,' Lewis replies.

'We are looking for a group with two, maybe three lowlanders and two islanders. That's all I know for now, but when you're on the go next, look out for folks that may be hanging out in that configuration.'

'In this haystack?' Lewis quips.

'The Grand Debtera grows impatient. I have been asking people questions and I find you Scottish magicians to be most unhelpful. Maybe "evasive" might be a better way to express it,' Kebede says, frowning. The stress on his face is evident and no amount of stoicism can hide it.

After all the things Kebede told me, I can totally understand why he's suspicious. There's a lot riding on this. How do they go back home having lost something so precious? I'll need to give them something, but in the meantime, hanging around here is getting us nowhere.

'We need more eyes and ears on this thing. I could ask the lads to help,' Lewis says.

'No,' I snap, more sharply than I intended.

'Maybe someone else can help, Ropa,' Jomo says timidly.

'Everyone is a suspect. Kebede, I'll make a progress report to the Grand Debtera in the morning. Jomo and Lewis, ears pricked, eyes sharp, find me a group that fits this profile. It's our best bet.'

Kebede drifts off without a response and I'm not digging his mood. After the threat his boss made to rip apart the castle, the last thing we can afford is to get them angrier.

Lewis heads off straight away, but Jomo lingers for a bit. I know he wants to tag along, but after his traumatic experience I'd rather have him on the bench. My hand throbs and I flex it.

Jomo gets it at last and weakly punches my shoulder before wandering off too, back to the castle. I go the opposite way, looping round the spooky Walled Garden to get to the Gardener's Cottage at the back. In the light of the aurora, it's plain to see this place is badly in need of repair. The slate roof is overgrown with weeds, the guttering rusted out. A plastic sheet covers a broken window. But even with a leaky roof, the shield above protects it from the elements.

It sits in a secluded spot surrounded by tall trees, their branches hanging over the ruined roof. This place needs a lot of TLC. I can't believe they put up anyone here, until I remember it's the Maccy Dees.

Cockburn clearly took care to place them as far from the castle as she could. I don't even want to know how that went down with this prickly clan. Still, the alternative was sleeping on the floor in the hallway of their rival's castle, or staying in the tents of the market sellers in the Round Garden, as some have been forced to do.

I knock on the door.

'Jesus Christ. Do you even know what time it is?' Dalziel shouts from inside.

'I'm glad you're awake. I need to see you for a minute,' I reply.

There's the sound of movement inside. It takes a wee while until he opens the door, then he steps out and shuts it behind him. Doesn't invite me in. Fair enough. There's no room left in the inn, Cockburn's got the place packed. Dalziel and his sons share the living room while Featherstone's got the main bedroom. The head of the Glasgow school's also staying here. It makes me bristle about the space Lord Samarasinghe's enjoying all to himself.

Dalziel gives off the vibe of clanging steel, chain mail and unsavoury medieval badassery.

'What do you want?'

'I heard you lot and the MacLeods don't get on.' Gruff men like him appreciate forthrightness.

'Is that what you came here for at two in the morning? Did Edmund set you up to this? He's not satisfied with insulting us by putting us up in this shack. No, he always has to go one better. You tell him, *by sea and land*, we'll remember this and get our own back.'

Don't know why he's bringing his clan motto into it. The sea and land have nothing to do with the sleeping arrangements. It's the story of these folk, petty vendetta after petty vendetta, rolling on through the centuries. It's insane and inane. And they don't seem to get tired of it. Gotta check my prejudices while I'm here. There've always been two Scotlands. Down in the lowlands, where Scots was spoken – the mercantile, 'civilized' ones. Up here it's the wild, wild west, Gaelic speakers with their clans and chiefs. They were raiding each other's cattle and doing savage stuff up here since way back when. Two different worlds. That history colours everything up to this day if you're not careful. It can blind you to what you really need to see. But I'm after facts.

'Can I take a look around?' Late at night, that would surprise them.

'If you were a man, I'd break your jaw with this fist for that affront.' Dalziel holds his big paw up in my face. 'My sons and I are honest men, like those of our clan. Were this conference held at Armadale Castle, as we've suggested in the past, we'd have ensured proper security, unlike these inept MacLeods.'

'I don't think anyone wants to do a conference in ruins, even if they have some historical value. Wouldn't be practical,' I reply.

'That's your second strike. Lass or no, I won't bear a third.'

'Surely you understand the optics here. I don't care about the games between the MacDonalds and the MacLeods, but everything going on here's put the Society in a bind. It's highly convenient that you and Avery were the first people to reach Mr Sneddon and Jomo after the attack. It was dark, so we don't know what you did before that.'

'We were nearest the exit, and we did what any person with an ounce of decency would do, which is try to assist.' He's shaking with rage, literally growling at this point. 'Do you know why I haven't slept? Have you flipped that question round and tried to look at it from the other side? It's not a mistake we've been stuck in a secluded part of the grounds where anyone can get to us easily. We're taking turns to watch because MacLeod wants to start a war.'

'And why would he do that?'

'Because he's broke. Strip away the shroud and all you'll see's a corpse wearing perfume. The MacLeods are done.

They've got no money, and without that you lose power and influence. So, he's hatched up a scheme to get it the old way. Looting and plundering. That's what they're really about. They've long eyed our well-managed estates and the wealth of the Clan MacDonald. All they needed was an excuse to start a war with us and we've walked into their trap. Lavvy heids, the lot of them. We're not going to take this lying down.'

I knew the folks in these parts were backward and did things old school, but this is insane. What Dalziel's saying about the condition of the estate is true, though. But is that why the MacDonalds chose to come back to the conference this year, after so long? They sensed vulnerability in their rival and came to undermine his position as its traditional host? And if Edmund MacLeod really wanted to start something with this lot, why did he try to pin things on Murdo, one of his own? Unless that was a feint. It'd buy him cover, make it look like he wasn't interested in setting them up, before he then made his move. Or maybe this is just Dalziel MacDonald deflecting to cover his own arse.

These people are driving me doolally.

'Never you mind, lassie. I'll have it out with MacLeod in the morning, man to man, in front of everyone. They'll see the MacDonalds are not to be trifled with.' Dalziel growls so low a shudder passes through me.

'What do you mean by that?'

'You'll see. We'll show you all.'

XXIV

I barely got a wink last night, but I've caught the worm and the early bird's going hungry tonight. We've skipped over bodies laid down on the floor to get out of the castle. The place is musty, smells of stale farts, sweat and morning breath. I couldn't brush my teeth this morning 'cause there ain't no running water in the taps. And there I was moaning about how wet and miserable this place was. It's gonna be a big problem for Cockburn when these people wake up demanding hydration.

Priya's proper cheery, ray of sunshine that she is. She's wheeling herself backwards as we go up the drive, then swivels and asks me to help her through the muddy woods. We head up through them to the Keeper's Cottage to see Callander.

'So, what did Lord Samarasinghe want with you then?' she asks.

'He said he wanted to offer his support with the case. Nothing concrete.' I don't tell her about the actual offer he made me. I feel sick just thinking about it.

'The *case* – look at you sounding all professional.' She laughs.

'Do you have another name for it then?' I shoot back.

'You've got me there.'

'I prefer investigation! It's more dramatic.'

We laugh our heads off. At least she's not prodding for more stuff about Lord Samarasinghe. Lies of omission are still awkward with your pals, though. And thinking about that offer's super-bugging me. Like when a tune won't stop playing in your head, but you can't even remember the name of it. So annoying.

It's clammy this morning.

A haze hangs in the woods. I'm not sure if it's just a morning thing or because of the Newton Barrier. Samarasinghe's fire last night couldn't have helped much. I'm feeling warm, but I ain't about to take off my gran's bulletproof coat any time soon. It's an astonishing piece of kit, come to think of it. I wonder why Gran needed it in the first place. Maybe she was tinker tailoring back in her prime. Ha, bollocks. Not Gran, that ain't her style. She just likes knitting in peace, watching crime dramas.

My itchy feet are driving me up the wall right now. It's awful.

'I swear if Callander doesn't turn on the air-con, I'm so done with this,' Priya says as we walk through the wooden gate separating the cottage from the castle gardens.

There's birds singing in the woods. I guess they're stuck in here with us. Their song . . .

No.

The world narrows in front of me. No. No. Not again. Curtains draw closed. Leaving me shut in.

'Hey, you alright? Ropa? Ropa?'

Yahweh. My heart. I clench my chest. Can't feel my hands. I'm having a heart attack. I don't wanna die. Don't wanna die. My ticker. No. Please. It hurts. I can't breathe. I can't breathe. I can't breathe. I can't I can't I can't I can't I can't I can't I can't I can't I can't I can't I can't. Breathe. Oh my God. I drop to my knees. My heart's going to burst. I'm dying. Nooo.

Help. Priya.

I can't speak.

She puts her hand on my back and strokes me.

'Breathe in through the nose and out through the mouth,' she says. Priya breathes in and out slowly, demonstrating. I can feel her breath against my skin.

I can't.

'It's okay. I'm right here. Let's slow down for a bit and just breathe. That's it, in through the nose, exhale through your mouth. Everything's going to be fine.'

I'm trying to . . .

So afraid.

What if this never ends and I'm stuck in here forever?

'You're doing great, Ropa. I'm here for you.'

My heart. Lemme just. Breathe. I concentrate on my breathing. In through the nose. Out through the mouth. I can breathe again. I'm fine. My heart. Wow. That's intense. Priya's moving her hand across my back and neck and arms.

I need a moment. It's all good.

Oh man. Proper nippler, that.

'There you go. Nice and easy. Let me work on your aura,' Priya says.

Christ almighty.

At least I've got air in my lungs now. My heart's pumping like I've OD'd on caffeine. Okay. At least it's not trying to break out of my ribcage anymore.

'We'll take our time. There's no rush at all.' Priya's voice is so soothing. It's like being immersed in a warm bath the way it touches me. Oh wow. No idea how long we're at it, but after a wee while I feel much better. Must be her miracle massage too. Although I'm embarrassed by this whole palaver.

'I'm good, pal,' I say. 'That was awkward, innit?'

'You've just had a panic attack, Ropa. But it's okay. I'm here.'

'No, you're wrong. I don't get panic attacks. I was just, you know, funky. Must be tired. I had a late night.'

'We need to get you help for this. It's not the first time, I've seen it happen to you before, hen.'

'Stop, okay. I don't have bloody panic attacks, Priyanka. Geez.'

'It's alright.'

'I had a wobble, that's all. I'm knackered. Now can we get on with it?'

Priya removes her hand from my back and draws away.

'I'm sorry, I didn't mean to snap at you,' I say. Now I'm ashamed I've had an outburst on top of everything. I've got to keep it together.

'Don't worry about me. I've got your back, always. Any time you wanna talk, I'll be right here.' She points her finger and taps my chest, right where my heart is. I feel extra bad. Priya's my girl.

'Thanks. It means a lot to me. Now let's go see the head honchos.' I try to sound lighter, but my voice comes out all odd.

The cottage reeks of cigarette smoke when we enter. Callander's the worse for wear. I've never seen him like this: veins showing under his skin, puffy eyes, all droopy. There's stubble on his chin too. He could drop off at any time. That's what happens when you go for too long without a vacation to Dreamland. Makes me feel like I've not been lifting my side of the yoke, though. The pressure's hitting me bad. All the time I've worked for the gaffer, he's given me a long leash, which is how I like it, but right now I'm wishing it wasn't on me. I'm new to this, but things must be *really* fucked up in Scottish magic to think he trusts me more than these practitioners he's known for yonks.

Esfandiar's fretting about him.

'Do you want another coffee, my love?'

'In a minute,' Callander replies with tenderness. The gaffer can be gruff, but he's proper loved up with his beau. This is the sweetest I've ever seen him. Cute, considering the circumstances.

'Priya, darling, I've been meaning to ask. Since this situation is dragging on, would it be possible to get some kind of stimulant to help Ian stay awake? It's awfully stressful with him holding this dreadful spell up. Look at him!'

'If you want a healer's advice, not sleeping is bad, especially for a man his age. Can't someone else hold up the barrier for a bit?' Priya replies.

'Few practitioners can wield a spell of this complexity.

There's only one other magician here who's capable of it, but he's not a viable option. We can't risk giving the criminal an out,' Callander says.

'In that case, you're already doing caffeine, which is helpful. Drink plenty of water to stay hydrated. The taps are dry on our side, so if you've got any here, I'd love a glass too. Dark chocolate, if you have any. Apple cider vinegar may help as well. Avoid alcohol and sedatives. Get him outdoors from time to time. Sunlight helps.'

'You don't have to refer to me in the third person. I'm right here, fully compos mentis,' Callander complains. Touchy.

'I was hoping for something a bit stronger. When I was younger we chewed khat to party. It's almost impossible to get ahold of now. Those were the days. We'd rave all night and go to work the next day, fresh as daisies. Perhaps you have something similar in your kit?'

'Sorry, no can do. I'd lose my licence to practise if I did anything like that.'

'Well, I didn't mean . . . He *is* the secretary, so I thought maybe . . .'

'Esfandiar, that's quite enough. The healer is right. You mustn't put her in that position. Not ever. I'm fine, honestly.'

The poet-magician's chastened. I get him, though. Who wouldn't bend the rules out of love? Love for king, country, family, money, a passion. Poor lad just wants to lighten the load for his husband. The powder and rouge do little to mask the worry lines on Esfandiar's face. He takes Callander's hand and pats it. Seeing these two, I realize I made the right call not to bail on the boss. Especially not at a time like this.

The atmosphere in here's a real downer all the same.

The strain of holding this spell together is too taxing. That's the thing about scientific magic, it emerges through your will. That, coupled with your knowledge. If only it was more like the hocus-pocus you see every day on telly. That'd be much easier.

Creaking stairs and footsteps sound. A few moments later, Kebede and the Grand Debtera emerge from upstairs. It was always the plan that the guest of honour should stay with Sir Callander. But I doubt any of them would have thought they'd be quartered together under these circumstances. Gran told me that when she was a little girl growing up in her village in Zimbabwe, they raised chickens for food, and rule number one was, you never put two cocks in the same small coop. They'd peck each other, fighting all the time.

I'm taken aback when the Grand Debtera approaches me and Priya. He then puts his hands on top of our heads and blesses us. I'm not into any of that religious malarkey, but it kinda feels nice. Could do with some divine intervention, the way things are going.

He says something very quietly to me and I have to wait for Kebede's translation.

'You are a traveller into the realms of the dead. I sensed this of you. Death seems to follow you wherever you go, little one. Perhaps this is why events here have occurred the way they have.'

'I don't understand,' I reply.

'*The Book of the Shaded Mysteries of Solomon* deals with the return of spirits travelled beyond the everyThere's hard border.

Such spirits have no business returning to this realm. We must keep it that way. I chose to bring this book because it was revealed to me that your magicians need to learn to keep the darkness at bay. But it seems the turmoil in your system cannot bear it.'

The Grand Debtera looks into my eyes with infinite patience and compassion. But what he's describing is impossible. Only the souls who remain in the everyThere can return to this plane, since it's tied to ours as surely as life is linked to death. Most souls rest there a while. But if they cross over beyond the everyThere they cannot come back. That's what my grandmother taught me. Are there exceptions? Is this why a minion of some geezer who calls himself the Black Lord might want the scroll? A deado actually coming back to life's a bit far-fetched, though. No one ever does that, second coming be damned, and certainly not from the Realms Beyond. The spooks who turn up from the everyThere we can handle with our Authority, as we've always done. I'm going Scooby-Doo on this and will bet that, at the end of the day, when we pull back the white sheet with little holes for eyes, the Black Lord will be one of the magicians gathered here at this conference.

Moments later, Dr Maige comes into the room too. Make that three cocks now. Him and Callander have been crossing swords since I joined the Society. He ensconces himself in the chair furthest away from everyone else – this is a man who prefers abstraction to people. Even his own son. But we've all got flaws, other people's just seem more jarring than one's own.

'Now everyone's here, Ms Moyo, if you'd care to give us

a debrief of your activities. I hope everyone in this room understands nothing we talk about is to be shared with anyone else.'

How to break it down in a meaningful way . . . I'm holding together all these strands, but none of them is secure enough to tie to Sneddon and the scroll in a knot that'll hold. I've got hints it's right there but I'm missing it. I'll have to keep tugging until something gives.

'Before we get into that, there's something I need your help to fix.'

Callander inclines his head.

'I've been to the tower and met the piper. His name is Stephen MacCrimmon and he pissed off the MacLeods centuries ago. They've been holding his soul—'

'Young lady, I'd advise you to stick within the remit of your office,' says Dr Maige. 'Matters concerning the islanders' peculiar customs are not for you to interfere with. They do things differently out here and we have to respect that.'

'I'm a ghostalker and I can't pretend this outrage isn't happening. I don't know how you can either. Set his soul loose.'

'Out of the question.'

'This matter lies outside the *remit* of your office too, Pythagoras,' Sir Callander says.

'I beg to differ. As librarians, we are tasked with arbitration pertaining to disputes within Scottish magic. I'm certain I have a more thorough understanding of the laws, customs and practices of the practitioners in these parts than anyone else in this room.'

Callander ignores him.

'Ms Moyo, thank you for raising this matter. I'll be certain to take it up with the appropriate person and see what, if anything, can be done.'

I was complaining about the heat earlier, but this room's suddenly gone Baltic. Sod that. I begin my debrief, since I've done what I can for now. I can't stand the idea of Stephen enduring more up there. This Newton Barrier's driving folks here mad after just a couple of days; imagine if they had to endure what he is. We'll see . . .

Back to the matter at hand. On one side we've got Euan Cleghorn and the Glasgow librarians. Dr Maige's posture changes when I mention them, especially as I lay out their dispute in detail. He tries to interrupt, disparaging Cleghorn's assertions, but Callander silences him. I make it clear the Weegies have an interest in all this. I also speculate the Edinburgh Library may have made enemies due to their harsh penalties and draconian rules. But that's much fuzzier. I soften this with the fact Sneddon was known to be a nice guy with no evident enemies. I then go through the Murdo mistake. How it's really so unlikely that he's the thief in this scenario. Here I make sure to say that the MacLeod staff's search of the castle grounds turned up nothing either. I'm due to check in with him, and I emphasize that a blanket search of everyone's gear, straight away, might have been more useful. Since this could be an antiquities crime, I've also checked in with the sellers at the Barras. I even get into stuff about the Black Lord and possible links with the Marquess of Linlithgow's library.

'And who is this Black Lord? Is he here?'

'I'm still looking into that. Don't even know if he's a real person, a ghost or what.'

Then I get into some detail about the MacDonalds and their thing vs the MacLeods. Ancient rivalries. Machinations about who gets to be the centre of Scottish magic in these parts. The use of the dirk from the Dunvegan Castle armoury suggests a personal, maybe even emotional, dimension to this crime. I reassure them I'm doing everything possible to put the pieces together. Mostly I regurgitate stuff I've seen from cop shows when they do press conferences. I think I come across pretty well.

'Are there any Eritreans at this conference?' Dr Maige enquires suddenly.

I have no idea what that's about. I've seen the guest lists with nationalities and personal details. There wasn't anyone Eritrean on there.

'We hope you're not seriously trying to shift the blame to our nearest neighbours, with whom we've enjoyed peace for so long,' Kebede says, translating for the Grand Debtera.

'Not at all,' I jump in.

'Then why do I get the sense you're holding something back from us? I thought we were promised openness.'

'There are operational matters only me and Priyanka can know right now. Other stuff is just dead ends I've hit, which would only be a waste of everyone's time.' I give it to him straight. It's best not to further fuel their distrust. If I say more than that, it will make my omissions even more obvious.

The biggie is my suspicions about Lord Samarasinghe.

The matter between English magic and Scottish magic is too sensitive for my liking. I've seen how Callander's desperately tried to avoid conflict with London – he values the independence of Scottish magic above all else. Right now, the last thing we need is for shit to kick off with our big neighbour south of the border. And that's what will happen if we so much as imply a suspicion about the Sorcerer Royal without proof.

When I'm through and done responding to their questions, I ask to have a word with Callander so we can get into this additional dimension in private.

XXV

Frantic banging on the front door. Here we go again. Me and Callander were in the kitchen conferring, and now we're interrupted.

'Hurry, please,' Sinéad shouts desperately. I rush to the door to let her in and she bursts through, pushing past me.

'At the castle. They're fighting. You've got to stop them. Frances Cockburn's tried, claiming she's in charge, but they won't listen to her,' she says, breathless.

Dr Maige jumps up from his seat. It's the fastest I've ever seen him move. But he's slower than Priya, who's made her way out already. The swiftest of us would be Callander, who can use the Hermes' Walk spell, but I'm not sure he can do it and hold up the barrier simultaneously. There's a thunder-clap in the direction of the castle.

I run outside behind Priya. She's now set the Horses of Helios spell whizzing her chair forward like a chariot and I can barely keep up with her, even though I'm busting a gut. After we get through the woods, she brakes, skidding to a halt. We find ourselves on the fringes of a war zone. Drastic entropic shifts. Smoke. Thermal discharges. The acrid scent hits us. Without the wind to blow the smoke away, it's as if we've wandered onto an ancient battlefield saturated with the discharge from cannons and muskets.

Two camps, positioned on opposite sides of the bridge leading to the castle's main entrance, are hurling spells at one another. The noise they make is deafening.

At this end, Dalziel, his sons and a dozen MacDonald supporters are raising hell. Holding the castle with far greater numbers are the MacLeods. But they stand on a narrow section, making it hard for them to take the bridge and spread their strength. If they could, their numerical advantage would count for something. It's proper mental, like. I don't know what to do. Doesn't seem like Priya does either. She's watching in stunned silence. This isn't what I was expecting at a professional conference. The flames of the magicians blaze across all colours of the rainbow and then some. The majority are yellow flamers, but you have your oranges, browns, greens, blues, reds, the full assortment and intermediate tones. The spellcraft on display is ridiculous.

Neutrals watch from the castle windows, some of which are broken from stray shots. From what I can work out, the two factions are mostly Highland magicians. No one from the central belt seems to be involved, and those not from Scotland are keeping well clear.

A gigantic fireball the shape of a hand, hurled from the MacDs, shoots across like a comet, fortunately missing Fenella, who leaps out of the way in time. It crashes into the castle and explodes, leaving a black soot handprint. She returns the favour with a grey horse's head–shaped concussive blast of air that strikes the opposing magician. He's thrown in the air and lands on his backside. Wowzers. I've read of magicians weaving sigils into their spells but never seen it done. It's peacocking of the highest order, and Clifford's against it. They chuck Celtic symbols at one another, a crescent moon, Chinese glyphs, some in the shapes of missiles, mythical creatures, and, bizarrely, a flying butt. It'd be pretty if they weren't trying to off each other.

'What's the play?' Priya asks.

'Wait it out,' I reply. There isn't much else we can do. This one's way over my pay grade. I couldn't even match these learned magicians in their element.

Someone on the MacLeod side attempts a Zeusean thunderbolt, but instead of crossing the bridge to hit the enemy, it leaps sideways, zapping a comrade. The guy twitches around like a rag doll, then goes limp.

The market stallholders watch from across the dried-up burn, and standing beneath the giant oak in the gardens are Lord Samarasinghe and Briggs. They're not doing anything to help. Even from this distance, I can see the smile on Samarasinghe's mug.

Avery and Fenella regard each other from opposite sides like Romeo and Juliet, each stuck on the wrong side of the fence. It doesn't stop them fighting. The only concession is they don't go for one another directly. While I understand this, their willingness to harm each other's clansmen disturbs me. I don't know if this is some weird thing that goes on in these islands or something.

Dr Maige rushes past us, the hem of his vestments swishing this way and that. He boldly walks through the

MacDonald camp, and they don't seem interested in fighting him. Even as the missiles keep flying, both sides are at pains to avoid him as he strides onto the bridge. There's a couple of near misses, including a green thermosphere that flies over his head, but he gets there safely and stands in the middle.

There he holds out his hands, instructing them to stop with the same firmness he showed on the rugby field.

Incredibly, they cease fire.

I've heard it said many times that librarianship is a sacred vocation, but to see these powerful practitioners bend to the will of this one man is astonishing. The question is, how long can he keep them from tearing each other apart?

It's a right old stramash and on both sides lie injured belligerents. Burns and broken limbs. It's awful. Priya rushes down the incline to aid the injured. But I think I'll stay right here for now. Lethington, too, steps out from the safety of the castle to treat the casualties on the MacLeods' side. I can only stand here like a pillock watching. Sin arrives, still panting, and hangs back with me.

'Who won?' she asks.

'We all lost,' I reply.

She gives me a funny look and goes back to rubbernecking.

'This is none of your business, librarian. Stand aside,' Edmund MacLeod says.

'Aye. On that we can at least agree,' MacDonald replies. 'It's our right as men to duel.'

'This isn't a duel, it's a brawl. There are young students here and foreign guests. What happens when your stray thermospheres and concussive blasts injure them? Look at those broken windows. No, gentlemen. The Library is the final arbitrator when it comes to disputes between magicians. You all know this. It's in the code you signed up to. We are no longer in the eighteenth century.'

'This isn't Edinburgh neither. We have our own rules in these parts.'

'I am well aware of that, since it is my duty as head librarian to interpret them. Gentlemen, would it satisfy you if we consulted the Rulebook?' Dr Maige is calm but firm. For once I'm glad he's such a stickler for the rules.

Lord Samarasinghe laughs mockingly as if to show how pathetic we are. I'm embarrassed the Sorcerer Royal should witness Scottish magic in such a state. It's as if we've made the point for him. They've always seen themselves as superior south of the border. But this thing isn't some sport. It's not a joke. Thank goodness for Dr Maige. Splitting hairs over legalistic minutiae seems to have taken the sting out of it. But I'm disturbed to see Euan Cleghorn standing at the window on the first floor watching with his arms folded. He makes no attempt to help Dr Maige. Surely, as a fellow librarian, it was his responsibility to try and stop this too, before we arrived? It seems he left it all for Cockburn to deal with on her own. These cracks in Scottish magic seem pretty messed up to me.

Callander makes his way through the woods at last. He has Esfandiar at his side. The poet's alarmed by all of this and I grab his hand to keep him with me, away from the madness. The secretary proceeds alone, calmly surveying the scene. But I know Callander. His gait is weary, shoulders hunched, which isn't normally him. This is a tired man shuffling. I'm even more worried now. Esfandiar's nerves are getting to me. He locks his arm with mine. I really think it'd have been better if they'd both stayed at the cottage. Signs of weakness could be fatal in this cesspit of vipers.

This is what I'm so desperate to become a part of? The glitter's wearing off for me. Scottish magic ain't what I thought it was.

The MacDonald faction parts to let Sir Callander through. They yell their grievances at him as he goes. He doesn't acknowledge them. Just strolls casually by like it's Sunday. For me, he's Scotland's great battleship. As he takes the bridge, Wedderburn and Hutchinson join him for support. There's levels to this game. You'd be a fool to challenge these three.

'What seems to be the problem?' Callander asks.

'My family has been host to the Society for a century. Now I find myself prevented from exercising discipline against those who insult me in my own home. These MacDonalds have enjoyed my hospitality, yet here they are impugning my good name with all sorts of vile allegations. We still remember Coire Na Creiche.'

There's vocal agreement from the members of MacLeod's party.

'Lies, lies, lies. That's all you lot are good for. We came here seeking peace. Because of your display, we believe now is the time for the Society to heed us. Let the Clan MacDonald take charge. There wouldn't be thieves and murderers crawling about if the conference was hosted by us. And we can afford it too.'

Dalziel's side, though smaller, is much more vocal in its support. Their ayes echo off the Newton Barrier.

'If you both had concerns, why didn't you come to me or speak with Frances Cockburn?' Callander asks. He's like a long-suffering parent dealing with errant kids.

'It sounds to me as if you're holding us equally culpable. That won't stand,' MacLeod says, stepping forward to square up to Callander. 'On top of that, you've got us all imprisoned here. There's no electric, now the water's gone too. My stores of food are nearly run through. If you won't resolve matters the right way, then I think it's time for a new secretary to be decided by duel.' There's gasps of shock all round. Even the partisans on his side weren't expecting that. Edmund MacLeod is throwing his weight about like his first name was Connor from the film *Highlander*. He might be lord of this castle, but he's not Christopher Lambert.

'I'd be very careful with the next words coming out of your mouth if I were you,' Wedderburn says in a chilling tone.

'Rector Wedderburn, stand aside. The rules are clear. Edmund MacLeod is allowed to make his challenge if he so wishes and none may interfere,' Dr Maige says. I now totally hate his sticklerness more than I've ever done.

'This is ridiculous,' Wedderburn says, stepping back all the same. Hutchinson also retreats.

Callander is left face to face with the chief of the Clan MacLeod. Knapf. It seems Gran's two-cock analogy applies everywhere now. This is an explosive situation. MacLeod's assessment of the situation is likely to resonate with tired, thirsty folks, fed up with being held against their will. But if Callander lets down the Newton Barrier and the scroll is lost forever, then we'll have to face Qozmos's wrath. I don't much fancy being drowned under a tsunami like what happened in Portsmouth. All them places buried under the sea.

I should be down there beside Callander right now. But I don't know what good I'd do and I console myself that I get to babysit his husband instead.

You could cut this atmosphere with a knife.

This shit's too heavy.

'Edmund, my dearest friend. It's been a trying time for all of us. I understand that. But we need to *hold fast*, together—' he turns to Dalziel MacDonald '—*by sea and land*, especially when the storm's threatening to tear us apart. There's more that unites us now than has ever divided us in the past. Let's all calm down. I'm certain the principles of desalination are known to the heads of the four schools, who will provide water for all. And while they do that, you, me and Dalziel will sit in the castle library over a cup of tea to resolve these differences. Would this be acceptable?' Callander reaches out and squeezes MacLeod's shoulder, keeping a hand there. All the while he has his eyes on Dalziel.

The neutrals murmur their approval.

This nonsense is getting in the way of my work. I'd be happy to see it quashed. There's plenty enough of the same sentiment here.

'Aye, that makes sense to me,' Dalziel says.

'If that's what you want,' MacLeod replies.

257

Phew.

Esfandiar rests his head on my shoulder, sniffling. His tears moisten my clothes. Callander's put a Band-Aid on this but it won't last for long. I've really got to crack this thing before things spiral completely.

XXVI

If you can keep your head when everyone else is going ape, you deserve an OBE or something. I figure I need to chill. It would do me some good to be in a place I can sit alone and think, try to figure out this mess once and for all. The great thing about the gardens here is there's plenty of space, and Murdo and the staff do a good job maintaining them. The gradual decay of autumn actually complements the run-down state of the castle buildings.

I take the path over the dried-up burn, looping past the waterfall. It's now a rock feature. This bit's called the Water Garden, and it borders the Round Garden where the market is. I'm headed past those to the New Garden, which I've discovered is often empty.

The topography of the garden is the gentle V of a small valley. The burn's down below and the land slopes upwards on either side. From here I can see water from the burn's flooding the road, then streaming towards the town. An insane piece of geoengineering. Unintended consequences have a way of gatecrashing the party. In my experience, that's the one thing you can always guarantee when you bend over to smell the roses with your arse hanging out. The bee coming for the pollen's gonna sting your backside instead.

Threads are gathering in my head and I've been weighing everything. But things have reached boiling point in this cursed castle. I have a move up my sleeve, one that may yet reveal all, but I need to consider my next steps carefully. Thinking first and acting later hasn't always been my forte, but I'm trying.

All around me are holly, pine and bracken.

Moss carpets the ground and climbs up the trees. No grass can grow here 'cause it's too shaded, very little light comes through. Dead leaves carpeting the path squelch under my boots. The air here's fresher than near the castle. It's a relief for me as I find a nook surrounded by bushes with a small opening. There's a wooden bench and I plonk myself down on it. Let me enjoy this solitude for a bit. It feels nice to get away from those magicians and their constant drama. The people at Hermiston Slum complain less than these guys. It's amazing.

I'd give anything for a deep-fried Mars bar right now.

I spot some mushrooms growing in the damp soil. They'll do well with the poor light here. I get off the bench to inspect them. I'm peckish. While the posh folks out there wait to be served, I bet I could feed myself off the earth here if I really wanted to. Maybe when this is over, I can teach the orphans to forage. Kinda like how Gran taught me. We'll see if there's time for that.

Uh-oh. No, thank you very much. That's death cap right there. It's large with a domed white cap and an off-white stem.

Gills underneath. Looks like an innocuous mushroom, but you don't want to try it. It will turn your insides to mush. Poisons the liver and kidneys, circling through the blood to do it over and over. You'll experience the most awful death. Stomach pains, diarrhoea, nausea for hours. And here's the kicker. The symptoms fade away after a day or so. So you think you're going to recover. But that was just the warm-up. Really, your insides are screwed. When round two comes, you're toast – there ain't no antidote for it. Mother Nature can be cruel like that. Nope, no death cap for me. What I'd really like is chicken of the woods, or cep, or hedgehog fungus – that's a good one – or morel, or Gran's favourite, chanterelle. Izwi's a vegan and she loves mushrooms, especially the ones with a meaty taste. I tell her that's because she's a carnivore in denial.

It's nice to think of something else for a mo. If you keep the machine running full revs all the time, it burns out and breaks down.

I close my eyes. Change the channel. Tune in to Zen FM. Nice.

'Sorry, am I disturbing you?'

'I was just resting my eyes,' I reply.

'This is usually my spot. I'm happy to share it with you.'

A woman carrying a laptop bag's come over. She's dressed in heels and a blue velvet suit with a single-button jacket. Hair tied in a ponytail. She walks awkwardly through the mud. Would be better off removing her shoes and going barefoot. I make space for her on the bench.

'Sahra Salat.' She offers her hand for a shake and gives me her business card.

'Ropa Moyo.'

I don't have a card to reciprocate with. I take a bit of time checking hers out. I read it's the polite thing to do. It says she's an associate at MacNally Lennox Blair with an LLM, specializing in magical delict. That means negligence in lawyer speak, I think. Sahra's positively beaming, and under normal circumstances I'd vampire off that vibe. But she's messed up my serious thinking time.

She waves her phone about, looking for a signal, and gives up.

'I feel funny without my phone. My whole life's on it. The office will be wondering why I haven't checked in. Won't matter much when they see the amount of work I bring in. We're going to be absolutely swamped,' Sahra says.

'Sorry.'

'Don't be. I chose this. Sixty hours a week, working my way up to partner. My big break has come at last. Isn't all this wonderful? To get ahead you've got to work hard. Lady Luck does the rest. That's how you wind up in the right place at the right time.' She's the only person I've met who's ecstatic about any of this.

Sahra explains she came to give a talk for newly qualified magical practitioners on registration and the importance of professional indemnity insurance. This is something MLB do at every conference. According to her, the schools are great at teaching the practical aspects of magic, but students seldom graduate with a proper understanding of business and the complex regulatory framework governing their profession.

'Disputes within the profession are easy. The Library

handles that. But if you work with the public, a malpractice lawsuit can devastate your career,' she says.

'I never thought of that. How does one become a magic lawyer?' I ask.

'You have to do magic school, like everyone else, and be registered as a practitioner before going on to complete a law degree on top of that. This is the only branch of law where you have to first have the underlying qualification in your speciality. That's why there's big bucks in it. I don't really practise magic anymore. There's more than enough legal work to keep me occupied.'

'Cool.'

There are moments you need to veg out but a random comes up to you. Sometimes it's whack, others suck you in. Sahra's got that excitement you get when you want to tell someone who doesn't know you that it's your birthday, and you're trying to stick it in there. Must be like that, since she can't speak with her colleagues.

'Everything that's been going on these last few days has been great for me. There's the criminal case, which is the librarian's murder. What was his name again? Never mind. Hope they find whodunnit because that guy will need representation. The victim's family might lodge a civil suit against the Library, the Society and the MacLeods. With a good lawyer they have great odds to win that. The Ethiopians might bring in some business too. But the big fight today – did you see it? – that's the icing on the cake. There's definitely going to be lawsuits in that too . . . Oh, I almost forgot about the stream that's been diverted. There's all sorts of environmental issues there. If it causes damage to life and property in Dunvegan, then that's even more business, potentially. The Society will be facing lawsuits for the next ten years unless it settles. Argh. I can't get a signal. I need my firm to move in, so we can hoover this up before our rivals do.'

Sahra speaks like a machine gun. Speed is essential if you're an ambulance chaser.

'I'm also looking into the legality of the secretary's Newton Barrier. The magicians can seek redress through the Library's arbitration process. But the castle staff have to go through civil court. You don't look like a magician. Seriously, if you want to sue for anything, you've got my card. I'd be more than happy to help. No win, no fee. Oops, how old again? Soliciting a minor's not a good look. Your parents will have to get involved. Give them my card. And don't forget to tell them it's free.'

Bollocks, there's always a cost. Free lunches went the way of the dodo. Seems to me whenever there's a bad situation someone's at hand to make a killing. What an age to be a vulture. The funny thing is that, not so long ago, I'd have been like, 'Get that money, girl.' Now I'm disgusted by it all. Scottish magicians are all so self-serving it makes me sick. I excuse myself from the scheming solicitor and decide it's time to get back to the castle.

As I make my way back there, I spot Fenella and Avery huddled up among the fir trees. The two are sooty and Avery's jacket is torn at the shoulder, but they seem otherwise unharmed from the affray. They look up at me and I smile and wave at them.

XXVII

As soon as I walk into the castle, Cockburn directs me up to Edmund MacLeod's private study on the second floor. As I climb the stairs I keep thinking, if only I'd done better on the night the scroll was taken and managed to catch the thief on the roof, all this could have been prevented. Everything would be kosher. But I was up against someone who'd planned this through. They knew exactly where they were going in these apartments. If it hadn't been for Callander's shield, they'd have got away with it too.

Priya comes with me this time. She's now finished dealing with the casualties of the kerfuffle earlier. It's a miracle no one was killed after all that.

Stressed out here.

Callander can't hold that shield much longer. It doesn't matter who you are, a man needs his kip. Instead of pressuring myself more, though, maybe I need to try the General Kutuzov strategy of letting it play out. Chance may yet turn the wind in our favour. The problem is, by nature I'm more like Napoleon. I want to control the battlefield.

MacLeod's office has a wonderful view of the sea. It's hazy, though, like we're in an alternate reality. There's a flicker of dark light, like black paint, running across the Newton Barrier. That's new. Whatever. This is a very practical office. None of that antique shit downstairs. The desk he sits behind is the product of flat-pack if I've ever seen it. There's paperwork everywhere and notes on the wall. Reports. Calendars. Bills and reminders. Inspection letters. The business side of running and maintaining a castle's not sexy at all.

The room contains a chaise-longue against the wall. The only other chair is the swivel one he sits in behind his desk. MacLeod gets up, goes over to the globe drinks trolley in the corner, near the window, and opens it. There's a mini fridge on the floor beside it.

'Do you ladies want something to drink?' he asks.

'G&T. It's been one hell of a day,' says Priya.

'The same.' I try my luck. She gives me a look.

Glasses clink. He fannies about for a bit and then comes over with our drinks. I notice mine doesn't have any alcohol in it. Just tonic water. Priya ain't complaining so hers must be the real thing. I can battle ghosts and all sorts, but I still can't legally drink. It tells me something about Edmund MacLeod, though. He's the sort of man who won't give underage teens a drink. There's a man of honour. The same trait that pulled him back from duelling Callander.

The tonic's lukewarm, though. Yuck. That's what you get with no electricity. The Dark Ages must have been better than this.

'I believe we got off on the wrong foot, Ms Moyo,' MacLeod says, taking a sip from his glass. 'Fortunately, today is a day of reconciliation. Your mentor and I have settled our differences. The MacDonalds too, for now. I think you and I should too. Scottish magic mustn't be a house divided against itself.'

That last line could have come from Callander himself.

'The last few days have been stressful for everyone,' Priya replies. It's the healer's way to soothe. That's why I adore her.

MacLeod raises his glass.

I wanna jump in but decide to be cool like Kutuzov, let it play out. It's MacLeod's castle, his guests that have been violated, his clan's reputation on the line. His ancestral home faces demolition by the Grand Debtera. He's going through the most. I'd rather bear my own cross than his right now.

'I can't wait for this goddamn thing to be over and have all these people off my property. This whole thing's a nightmare,' he says.

'We're nearly there,' I reply.

He starts pacing back and forth in front of us. One hand's in his pocket. He looks well zonked. It seems Callander's not the only one going without sleep.

'Can I take you ladies into my confidence?'

'That's what we do,' I reply.

'Yep,' says Priya.

He continues his pacing. This must be something he does often, because I notice a line worn away in the carpet, running across from the window opposite to the door. Let him take his time. Folks get spooked if you rush them, best to leave it till they're good and ready. I do this with my little sister sometimes.

'I never wanted to be chief. My elder brother Hugh was

meant for that, but he was killed. It's a thankless task, this. I want to leave it all behind, but I have to press on for the good of Skye.'

'That's tough.'

'You don't know the half of it. I envy young people like you. This island would fall apart if it weren't for what I've done.'

'I've heard rumours you're virtually bankrupt,' I say. 'Your old man didn't leave much behind for you in the first place.'

He bows his head and takes a swig. I'm thinking he needs to take it easy, lift himself out of this funk and help us get some work done. Gran's always told me I should be more compassionate. The problem is I find it much easier to feel for the orphans freezing outside the gate than to be sympathetic to a laird with his own private castle. Boohoo, cry me a river.

'We'd appreciate anything you can give us that might help crack this,' says Priya, who has a better bedside manner than I do.

'Do you believe in curses?' he asks.

'Not really,' I reply.

'I'm fifty-fifty,' Priya hedges.

'There's an old man who lives atop Druim Na Creige, the hill yonder. It's the one with the big rock on top. Have you seen it from the road?'

'Ropa's hiked up there before,' Priya replies, pointing at me with her thumb.

Something called me to that hill a few days before conference started. You get to the kirk beside the road headed for the village, and a circular walk starts from there that's supposed to take you all the way round, up and over the hill.

It was an eerie feeling walking through the pines that grow at the base of the hill. Skye doesn't have too many trees on it, but in the dim, cool shade, I noticed memorials nailed to the trees. They had the names of loved ones who'd been lost. It was touching and unsettling too. Strange poetry was also glued to the trees about the Fae who'd once ruled this island. Offerings made of seashells and painted rocks. The island has had newcomers throughout the ages: the MacLeods are descendants of the Vikings, dating back to the thirteenth century. But there were those who lived here before that. Gaelic-speaking Scots. Men who fought alongside the Fae. Morag told me the descendants of the Gaelic speakers remember what the Norse did to the immortals. And they tell a different story of the Fae. One of harmony and brother-hood that was broken by the conquerors.

I pressed on up, drawn by something feeding off the vestiges of the old powers of the hill. It's that feeling of being hailed by a whisper. It gets louder as you approach and fades if you move in the wrong direction. You can choose to answer or ignore the call.

It was peaceful walking between the near-bare trees which had shed their needles to carpet the path. Their branches seemed to reach out. These are places dangling on the vesti-bule of elsewhere.

A lone sparrowhawk circled above as I reached the summit.

In the distance I heard a ringing bell.

There were no trees up top, only the golden, purple and

green rolling landscapes of grass and shrub. The sun battling to come through the clouds in this preternatural dusk. Old pylons, with cables dangling, ran alongside the path. I'd fallen inside of a picture. Perfect. The rocks embedded in the ground had straight cracks. Freeze and thaw.

I was pulled to the Duirnish Stone standing bent like a man bowing. In the scattered yellow light, it seemed other-worldly. I made my way to the stone and looked down below to see the village of Dunvegan, white houses running along the salt loch. Hills beyond.

I say to MacLeod, 'I heard there was a bum who lives atop this hill who rings his bell every evening and spits at the ruins of St Mary's.'

It's a sensitive issue, because the abandoned church's grave-yard is where a lot of prominent MacLeods are buried. I daren't visit 'cause of all the old ghosts lurking. It can be pretty distressing to see them in their hideous shapes.

'We were taught never to go up there as children. They scared us with rumours of a monster that would cut your heart out. But I went there to seek answers this summer. I could not sleep, and I was troubled. I met a vagrant who offered me bread and water, and he reminded me of the curse of the MacLeods. We won the war against the brounies, but we didn't completely get rid of the problem. This man warned me that after we'd bested the Fae, the Fairy King cursed our bloodline as vengeance and we'd be reaping of that soon,' Edmund MacLeod explains.

'That's a right nippler,' Priya replies.

'It's foretold our clan will fall, and I fear if we don't resolve whatever is happening now, this might be the beginning of the end. Why else would the MacDonalds re-emerge from the cesspit as they have now? They are up to something, and it's all connected to the theft of that scroll, I'm sure of it.'

There they go again, casting aspersions on one another. Proofs be damned.

'All doom based on the ravings of a bum living atop a hill?' I say. It's got to be some old wives' tale that's been handed down for generations. But it occurs to me that MacLeod's talk of the Fairy King's curse is pretty damned similar to what Adamina told me.

'It was not his own gift. The radiance of the Duirnish Stone allows him glimpses of what's to come and what was. Knowledge of this curse was hitherto only known to us. This was a warning given him for a reason.'

I get why he's so wired. Scientific magic doesn't believe in curses and hexes; those are vestiges of the age of superstition. On this isle, though, the old ways may be suppressed, but they can't be erased. They linger in the twilight. Touch wood. Black cats. Four-leaf clovers. Broken mirrors. White rabbits. Spilt salt. Meeting two or three ravens. They creep along the edges, never quite coming into the light. Only a man keeping a nest of angry Fae in his tower might understand these things.

We're all trapped by history. Choices made aeons ago reverberate today. These are the currents that buffet us as we paddle the river of time. And MacLeod has his own family curse to account for, on the poor piper.

'If we fall, Skye falls with us. We've been lords of these

islands since our forefathers sailed here and settled. Do you understand this?'

These descendants of Leòd – Morag had tried to teach me some of their history. Of how they traced their line from the Norsemen who used to raid these shores. How they came and conquered. Now yours truly has to help break this ancient curse, which I don't even believe in. If Gran was here, she'd know what to do. But I can't even call her for advice. I still think it's a load of bollocks, but I spot an opportunity to get something I want out of this. It means taking advantage of MacLeod's fears. He's spooked enough to be a sucker. Sometimes that's the right thing to do.

'I need a favour from you,' I say, standing and walking over to him.

'Only if I know you're on my side in all this. For some reason you have the secretary's favour, and I need to know that, alongside the Society's interests, you're looking after those of Clan MacLeod in the work you're doing on his behalf.'

Priya frowns and shakes her head, asking me not to.

'Your piper in the tower, Stephen MacCrimmon, angered his chief and was punished for it in life. They handled things differently then. When it came to matters of honour, they were hardcore. I have no qualms with what they did to him when he was living, but now he's dead, centuries later, I think it's time to let him rest. Release his ghost. Allow him to go to the halls of his forefathers. If you do this, I'll scratch your back.'

I hold out my hand and Edmund MacLeod takes it, gripping me with both hands.

'I, Chief of the Clan MacLeod, defender of Dunvegan Castle, consider Stephen MacCrimmon's just punishment served and set him free,' he says.

There's a mini tremor. I hear the sound of chains hitting the floor and the castle seems to flex then sigh. It's done.

XXVIII

There's a knock on the door and Edmund MacLeod lets go of my hand. Paudric, one of the castle staff, comes in looking very excited. He gives me and Priya a quick nod of acknowledgement.

'Sir, the scroll. The box containing the scroll has been found on the grounds.'

'Where exactly?'

'In the bracken opposite the archway under the bridge.'

'I'm on my way.' I can't help but smile.

Finally, some good news. Kutuzov's patience is paying off, things are coming to me. Chance is the sleuth's friend after all. You just don't want to play your whole hand counting on her alone. Right now, I'll take what she's thrown our way.

Priya's ahead of me on the way out.

If the box has been found, someone's gotten sloppy. More likely, they're getting cold feet. There has to be some way of using this to our advantage. The scroll itself is valuable because of its ancient history and secrets about the Realms Beyond. But the information would have been made available to Scottish magicians eventually. And if it was that information the thief truly valued, then by now they've had a fair chance to take photos. They'd have whatever incantations it may contain, so they can now get rid of it. But if this is an antiquities heist, then they'd need to move the scroll intact, box and all.

So what do they think to gain by getting rid of the box? That's the thing that's bothering me. It could be misdirection. The lowest form of magic. To what end? Buying time? Make folks look one way while you go the other.

We encounter Jomo in the corridor on the first floor. He rushes to us, a hopeful look on his face. His dad's giving him the frozen pork shoulder joint, but this might be his way back in.

'I've been looking everywhere for you guys. Did you hear the good news?'

'That's where we're headed right now,' Priya replies.

Seems like word's got out and everyone knows already. That's what happens when folks have nothing better to do. It also means whoever's behind all this gets a steady stream of information. Feedback about what they've done. If this is a mistake, they'll be covering their tracks already.

Oh no.

Not again.

I feel the pressure rising.

I dash down the stairs to the ground floor, through the door on the left and into the corridor. There's an open utility room, so I get in and lock the door. I don't want anyone seeing me. This thing's overwhelming. Dread like it's the end of the world. My heart. How many times must I die? The room, everything comes crushing in on me. I'm on the floor, my head near a red mop bucket.

Breathe.

Just like Priya taught you.

In through the nose.

Out through the mouth.

My bloody ribcage. I wanna tear it off. Tingling hands. I lie back and try to take off my jacket. Barely wriggle out of it. I pull my T-shirt off over my head. Passing it over my mouth and nose is a harrowing ordeal. I push up with my legs, trying to stop myself from being crushed.

'Ropa, open this door right now. Let me in,' Priya says.

I need to breathe. That's all. My ticker's about to explode like it's Guy Fawkes Night. Oh God. It's too hot. The air's so humid. It's like I'm inhaling lava. A dark cloud of irrepressible dread shrouds me. There's no way out. This is how it's going to be from now on. Forever. Please make it stop. Please . . .

I can't tell how long I'm on that floor for. Eventually something happens. The slow lifting of a hydraulic press. The darkness overwhelming me lifts and I just feel light-headed.

I slowly get up off the floor. I discover I must have been crying and wipe the tears off my cheeks, then take a deep breath and pause. I feel grateful this thing's done now, but I'm going to have to take care of this. Something's changed inside of me, I used to be able to grind through anything like I was Mr Fantastic.

This is pathetic.

I'm weak.

It isn't supposed to happen to someone like me. I close my eyes and rest my head against the door. Priya's gently knocking, but I can't let her in. How do I fix this? I can't afford to keep breaking down, or for it to happen out there, in front of everyone. At least this time I sort of anticipated it was coming. It's one thing not to be able to control circumstances, that's the story of my life, but if I can't have mastery over myself, I'm done.

I get my phone, turn on the torch and use the selfie camera to check my face. Then I get dressed, straighten myself out and grab my gear. Game face on. Let's do this. I open the door and walk out.

'What's going on?' Jomo asks.

'There was something I had to check on.'

'In there?'

Priya gives me a sharp look but says nothing. She knows my secret, and that I can't be dealing with it right now.

'Let's go, guys,' I say, leading the way.

We head back into the entrance hall, past gossiping attendees and out the main door.

'God save the king,' someone says as we pass.

'Long may he reign,' we reply.

Down the stairs and out into the open. A smog hangs in the air, like the Clean Air Act was never a thing. I feel sorry for any asthmatics right now. We cross the bridge and bear left. Past the block of outdoor toilets, all the way down the footpath, till we loop right. This leads us to the archway under the bridge.

Cockburn, Wedderburn and the Edinburgh boys are here. So is Edmund MacLeod. He got here before us 'cause of my little detour. You have Octavius Diderot, who works at the

Society. We've never spoken much. Mary Hanley, an ordinary member of the Society. Kebede and the Grand Debtera. Abdul and Aurora from the Hamster Squad. Also watching from up on the bridge are Hamish Hutchinson, Lord Samarasinghe, Briggs and a few other honchos.

'You show no sign of urgency,' Cockburn says. 'We expect you to take this more seriously.'

'I needed a bathroom break if that's fine with you,' I reply.

'Go look then.'

'Who found the box?' I enquire.

'Nathair Walsh. Sterling work,' Wedderburn replies.

I take the box from him, looking at him suspiciously, and inspect it. There's marks on the wood. Wear to be expected given its age. It's open and empty, but not in the fancy way Qozmos did it. It looks a lot more ordinary without the glow. But I suspect that was more of the Grand Debtera's special effects rather than anything the box can do.

'Where exactly did you find this?'

Walsh points to a spot in the bracken. I check it out. A few holes in the lawn there, like someone wearing heels came this way. Cockburn and Hanley are both in heels, which means I don't know if it was them or someone else.

'Did the castle staff inspect this area?'

'Aye, we did.'

'And you missed this box placed there so obviously.'

''Twas early morning when we checked. The lighting was different.'

'You didn't look hard enough, that's what it is,' MacLeod spits.

The staff know these grounds better than anyone else. They'll have scoured every nook and cranny. It's rather strange the box should only be found now. And by Walsh.

'What were you boys doing here?' I ask. There's nothing remarkable about this spot.

'We got bored. There's nothing to do, so we decided to poke around,' Nathair Walsh replies. With his dominie Wedderburn here, he's being a lot more polite than usual.

Still, this bunch of posh twats? The same ones that fingered Murdo. Lewis avoids making eye contact. Obviously lost some cred with the others because of me. I'm to believe they decided to do the menial task of tramping about in search of the scroll, when those searches had already been done? And then they happened to find the box straight away? I weigh the different options. Everything they're saying might be true. When it comes to them, I've got a chip on my shoulder you could hit the Vegas jackpot with. If I'm not honest about myself and my motivations, that only serves to cloud my judgement. It doesn't get the job done. And it does have to be pretty boring for them hanging around in here. Here's all of us milling about. Checking bushes and looking inside an empty box.

The Newton Barrier strobes an ominous black. There's a loud crack and the top of a tree high up in the woods comes tumbling down.

'Goddamn Callander. He's gonna chop someone's head off by mistake if he can't keep that damned force field of his stable. It's been pulsating too,' says Hanley. 'He should let it go, this is dangerous.'

Callander's weakening with every moment. You can't drive and nod off at the same time.

'What are you going to do now?' Cockburn asks.

It feels like I'm standing upon a trap door. Callander's no longer managing his force field properly. Dealing with events this morning can't have helped with his strength either. It's probably left him even more exhausted. He's not in full control anymore, and I can feel everyone's dissatisfaction lasered on me like a dozen sniper rifles.

'I'll continue with this investigation.' I offer a neutral reply. 'We're nearly there now.' I try to give some reassurance.

'More of the same then.'

'These schoolboys have turned up a lot more than you have and it's not even their problem.'

'Callander's girl doesn't inspire confidence.'

'Something needs to be done.'

'It bloody well should have been right at the start of this whole affair.'

'Please give Ropa Moyo a little more time,' Wedderburn says. 'She's working very hard, and I trust in the faith Sir Ian Callander has invested in her. If we, perhaps, grant her the opportunity to allay these legitimate fears, we might all rest easier tonight.'

I hold my breath. Any one of these people could be behind this thing. I can't go feeding them any more information than they already have.

'I only answer to Sir Callander,' I say.

There's a collective groan. I've put my foot in it now.

'There we have it. Zero accountability,' Hanley says.

'Are you sure about this?' Cockburn asks. 'All we're asking for is something to allay our concerns. Proof you're actually getting somewhere with this.'

Cockburn looks up at the bridge to Hamish Hutchinson, who signals with a nod.

'I'm sorry, Ropa. We are calling for an emergency meeting of the Extraordinary Committee in the Dunvegan Castle library in five minutes' time. There you must appear and give a satisfactory account. The Committee will then make a determination on how this investigation will proceed. Failure to appear when summoned by the Committee will result in dismissal, and with that the end of your ability to conduct business for the Society within the umbrella of the General Discoveries Directorate. Is this clear?'

Priya's stiffened up, otherwise her jaw would be on the floor. I'm being railroaded. I don't know nothing about the Extraordinary Committee. They've given me no time to confer with Sir Callander either.

XXIX

Priya's barred at the door of the library. The whole thing's supposed to be 'confidential'. So it's just me standing on my own in the middle of the room. You've got Cockburn, Wedderburn, Hamish Hutchinson, Octavius Diderot, Mary Hanley, Lady Rethabile Lebusa and Dr Maige in the room. They are sat around me in a semi-circle. I'm proper anxious, like. I hope I don't break down again.

Keep it together, Ropa.

At the back of the room, you've got Lord Samarasinghe, Edmund MacLeod and Kebede. They've got heavies here, but I can't have my mentor. No wonder my pal Nicco taught me politics have no relation to morals. Hatred is gained as much by doing good works as by evil. I've been on the streets long enough not to be surprised by this shit. You learn to differentiate between the kind that sticks to the soles of your boots and the kind that doesn't.

All the same, you're bound to step into a steaming pile sooner or later.

'Has anyone explained to you what the Extraordinary Committee does?' Dr Maige asks.

'I don't even know why I'm here. I've got stuff to do.'

'I'll take that as a no,' he says. 'I am not part of the Committee, but as head librarian it is my job to know the standing rules. I'm here to ensure everything that happens is above board. In the event of the secretary being incapacitated, the Extraordinary Committee convenes to assess and, if necessary, assume his powers for a limited period.'

'Sir Callander is still very much "in capacity",' I reply.

'Allow me to finish. The Committee also plays the role of checking the secretary's power. It is only ever convened in extraordinary circumstances. It comprises the head of the Edinburgh School, plus one of the other three schools, who hold the post in rotation. This year it's St Andrews' turn. Frances Cockburn you already know. Lady Lebusa and Mr Diderot are board members of the Society as well. Mary Hanley is an ordinary member of the Society who's drawn by lottery, serving for five years. This is to ensure ordinary members have a voice in the decision-making process. The Committee has informed you they wish to hold a hearing on your investigation.'

'Then what are these other guys doing in here?'

'Observing. It is the right of the Committee to invite any observer it sees fit.'

I can understand Kebede and MacLeod being here, they've got skin in the game. Samarasinghe? Someone's done the exact thing Callander's been trying to avoid. They've brought the Sorcerer Royal into the heart of Society business. I recall Wedderburn and Hutchinson leaving his cottage last night. That's the plug right there.

'If this is a hearing, then am I not entitled to an advocate?'

'This is different from the Library. You don't have that right here.'

'We are here to help you,' Lady Lebusa says.

I have to stop myself from laughing. This lot here to help me? Cockburn doesn't even want me in this organization. Mr Diderot has not once said hi to me in the corridors of the Society HQ at Dundas House. Wedderburn's alright by virtue of being Callander's mate, but he's just one man. Hutchinson and me don't get on. I don't know where the rest stand, but look at me vs them in their designer gear, with their diamonds and Vacheron Constantins.

I shove my hands in my pockets and chill. I'm less anxious now I've got an idea where this train's headed. These vultures wouldn't dare if Callander was here. His colleagues are making a move on him at last.

'What's supposed to happen now?' I say.

'I'll hand over to the chair and the meeting shall begin in earnest,' Dr Maige replies.

All I've ever wanted was to be part of the Society. But when you're inside it, a part of it, man, does that sheen fade so fast. Here we are in this old library, surrounded by Old World trappings. We're supposed to be solving a problem. What's actually happening's power play, 'cause X wants to shaft Y. To think I gave up being my own boss for this.

'Ropa, I need to make it clear that we are on your side,' Rector Wedderburn says gently.

I've had enough run-ins with the fuzz to take such statements with a pinch of salt. But he is one of the nicer ones and I know he's on Callander's side. So I give him a nod and hope anyway.

'Everyone in this room is vetted and highly trusted,' Diderot says. 'You are part of the Society now. We should all be working together to resolve this situation.'

'It's not your fault, Ropa. You're far too young for the responsibilities the secretary has put on your plate,' Lady Lebusa says. She has high cheekbones and gives me the vibe of a python, slowly encircling to crush you.

'Good. We've established everyone is working together,' says Cockburn. 'Perhaps now you can tell us what you've unearthed in your investigation so far.'

They used to draw and quarter people on these isles. Tie their limbs to four horses and smack them, sending the horses galloping in different directions till you were torn apart. Cruel and unusual punishment. That's what this lot have in store for me.

'Speak up, so we can hear you,' Diderot says.

'I already told you people: I only answer to Sir Callander.'

'Come now—'

'Is the General Discoveries Directorate, which I work for, independent or not?' I turn to each of them in turn. Lord Samarasinghe gives me a playful wink. He looks amused, as he always does when we're fighting amongst ourselves.

'Young lady, this is a serious matt—'

'She is correct on that point,' Dr Maige says. 'The GDD reports directly to the secretary in his role as Scotland's Discoverer General. As you all would be aware, this is a quasi-governmental position, thus not falling within the remit of the Society per se.'

'But in order to hold that position, she has to be approved by the Society.'

'Correct.'

They do love nitpicking, this lot. I should give them my dreadlocks to unpick at this rate.

'There's a dimension you haven't looked at, Dr Maige,' says Diderot. 'This crime is Society business, since it's happened during conference. It means the Society sanctions the GDD for this investigation. We take precedence.'

Dr Maige looks up and considers the matter. He blinks as if accessing random files in his memory banks. I say nothing, but by this same logic, it could be argued the crime was against the Library, since Sneddon was murdered, and the theft of the scroll was against property loaned to them. Then again, the Library relies on security from the Society, so we're back biting our own tail. Maybe the MacLeods as the property owners have a stronger claim of precedence. I'm not sure, so stay schtum.

'Technically you're correct, Mr Diderot. But I must consult the specific wording of the rules before I say any more,' Dr Maige declares. Or dodges. 'What is clear is the Secretary of the Society of Sceptical Enquirers has sanctioned Ms Moyo's activities, so it would be irregular to dispute that at this late stage.'

'Irregular but not illegitimate, since Sir Ian Callander is, technically, incapacitated while holding up this Newton Barrier of his. He is unable to perform the full scope of his functions. He could simply let it go and resume his duties as normal.'

Dr Maige concedes. After all that, I'm back in the viper pit.

'Good. Now that's settled, we can return to the matter under discussion,' Wedderburn says. 'Ropa, be reasonable. Everyone in the Society has to be held accountable. We need you to divulge any pertinent information to us for review going forward.'

'I only answer to Sir Callander.' I'm prepared to die upon this hill.

Wedderburn closes his eyes for the longest blink ever. When he opens them, there's pity in his eyes.

'You've heard it for yourselves now. Working with her is a nightmare,' Cockburn says.

'Oh, piss off. I do every other thing you ask of me,' I reply, mouth running faster than brain.

'That's enough from you, young lady. You leave us with no choice. I would suggest a change of direction at this stage since we've wasted valuable time as it is. We should hold a vote. I'm in favour of assigning this investigation solely to Rector Wedderburn, whose students have turned in valuable evidence already. The only tangible progress made thus far. Ms Moyo, please leave the room. We'll call you back in when we've reached our decision.'

I ball my hands into fists and bite my tongue. Total stitch-up, this. I step outside and meet Priya waiting for me. She asks what's happening and I tell her we're done. We've been turfed out.

XXX

I've still got to attend dinner that evening, as the secretary's intern. Pass the salt shaker to the same faces who've just shafted me. I've learnt to take my wins and lickings with equanimity and a swig of Irn-Bru, though. The chemical haze hanging in the air's blue grey, the colour of a corpse's lips.

Lord Samarasinghe enters last. He's kept us waiting a good few minutes, as dinner can't start without him. He takes the empty chair at the head of the table. Callander's usual spot.

'Sorry I'm late. Looks like this one's free tonight,' the Sorcerer Royal says, dragging the chair back. 'God save our gracious king.'

'Long live our noble king,' we reply in unison.

Next line of this thing goes 'Send him victorious'. Where there's victory, someone else tastes defeat.

Lord Samarasinghe's power and influence increases as Callander's wanes. If it's a hold over the Society he wanted, the Extraordinary Committee has opened the door a fraction, and I look around, pondering again who he could be in league with. His self-satisfied air pisses me off. I should leave, but I'm starving. If you've ever been hungry, you learn nothing's ever worth wasting a plate of warm grub over.

Esfandiar isn't here either. Right decision. He wouldn't stand a chance with this lot. I daren't imagine how bad the sleep deprivation is for Callander now. I hear it was a method of torture in many places. Keep someone awake long enough and by the end you'll have a disoriented wreck.

I'm zonked here too. But my shift is done. Cockburn's already given me orders to help the cleaner tomorrow. That's designed to keep me occupied and stop me noseying about anymore.

Our roast lamb and tatties arrive.

Forks and knives are scraping bone china from Stoke-on-Trent.

I try to eat, but each mouthful I swallow feels like it's gonna come back out the same way. The toxic scent of the haze permeates the air. I push my food around my plate. Everyone on the table's trying to act normal, but the conversation feels forced. Too many posh twats throwing their weight about. Too many hidden agendas. Old scores to settle. Chefs and broth.

They praise the handful of events Cockburn's managed to run under trying circumstances. It's a self-congratulatory wank all round. They even talk about the weather, as if we're not ingesting toxic fumes. It occurs to me that their greatest magic lies in their ability to bend reality. To turn bad into good, darkness into light, and to play a game whose unwritten rules are more bewildering than those of the rugby we watched last night.

I wonder if Dr Maige truly is the impartial ref he believes he is, or if they play him like another pawn. The losses have been greatest on his side of the ledger. It's his librarian who paid the ultimate price for the game to start.

Forgotten in all this is poor Sneddon, whose fault none of it is. What does he get out of it? A shelf named after him in some obscure alcove within the Library of the Dead. Maybe they'll flay him and write him into a book. I doubt that. It's reserved only for the greatest minds. Their own. Gran tried desperately to warn me about what I'd signed up for. She said I was better off practising her kitchen-table magic. I didn't want to be stuck in a trailer park for the rest of my life. I brushed her off and did my own thing. With 20/20 hindsight, I see she knew something I didn't. Everyone at this table's bleeding some place. A slow puncture leeching out the ecto-plasm of their soul. But I've come this far. I must push on. Sunk cost fallacy – heard about it on a podcast the other day. The casino's dealt me a loaded dice and still expects me to play under normal rules. My fate's tied to Callander's. If they squeeze him out, that's me gone. He asked me to flank him, find the murderer, recover the scroll. Do that and we'd come out tops. As it stands, my great ship and I are sinking together. They might have thrown me off this thing, but I must press on.

Tyche, give me something, pal. It seems the manner in which events have panned out demands I pull that move I have out of my sleeve. There's a feature of this estate's Walled Garden which deserves an entire episode on *Gardeners' Question Time*, my gran's favourite radio show. Let's see if I can harvest a carrot from there to dangle.

Dessert arrives. I'm super-grateful for it 'cause sugar's my drug. Appetite or not, I'll have it. Don't judge me, I'm an addict.

'Cousins, English magic has not been blind to your plight. Events unfolding here have pained us much,' Lord Samarasinghe says in dulcet tones.

'Hear hear!'

'I tried to speak of this before. Perhaps I was too hasty, and my sentiments caused confusion. I still believe we're better together. It's just that the time is not yet ripe.'

'It is already ripe. The important thing is not to let it rot in the field before harvest,' Octavius Diderot says. Without Callander here, true colours are showing in ultra-HD.

'We have endured much together for three hundred years, and so we learn the virtue of patience. I've decided to offer you, should you accept, our professional investigators. Once we can use our mobiles again, it will only take one phone call. They are experts in antiquities crime and will find that missing scroll . . . I will inform Qozmos of this. We might not be the force that once ruled the waves, but I will make it clear that his threat against life and property here will be met with the full weight of English magic behind yours. That he cannot hope to prevail against a United Kingdom.'

'My lord, I really think these matters ought to be discussed with the secretary here,' Wedderburn says.

If any agree with him still, they are too cowed to speak up. Cockburn sits cold and neutral. Dr Maige, for all his talk about the rules, is silent on this matter. I felt the burn about 'professional investigators'. But since one has to be both fox and lion, I lean into my vulpine nature. My big mouth has already cost me. With this chair at the table, I might at least still collect information and pass it on to the gaffer.

These petticoat tails are delicious. I wish I could pocket some for Priya, but I can't. The Hamster Squad floats around the table refilling drinks. Pity. I was just getting used to these luxuries.

'You know, this isn't the first time we've been estranged and the Sorcerer Royal has come up from England to put our house in order,' Lady Lebusa says.

'I believe you're talking about '76,' Mr Gupta says.

'No. '76 was the Donlevy debacle. I'm referring to '64, during the Abernathy schism. If that had gone through, you'd have had two separate bodies regulating Scottish magic. It was only because the English refused to recognize Abernathy's faction that we remained intact.'

I'm not a hundred percent about the specifics of all that. It's tedious how they can sit here regaling each other with tales about the past. I'm sick of the performance. This polite conversation masks cunning and conniving. It's now a matter of time before they depose Callander. Even though he's taken my gig, I'm grateful the head of the Edinburgh School has stayed true. That might make it harder still.

Where does MacLeod stand now?

God, I hate politricks.

The Hamster Squad removes our plates before returning with the coffee. I don't get this habit of drinking the stuff at night. They claim it helps with digestion, and that you'll lose weight 'cause the food won't linger in your belly. That's never been my problem.

'The chief has a plan for helping handle this problem, and I believe now is the time for him to tell us,' Wedderburn says.

'We'd love to hear it,' Samarasinghe replies.

'I'm going to grant permission to the new investigative task force to search everything fully on this property. Doesn't matter whether it's personal material or not. This isn't a decision I've taken lightly. I've come to believe it's an absolute necessity given the situation we're now in.' MacLeod puffs himself up as he says this, the portraits of his ancestors looking down approvingly.

'Excellent idea,' Calista Featherstone says. 'That should flush them out.'

Wedderburn wipes his mouth with a napkin and places it on the table.

'Bravo. That's the first real display of courage I've seen in all this. Imagine how far we'd have got had it not been for Callander's obstructionism,' Diderot says.

I'm proper seething now. I suggested this ages ago and got blocked with some spiel on ethics and whatnot. Now it's been repackaged by MacLeod, it's suddenly the right thing to do. It still works to my advantage, though. There are going to be gamekeepers walking about with sticks flushing the quarry while I lie in wait. This will leak, and I'm sure it's going to spook the thief out. They're due a mistake now. I'll keep an eye on my hit list.

'It will be a full moon later tonight. The first of the autumn. I hope you will all be joining us for the ceremonial unfurling of the Fairy Flag,' MacLeod says, beaming with pride. 'Whenever the MacLeods have been in trouble in battle in the past, we only had to unfurl the flag and victory was guaranteed. We remember the Battle of Glendale when we routed the MacDonalds with its aid. In our most desperate moments, the flag united us and gave us strength to defeat our enemies. When we unfurl it tonight, you will all be reminded why this conference is held here, because the MacLeods are the truest friends of Scottish magic in the Highlands and Islands.'

'I wouldn't miss that for the world,' Wedderburn replies, raising his glass to the glowering figure of Dalziel MacDonald.

'I've heard it's an incredible event,' Lord Samarasinghe say. 'I'll try to stay up for it too, seeing as I missed your exciting last reception.'

I've had enough of this chit-chat and the back-scratching. I'm not out of the game yet. Before the hunt starts, I've got one more thing to fix. I excuse myself and leave the table. Let them do their thing while I set my own bear trap under the autumn leaves.

XXXI

Priya's in bed already. She's fiddling with her phone, maybe for the placebo effect. There's not much she can do without reception. Look at photos, old messages. Play games. Repeat. It's not the same as being online. This is the worst thing about this gig. I take off my gear and chuck it on the desk where she's got her stuff too. There's a small tube with ointment. She's stuck a note on it that says 'For your athlete's foot'. I apply it, rubbing it all over and in between my toes, which are the worst.

'Thanks. The itch was killing me. How did you know?'

'Healer's intuition. Did anything interesting happen at dinner?'

'They're making a move against Callander now.'

'That was bound to happen. At least you witnessed it with hot food down your belly. We got a spam sandwich and about three chips each. They were generous with the mayo, though.'

'That's good enough for the riffraff. Now budge over.'

I hop into bed and lie down. Priya leans over my chest to put her phone on the floor, then she snuggles into me. She's better than any hot-water bottle I've ever had. Reminds me of when I get to cuddle in with Gran. Except there's a lot less of Priya and she doesn't snore like a tractor. I didn't get too many sleepovers as a kid, so this makes up for lost time.

It's nice to even have a bed.

Our solar lamp flickers. Battery must be dying. It blinks a couple more times then we're in darkness.

I forgot to close the curtains.

From outside comes the eerie glow of the Newton Barrier reflecting whatever light is coming from the practitioners milling about. They have no idea how good they have it. I wouldn't be any different if I'd been born into this magicking racket. Blind. Clueless. Always chasing more. Gran warned me you can't ever get enough of it – whatever it is you desire. Money or power. I told her that not having any was the true tragedy. That we only say these things to make ourselves feel better about being on the wrong side of the fence.

I should be more like my friends. Priya's got her free spirit. Jomo's still got that big bleeding heart of his. Whatever I'm searching for's right here in my friends.

'Penny for them,' Priya says.

'It's always the human element.'

'Back up and start from the beginning for me.'

'This was a brilliant heist. Tracks well covered. But the dumping of the box was clumsy and obvious, and shows that someone's spooked or had already predicted the outcome of events. They've played a good hand, but they didn't anticipate Callander setting up the Newton Barrier and holding everyone here. The murder of Sneddon and theft of the scroll should have thrown the conference into disarray, but it's limped on thanks to Cockburn's cobbled-together programme. I'm certain they'll be desperate for a way out now.'

It was right there, niggling at me. I'm channelling my inner Machiavelli PI. The dots are already lined up. I just need a wee nudge to join them. Then you factor in the cast-iron law of unintended consequences. Getting rid of me got MacLeod doing something else. Thorough searches. Room by room. Somebody's going to crack.

'*They* – plural or singular?'

'Five people were in on this. That much the ghosts have confirmed for me. We worked in teams back when I was burglaring and it takes some level of coordination. But we always wanted to get out of there fast. Nothing sets off the nerves like having to sit there with stolen goods while a search is going on. Trust me, I once stole a rubber in school and had to sit there as the teacher went through everyone's stuff.'

'Go on,' Priya says.

'The drawing room has two entrances. You can come in via the first-floor corridor. Then once you've shown your face for long enough, there's the route out on the opposite side. Out the back of the drawing room, past the dungeon and left down the stairs to the ground floor. From there you can use the other corridors to get anywhere else in the building. Someone had to disable the power supply and the backup generators plus the security cameras and that's a two-person job. There was also someone else to deal with Jomo and

Sneddon. That could have been the murderer who took the scroll. But when I chased them through the castle, in the heat of the moment, I didn't take into account one very crucial factor.'

'Which is?'

'They weren't carrying anything up on that roof, Priya. They were empty-handed. I didn't see the box containing the scroll.'

'Which means they could have stashed it for someone else to retrieve with all the chaos going on.'

'There you go.'

'And it's not just for the money, because there's plenty of other stuff one can steal in this castle. I saw you casing the joint, FYI,' Priya says archly.

'Old habits,' I reply.

'Given the situation the Society is in now, I know there's something more going on.'

'That's what we'll find out.'

I love bouncing off Priya. There's all these power-hungry magicians about. This thing has to be about the future direction of Scottish magic. Something much bigger is coming.

'What do we do now?' she asks.

This is so bloody hard for me, I can't afford to get this wrong now. My edges are fraying. Nerves fried. I'm too used to grinding through everything like Carol Danvers in a kilt. We all need someone to lean on. If Priya can know to heal my itchy feet without me even asking, she could do more if I only opened up. I should have done this ages ago, if only I weren't so bone-headed.

'I need you to fix me, Priya. I'm cracking up.' This comes out in a hoarse whisper. Doesn't even sound like my own voice.

'Come here, you silly sausage.' She gathers me up in her arms and embraces me.

'I can't do this if I might break down at any time.'

There's no roadside assistance out here. Half the time I'm anxious, hoping I don't make a fool of myself. It's impossible to keep it together. If there's anything my pal Nicco's taught me, it's that you have to confront the facts as they are. The hardest ones to grapple with are the ones about yourself. If you don't, though, you're screwed.

'Everything will be fine. I'm here for you. Always.'

I exhale and let it all go.

'Is there like herbs or something you can give me for it? Just to keep me on the even until this thing's done?'

'It's not that simple, Ropa.'

'A magic spell? Anything?'

If only. She tells me there's remedies that might ease my anxiety. Valerian helps some people, not all. Downside is they were still looking at the side effects. You could get headaches, dizziness or drowsiness with it. Chamomile tea was a safer option, if I was not allergic. Reishi and lion's mane mushrooms too, but not long-term because of potential liver damage. She could also try aromatherapy at the Our Lady of Mysterious Ailments, the clinic where she works. There were loads more options. But as with drugs, there could be downsides. And none of them were a hundred percent effective. The key difference in approaches between medicine and healing is they're not just interested in managing symptoms. She said they were more holistic. They'd try to drill down to the cause and help fix that.

'The cause is dealing with crazy shit all the time. Give me something while we figure it out. If this was a tumour, I'd want you to get in there and cut it out. No mess, no fuss.'

'That's not how it works.'

Priya chuckles and my head bobs up and down on her chest. At least she's not acting like I've gone completely cuckoo. And she's not doing the whole drama of feeling sorry for me. I ain't into that.

'This sort of thing happens to most of us at some point. We're not machines. It's life,' she says.

'If I'm to be honest, I love the pressure the same way you enjoy extreme sports. I've lived with fear all my life and I can handle it. At least I could, until now.'

'That's not healthy. Too much cortisol flowing through you will mess you up . . . Look at all the things you do, Ropa. Looking after your family, taking care of ghosts, helping people out, solving mysteries. You never take time out to look after you.'

'I like being on the go.'

'Maybe you keep pushing forward to avoid stopping and reflecting on your own feelings. On what all this is doing to you. It's been mad ever since I met you. Don't get me wrong, I love it too – you're not the only junkie. But there's a toll on your mental health. These panic attacks you're experiencing may be the manifestation of some deeper underlying trauma.'

Great. Now I've got trauma too. I feel my temper rising and have to check myself. I asked for this. But I ain't got no trauma. You get so much as a paper cut in nursery school these days, and they say you've got trauma twenty years later. I wanna get on with things. I don't want to feel sorry for myself. Take a deep breath. Close your eyes. The warmth of her skin against mine. Priya's right. I'm in denial.

'What can I do?'

'You've taken the first step in acknowledging there's a problem. It's probably the bravest thing you've ever done.'

'Over battling spectres and dodgy practitioners?'

'Infinitely more so.'

'I'll take that.'

'I'm your friend and not a psychohealer who can give you the specialist therapy you need. The good thing is, I know a great lass who I usually make referrals to. I used her myself when I was having issues at uni. We can get you referred and see what she can do for you.'

'I can't afford it, man. I've heard about how much those shrinks cost.'

'You seem to be conveniently forgetting you work for the Society now. There's perks to that, even if they won't pay you. As soon as we can get a signal, I'll make some calls so we can get this sorted out. We've got this.'

Priya squeezes my hand.

Great, now I have to get my head fixed. One more thing in a long line of things I've got to do. I shift about to get proper comfy. Then I relax, listening to Priya's heartbeat. I feel better. It does wonders getting things like this off your chest. Otherwise, your head explodes like one of them zombies taking a headshot. I've got to look after me a bit better. If I don't, then I can't look after Gran and Izwi. And my friends. And my fox. This is nice. I feel warm. Yawn. Let me just rest my eyes. Heartbeat. Good night . . . No, I have to get up. There's work to be done now.

'Priya, we're going to get a little help from our friends,' I say.

Me and Priya are suitably downcast as we make our way to the old butler's room on the ground floor. There's laughter and the sound of voices bantering within. I blow out air through my mouth and knock on the black door. The paint is flaky and there's an illegible plaque on which someone's name from the past must have been written, once upon a time. Lewis Wharncliffe opens the door, looks shocked to see us and steps out into the corridor, hurriedly shutting it.

'Not here,' he whispers.

'Lewis, who is it?' a posh voice asks from within.

'It's okay, we've come to ask for your help,' I say to him.

'I thought you said you didn't want the guys involved,' he replies, all confused.

'A lot's changed since then. We're on the ropes and need all the help we can get.' I can feel Priya looking at me quizzically, but she goes with it.

The door's swung open and Nathair Walsh stands there, looking proper smug. He runs his hand through his hair and then nudges Lewis to one side so he can take a good look at me and Priya. Despite everything that's been going on, he's impeccably dressed in his uniform.

'Looks like Lewis's girlfriends have decided to pay us a visit, lads,' he says, turning back to glance at whoever's in the room. 'Please, come into my office.'

Walsh steps back and goes to take the sole seat, an old chesterfield by the window. The butler's room is a bit larger than the room me and Priya are sharing. The three members of the Edinburgh School's rugby team were meant to be sharing it. There's a single bed on which Avery MacDonald and Fenella MacLeod are lounging, each holding a hand of playing cards, with the deck on the floor. A game interrupted midway through. Two mattresses are also placed up against the wall to the right and there's bags on top of them. I wonder where the other rugby player is who's meant to be sharing the space with them.

'I would offer you ladies a seat, but . . .' Walsh gestures to the spartan nature of the decor. 'Lewis, sit down. I can't have you hovering by the door like some loon.'

Lewis scratches his head then wanders over to the mattresses and plonks himself down. He reclines there, placing his weight on his left elbow, but he looks uneasy. I guess he was always embarrassed to be seen with us. Lewis has a very middle-class accent, but Walsh's is proper posh, and I can see why he'd be the skivvy here. Obviously must think we'll mess up his rep.

'I always did wonder how you got in as the secretary's apprentice without any qualifications,' Walsh comments.

'That's not why we're here,' Priya replies, sharp like.

'The role's always gone to someone from our school. I worked hard for six years to be in line for that apprenticeship. Top marks. Aced everything. Captain of the rugby team. Deputy head boy. Then all that wasted because they gave it to a *ghostalker*? That's not even real magic.'

'Walshy, come on. She's alright,' Lewis says meekly.

'I heard a rumour that her grandmother used to work for the secretary,' Fenella says.

'Doing what exactly?' Walsh asks.

'Don't know. Domestic, probably.'

'It's still nepotism then. That's the only way someone like her can get in without doing the work like the rest of us.'

'Boo-fucking-hoo, must suck royally being you,' Priya quips.

Walsh laughs, like he's taken it in good humour, but there's no mirth in his eyes. I grit my teeth and battle to stop myself balling my hands into fists. Instead I nod my head.

'Yeah, you're better than me. More talented, better educated. There, I admit it,' I say.

'Ropa, what the—' Priya begins, but Walsh cuts her off.

'Please, let her finish. I'd like to hear this.'

'There's one other thing you're better than me at too, and that's finding stuff. It was my pride that stopped me, but I should've asked all of you lads for help earlier. We could have covered more ground together. I just couldn't bring myself to do it. Not after the way you embarrassed me at dinner the other night.'

'Everyone already knows you've been kicked off the investigation. So why are you here now?' Walsh asks.

Give me strength. Humble pie, my old friend, you've never tasted sourer than you do tonight. But needs must.

'It's for my mentor, Sir Callander. He really is weakening and can't hold that Newton Barrier up much longer. Maybe a day or two at most. But I spoke with him earlier and he's worried the thief might just go to the Walled Garden and use that place to break out.' I throw in a wee sweetener: 'And I'm sure after this he'll be in search of a new apprentice.'

'What does the Walled Garden have to do with this?' Walsh asks.

Fenella perks up.

'It's an unusual area of far lesser natural resistance to magic than anywhere else in the castle grounds. Which means it amplifies the power of a practitioner working in it. I used to practise there as a little girl. I haven't thought about it in a long time. Now we mostly just grow stuff in there,' she says.

'You found the box, there must be something you've seen over the last few days that can help me to crack this thing,' I beg.

'Of course we'll help. What do you take us for?' Walsh replies irritably.

'Thank you.'

'I'll lead this, naturally. I didn't make captain of the rugby team for nothing. Let's start by sharing information. You tell us what you know and we'll tell you what we've seen.'

'This is great. We can all work together,' Lewis says excitedly.

'Shut it, you. I already know you were helping her on the side. I'm not a complete idiot,' Walsh says in good humour.

'And about the dinner thing. I wish you hadn't taken it so personally. That's how we debate at our school. It's meant to be sharp and fun, otherwise how else do you test out whether your ideas are true or not? Try not to hold it against me.'

I breathe a sigh of relief and place my hand on Priya's shoulder. Hopefully now we can really get things moving with this lot.

XXXII

No rest for the wicked. Me and Priya resemble the walking dead, given how knackered we are. She was a bit miffed with me after we left the butler's room, but once I told her my real plan, she came round. I get dressed and make sure to check my gear. The stuff's laid out on the small table: katty, ammo – six smooth round stones I picked up on the beach, my loyal scarf Cruickshank, dagger. I don't forget to put on my brounie-busting bulletproof coat too. Plus, I've got my mbira in my backpack, just in case there's a poltergeist in play.

Machiavelli's most important piece of advice comes to mind: 'Before all else, be armed.'

He knew that when all the court drama, the scheming and subterfuge were done, only one thing mattered. The final outcome would likely be determined by brute force. Everything else pales in comparison, it's the most primal thing out there. The sword is mightier than the pen. Power in its purest, gluten-free, unadulterated form.

I make sure the rubber bands on my katty are okay. You can't have no nicks or nothing on them. Sheath my dagger on my hip for a quick draw. Drape Cruickshank round my neck, then button up my coat. Lastly, I put on my boots and tie my laces.

I feel like John Rambo all decked out like this.

Priya's sorting herself out too. Getting dressed is a wee bit of a mission for her. It's like that with my gran too: you don't help unless she asks. So I give her the space to do what she's got to do.

We have the element of surprise. And so I've got Priya, who can handle herself, to back me up. I've seen her in action a couple of times, and I'm always glad she's on my side rather than against me. She's a badass Yu Shu Lien on steroids.

Priya takes her time checking over her most important piece of kit, her wheelchair. She's damned serious while she's at it. The last thing she takes a look at is her medkit, but I'm hoping it'll only be the other side that'll need it. Not us.

'You up for this?' she asks, settling into the chair.

'I was born ready, motherfucker.' I channel my inner *Blade*.

'Motherfucker – I like that.'

We giggle for a sec, then get all pro again. But, yeah, when this is done, we're deffo pirating that old movie. We'll binge the trilogy, me and her, sipping slushies and chowing popcorn. I tell her this and she says, 'It's a date.'

Now we're both finally ready, we sneak out of the castle.

The fog outside's so thick hardly anyone will see us. And if they do, we have an excuse as we're headed first for the Keeper's Cottage. We'll then loop back round away from the castle on our way back.

A couple of times in the past, I've rushed into situations and got my arse handed to me. This time around, I'm taking precautions. I may have Priya, but we need an even bigger gun as backup. I know everyone around here's a better magician than I am. Stings, but it's the truth. And so I'm not going to take to the field without a tactical advantage to give us the edge.

Have to help Priya over the boggy mud like before, which gets my socks wet through again. My kingdom for a new pair of boots.

There's an ominous silence through the woods – no wind, 'cause of the barrier. It means we sound loud trundling through the fallen leaves. We get to the place I had a panic attack, but I don't feel anything coming on in the same spot, which is great. Put that at the back of my mind – it'll be alright. We can worry about it later . . .

Priya knocks on the door of the Keeper's Cottage.

It takes a couple of minutes but Esfandiar answers finally. He's well haggard. Stubble's growing on his chin, his make-up's smudged. It's a sign of his exhaustion that he lets us in without question.

Sir Callander's leaning against the far wall, eyelids drooping. He regards us. It takes a couple of seconds before he registers, then he speaks.

'Ms Moyo and Ms Kapoor . . . Very—' he yawns '—to see you. Esfandiar, my love. Another brew, if you will.'

Esfandiar throws us a look as if to say 'You see?', before answering: 'Sure, darling.'

'I've been informed the Extraordinary Committee has made its own decision as to the direction of things. They've advised I set aside the Newton Barrier to better carry out my duties, but I have so far declined their request,' the gaffer says. If he's rattled by this, his demeanour gives nothing away. I don't know if he's all stoic or just too knackered to care.

'When you first met me, I wasn't working under no official channels. I had nothing to do with your Society. Didn't stop me then,' I reply. 'And I already told them, I only answer to you.'

Callander lets out another long yawn. His head drops and he manages to raise it again. In the struggle to keep himself awake, he begins walking around the room. But it's clear he's disoriented. I'm not going to get the naval destroyer I was hoping to bring into play. Bugger. He's no good to me in this state. Callander seems at points to forget we are here, pacing around in his daze. Must be a feat of superhuman will holding the Newton Barrier up in this state. Just a little bit longer, that's all I ask.

'Progress report,' he says. 'What's happening with Max Wu?'

Jesus Christ, he's really not here. I feel a wave of panic wash over me.

'That was ages ago. We're working on something else now,' I reply.

Callander shakes his head to clear the fog in his mind.

'Of course. You're quite right. The scroll.'

Then he begins pacing around again. He strokes his chin, thinking. Tonight better be the night we catch them, get the scroll back, else we'll have to shut this circus down anyway. To hell with the consequences. Sucks for me to see Callander like this.

Esfandiar returns with a coffee so strong the aroma fills the room. That'll bring back Lazarus from the dead.

I consider something radical for a second, but Priya looks at me and shakes her head like she's read my mind. Esfandiar isn't made of the same stuff his husband is. He's the gentler sort. He's a fucking poet, and those aren't much good to anyone in a situation like this. Unless, perhaps, he was a drill rapper. I stood next to him when the kerfuffle between the MacLeods and MacDonalds was kicking off. Violence ain't his thing. No, he won't do at all.

'Esfandiar, I need you to get me Kebede.'

'Anything you want, Ropa.'

I've seen Kebede on the field and had the privilege of ducking his lightning. Reckon he serves as the Grand Debtera's bodyguard too. He's got swagger. It's that Ethiopian thing: never been colonized. Balls of steel. I could use some of that fire tonight.

'What do you need him for? I'll come with you,' Callander says, stifling a yawn.

'We need you to stay here and make sure the Grand Debtera is safe,' I lie.

He's way too tired to contest this.

It doesn't take too long before Kebede comes down in his flowing white clerical robes. Not the most subtle camouflage.

'Don't you have something darker?' I ask.

Kebede runs his hand diagonally from his right shoulder, across his chest, down to his left hip. Right away, his robes change to black.

'You're going to have to give me a copy of that spell,' Priya says.

'I heard we are going to a party,' he says.

I give him the rundown. Tell him that whoever stole the scroll could be making a break for it tonight, because of the searches MacLeod's got lined up and they believe Callander can't hold this shield up any longer. I give him everything, my idea of what's going on and the stuff about the Walled Garden, etc.

'This is our best chance to end this,' I say.

'And you're certain of it?'

'We'll soon find out.'

'It is good that you've asked me to help. I come from a long line of magicians who used to guard the emperors of Ethiopia. If anyone tries anything, they'll answer to me.'

That's the energy I need. But I don't bother asking him what happened to the last emperor. Haile Selassie was strangled in his bed by the Marxist army officers who overthrew him. Let's hope Kebede's a wee bit better than those imperial guards. Must be that with no emperors left to protect, his lineage has had to find new employment. The new regime wouldn't trust them not to try seeking vengeance.

I go over to Esfandiar and grab his arms. The poor poet's eyes are red, thin film of water in them. He's ready to cry.

'Look after Callander, okay? This is nearly over.'

He sniffles and nods.

'Priya, Kebede, let's get to work.'

I lead them back outside and over to the woods. We try to be as quiet as possible. Instead of taking the main route towards the castle, we keep to the fringes, following the paths nearest the main road. No one can see us all the way from the castle in this thick fog. Allah, the humidity. Makes breathing feel more like drowning. We go round the dried-up Water Garden and through the New Garden, circling the Round Garden. The Walled Garden finally comes into view.

I stop at a discreet, elevated point.

'What's the play?' Priya asks.

'They won't be expecting us, so they'll probably take the road up from the castle. We don't want to spook them before they're boxed inside the Walled Garden. Kebede, you remember how hard it was cornering them last time, just after the scroll was taken.'

'This place is very large,' he says.

'Exactly. We may only get one chance at this, so I think we need to let them go into the Walled Garden unimpeded. Nothing, absolutely nothing, should scare them before then. Once they're inside, just observe until my signal. Kebede, you're coming inside the garden with me too. We'll confront them there. Priya, stay here. On my signal, you shut the trap. No one comes out unless I say.'

She grins. But I can tell from the intensity on her face she's well psyched up. Almost scares me too, she does.

'I like this plan of yours,' Kebede says.

'It'll work. Priya, make yourself the Invisible Woman. We might be here a good while yet. Phone me if . . .' I then recall our mobiles aren't working. 'Hold tight and wait for a signal. I know you like sparklers.'

'Wait,' Kebede says. He touches the silver push rim of her chair, muttering an incantation, and it turns black, along with all the shiny metal parts on it too. 'Now we're matching.'

I give Priya a fist bump and she retreats behind the bushes.

Me and Kebede scurry silently along the edge of the road, keeping a lookout. We pass undetected and undisturbed. The Walled Garden has a massive green wooden gate set into the arched entrance in the high stone wall. Must be at least ten, maybe twelve feet tall. We enter and our feet crunch on the gravel pathway.

'Where do you want me?' Kebede asks.

'Hide in the Glass House. It'll be hard to spot you in there with all them plants, and you'll have a good view of the entrance. Don't make a move unless I call.'

I'm chuffed when Kebede holds his fist out for me to bump too. I guess that means he's an honorary part of the team now. He makes his way to the greenhouse built against the wall which runs to the entrance. Even in this haze, he'll be able to easily spot anyone coming into the Walled Garden. I stick to the shadows, navigating the hedged paths within the garden, trying to scope out a good location to hide in.

Ghostalking was so much simpler.

I'm trying to map out where I can move quietest and out of the line of sight of anyone coming in. The slightest sound kinda rings out. I hide behind the hedges at the furthest end of the garden. This way I'll be able to move in the shadows and track anyone coming in. Then, should they attempt to back out, Kebede's my defence and Priya's the goalie.

I take my place and squat.

Can't get comfy, so I kneel.

I don't wanna sit down 'cause my butt will get wet and I've already been soaked once in this bloody place. Stake-outs aren't fun like in cop shows, where they sit in squad cars eating donuts. I always wondered how they got to pee.

The other advantage this place has going for it, beyond the lower natural resistance, is how isolated and private it is. Used to be they grew veg for the chief and his family here. Then they touristified it with flowers and shrubs, back when they used to have visitors. Murdo and his crew still look after it nicely now. But yeah, someone can come in at night and work spells in seclusion. Earlier Priya was talking about teleportation and stuff – if you needed a boost to do that kind of difficult spellcraft, this would be the perfect spot for it.

I feel the temptation to reach for my phone and muck about a bit. Can't, though, because the light would give up my position.

Stay alert, Ropa.

It's small consolation the other two are probably just as bored. Waiting sucks. Any time now, villain. Still. Nothing's happening. Where are they? This better not be a dud – I was so sure I'd got them hooked. Time really stretches out. It's a total drag.

Stay awake.

The plan's tight. We're no different to those ancient hunters who dug a pit, waiting for animals to drop. Come on. I should be in bed right now. Warm under the covers. Yep, I should have just left it when they kicked me off this investigation.

XXXIII

Oh, my days. Been knelt behind this shrub for so long, I can't feel my knees. Hoping I haven't brought Priya and Kebede out for nothing. I'm starting to feel sleepy. That warm bed, just waiting for me.

The moon's risen now. It hangs over the treeline beyond the wall surrounding the garden.

It's got a spooky, blood-coloured aura 'cause of Callander's shield. We're ants inside a jar, staring out. Maybe I got it wrong. Lemme go over to Kebede. Or maybe wait just a little bit longer. Any kicks I got from this have long since worn out. I wonder how Priya's getting on, what she's doing to keep herself alert.

Worst gig ever. I'm fed up now . . .

Suddenly the gate swings open, hinges squeaking.

A black figure enters, hidden in the haze. Confident stride. Too tall to be any of the Edinburgh boys, but the light's too dodgy to see who it actually is. Seems to be wearing a hat, making it harder to identify them. The figure comes to a standstill, checking all around. I'm literally holding my breath, scared to make a sound. Tickly throat. I swallow, trying not to cough. They wait for a good while, assessing every part of the garden, before turning their back to lock the gates.

Is this it? Just the one person? I thought there'd be a couple more at least.

Advantage: us.

Wasn't expecting to get locked in, though. There's gates on the northern and western walls too, but those aren't in use and are always locked up. These walls are too tall to climb as well. I don't like this. Always have an exit strategy. Still, three-vs-one odds – I'll take that in any game of chance.

Their feet crunch on the gravel as they finally move forward.

Bloody haze. I wanna take a better look, but I can't.

They walk past the pond with lilies, closer to the entrance. Here's hoping Kebede hasn't nodded off. They take a right, walking towards the centre of the garden, and I watch, crouching and still hidden behind the hedge. I shift a little. Crack. Bollocks. I've stepped on a twig.

The figure stops and takes a look around.

I hold my breath.

They incant something I can't quite catch, and a golden ball of fire blazes atop their open left palm. They then throw the thermosphere in the air, where it hovers. It's not high enough to clear the wall but it stings my eyes. Colours swim. I have to readjust to the light. It gives the haze a molten glow.

The man, and I'm pretty sure it's a man now, walks further through the gardens until he reaches the seventeenth-century lectern sundial. I find it curious that of all the things here, he's chosen to stand at this symbol of time. It doesn't work under moonlight.

But if this is an area of inverted natural resistance, then

maybe the sundial was placed at a nexus point. He's also holding some sort of poster tube.

I realize I can breathe again, and crawl nearer.

Take care not to be seen.

He opens the tube and pulls out its contents. It looks like the scroll! Finally I have it in my sights! It worked. He unrolls it and then starts reading from it, next to the lectern sundial. I just need to get closer to take a proper look and hear what he's saying. Slowly. Silently. This bloody thermosphere makes my job a lot harder with the brightness it's radiating. Neat spell suspending it like that, though. In the haze, it has a ring of concentric halos.

I inch closer still.

'I know you're there, Ms Moyo. Come out.' Montgomery Wedderburn's voice cuts across the night.

I freeze. *Him?* I thought he was Callander's friend?

'Don't make this any harder on yourself,' he says.

Busted. How the hell did he know I was out here? I don't see too many options other than that Lewis and Walsh must have realized I was setting them up and told him I'd be here. Maybe I was wrong about them and Wedderburn's just found the scroll? He's the main one investigating this thing now, after all. But if he did, why would he come here and not go to the Keeper's Cottage to give it to Callander and Qozmos?

In my confusion, I suddenly find myself worrying whether this heist might be pinned on me somehow. Good thing I've got my own witnesses.

'This thermosphere's going to zip through the air and

barbecue both you and that bush you're hiding behind if you don't come out now.' He's not playing.

I stand up and edge around, maintaining my distance. I'm about ten feet away. I suddenly recall his strange words to me a few days ago: 'All will be revealed under the silver light of the full moon.' It might not be silver now, but once that barrier comes down, we'll be bathing in it like Judas. I'd not paid attention to him at the time – just thought he was spouting some other literary quote. Something doesn't feel right. This whole thing's off.

'Fancy meeting you here,' I say, getting out into the open. 'Out for a stroll?'

'This air's rather refreshing, isn't it?' he says sarcastically.

'I agree. Maybe we should go back to the castle and tell the others you found the scroll. Congratulations.'

Wedderburn chortles like he's at a polite dinner party.

'Didn't think it'd be you,' I say.

'Come now, you're a smart girl. It's the only quality you've got going for you. I think you'd have made a half-decent practitioner. Which is exactly what Scottish magic needs in order to rouse itself from this stupor.'

'I thought the students were doing their own thing but it was the Pied Piper.'

'Pardon?'

'I imagine you're the one leading the kids to this glorious new future. I heard part of your lecture – all that bollocks about reviving Scottish magic. Get them to do your dirty work for you while you wine and dine with your nose clean. The night of the murder and robbery, you were there at the reception, glass of bubbly in hand, with the perfect alibi. And I've been so busy chasing the Angus beefs in Scottish magic, looking for motive, I initially overlooked the students, but their missteps grew like a cartoon snowball.'

'Humour me,' he says with a chilling laugh.

'Put two people together and no secret's safe. There's always a leak . . . It can come through a misspoken word, like when Fenella MacLeod saved me after I blundered into the prison where they hold the remaining Fae. She told me they didn't want any more "collateral damage". I found the phrasing odd, though I was grateful at the time. Is that all Sneddon was to you lot, *collateral damage*? The little princess in her father's castle, desperate to escape his tyrannical shadow, dreaming of a better world. And you sell it to her. Who else has easy access to the armoury? Who else knows how to sabotage the power supply, and can move around the castle in the dark with ease? Fenella MacLeod. "Hold fast," she said to me on the roof. That's her family motto. But she'd only betray her clan if she was sold something more seductive. The chance to show her father she could be her own woman. I cast this net for them and seem to have caught a bigger fish instead. I can understand now, Fenella just found a substitute father: you. That's your speciality. Grooming kids. I've seen how you wander around the castle grounds philosophizing to your young audience.'

'Is that all you have?' he asks, acting very amused.

'Lewis Wharncliffe was very keen to help, a little too keen. But by then it was already clear to me he was an underling to a more forceful personality, Nathair Walsh.'

Wedderburn laughs and points an acknowledging finger at me. Even now, in this moment, his allure is irresistible. All those young people who follow him about. When I met Wedderburn taking a stroll with his gaggle of students drawn from the different institutions, Lewis blurted out that whoever was doing this must be the 'Fifth School', in a bid to appear helpful. But Scotland only has four schools of magic: Aberdeen, Edinburgh, Lord Kelvin and St Andrews. I begin to wonder if this Fifth School really does exist – could it even be a new alliance Wedderburn's created? It would do away with all the petty rivalries. One school to rule them all, and bind them together in secret under him.

I think back to that night on the roof as I chased the thief, and can't believe I didn't realize sooner they weren't carrying anything. Could it just have been Fenella running, leading me away? And I, seeing red, pursued her regardless. Her job was to make it seem as though the scroll had left the property. Mr Holmes would be ashamed of me. Misdirection, the lowest form of magic. Avery MacDonald and his father had been at the reception, which made it harder to suspect them, but they were also the first upon the scene. That means there was one player close by who could collect the scroll and stash it. While we gave chase, the scroll remained in the castle, ready to be shifted at a more auspicious time.

'That's your little team, isn't it? Walsh and Lewis to cut the power, Fenella to deal with Jomo and Sneddon, then cause a distraction, and Avery to collect the prize,' I say, buying time.

'An excellent summary. Not a hundred percent accurate,

but you seem to have understood the thrust of it. It's such a pity you're not a student. I could have used you.'

'Which bits did I get wrong?' I have to keep him talking.

Kebede stealthily moves out of the Glass House. Wedderburn has his back to him, so he doesn't spot him approaching. I carry on as if there's no one else. Buying time with this talk.

'Funny how at every turn you seem to have taken Callander's side. Lured us into complacency. It couldn't be you, his dear friend. But really you've been working to undermine him. And murdered a good, innocent man,' I say, when Wedderburn doesn't respond to my question.

'Sir Ian Callander is an excellent practitioner, and he was my mentor a long time ago,' Wedderburn says wistfully. 'There was a time I was in your shoes. I idolized him. But he's been holding back Scottish magic for thirty years. It's time for a change. Don't you see this? Sneddon's death was unfortunate, but he was just in the wrong place at the wrong time. Nothing personal; Fenella did what she had to do. The bit you missed out, since you asked, is the fact that it was actually Avery who gave Jomo Maige a knock on the back of the head. Two deaths would have been gratuitous. Nobody loves librarians more than I do.'

'All I see is greed and ambition. How disappointingly pedestrian. Using kids to commit murder too; you really have your claws deep inside of their heads.'

He scowls. There's a real darkness about him. Men like him who do evil things then try to justify them with fine words. Even as they do, they want to be understood as the good guys. There's always a larger objective that steamrolls over everyone else and every moral consideration. There's always a utopia waiting at the end of it all. It gets tedious.

'You're out of time. There's still factors outside of your control, like MacLeod discovering the scroll when he does his search. So you're desperate to leave, and that's why I planted a seed with your students, telling them that the Walled Garden offers an escape route. But it doesn't. Callander's shield will hold and you'll still be stuck here. Give me the scroll and we'll call it evens.' I hold out my hand.

'This old thing? It's no use to me. I'd rather shred it.'

Oh dear. I know Wedderburn's taking the mick, but Kebede comes flying out from behind with a scream. He hurls an almighty concussive blast at Wedderburn, who moves smoothly sideways, stepping out of the way as the wave of air roars off, crashing into the wall. Wedderburn then shifts back, keeping both of us in his peripheral vision.

'It's the little debtera. Good of you to join us,' he says, throwing the scroll onto the ground. 'Superstitious rubbish. This can never defeat science.'

I feel a sudden tightness take hold inside my chest.

No, not now. Please.

Come on.

Wedderburn waves his hand and his floating golden light whizzes towards me. I'm frozen. Paralysed by an overwhelming dread that turns my limbs to marble. Cruickshank yanks me to the ground and the fireball explodes in the bush next to me. The world narrows around me and I struggle to stand. Can't breathe. Cruickshank then roughly drags me further away from Wedderburn.

I hear whooshes and loud booms.

Sparkling gold against blazing blue.

'You really ought to help your friend, Ms Moyo,' Wedderburn says. 'He's no match for me.'

I force myself up onto my knees. Fireworks are lighting up the garden while my heart's pounding out of my chest. Feels like a cardiac arrest. Breathe. Another thermosphere comes my way and Cruickshank moves my arms to protect my face. It explodes against my sleeves, but all I feel is a bit of warmth. Thanks, ninja coat. An acrid chemical scent hits the back of my nostrils. Backwards my scarf drags me. Away from the fight.

Wedderburn turns his hand round over his head, like a cowboy with a lasso. The air churns violently. A mini tornado spins away from him, tearing up leaves, throwing up dust as it heads for Kebede. That's a new one. Kebede tries to evade it, but the damned thing chases him. Wedderburn stands at ease, watching as his target runs between the plants. The tornado grows and whistles, stirring up the haze, and eventually catches Kebede, spinning him like a centrifuge before spitting him out. He flies in his black robes and slams against the wall before falling to the ground.

'Stay down, boy,' Wedderburn says.

But Kebede stands slowly, fury written all over his face. He shoots off a concussive blast of air. Wedderburn moves his hands in a circular pattern, stopping the wave of air midway, spinning it round and returning it to sender. But Kebede leaps out of the way, just in time.

The air's now filled with debris and leaves floating about.

I should be in the fight, but the dread's got me paralysed.

'Really, Ms Moyo, this is pathetic,' Wedderburn taunts. He's deriving some diabolical pleasure from all this.

I'm gasping for air, like a fish out of water. Wedderburn sends a malicious potted plant flying my way. Cruickshank catches it, thank goodness, spins around and throws it back. Kebede then hurls another fireball, but Wedderburn sleekly moves out of the way. The potted plant and thermosphere collide and explode, sending earth and ceramics flying.

I can't.

I can't.

Breathe.

Oh no. Make it stop.

I'm trying to pull it together but am dragged under a current of dread. Kebede's on his own. The human element, again – I'm the weak link.

Wedderburn fires an incredible barrage at him.

Kebede runs, ducks and evades. It's clear he's no match for the more seasoned practitioner. He breathes hard in the thickening smog, exhausted already. It's like tennis. Wedderburn's only circled the lectern sundial, while Kebede's been up and down the length of the wall, trying to dodge his missiles. He's done all the work. And there're longer intervals between his attempts at firing back new spells.

On the other hand, Wedderburn very coolly maintains his attack. It's not taxing him anything. Flame and blasts of air shred the hedging and flowers. His magic is loud, casting shining strobes of golden light through the air. He's not subtle about it, someone's bound to hear. I hope.

I try to incant a Promethean fire spell to distract Wedderburn, but nothing happens. My mind's racing. I can't find the nexus point to make the spell work. Too much fear in my mind.

Come on, Ropa. Breathe.

I try again. Nothing happens.

Kebede waves his hands about, raising the dirt, broken pottery and debris from the ground. He yells out and shoots it all at Wedderburn, blue light flashing everywhere. But the older magician merely cloaks himself within a golden mini tornado which nothing can penetrate.

I'm sprayed by some of the stuff Kebede's cast.

Glass breaking.

Potted plants from the Glass House fly out. Kebede runs and ducks and rolls, but when he recovers, he's caught on the chest by a flying plant pot. It knocks him to the ground, stunned. A hail of other pots come at him, plants, dirt and all. Beaten, Kebede can only roll himself into a ball and cover his head.

Bloody hell. He's going to be murdered, while I'm frozen like a knob.

Trying every spell I know.

Nothing happening.

A dark object vaults through the air, landing with a metallic clank upon the southern wall. It's Priya! Incredibly, she's balancing her chair on one wheel, the walls too narrow for both, maintaining her weight at an angle. This startles Wedderburn, and the flying pot plants drop onto the ground.

Priya speeds along, lobbing green, plasmic thermospheres

at Wedderburn. Taken by surprise, the rector is forced to dodge a couple. He then waves his hand, raising the water in the pond as a screen between them and extinguishing the fire Priya's chucking at him as she zips across. Her chair vaults from the wall onto the slate roof of the derelict building bounded by the western and southern walls. From there, she leaps onto the ground, making an almighty racket.

Wedderburn laughs.

'Priscilla to the rescue!' he shouts.

'I told you before, it's Priya!' she replies angrily.

'Perished is a more apt descriptor.'

The water from the pond freezes in an instant and Wedderburn hurls this wall of ice at Priya. As it flies, she reclines, falling backwards in her chair. The wheels and base shield her from the ice block, which smashes and breaks against them, spraying shards of ice everywhere.

The wheels of Priya's chair turn and she rights herself, in the same motion sending a concussive blast of air towards Wedderburn. But the skilled rector merely holds up his hand and it dissipates into a strong wind that knocks his hat off.

'You amateurs,' he taunts.

Kebede uncurls and gets up from the ground. A bit wobbly. Clumps of earth fall off him. But he's ready to go again, while I'm still cowering in the corner protected by my scarf and coat. I'm isolated behind Wedderburn by the northern wall, closest to the sea and castle.

The temperature in the air's risen, with three practitioners casting so fiercely in this small space.

'Ropa, you alright?' Priya shouts.

'Your little girlfriend can't handle this. I think she wants her granny. I'll make you a deal. You can just take her and walk away from all this. None of you needs to get hurt. What's going on right now is beyond your level of comprehension.'

'I am not going anywhere without *The Book of the Shaded Mysteries of Solomon*. Return it to me at once,' Kebede says.

'Young man, you're in no position to be making threats. I've seen your skills, they're below par. Even Priscilla here casts better than you. Ethiopian magic – what a joke. It's nothing more than superstition that should have ended two hundred years ago. But I guess the Enlightenment didn't reach your savage part of the world.'

That's right, keep him talking, I think. The arrogant bastard is so loud, someone's sure to hear. I've been so wrong about this man.

The edges are lifting, but I'm still crushed under this avalanche. When I tried to take off my coat, Cruickshank wouldn't let me. You don't take off armour in the middle of battle, I s'pose. Oh man. This is horrible. I can't help my friends. Can't form a coherent spell in my head. You need will and focus to do magic. I ain't got none. My hands are shaking so much, I can't even use my katty.

I'm useless.

'Enough of this,' Wedderburn says, weaving a golden soliton of flames beginning as a circle where he is and growing as it spreads out in a flat disc.

There's a roar as it runs over us, singeing the walls. Such power!

Kebede ducks, while Priya creates a heat shield around her,

absorbing much of the fiery soliton's heat. Smoke billows in the air. It smells like burning tyres in here. I've fought a couple of magicians but never anything like this.

'Kebede, the sundial! It's the nexus of this place's inverted natural resistance. It's amplifying his power. We need to take it,' Priya shouts.

'Come and get it,' Wedderburn calls out.

Why is he making so much noise? It's like he doesn't care who hears. There's a showiness about most magicians, but this makes no sense.

Priya and Kebede try to circle the rector. Classic pack animal tactic. But Wedderburn is too wise to that, moving to neutralize their angles, so they remain in his field of vision. Kebede notices this and stops, allowing Priya to keep moving. If they stand on either side of him, he'll only have one of them in sight at any given time. Wedderburn moves back, adjusting, forcing Kebede to abandon the manoeuvre.

The rector is too wily.

'Now,' Priya yells, and they lob everything they've got at him.

But Wedderburn matches them volley for volley, redirecting Priya's thermospheres so they aim for Kebede instead. With each exchange he knocks them back and keeps his place by the sundial.

'Cruickshank, take me as close to him as you can,' I whisper. The scarf ignores me. 'Do it,' I command.

Almost reluctantly, it helps me up and steadies me as I sneak behind Wedderburn. The dread's still lodged in my nerves. A concussive blast hits Priya, knocking her, chair and all, back into the wall. She cries out in pain but moves quickly with a Helios spell before Wedderburn catches her a second time. He next forms the air into sharp arrows and sends them after her. One catches Priya's cheek and again she yells. Holding Kebede off with fire, Wedderburn steps up his anemoic attack on Priya.

This is incredible. He can cast two spells near simultaneously.

No way they can beat him like this. I have to help them. I crawl on, aided by Cruickshank where my numb limbs fail. I sense the drastic entropic shifts as Wedderburn works. Reckon I need a few more feet.

Just a bit more.

If he spots me, I'll be cooked, well done.

Careful.

Quietly.

The noise of his spells is deafening.

Almost. There.

Priya screams, parrying Wedderburn's sharp darts of air, as Kebede's caught by a huge fireball. He tears off his burning robe. Priya quickly mutters a Hyades spell, named for the Greek goddesses of rain, and a thick grey cloud appears over Kebede, showering him with water. She keeps on moving, dodging Wedderburn, who casually spars with both, pressing his advantage.

Almost.

There.

I feel something different in the soil. It's like you've been running uphill, which is what doing magic feels like most of the time, then you're hit by a surprise downhill stretch. A sudden decline so sharp you automatically try to slow yourself down. That's what this area of inverted natural resistance to magic feels like.

Strobes of blue, green and golden light flash against the smog.

Underneath the red moon.

Beneath the Newton Barrier.

I battle just to breathe as my companions fight to survive. But there's something in the earth near this spot that drains the stress away somewhat. The constriction around me eases. Not totally, but just enough. I'm starting to feel like my body is mine again, without a chestburster breaking out of it anymore.

Kebede cries out, struck again. He flies through the air, smashing into what remains of the Glass House. Priya yells in a desperate rage, hurling green thermospheres as Wedderburn laughs at her efforts.

I dig deep into the earth.

My grandmother taught me this is where everything comes from and where all shall return.

I close my eyes and incant my spell:

'Father Zeus, almighty king of the gods, shake the earth with your thunderbolts, till all quake before you.'

Tiny flashes of white.

Static builds up in the humid, smoky atmosphere. Sparks dance in the air, gathering and gaining strength. The hairs on my body rise.

Wedderburn turns and sees me.

'You stupid girl. An upper-level Zeusean spell in this hyper-ionized—'

A strobe of astonishing white crawls through the air like veins. Blinding. A crack, then an explosion, and streaks of lightning flash out in every direction. Wedderburn is struck and lifted off the ground. Priya screams like Old Sparky's been lit under her. Kebede howls in agony too, and I'm thinking I've bollocksed this up royally when I'm hit by something awesome I've never felt before. A microsecond of intense heat like the surface of the sun. My whole body just seems to stop. I'm surrounded by brilliant white light and the whole world moves in slow-mo. It's pain beyond putting your finger inside a light socket. Even though I'm already on the ground, I'm thrown several feet, landing in a flower bed.

My body fits, jerking about.

I've been zapped. My ears ringing, my eyes seeing white. Strange shapes float in my field of vision. I hurt so much I know I'm definitely still alive. But everything inside me's scrambled up, a mess of hot soup.

Someone's coughing. Groaning. Moaning.

Dazed, I can only just about lift my head up. I survey the damage and let my head fall back to the ground.

XXXIV

Wowzers. The air smells of ozone. My tongue tastes like I've licked a battery or something. But my head feels alright. Nothing a bit of electroshock therapy can't fix. Let me just get . . . ouch. Okay, lie here for a minute. Just one sec . . . Someone coughs. Sounds like Kebede.

I overcooked this one. Lesson on natural resistance noted. Where's—

Uh-oh.

'People like you shouldn't be doing magic,' Wedderburn says, standing over me.

'I see you've changed your mind on the subject,' I croak.

His jacket's tattered, clothes hissing with smoke. The left side of his face is also burned out. Seems like he took the brunt of my high voltage thunderbolt. I push up onto my elbows and he kicks me in the ribs, forcing me to roll over onto my front. Ouch. Wedderburn's proper radge. I pull out my dagger and slash at his shins, but he spots this and stomps on my hand, his boot pinning it down. Then he raises his own hand, with an almighty ball of golden fire blazing in it. This is it. This is how I go out. I close my eyes and flip him the V.

The sound of a million angry bees fills the garden.

Something that feels like grains of sand washes over my face. I open my eyes just in time to see this dark swarm slam into Wedderburn, throwing him backwards. He falls into the empty pond. The swarm circles the air, gathers and then coheres into the shape of a man. A tiny old guy.

The Grand Debtera, Qozmos is here.

Fury flashes in his eyes as he walks along the ground and picks up the fallen scroll, securing it in the sleeves of his robes. Then the Grand Debtera surveys the scene. Kebede stands up and staggers to him. Bare-chested with burns on his torso, he grits his teeth to endure the pain.

Priya's wheelchair flips up, righted again.

'I'm okay,' she yells. 'Just a bit shocked, that's all.' The hairs on her head are standing up all spiky. I think the new hairdo suits her.

I finally get up too. My limbs feel like rubber, and my hand hurts from being stomped on, and I waddle over to stand near Qozmos. You can feel the power radiating from his entire being. It's like standing in the presence of a planet-wide sandstorm. In this moment, I truly understand his threat to tear the castle down was no idle thing. He nudges me to stand behind him.

Wedderburn picks himself back up too. He's shaken. Winded by the Grand Debtera's power. He angles himself so that Priya, at the other end of the garden, is also in view. His eyes dart between her and us. It's clear he's scheming, weighing his options, whether to take a shot at Qozmos or not. But the scales are now weighted decidedly in our favour.

'You have no standing here. It's unlawful for you to practise or interfere with Scottish magic. You bloody translate that for him,' Wedderburn shouts out. Funny how he had no objections taking on Kebede before.

The assistant translates faithfully. The Grand Debtera replies, which in turn Kebede relates:

'God and history will remember the things you have done, my son.'

Wedderburn smirks.

The locked gate to the garden explodes, blowing fragments and splinters of wood through the air. Once they've cleared, we see Callander standing with Esfandiar Soltani at the broken entrance. Between us, there's now no way out for Wedderburn. He's cornered like a rat. But that just makes him even more dangerous in my eyes.

'Stay here,' Callander tells his husband as he walks into the garden.

'Ian, old chap, we've got them at last,' Wedderburn says. 'These three had the scroll all along. They meant to sell it, you see . . . The Extraordinary Committee tasked me with the investigation because we didn't trust your intern. A hoodlum from the slums. You know what these people are like. Taking advantage of your charity. But we've got them now. You should—'

'That's enough, Montgomery,' Callander says. He looks tired, both in body and soul. Wedderburn was his protégé, after all. I recall the evident affection with which both men looked on each other when I took my test to join the Society in the Dundas House, Edinburgh. That already feels like a long time ago.

Some of the conference attendees start trickling in through the broken gate. There's looks of surprise when they see the state of the Walled Garden. Smouldering bushes, uprooted shrubs, the empty pond and broken windows in the Glass House. The gazebo's twisted and bent out of shape too. Yep, we've done a great job here.

It's like the rubbernecking that happens at the scene of an accident.

They continue to pour into the garden.

Lethington rushes straight to Kebede and starts administering medical aid, while Cockburn makes her way over to stand next to Callander, looking horrified. This must be the most exciting conference she's hosted. And Edmund MacLeod looks absolutely furious at the state of his historic garden.

In no time at all the garden's full. We've been making quite the racket – they heard us and came out. Finally. At the centre of it all, standing in the empty pond, is Wedderburn. I track his eyes and can see he's looking for support. There's obviously some out there, especially amongst the young students, who are still in his grip. But what he's done is now out in the open – I don't see much chance of anyone supporting him anymore.

Yet something feels off, even though I can't put a finger on why. I should be celebrating getting the scroll back and finding the culprit, but I'm still unsettled. We have him surrounded; there's no way out, is there?

I check out Priya, but her herbology friends are gathered around her. Mrs Guthrie, the groundskeeper at the Edinburgh School, is quizzing her, pointing now at Wedderburn and then back to Priya.

The heads of the other three schools of magic are also here, witnessing their most prestigious colleague's fall from grace. Featherstone has a satisfied air about her. Cattermole tries to be stern but can't seem to suppress the corners of his mouth, which are straining on the edge of forming a smile. St Andrews' Hutchinson is unreadable. He watches without expression.

There's a bunch of angry folk about. They've been sleeping on floors in hallways. Eating rubbish food. Prevented from leaving the castle because of this whole affair. Wedderburn is so screwed.

Being a thief, I've always lived with this visceral dread of one day being exposed. It's not a good look. Wedderburn is naked and shamed in front of his peers, responsible for the death of a valued, popular librarian. It's disturbing to see him there in his burnt Savile Row suit, even as the fog begins to lift, the red moon above us shining down. The truth is revealed, but I'm even more anxious than I was. He's already tried to pin this on me, and if there weren't witnesses, I'd never have won that one. The truth morphs and changes depending on the situation, and in my experience most people prefer lies. Especially ones coming from fork-tongued rich geezers like Wedderburn.

'Sir, explain yourself,' MacLeod says angrily.

'We ought to handle this in private,' Octavius Diderot suggests.

'Don't you dare tell me how to conduct business in my own castle,' MacLeod snaps. He's in no mood for niceties. This whole affair's taxed him to the max, and he's got so much to lose. His home. His honour. I wouldn't dare cross the chief just now. At least the scroll has now been safely recovered, the true perpetrator caught. Perhaps his worries about the Fae curse and imminent fall of his clan can be eased now.

Diderot wisely retreats with his tail between his legs.

I've seen how these people do justice 'in private'. Words are twisted, pockets lined, favours exchanged. Dark becomes light. Better to have it here in the open. But no one's asked me, so I keep schtum. This is their problem now. My bit's done.

The Grand Debtera retrieves the scroll from his sleeve and points at Wedderburn. Kebede translates:

'This man has done a truly grievous thing. A harm barbarians from three different continents have hitherto failed to do. He has stolen *The Book of the Shaded Mysteries of Solomon as Recounted by the Queen of Sheba*, and now he stands before you without remorse, making false claims. Do with him what you will or fail to act. It is all the same to us. For from now on, and until the end of time, none of our sacred texts will we share with you. We return the book you offered in exchange for this loan. You will keep what's yours and we what's ours. Our Orthodox magic will have nothing more to do with the magics on these islands.'

There's a murmur through the crowd. Even Lord Samarasinghe, skulking in the corner of the garden, looks disturbed. I did warn him this would spill over to English magic too. Qozmos's words apply to the Royal Society of Sorcery and the Advancement of the Mystic Arts as much as they do to the Society of Sceptical Enquirers. But this also vindicates his position that we need the English with us here, because we're tied together. I suspect he'll spin this somehow to suit his agenda of swallowing up Scottish magic. Perhaps the complaint that we're unable to handle our affairs, that our issues are tainting London too, will reach the king's ears.

Can I fix this?

Qozmos seemed to like me, on the handful of occasions we've interacted. Maybe after he cools down I could appeal to him, using Kebede to support me? *Nah, leave it. You've done your bit.*

Wedderburn begins to laugh. He looks around the crowd, cracking up as he does. The lawyer Sahra Salat's been sneaking her way through the throng, getting nearer to Wedderburn. She whispers, 'Don't do or say anything without representation,' and holds out her business card. But he waves her away and she shrinks back.

'Look at us. To think, Scottish magic, the cream of the second science around the world, has sunk so low as to be begging for worn-out texts filled with superstitious drivel from the tenth century BCE.' Wedderburn is beginning to weave his spider's web, I can feel it. Fine words. Will they sway everyone over as they do his pupils? 'We are the nation that took magic by the ear and made it the second science. But how far we've now fallen. More so under this man's stewardship.' He points at Sir Callander. 'We used to be a first-rate nation doing first-rate magic. I've done this to show you all that being a magician in Scotland doesn't mean anything anymore. I knew it would take something drastic to open your eyes. And so I acted. Here you all were, the finest practitioners in your field, yet it took little for one man to deprive you of your rights, your very liberty. There was a time when our magicians were lords and treated as such. And because of that, we drove this nation forward. Now they make you sleep on the floor like dogs because they can. But I ask you to stand with me against this tyranny. Together we shall rejuvenate Scottish magic and make it the envy of the world again.'

How easily he twists his villainy into heroism. He looks up as if staring at the bright future he's about to propel us into.

'This is absurd,' someone says.

'Let the man make his case,' replies another.

'He should be put in jail.'

'Innocent before proven guilty. What happened to habeas corpus?'

'Our long, proud traditions.'

'Let him speak.'

'Common criminal.'

Angry voices rise around us. Men shaking their fists as they speak. Wedderburn's struck a nerve for some; others are still appalled by his actions. It's getting a bit mad.

'That's enough from you all,' Callander says. But his voice sounds so, so tired. 'His words do not excuse the criminality of his actions, and how grave those crimes are. A man lost his life over this folly. We are a Society of rules. Nothing should ever make us forget that.'

'Quite right. This is not up for debate. Wedderburn has

been caught red-handed here. If this were the old days, I would—' MacLeod begins.

'Let us, together, revive our former glory!' Wedderburn interrupts.

'I have no choice but to send you to the dungeon under the hill. Seize him,' Callander orders.

'No! I challenge you to a duel for the right to the secretary-ship of the Society of Sceptical Enquirers,' Wedderburn shouts even louder. So that's his game. This must be why he was hostile to Edmund MacLeod challenging Callander before, when the brawl with the MacDonalds happened. He was saving this option for himself as a last resort.

The crowd gets noisier. Outrage. Incredulity. A mix of views are expressed, most of them unfavourable to the rector. He had a weak hand and he's really messed it up now.

'You lost that right when you committed crimes completely unacceptable to the office, Montgomery. Don't be pathetic,' Callander says testily. 'Take him away. Tonight, we will inter-rogate him and identify any accomplices. Only once all these have been apprehended may we take down the Newton Barrier and get on with our programme. I'm sorry for the inconveni-ence this has caused everyone, but the matter is nearly at an end now.'

Mrs Featherstone and Professor Cattermole move forward to take their peer into custody. He ain't challenging anyone right now and there're loud cheers in the crowd. Everyone's turned against Wedderburn. Even Lord Samarasinghe's smile appears less malicious, morphing into approval. Wedderburn looks around wildly, but none of his supporters come forward.

He's miscalculated. Even the castle staff are here to jeer at him. Murdo, abused for a crime he didn't commit, watches alongside them. Now justice will be served. It's not exactly a panacea for what's happened to him, but I hope it may be a soothing balm for both Murdo and his mother. Sometimes that's the best you can hope for. Featherstone and Cattermole reach Wedderburn and seize his arms, placing their hands on his shoulders.

'Montgomery Wedderburn, rector of the Edinburgh Ordinary School for Boys, do you consent that we bind your will? Vow you'll do no more magic and come peaceably. Do we have your word as a gentleman, or shall we neuter you the old way?'

Magic stems from the magician's will, in accordance with the Somerville Equation. Without it there can be no power. The human body is a vessel of will. This is why consent is sought by people like Priya before they heal someone. She once told me the alternative is compunction or connivance, or something like that. I've read about this. A magician who consents to having his will bound loses his ability to do magic. It's a sanction for wayward practitioners. Some have it taken away for a period, others for life. Neutering, the alternative, is like a lobotomy and is performed forcibly. You don't come out the same after that. Like, ever. It destroys your entire being and is only used as a last resort. Wedderburn has no choice; he must accept.

The rector looks agonized. He opens his mouth but can't say the words. His pride won't let him consent. It takes a few seconds, as we all wait with bated breath. Finally, he exhales and speaks.

'I, Montgomery Horatio Wedderburn II, hereby—'

'Stop,' Dr Maige says, stepping forward. 'There's been a misinterpretation of the rules. They state clearly that only if *convicted* of a crime, whether magical or not, is a practitioner considered unfit to hold the post of secretary and therefore may not challenge for it.'

'But he stole the scroll. This is clear to everyone. He can't be allowed to do this,' Esfandiar protests.

'You're an interested party and I empathize, but the rules are clear. This man has been neither tried nor convicted of the alleged crimes. Therefore, his standing within the Society of Sceptical Enquirers remains the same. The challenge against Sir Ian Callander is valid and should be upheld.'

'But no head of one of the four schools can be secretary.'

'The rules are clear. If he ascends to secretary, his academic position will then be automatically forfeit.'

I could deck Jomo's dad. I swear I wanna take him out. Fucking psycho. All he had to do was shut up. How hard is that? This could have waited, but no, Dr Maige is all about the rules. This is an almighty disaster. I then begin to wonder if he's in on something with Wedderburn himself.

'Then he must first clear his name at least, before he can challenge,' Esfandiar pleads.

'I've already ruled on this matter,' Dr Maige says.

'Excellent. So it is my right to declare I do not wish for the matter to be put to a vote. I demand we do it the old way. In a duel,' Wedderburn says.

'Right, the old way it is. Unless one of the participants decides to yield, we shall proceed.'

Lord Samarasinghe laughs. He's back to enjoying himself at our expense. After all that, and what Priya, me and Kebede have just been through, Wedderburn gets a shot at going scot-free? My whole life, I've seen how the rules are tilted in favour of people like him. Qozmos should have taken the bastard out. Callander ain't had no sleep in three days; this challenge can't be held now, surely. They will have to wait a couple of days at least.

'We shall have this duel at ten o'clock this morning,' Dr Maige says. Thank heavens. Callander has to rest immediately.

'I am sorry, Doctor.' Wedderburn shakes free of his captors, who can do nothing now. 'I believe the rules state the duel must be had at a time and place of the challenger's choosing.'

'That's correct, but surely you don't mean to—'

'Then I must insist on exercising my right here, right now.'

Esfandiar cries out and runs to Sir Callander. He grips his arm, tugging at him, pulling him away from the scene. Callander gently removes his husband's arm.

'Don't do this, Ian. Darling, just say no. Let us go away,' Esfandiar says. 'Don't waste this breath, if your heart isn't crazy, since "the rest of your life" won't last forever.'

In despair, he's turning to verse.

Callander replies to him gently:

'I can't just hand it to him. Everything rides on this now. *One day your soul will depart from your body and you will be drawn behind the curtain that floats between us and the unknown. While you wait for that moment, be happy, because you don't know . . .*'

'*. . . where you came from and where you will be going,*'

Esfandiar finishes off his husband's Omar Khayyam quote. I've never known Sir Callander to be so tender. He holds his husband's cheek first, then his heart, and pushes him away.

And when Callander looks at Wedderburn, his face is full of pain. This is the stuff of a broken heart. Betrayed by his friend, now of all times.

'Choose your seconds,' Dr Maige says.

'Ms Moyo, will you be my second?' Callander asks.

I could weep. What possible use could I be to Sir Callander now? He truly has lost all faith in his peers. I'm like one of those hobbits Gandalf used to ride with into battle on his horse in the movies. I place my hand on my heart and give him a slight bow.

The magicians gathered there jostle for the best spots around the four walls of the garden. Someone brings a ladder from the nurseries and a few young men climb up it to sit atop the wall and watch from there. Dr Maige asks Wedderburn to retreat to the northern wall and Callander to the south. He calls me and Hutchinson to the centre to parley.

Turns out the Society uses a modified version of the Irish Code Duello, created in 1777. This was the popular set of rules that governed duelling in Europe and the Americas, standardizing the barbarism until most places banned the practice. Save for magicians, duelling is still banned in Scotland. Dr Maige goes through the rules one by one. He approaches it as if he was talking about rugby. I wish I could be as cold as him, but my hands are shaking. I ball my fists up in my pockets so no one can see. Hutchinson nods in agreement to Dr Maige's instructions, seemingly keen to get this thing started.

'As seconds, you are encouraged to seek reconciliation at this stage, so bloodshed may be avoided. Is there any set of circumstances in which you can see your principals return to amity?' he asks.

'Only if Sir Ian Callander surrenders the secretaryship and withdraws from magic altogether. These are the same terms his predecessor Sir Robert Latimer received,' Hutchinson says.

'Is this agreeable to your side, Ms Moyo?' Dr Maige asks.

'As agreeable as a poke in the tit,' I reply.

'Very well. Then it is my duty to inform you of the rules on the field. As seconds, you are to ensure no one else interferes in the duel by means magical or mechanical, whether to the advantage of your party or the opponent. This is a duel to the death, but should one of them yield, combat is to cease immediately and the winner declared. Is this clear?'

We both nod. The trembling in my hands spreads to my entire body. Can this really be happening? It's like some *Highlander* bullshit – 'There can be only one'. Pure madness.

'Any questions?' Dr Maige asks calmly.

We shake our heads.

'Then return to your principals. You have five minutes to inform them of everything we've agreed here. After that, at my signal, they are to take their places here in the centre of the garden, ten paces away from each other. You will be a further ten paces behind them and to the side, avoiding fire. From there you shall observe the duel and carry out your responsibilities as seconds. You are allowed to move and protect yourselves from stray spells, but you may not retaliate or otherwise intervene. Thank you, gentlemen . . . erm, lady and gentleman.'

This is it, I guess. I return to Callander and give him the rundown. I advise him to drop the Newton Barrier and focus entirely on the battle, but he doesn't seem to be listening. He's tired and broken. Old. I wanna slap him, to shake him out of this funk, but he's my boss, after all. I'm hoping what me, Priya and Kebede did has tired Wedderburn out a bit, which would be a slight advantage.

A man on the sidelines goes round taking bets.

Sigh. How we monetize absolutely everything. It's disgusting.

Dr Maige calls out from the centre: 'Gentlemen, it is time. You may approach.'

I look round the crowd. Even with so much at stake, this is just a game. We're more loathsome than I truly realized. I break off and leave Callander, drifting over to what's left of a burnt-out hedge. He continues stoically and stands several feet from the head librarian. Wedderburn too has taken his place, and I notice he is back near the lectern sundial. This will give him the advantage due to its magic-boosting location.

I quickly run over to protest to Dr Maige. He accepts and asks Wedderburn to move further away from it.

'But once the duel starts, the sundial is part of the landscape and open to anyone who can take that position,' he confirms.

I accept this and retreat back to my station.

Esfandiar's sobbing somewhere behind me. Men of fine feeling, poets like him, are unafraid to wear their hearts on their sleeves. As I wear a straight face, I realize Esfandiar's possibly the bravest person here.

'Gentlemen, you may begin. Good luck to you both,' Dr Maige says, stepping back from the combatants.

Then something strange happens. Callander and Wedderburn stand there, staring at each other. It's almost as if neither can believe it has come to this. There's confusion in the crowd too, as this goes on longer. Finally, Callander raises his hand, aims it upwards and forms a brilliantly black thermosphere which he fires into the sky.

'Nicely done, sir!' someone yells in the crowd.

I've heard of duels with pistols where one of the fighters deliberately fires away from his opponent. This is exactly what Callander has done. Wedderburn grits his teeth and spits.

'I may spare your life, but only your complete surrender will do,' he says, waving his hands and launching a barrage of concussive blasts at Callander. The sonic booms are deafening. It's clear to me that Wedderburn was holding back when he fought us.

A shock wave catches Callander on the chest, violently throwing him to the ground. I bite my lip and pray to gods I don't even believe in. Callander slowly gets up. As he fell, Wedderburn rushed over to take up his favoured place by the lectern sundial, where he can now cast even more powerful spells. There's malice in his eyes. I look to his second, Hutchinson, who exhibits nothing if not a professional aloofness.

'Montgomery—'

'Yield, sir.'

Wedderburn waves his hands and the air hisses like a thousand snakes. He twists them in a circular motion, sending an anemoic chainsaw blade of sharp air flying towards Callander, who staggers out of the way just in time, but not before the sleeve of his jacket's shredded, blood dripping from his arm. The audience gasps, but the blade dissipates just before it reaches them. Wedderburn next launches a volley of thermospheres, and Callander crosses his arms in front of his chest, creating a heat sink that diverts most of the energy. Even from here, I feel the heat.

The Newton Barrier flickers as though failing.

When Callander uncrosses his arms, he immediately returns an even more powerful thermosphere. But like the last, it is aimed too high, harmlessly sailing above the wall, into the night.

'Fight me, damn you,' Wedderburn shouts.

'This is foolishness. I knew your father, he'd not want this. Let's stop, Montgomery. There's always another way,' Callander says.

The temperature of the air rises as Wedderburn unleashes a flamethrower. Smoke billows out, causing some of us to cough. Callander shields himself, fire spraying all around him. The barrier between him and the flames glows white-hot and the force of Wedderburn's attack pushes him back a few feet. But his opponent launches arrows of sharp air which pierce the barrier, allowing some of the flames through. Callander shifts his position, away from the breach. Yet still he doesn't fight fire with fire. Instead he draws moisture from the air, dousing the flames. The normal rules don't seem to apply to these two. They can hold multiple spells at the same time, as I've observed of Wedderburn before. I've read of it. A technique called coupling, which layers spellcraft together and allows the magician to deploy them near simultaneously. The fine, almighty splash of moisture douses Wedderburn, but he raises some broken pottery behind Callander's back and stones him with it.

Once again the secretary is felled to the ground. He gets up, touching the back of his head, and his hand comes away bloodied.

'After I end you, I'll kill your little ponce too,' Wedderburn shouts.

Callander frowns. I feel the gun ports on Scotland's mighty battleship opened up and pointed. The Newton Barrier falls away and the silver moon shines brightly down upon us.

We're fortunate, because the thick toxic smog was becoming unbearable. The air around us shimmers, a haze of glinting black and gold.

'Goun yersel, big man,' a woman shouts from the audience.

Wedderburn launches ten more thermospheres at Callander, all with different trajectories. Callander steps one way and in an instant, there's two dozen of him in various positions on the field. The thermospheres explode harmlessly. Wedderburn launches spell after spell, hitting mirage after mirage. Seismic entropic shifts. The illusions of Callander all seem to move independently and human-like. Even I don't know where the real him is anymore. These figures seem to weave different spells. Some illusory, but others real, because something dark strikes Wedderburn and he's thrown onto the ground. The

Callanders then converge upon him and in desperation he sets off a soliton, erasing the illusions. Too slow. The real Callander is now upon him and punches him in the mouth.

All around us, people's phones are suddenly beeping and ringing, 'cause we've got a signal back.

On the downside, though, we're now inside a magical volcano. The air around us is growing uncomfortably hot as the two men punch and kick each other. Every blow loaded with magic lands with a crunch. From close quarters, they blaze their colours.

Wedderburn tries to retreat to his previous position at the lectern but is sucked back by a vortex of air into Callander's waiting fist. He crumples to the ground. Then Callander levitates him, raising him bodily into the air, spinning him round and round, before dumping him onto the ground beside the empty pond. The secretary moves strangely, appearing here, now there. Covering the ground in an evasive pattern so you don't know where next he'll show up.

Darkness draws itself around Sir Callander, weaving into the tentacles of a kraken. Rage is written upon his face. The fabric of space bends.

'I yield,' Wedderburn calls out. 'I surrender. I'm done.'

But Sir Callander strides towards him, seemingly drawing energy from the dark, ready to smite him. Dr Maige rushes in, as do me and Hutchinson, who stands over Wedderburn, shielding him from the wrath of this night Callander has conjured.

'That's enough. It's over, he's surrendered,' Dr Maige says, blocking Callander's path.

The secretary glowers at him.

'We've won,' I say cautiously, like Romanoff trying to calm the Hulk.

Esfandiar runs to his husband and throws his arms around him. The magicians around us burst into applause. Cries of 'Bravo', 'Fine show, gentlemen', 'Absolutely brilliant', 'Duel of the century', and other such vapid salutations. I'm just happy this whole thing's over. And Callander's safe. We soak up the applause and watch the heads of the other schools, including Hutchinson, apprehend the rector. They make him kneel on the ground and submit to the victor.

It is Hutchinson himself who binds Wedderburn's will.

And yet, after the deed is done, in the smoke-filled atmosphere, Wedderburn smiles. Blood is streaming down his face but he seems satisfied with himself. I know what it is to lose a fight. That's not how you're supposed to take it. And even though he's facing prison, he just looks smug. He moves his gaze up towards the moon and I follow his eyes.

No, no, no, no.

This isn't right.

I look around the crowd, scanning the faces there, and realize who isn't present. Son of a bitch.

'Priya, with me,' I shout, and run for the gate. I shove people out of my way, barging through. And soon I'm out the Walled Garden, on the road that leads down to the castle, busting a gut with Priya close behind.

XXXV

Misdirection, the charlatan's corruption of magic.

Magic alters reality. In its most vulgar form, the seemingly impossible is made manifest. Rabbits are drawn from hats. Women sawn in half and put together again. Our eyes and ears are deceived.

I'm tearing along the smog-filled road with Priya in tow. Everyone else is left behind, captivated by the spectacle of the duel and its aftermath. I'm praying I'm wrong, but there's this awful feeling deep within my bones. I pump my arms to go faster and nearly slip on the wet, treacherous fallen leaves stuck on the road as I turn by the path next to the oak tree. The one just over the bridge, where the burn roars once more, now it's free to run its natural course again.

We run up, past the toilets, heading for the castle.

'Come on,' I shout at Priya, leaping onto the steps, bursting through wide-open double doors.

I whip out my katty and load ammo as I hurry up the stairs into the entrance hall, then over to the drawing room on the right. Cautious, but hurrying still. The door's open. I peek first then enter. Rushing over to the far wall where the frame with the Fairy Flag is supposed to be. The MacLeods' most precious artefact, and root of all their power on Skye.

Knapfery.

The flag's gone. My boots crunch on bits of broken glass and wood from the picture frame that once housed it. All that remains is the imprint of the frame against the wallpaper, marking its absence. MacLeod said the flag was shielded, that it was 'as impenetrable as though it were in a bank vault'. Fuck me. I hold my head in my hands. I need to think, to make a plan. *Come on, Ropa.* Where to next? How much time do we still have?

'Holy crap,' says Priya, wide-eyed.

'They can't be that far ahead of us,' I say.

'Who?'

'Lewis-Cocksucking-Wharncliffe, Fenella MacLeod, Avery MacDonald and Nathair Walsh. They weren't at the duel. All that noise, the light show, it was a distraction. Wedderburn really just wanted Callander to take down the shield. If he won the duel, it'd be a bonus, but this right here was the plan,' I say, gesturing to the empty wall.

'The shield protecting the Fairy Flag only comes down on the first full moon of the autumn. To allow the celebratory unfurling of it. That was today.'

'All them people out there watching the duel were supposed to be in here tonight for the unfurling. No one could ever have hoped to steal it then.'

'So what do we do now, Ropa?'

'Organize a manhunt. Sweep through the island. Get MacLeod to call his people in Kyleakin. Road-block the Skye

Bridge that leads to the mainland. The phones should be working now the shield's down. We need eyes on every road.'

'What if they went by sea?'

'MacLeod could rouse the fishermen and have them on patrol. He needs to contact folks in Rum, Eigg, Muck and Canna, all the small islands. But if they're already on their way to the mainland, I don't know, Priya. We need to cover every base we can. Talk to the other Edinburgh students, find out if they know anything. But right now, we've just got to get moving. Come on!'

We've been here barely a minute, but it already feels like I've wasted too much time. If we don't get it right against this organized, determined bunch, then we lose again. I put my weapons back and briskly leave – back down the stairs and outside.

There's a couple of magicians trickling back from the duel. They speak in loud voices, excited but oblivious to the heist that's just happened. Jomo's ahead of them all, floating happily now the scroll's been recovered. I stand at the bridge and shout:

'The Fairy Flag's been nicked. Get everyone here, right now, Jomo.'

'Tell Callander and MacLeod. Hurry!' Priya adds.

That gets Jomo's and everyone's attention, right enough.

'The Fairy Flag's been stolen,' they shout to the people behind them. The call goes out quickly and Jomo's running back to the gardens.

Some of the castle staff start running this way too.

I need to hit the streets, but we have to spread the word

and get organized first. Nah, screw that. I tell Priya to talk to MacLeod and Callander, for them to call everyone they can who might block the thieves' escape. But I'm gonna take a chance and give chase right now. If I spot them, I'll call for help before jumping in.

'Tell the others the plan, then follow me,' I say.

'No, wait, Ropa.'

'Just do it!'

I sprint up the driveway and then out the gate. If they came this way, they'd have a couple of options. One's going right on the road. That would take them down to Dunvegan, from where they could head south onto the mainland, or they might have gone to Portree and be hiding out there. Secondly they might have gone left, headed towards Coral Beach, where they could catch a getaway boat. I wouldn't be too surprised if one of them posh kids knows how to sail. Option three takes them through the car park and into the woods. Maybe they've decided to just hide out there until the coast is clear.

Which one?

It's a crapshoot. What would the four of them do? Or would they split up? The first option, going towards Dunvegan, is too obvious. They'll know we'd want to go that way. The boat option's pretty slow too. So I go with my gut and run across the car park into the trees. There I head up the track a bit, guided by the moonlight. There're footprints in the mud, but I can't be sure whose they are. I press on, hoping to see, hear or even smell something.

Messages pinging through onto my phone now we've got reception.

Branches catch at me as I hurry up the path along the burn. I head in deeper, but there are no signs of life. Next my phone rings. Priya. I answer and tell her where I am. She in turn lets me know a search has been launched and that she's going with a posse to Dunvegan and beyond. The police and comrades of the MacLeods have been notified. Even Dalziel MacDonald has offered to help, calling in his connections.

I concentrate on what I can do right now, hurrying through the woods. But even as I go, I have this awful feeling we're too late. Those four kids, Fenella, Avery, Lewis and Nathair, have outsmarted us. Wedderburn's behind this, I'm sure, and he's planned this stage of the heist. But why that flag is quite so important to them and what they intend to do with it is yet to become clear to me.

Can't help but admire the cunning behind it. It's like Machiavelli said: 'One who deceives will always find those who allow themselves to be deceived.' Breathless, I stand under the bright moonlight, realizing we've been completely outplayed. It's a bitter pill to swallow, I'll tell you that.

XXXVI

I'm beat. Going back to the castle, since my search has borne less fruit than an apple tree in winter. I check my phone and see messages from Izwi, telling me they've been taken back to school in Aberdeen since they can't get in for the conference. After all this, I won't get to see my sister. When she'd been just down the road.

I message her back and tell her it's okay. We were dealing with a little problem, that's all. I tell her I love her and send her a kissy kiss. Next I message Gran to apologize for not staying in touch. I say we were having difficulties with the network. This is rural Scotland, after all.

Everything still hurts since I zapped myself.

But I've got more work to do. I need to interview whichever students I can find for information on where the Fab Four might have fled to. The worst thing about all this is the sense that we've only hit the tip of the iceberg. Were Wedderburn and them kids working alone? Could there have been even more sleepers amongst us while all this was kicking off?

I'll have to talk to Callander.

But he needs to rest first. After all them days with no sleep, he'll be half-man-half-zombie.

My head's spinning as I walk down the muddy path. A key artefact of Scottish magic has just been stolen, and one closely tied to the fate of the MacLeods on Skye. It seems Edmund MacLeod wasn't wrong to worry about the prophecy coming true, predicting the downfall of his clan. It's said whenever the MacLeods got in trouble on the field of battle, they only had to unfurl the Fairy Flag for the tide to turn. Now, without it, they lose whatever strategic advantage they ever had. And we all lose the flag's ability to manipulate and facilitate the linkage between our dimension and others. In the wrong hands, could the flag be used to release the Fae back into this realm? I've had my own encounter to give me a sharp fear about this.

This makes me wonder what the students want it for. What's Wedderburn cooking up? I'll have to question him first. If this is a chess game, then he's one of the most powerful pieces. They've sacrificed him for a reason.

Back at the castle now, I rub my temples to ease the stress.

The good thing is most of the folks who were here are now out on the hunt. Or they've left, fed up with having been held here. Those that remain, I avoid. I hurry through the grounds and the building until I get to the relative sanctuary of my bedroom. There I take off my coat and set Cruickshank aside, as well as my dagger and katty. These bloody boots come off too and I finally fall back on the bed.

My phone beeps.

Ignore it.

I stare at the ceiling for a wee bit then close my eyes. Not to sleep, my mind's racing too fast for that, but to breathe in and out. Daylight starts to pour in through the windows. Let me veg for a mo and recentre, then I'll head out again.

Priya comes back absolutely shattered. She's all hot, bothered and sweaty. It's been a mad night. She shuts the door and wheels herself to a spot beside the bed, looking out the window.

'You're hopping in?' I ask.

'I need a shower. Actually, make that a nice hot tub with bath salts.'

'Sounds like a plan to me.'

'You don't look too great,' she says. 'Stressed out? I went all the way to Orbost chasing a dud. Some farmer saw a bunch of kids in a camper van going out that way. All I got was a bunch of surfers with zero magical ability. No one else seems to have turned up anything either.'

'There we go then.'

There's a knock on the door. I don't want to deal with anyone right now, but Priya says enter and in walks Jomo. He's looking all nervous as he plonks himself at the foot of the bed, then shifts to lean back against the wall. He grabs my foot and places it on his lap, pulling at my toes to make them crack.

'Did we win?' he asks.

'Depends on how you score it,' Priya replies. 'We got the scroll back. That was our mission. The flag had nothing to do with us, so technically it's a win.'

'It was all about the Fairy Flag, don't you see it? The

Ethiopian scroll was a false flag operation that lured us away from the true objective. Adamina MacLeod's ghost kind of warned me that the MacLeods would lose what they treasure the most, and so they have,' I say, burying my face in my hands. 'If we've won anything at all, it's a Pyrrhic victory, Priya.'

Old King Pyrrhus of Epirus defeated the Romans in BCE something but lost so many of his troops doing so, the cost was way too great. I recall my promise to Edmund MacLeod to look after his interests alongside Society business. Dumb move. Sneddon's murderer got away and the accomplices to the robbery have bailed on us. And it was MacLeod's own daughter aiding in a theft that could lead to her family's downfall. Although having Wedderburn doesn't balance the ledger, I suppose it's still better than nothing.

'Erm, Ropa. The Extraordinary Committee wants to see you in the castle library,' Jomo says.

'What for? They kicked her off the case,' queries Priya.

'I don't know.'

'Tell them I'm on my way,' I say. 'I guess I should be packing my things then.'

'Why?'

'Just tell them I'm coming.'

I sit up and swing myself off the bed after Jomo leaves. Go over to the window and put my hands on Priya's shoulders. We stare out into the gardens. Without the Newton Barrier, nature's been restored and gulls no longer break their necks against it. All things considered, this is a beautiful morning.

'I'll come with you,' Priya says, stifling a yawn.

'You should get some sleep, lassie. Last night was hectic.'

'I'm a bit zonked but—'

'Get some rest. I'll wake you when it's time.'

I help Priya into bed and tuck her in, kissing her cheek. No bedtime story, no lullabies, 'cause in no time she's knocking them zeds out. Then I put on my gear, replacing my weapons – this is still Scotland, after all. Grab my backpack with my mbira and scan the room one last time to make sure I've left nothing behind. I close the door quietly behind me as I leave.

XXXVII

Carrie, Abdul, Sin and Aurora waylay me en route to the castle library. The Hamster Squad's always up for a bit of gossip. I really should be getting on, but I give them a wee rundown anyway. In return they fill me in on bits they've heard, including the fact the police are on the case, 'cause MacLeod's connected like that.

I leave them to it, heading straight to the venue where Cockburn, Diderot, Cattermole, Hanley and Lady Lebusa are waiting, sat in their chairs. Hutchinson seems to have taken Wedderburn's position of prominence on the Committee, and Dr Maige's still there, observing and refereeing, as is his way. Edmund MacLeod's there too, looking surly.

Ever walked into a situation and been hit by an overwhelming sense of déjà vu? That's what it feels like with this lot. I decide to shake up the Matrix a little by not standing in the middle this time, but instead going right up to the desk and sitting on it.

'Perhaps you'd like to stand over there,' Cockburn says, pointing.

'I'm fine right here,' I reply.

'Let's get on with this, shall we?' Diderot says. 'Ropa Moyo, we need a full report on what exactly happened last night.'

'Why don't you ask Montgomery Wedderburn? Last I heard, he was running your investigation.'

'This isn't the time for games, young lady.'

'I'm surprised. It always seems to be like that with you lot.'

'That is outrageous,' Lady Lebusa says. 'Your mentor will be hearing about this.'

'Your entire internship depends upon your cooperation with this Committee. You'd do well to remember that,' says Cockburn.

There it is. This is their cock-up and now they're looking for someone to blame. Something they can file in their official reports. I'm always amused by how historians value written records as primary sources. They're full of lies anyway. Power doesn't care about the truth.

'Because of your carelessness, we've lost the Fairy Flag,' MacLeod says furiously. 'This, after you assured me you would look after the interests of my clan. Your ineptitude has ruined us.'

Thing about kangaroo courts is, the conclusion's baked in before the dough's in the oven. It gets tedious. They pretend to have forgotten that a few hours ago we were all in this room, doing this exact same thing with Wedderburn, who they entrusted this thing to. Their bad judgement's been erased. And once again, they've chosen to meet without Callander. I remember him lecturing me about how I'm supposed to deal with this lot. Like, I'm the one who has to shrink myself to fit their schema.

I pick my nails as they prattle.

'You're not taking this seriously at all,' says Mary Hanley, all righteous.

'I really think we ought to start talking about expulsion, or her suspension at the very least for this insolence. Dr Maige, this is within the rules, is it not?'

'Ladies and gentlemen, you can all eat my vag,' I say, flipping the bird on both hands. 'I'm done with this bullshit. This thing's your problem now. You took it off me, so now you must own it. Guten appetit.'

Frances Cockburn smiles triumphantly. Even now, amidst all this trouble brewing, despite everything I've done for the Society, she can't hide her disdain for me. Well, she's got what she wanted at last – good for her. I leap off the desk to their deafening silence, stride across the room and leave, slamming the door.

. . .

Man, that felt good. If you're gonna fall on your sword, that's how you do it.

. . .

I am *so* done with Scottish magic. Ain't going to waste any more time going back and forth with this lot. The whole thing's a sham. They can put all the lipstick they want on it, but that damned oinker stinks.

Callander's not going to like this, though. He's expended capital getting me in, and I'm grateful for all that. But I can't be doing this no more. Still, I'll have to tell him my decision straight, that I'm out. It'd be cowardly not to. Plus, he's alright, you know? I've really enjoyed working with hi— working for him.

I don't know which it is anymore.

Next stop, the kitchen – there's something else I've been meaning to do for days. They should open the windows. The castle's reeking from all the folks who were sleeping in here. And since the air wasn't circulating, it's bad. I pop into the kitchen, where there's swanky stainless steel everywhere. One of them industrial stoves is in the middle and then cupboards and units up against all the walls.

It's bigger than our caravan.

'Excuse me?' the chef says. He's in white, wearing one of them funky hats too.

'Give me a sack of ingredients and a sack of leftovers,' I say.

'Who are you?'

'That's the lassie who stood up for my Murdo. Give her what she wants, Jocky,' Morag says, beckoning.

'This isn't done, you know?' he replies. 'If we get caught, I'll say it was you and you'll be the one getting the sack.'

'Just give it tae her, you miser,' Morag orders as she sits me down and gives me a nice cuppa. Plenty of sugar, cream and marshmallows too. I get that down me gullet and I'm less radge than I was a few minutes ago. Must have been my blood sugar acting up. I know all about that 'cause Gran's diabetic. I really can't wait to see her.

'This tea's ace,' I tell Morag.

'I see yous all packed up tae scoot. They ending the conference already? I heard Frances Cockburn say they were pressing on.'

'I don't care what they do. I've done my bit.'

'Cannae blame yous. There's lots of them out there leaving for hame as it is. Beats being cooped in here.'

'Amen.'

The chef drops two sacks of grub on the table, begrudgingly, and gets back to his work. The one with all the Tupperware's got leftovers. The other one's got bread, apples and some potatoes. Brill. This is my payment. And now I've got it, I best skedaddle. Don't want to be wandering about too late. Not with everything that's been going on.

I thank Morag for her tea and leave the castle, next heading up through the woods for the Keeper's Cottage.

Golden light streams in from behind the clouds above. Soft rays of sunshine, the sort that lick your skin like a Labrador puppy.

I knock on the door and wait. Doesn't take too long before Esfandiar appears. He's looking bright and cheery this time, the gloom of last night lifted totally. Seeing him like this buoys my soul. Other people's happiness is a beautiful thing. You can feast off it like a vampire.

'Darling!' he says. 'Come in, come in. What a lovely morning it is.'

'I love your eyeliner,' I say.

'I can look pretty again now Ian's nearing the end of this ghastly ordeal. I'm very happy.'

'That's how it should be,' I say. 'The Ethiopians still here?'

'They're preparing to go. You want me to get them for you?'

'I came for Sir Callander.'

'I'm afraid he's busy down in the dungeon interrogating

that awful Montgomery Wedderburn. After that, I'll be sure to tuck him in and make certain he won't wake up for at least a hundred years.'

'I thought your fairy tale was more *Beauty and the Beast.* You're Belle, of course.'

'Don't flatter me, Ropa. I'm vain enough as it is.' We giggle. I like Esfandiar. Pity this is farewell. But we meet to part and that's how it's always been.

When we stop, Esfandiar takes both my hands in his own and looks me in the eye. I smile at him like everything's okay. But he doesn't seem to be buying it. He frowns slightly, raising his eyebrows a fraction, inviting me to speak. I'm trying my best to maintain a neutral air but am struggling. I break free and turn away.

'I need you to tell Sir Callander that it's been a blast, but I'm going my own way now.'

'Darling, I could tell something was wrong. Why don't you sit down with me on this sofa. Let's talk over a cup of tea, hey?'

'I've already had tea, thanks. You tell him I said he's a stand-up guy, and thanks for the train ticket, but this is my stop, okay? He should find a new intern.'

'Ropa . . .'

I walk away. Goodbyes suck. And it's a long way to Edinburgh. But before I reach the door, the Grand Debtera, Qozmos and his assistant Kebede are standing there. Didn't hear them come down the stairs. They look resplendent in their white robes.

I guess I have to say something cinematic now.

'Thanks for saving my neck last night. That bee thing was a neat trick,' I say.

Kebede hesitates and then proceeds to translate. The way Qozmos chuckles tells me I'm funny in Amharic too. That's a great boost for my CV, since I'm freelance now. I wonder if there's any Ethiopian restaurants in Edinburgh.

Qozmos replies, Kebede translating in real time:

'You have shown honour, integrity and courage, young flower of Scotland. We will remember you always in our hearts and pray for you and your family. May the cobblestones in your path smoothen out.'

Then he makes the sign of the cross on my forehead with his right thumb. I'm no believer in faith-based magics or any of that hocus-pocus, but when you get it like that from a sincere believer, it feels pretty strong.

'I guess you guys have a long journey back,' I say.

'Very. From here we are going to see our friends in Mali. The libraries in Timbuktu rival our own and their magical scholarship is unparalleled. At one point they had the largest collection of books in Africa since the Library of Alexandria.'

Yes, I've read somewhere that Timbuktu has the oldest magical university in the world. It's called the University of Sankoré and was established by Mansa Musa back when Mali had an empire. I can totally see why these guys would want to go hang out there. African magicians have been going there for over a thousand years and the thing's still standing. I know I'll never go there 'cause I don't have the cash to travel, but it was still nice reading about it and checking out the pictures.

The two step out of my way, and I head out, with Esfandiar

in tow. He stands by the door and, as I look over my shoulder, he gives me a little wave.

'Hey, this coat you gave me, I don't have to give it back, do I?'

'No, darling, it belongs to you now.'

I nod, then ask, 'And this scarf I've got. Was it my grand-mother's too?'

'Her skill with fabrics is unparalleled,' he replies.

'I figured.'

I've got two sacks of food. Nice Yorkshire tea in my belly. All my most important possessions are on me and the wind is behind my back as I cut through the woods, trampling the fallen leaves. Some random lounging on the wooden bench gives me the 'God save the king' schtick and I answer, 'God save us all.' Soon enough I'm on the driveway headed to the gate. Then I see Dr Maige hurrying up the road towards me. His scarlet robes swish about in the wind. I wanna bail but he hails me.

Can't a lass leave in peace?

I'm lectured out.

'Ms Moyo . . . I'm sorry about everything that happened with the Extraordinary Committee . . . It's all within the rules.' He hesitates. I don't know what's caught his tongue. He continues: 'But, in light of your service to the Library, restoring stolen property and protecting our reputation, I would like for you to know that you may continue using our facilities in Edinburgh. That is, at least until the Committee submits a letter of objection to your presence. They have plenty to do and I'm certain they won't get round to it straight away.'

I just stand there staring at him. Like, what does he expect from me – thanks? There's a hole in my pocket, so I'm all out of those right now.

'Well, you should be getting on, but I just thought I should let you know.'

'What I want is for you to reinstate Jomo on your staff without condition.'

'Ms Moyo—'

'I don't care, okay? Just do it already.'

'Very well. I'll do that.'

'He's a good lad,' I say, walking away.

I take one more look at Dunvegan Castle over my shoulder and decide it ain't half as pretty as Edinburgh Castle.

XXXVIII

I'm out those gates and that posh estate. Beyond me lies the open road. Bliss. I walk across to the car park where the urchins are stood begging. There's only six of them today. Some of them gave up the longer the siege of Dunvegan Castle went on. There ain't a lot I can do for them, but with winter on the way, I'll be a hummingbird.

'Come here, all of you,' I say.

They run to me, dirty paws outstretched. Cheeks and noses red from the cold. That was one thing about the Newton Barrier, we lost very little heat. It kept us warm. These kids have it rough. I give them my sacks of food and tell them to share it all. Should see how quickly they dig in. It's a free-for-all and I'm happy to let it be, so long as they don't brawl. I stand there for a bit, making sure everyone, including the littlest, gets their share before I piss off. Wish I could do more, but good luck to them.

I then cross the road again to get onto the footpath.

Walk down the slope towards Dunvegan.

I carry on through the mud that's been deposited by the burn as it was stopped from flowing through the castle grounds to the sea. It's left a right old mess here. But I'm used to the wet toes. To the cold and all that.

Feeling so much lighter.

Freer too.

Something new'll come up. Always does.

At least I don't have to worry about sis's school and stuff. It's taken a lot of pressure off. Looking after me and Gran's easier. Her 'companion' helps out too, which is great.

Three ghosts walk down this road with me. One's Adamina in white, though her garment now looks less like a nightie and more like a wedding dress somehow. The other's in a kilt, now fully formed into a human shape. The bagpipes that were glued to Stephen MacCrimmon are also gone. The two hold hands in death as they were denied in life. We don't say anything to one another as they accompany me part of the way and then vanish into the ether, going to the great beyond where I hope they find peace for all eternity.

The last of the ghosts lingers for a good while. It's a newbie, still formless, much like a plume of smoke, but I make out the wee crinkles of a librarian's robe. That will be Sneddon. He doesn't attempt to speak. I don't know what to say to him either. His soul belongs to the everyThere now and from there he can make his way to the land of the tall grass. But for a while he keeps me company as I walk across Skye. This ancient, mysterious island where horse hairs are said to turn to eels, peat fires still smoulder in hearths, the goddess Skiach held a school of war and gave her name to the place, and the few cattle that remain still have fairy blood in them. It's an alien place for someone from the lowlands to end their life in. Eventually, Sneddon's ghost breaks up like the pages of a book shredded, tiny pieces rising into the grey sky lofted by a strange and sombre wind.

A load's been lifted off my shoulders and I can walk tall again. I come to the junction where the road forks. I could go left up the A850 to Portree and maybe try to hitch a ride from that side. Portree's the largest town on the Isle of Skye. There's buses still running from there to the mainland, I've heard. They tend to be erratic, though. And this way takes me across the other side of Skye, before I've even started making my way south. Or I could take the A863 through the town and straight down. That's the fastest route, but this way I have to hitchhike and hope I catch an electric going all the way, at least to the Kyle of Lochalsh back on the mainland.

From there I'll need to find someone going south to Fort William or, if I'm lucky, all the way to Glasgow. It's a doddle getting back to Edinburgh from there. Alternatively, I could maybe find someone going east, past Inverness to Aberdeen. And from there I could hitch my way south.

Might have been simpler if the trains were still running in the Highlands.

Decisions, decisions.

I eventually choose to go south and hope someone comes along.

It's a nice stroll through the run-down town. I meet very few people along the way. It's dead here after summer.

Sore legs start troubling me already. This'll be fun.

Wish I had my bike. And River too. I could use the company. Ah well.

Ten-odd miles in. Is anyone coming this way?

The few cars I've seen have all been headed in the wrong direction, towards Dunvegan. Maybe this was a bad idea. I could have waited to go back with Callander and Esfandiar. Or hitched a ride in the Hamstermobile with the Squad. Nah. My pal Nicco said you should never fall in the belief that you will find someone to pick you up. I'm on my own and that's alright.

Lone wolf. Howl. Bollocks.

Gets a bit scary on these desolate country roads, though. I prefer the city, where there's always someone going by.

Clippety-clop. Hooves on tarmac. Can't do me much good. I need someone with an electric vehicle. Don't even bother sticking my thumb out. I just move out of the narrow country lane and walk on the grass on the verges. Pain in the arse cause it's overgrown and stuff.

Horses trot past me.

I keep my eyes on the horizon.

A coach pulls up beside me and I'm expecting it to go past, but it continues for a good while, staying alongside me. Jog on, pillock. We go like this for a while, until I turn to look at the black carriage. I stop and the coachman goes 'whoa', bringing his beasts to a halt.

The window drops open and Lord Samarasinghe looks out at me. He's sipping his tea in a china cup.

'We headed the same way?' he asks.

'Edinburgh?'

'What a delightful coincidence. It happens I have the king's business to attend to there. Fancy a ride?'

Not really, but I look up and down the road. Ain't exactly like there's too many other options going. So I nod and the coachman leaps down to open the door for me. It seems doing that's beneath the Sorcerer Royal. Whatever. I hop in and sit opposite Samarasinghe. He sips his tea with a faint smirk, his eyes reflecting the lush velvet interior. Out in the wild he appears even more dangerous and beautiful, just like the tiger on his cane.

'Tough conference, eh?'

'I'd rather not talk about it.'

'Hiya,' the coachman shouts, and I'm thrown back in my seat. The ride's bumpy and the carriage isn't as comfortable as I thought. Takes a bit of getting used to, this bouncing about. But Samarasinghe drinks his tea unbothered.

The horses run faster. The crack of a whip sounds. And again, then again. Faster we go. This thing needs seatbelts. I'm really being thrown about. The landscape outside starts to blur and with one last 'hiya', the coach jerks up, and suddenly we're rising through the air.

I look outside. The trees, the houses, everything gets smaller and smaller. I can see the sea in the distance. This is wild. Higher and higher we climb. Still that whip cracks again and again.

I turn away. I can't look outside anymore.

'I hope you don't get sick. I've just had this coach reup-holstered. Cost a fortune,' Lord Samarasinghe says. 'But if you want the best, you have to pay for it.'

'I googled your family. You lied to me. Your parents are still very much alive and doing well in business.'

'Still made for a great story, though. Rags to riches and all that. If it makes you feel better, everything else I promised was true. Cross my heart and hope to die.'

Yep, I feel queasy.

After a while, the coach stops climbing and levels out. The ride's much smoother after that.

'Do cheer up, Ropa Moyo. I hope you're not planning on being a bore the entire ride. I'd rather chuck you out mid-flight than stare at that sullen face.'

'Thanks for the lift.'

'See, manners maketh the woman. Would you like a cup of tea?'

'No thanks, I've already had some.'

'Smart move. At my age it runs through me. I can't have us landing every five minutes, so I simply open the door and do my business there. I've micturated over all of Scotland, I believe. England too. Golden showers for all.'

'I'm sure they'll love you for it.'

Lord Samarasinghe looks outside and blanks me. It's almost like I'm not there to him anymore. Was it something I said? Nah. He's weird like that. To be fair, I prefer the silence. Lets me think about shit. My mind naturally drifts to the events of the last few days. The giant jigsaw I was piecing together. It didn't all quite fit. Never does. But hang on a minute. The more I think about it, the more I realize there's an awkward piece I left off the board.

'Lord Samarasinghe, are *you* the Black Lord?'

He jerks up, startled. Then he raises his eyebrows and, for the most uncomfortable length of time, stares me in the eye. When it gets unbearable, the corners of his mouth very slowly draw towards his ears, revealing Hollywood whitened gnashers. Then the Sorcerer Royal throws his head back and bursts out laughing. He laughs so hard and so loud it fills the carriage, rocking it. Voluminous tears stream down his cheeks. He clasps his stomach like it's all too painful. The cup clatters in its saucer, spilling tea everywhere. He laughs and laughs. My, how he laughs.

About the Author

T. L. Huchu has been published previously (as Tendai Huchu) in the adult market, but the Edinburgh Nights series is his genre fiction debut. His previous books (*The Hairdresser of Harare* and *The Maestro, the Magistrate & the Mathematician*) have been translated into multiple languages, and his short fiction has won awards. Huchu grew up in Zimbabwe but has lived in Edinburgh for most of his adult life.

Twitter: @TendaiHuchu
Instagram: @tendaihuchu